W9-DBO-259

SELECT EDITIONS
LARGE TYPE

SELECT EDITIONS

LARGE TYPE

**This Large Print Book carries the
Seal of Approval of N.A.V.H.**

Reader's
Digest

CONTENTS

THE MOUNTAIN BETWEEN US

CHARLES MARTIN

A SMALL plane goes down in the snowy mountains of Utah. And two strangers have nothing but their wits to save them.

Hey . . .

I'm not sure what time it is. This thing should record that. I woke a few minutes ago. It's still dark. I don't know how long I was out.

The snow is spilling in through the windshield. It's frozen across my face. Hard to blink. Feels like dried paint on my cheeks. It just doesn't taste like dried paint.

I'm shivering . . . and it feels like somebody is sitting on my chest. Can't catch my breath. Maybe broke two or three ribs. Might have a collapsed lung.

The wind up here is steady, leaning against the tail of the fuselage—or what's left of it. Something above me, maybe a branch, is slapping the Plexiglas. And more cold air is coming in behind me. Where the tail used to be.

I can smell gas. I guess both wings were still pretty full of fuel.

I feel like I want to throw up.

A hand is wrapped around mine. The fingers are cold and calloused. There's a wedding band, worn thin around the edges. That's Grover.

He was dead before we hit the treetops. I'll never understand how he landed this thing without killing me, too.

When we took off, the ground temperature was in the single digits. Not sure what it is now. Our elevation should be around 11,500, give or take. We couldn't have fallen more than 500 feet when Grover dipped the wing. The control panel sits dark, unlit. Every few minutes the GPS will flicker, then go black again.

There was a dog here somewhere. All teeth and muscle. Short hair. About the size of a bread box. Looks like he's jacked up on speed. Wait. . . .

"Hey, boy. . . . Wait. . . . No, not there. Okay, lick but don't jump. What's your name? You scared? Yeah . . . me, too."

I'M BACK. . . . Was I gone long? There's a dog here. Buried between my coat and armpit. Did I already tell you about him? I can't remember his name. He's shivering, and whenever the wind howls, he jumps up and growls at it.

The memory's foggy. Grover and I were talking. He was maybe banking right. The dash flashed a buffet of blue and green lights, a carpet of black stretched out below us, not a lightbulb for sixty miles, and . . . there was a woman. Trying to get home to her fiancé and a rehearsal dinner. I'll look.

I found her. Unconscious. Elevated pulse. Eyes are swollen shut. Pupils are dilated. Probably a concussion. Several lacerations across her face. A few will need stitches. Right shoulder is dislocated, and left femur is broken. It didn't break the skin, but her leg is angling out and her pant leg is tight. I need to set it once I catch my breath.

IT'S getting colder. I guess the storm finally caught us. If I don't get us wrapped in something, we'll freeze to death before daylight. I'll have to set that leg in the morning.

Rachel, I don't know how much time we have, don't know if we'll make it out . . . but I take it all back. I was wrong. I was angry. You were thinking about us. Not you. I can see that now.

You're right. Right all along. There's always a chance.

Always.

Chapter One

Salt Lake City Airport, Twelve Hours Earlier

THE view was ugly. Gray, dreary, January dragging on. On the TV screen behind me, some guy sitting in a studio in New York used the words "socked in." I pressed my forehead to the glass. On the tarmac, guys in yellow suits drove trains of luggage around the planes, leaving snow flurries swirling in their exhaust.

To the west, clouds covered the runway, visibility near zero, but given the wind, it came and went. Eastward, snowcapped mountains rose above the clouds. Mountains have long been an attraction for me. For a moment, I wondered what was on the other side.

My flight was scheduled to depart at 6:07 p.m. but, given delays, was starting to look like the red-eye. If at all. Annoyed by the flashing DELAYED sign, I moved to a corner on the floor, against a far wall. I spread patient files across my lap and began dictating my reports into a digital recorder. Folks I'd either seen or treated the week before I left.

Years ago Rachel, my wife, convinced me to focus on sports medicine in kids. She was right. I hated seeing them limp in but loved watching them run out.

The battery indicator was flashing red, so I walked to the store in the terminal and found I could buy two AA batteries for four dollars or twelve for seven. I paid seven, replaced the two in my recorder, and slid the other ten into my backpack.

I was returning from a medical conference in Colorado Springs. The conference satisfied several of my continuing-ed requirements, and most important, it gave me an excuse to spend four days climbing Colorado's Collegiate Peaks. Many doctors buy Porsches, big homes, and country club memberships; I take long runs on the beach and climb mountains when I can get to them.

I'd been gone a week. My return trip took me from Colorado Springs to Salt Lake for the flight home.

Her walk caught my attention. Long, slender legs; purposeful gait yet graceful and rhythmic. Confident and comfortable in her own skin. She was maybe five foot nine or ten, dark-haired and attractive, but not too concerned about it. Maybe thirty. Her hair was short. Not a lot of fuss, yet you could find the same style up and down Manhattan with girls who'd paid a lot of money to look that way. My bet was that she had paid very little.

She walked up, eyed the crowd at the gate, and then chose a spot ten or fifteen feet away on the floor. Dark pantsuit, a leather attaché, and one carry-on. She set down her bags, tied on a pair of running shoes, then sat and stretched, touching head, chest, and stomach to her thigh. After she stretched a few minutes, she pulled several legal pads from her attaché, flipped through pages of handwritten notes, and started typing on her laptop.

After a few minutes, the laptop beeped, and she began eyeballing the wall for an outlet. I was using half. She was holding the swinging end of her laptop's power cord. "Mind if I share?"

"Sure."

She plugged in and then sat cross-legged on the floor with the computer, surrounded by her legal pads. I continued with my files.

"Follow-up orthopedics consultation dated January twenty-third. This is Dr. Ben Payne. Patient's name is Rebecca Peterson. Date of birth, seven six ninety-five, Caucasian female, star right wing on her soccer team, leading scorer in Florida; surgery three weeks ago, post-op normal, presenting no complications, followed by aggressive physical therapy; presents full range of motion, strength test shows marked improvement, as does agility. Rebecca reports movement is pain-free, and she is free to resume all activities . . . except she is to stay off the skateboard until she's at least thirty-five."

I turned to the next file. "Initial orthopedics consultation dated January twenty-third. This is Dr. Ben Payne. Patient's name is Rasheed Smith. Date of birth, two nineteen seventy-nine, black male, starting defensive back for the Jacksonville Jaguars. MRI confirms no tear in the ACL or MCL; recommend that he stay off the YMCA basketball court until he's finished playing professional football. Range of motion is limited due to pain, which should subside given therapy during the off season. Schedule two-week follow-up, and call the YMCA and tell them to revoke his membership."

I slid the files into my backpack and noticed she was laughing.

"You a doctor?"

"Surgeon." I held up the manila folders. "Last week's patients."

"You really get to know them, don't you?" She shrugged. "Sorry, I couldn't help but overhear."

I nodded. "Something my wife taught me."

"Which is?"

"That people are more than the sum of their blood pressure plus their pulse divided by their body mass index."

She laughed again. "You're my kind of doctor."

I nodded at her pads. "And you?"

"Columnist. I write for several women's magazines."

"What kind of topics do you cover?"

"Fashion, trends, a lot of humor, some relationships." She glanced at my recorder. "Most doctors I know loathe those things."

I turned it in my hand. "It grew on me. Now I couldn't live without it."

"Sounds like a story here."

"Rachel . . . my wife, gave it to me. I was joining the staff at the hospital in Jacksonville. She was afraid of never seeing me. This was a way to hear the sound of the other's voice, to not miss the little things. . . . She'd keep it a day or so, speak her mind . . . Then I'd keep it and pass it back."

"Wouldn't a cell phone do the same thing?"

I shrugged. "It's different. Try it sometime and you'll see."

"How long you been married?"

"We married . . . fifteen years ago this week." I glanced at the single diamond on her left hand. "You got one coming up?"

She couldn't control the smile. "I'm trying to get home for my rehearsal dinner party tomorrow night."

"Congratulations."

She shook her head and smiled, staring out across the crowd. "I have a million things to do, and yet here I am making notes on a story about a flash-in-the-pan fashion I don't even like." A shrug. "Jacksonville still home?"

"Yep. And you?"

"Atlanta." She handed me her card: ASHLEY KNOX.

"Ashley."

"To everyone but my dad, who wanted a

boy. He calls me Asher. Instead of ballet and softball, he took me to tae kwon do."

"Let me guess. You're one of those crazy people that can kick stuff off the top of other people's heads. What degree?"

She held up three fingers. "There was a time when my orthopedist was on speed dial. So is this trip work, play, or both?"

"I'm returning from a medical conference and got in some climbing on the side."

"Climbing?"

"Mountains."

"Is that what you do when you're not cutting on people?"

I laughed. "I have two hobbies. Running is one—it's how I met Rachel. In high school. The second is climbing mountains, something we started while I was attending medical school in Denver. There are fifty-four peaks in Colorado higher than fourteen thousand feet, called Fourteeners. I climbed one this trip. Mt. Princeton. Fourteen thousand one hundred ninety-seven feet."

She thought about that a minute. "That's almost three miles above sea level. How long does something like that take?"

"Normally a day or less, but this time of year it's tougher."

"Was it bitter cold, snowing and blowing like crazy?"

"At times." I laughed. "I'll bet you're a good journalist."

One eyebrow raised. "So you're the 'man versus wild' type?"

I shook my head. "Weekend warrior. I'm most at home at sea level."

She stared down the rows of people. "Your wife's not with you?"

"Not this time." My stomach growled, and I stood. "You mind watching my stuff?"

"Sure.

"Be right back."

I returned with a Caesar salad and a plate-size pepperoni pizza as the loudspeaker cackled. "All passengers for Flight sixteen seventy-two, please board. If we load quickly, we might beat this storm."

I grabbed my pack and my food and then followed the other passengers—including Ashley—to the plane. I found my seat and buckled in. We began backing up; then the plane stopped, and the pilot got on the intercom. "Folks, we're in line for the deicer. The controllers tell us we've got about an hour's window to beat this storm, but the ground crew just informed me that one of our two deicing trucks is inoperative. We're twentieth in line on the runway, and long story short, we're not getting out of here tonight."

Groans echoed around the plane.

The pilot continued. "If you'd like a hotel voucher, please see Mark in the red coat at the gate. Once you reclaim your baggage, our shuttle will take you to the hotel. Folks, I'm really sorry."

We walked back into the terminal and watched the DELAYED signs change to CANCELED. I walked to the counter. The attendant stared at a computer screen. Before I opened my mouth, she turned toward the television, which was tuned to the weather channel. "I'm sorry. There's nothing I can do."

Four screens showed a huge green blob moving east-southeast, and the ticker at the bottom of the screen called for snow, ice, single-digit temperatures, and wind chills in the negatives. I had one carry-on—the daypack that doubled as my briefcase—and one checked bag. I walked toward the baggage claim. Standing around the conveyor belt, my eyes wandered. Through the sliding glass doors, I saw the lights of the private airport less than a mile away. Painted on the side of the closest hangar, in huge letters, was one word: CHARTERS.

The lights were on in one of the hangars. My bag appeared. I hefted it atop my shoulder and bumped into Ashley, who was waiting on hers. She eyed mine.

"You weren't kidding when you said you got in some climbing. You really need all that?"

My bag is an orangish Osprey 70 backpack, and it was stuffed with my cold-weather hiking gear. Sleeping bag, Therm-a-Rest pad, Jetboil stove, Nalgene bottles, a few layers of polypropylene, and several other odds and ends that help me stay alive and comfortable.

"These are just the essentials. Good to have along."

She spotted her bag and turned to run it down, then turned back, a pained expression on her face. Apparently, the idea of missing her wedding was starting to sink in, bleeding away her charm. She extended her hand. "Great to meet you. Hope you can get home."

"Yeah, you—"

She never heard me. She threw her bag over her shoulder and headed toward the taxi lane, where a hundred people stood in line.

I FLAGGED down the airport shuttle. Normally it would be busy taxiing people between terminals and the private airport, but given that everyone was trying to leave the airport, it was empty.

I stuck my head in the passenger window. "You mind giving me a ride to the private airport?"

"Hop in. Got nothing better to do."

When we arrived in front of the hangar, the driver sat in the van with the engine running while I ran in.

Inside, I found a red-hot space heater and a white-haired guy standing next to one of three planes, a small single-engine. On the side of the plane, it said GROVER'S CHARTER, and below that FISHING AND HUNTING CHARTERS TO REMOTE LOCATIONS.

He was facing away from me, aiming a compound bow at a target against the far wall. As I walked in, he released an arrow that whistled through the air. He wore faded jeans, and a shirt with snap buttons and the sleeves rolled up. GROVER was stamped across the back of his leather belt, and he carried a Leatherman multi-tool in a holster on his hip. A Jack Russell terrier stood at his heels, sniffing the air and sizing me up.

I waved at the man. "Hi."

He relaxed and turned. He was tall, handsome, and had a strong square chin. "Howdy. You George?"

"No, sir. Not George. Name's Ben."

He raised his bow and returned to his target. "Shame."

"How's that?"

He came to full draw and talked while staring through his peep sight. "Two guys hired me to fly them into the San Juans down near Ouray." He released the arrow. "One of them is named George. Thought you might be him." He nocked another arrow.

I came up alongside him and stared at his target. The evidence around the bull's eye suggested he'd spent a good bit of time shooting that bow. I smiled. "You look like you're new at that."

He laughed, came to full draw a third time, and said, "I do this when I'm bored and waiting on clients." He released his arrow, and it slid into the target, touching the other two. He set his bow down on the seat of his plane, and we walked toward the target.

He pulled out the arrows. "Some guys retire to chase a little dimpled ball with an expensive piece of metal." He smiled. "I fish and hunt."

"Any chance I could convince you to fly me out of here tonight?"

He raised an eyebrow. "You running from the law?"

I shook my head and smiled. "No. Just trying to get home ahead of this storm."

"I was fixing to head home myself and climb into bed with my wife." He noticed my wedding ring. "I 'magine you'd like to do the same." He smiled a broad smile. "Although not with my wife." He laughed. It was easy, and there was great comfort in it.

"Yes, I would."

He nodded. "Where's home?"

"Florida. Thought if I could get ahead of this storm, maybe I could catch a red-eye out of Denver. Or at least the first flight out tomorrow."

"Why the hurry?"

"I'm scheduled for a knee and two hip replacements in"—I checked my watch—"thirteen hours and forty-three minutes."

Grover laughed. Pulled a rag from his back pocket and rubbed the grease around his fingers. "You might be sore tomorrow night."

I laughed. "I'm performing them. I'm a surgeon."

He glanced at the airport in the distance. "Big birds not flying tonight?"

"One of their deicing trucks broke down."

"They do that a lot. You know, they can reschedule surgeries. I've done that a few times myself." He tapped his chest. "Bum ticker."

"I've been gone a week. Need to get back. I don't mind paying."

He stuffed the rag into his pocket, fed the arrows into the quiver hanging on his bow,

then slid the bow into a compartment behind the backseat of the plane. Alongside the
bow were three tubes. He tapped the ends.
"Fly rods."

A hickory-handled something had been
fastened alongside the rods. "What's that?"

"Hatchet." He tapped a stuff sack beneath
the seat, compressing a sleeping bag. "Where
I fly, it pays to be self-sufficient." Behind the
seat hung a vest covered with flies, small scis-
sors, and a net. He waved his hand across it.
"My clients take me to some places I couldn't
afford to get to on my own, so I use them as
an excuse to do things I love. My wife even
goes with me from time to time."

"You own the plane?"

"Yep. It's a Scout. A hundred and eighty
horsepower. Top speed is a hundred and
forty at full throttle."

I frowned. "That's not very fast."

"I gave up speed a long time ago." He put
his hand on the three-bladed propeller. "She
can land at thirty-eight miles an hour, which
means I can put her down in a space about
the size of this hangar. Which means I get to
hunt and fish some rather remote places.
Makes me popular with my clients." He

stared at a large clock, calculating the time and hours. "Even if I get you to Denver, you may not get out of there tonight."

"I'll take my chances. Folks at the counter say that storm may dump enough snow to ground everything tonight and tomorrow."

He nodded. "Won't be cheap. One-fifty an hour, and you pay my way going and coming. Cost to you is about nine hundred dollars."

"You take a credit card?"

He squinted one eye and considered me. Finally he smiled and extended his hand. "Grover Roosevelt."

I shook it and handed him my business card. "I'm Ben Payne."

He pulled a pipe from his shirt pocket, packed it, then pulled out a brass Zippo lighter and flicked it open. "Orthopedics, eh?"

"That and emergency medicine. The two often go hand in hand."

"Give me fifteen minutes. Need to let my wife know that I'll be late but that I'm taking her for a steak dinner when I get back."

"Has this place got wireless?"

"Yep." He walked away. "Password is tank."

I flipped open my laptop, found the network, logged in, and downloaded my e-mail, which included my business and personal voice mail, which had all been forwarded as audio files. That done, I synced my recorder with my computer, then e-mailed the dictation file to our transcription office.

Grover reappeared, and I said, "How many people do you carry?"

"Me and two more if they don't mind sitting hip to hip."

I stared at the airport. "You mind waiting ten minutes?"

"I'll be working through my preflight. But you need to hurry."

My friend in the shuttle van returned me to baggage claim and offered to wait again. I found Ashley standing on the curb waiting on the next taxi.

She had zipped up a North Face down jacket over her suit coat. I pointed over my shoulder. "I've hired a charter to fly me to Denver. Maybe get ahead of the storm. I know you don't really know me from Adam's house cat, but there's room for one more."

"You're serious?"

"I know this can look a little . . . whatever. But I've been through that whole wedding thing, and if you're anything like my wife, you won't sleep for the next two days trying to make every detail perfect. It's just an honest offer from one professional to another. No strings."

Skepticism shaded her face. She looked me up and down.

I spun my wedding ring around my finger. "On the back porch of my condo, my wife placed three bowls to feed the Dumpster cats that hang out in the parking lot. Now I've got names for them, and I've gotten used to that little purring thing they do."

A wrinkle appeared between her eyebrows. "You saying I'm a stray cat?"

"No. I'm saying that I never noticed they were there until she pointed them out. Now I see them most everywhere." I paused. "I don't want you to miss your wedding. That's all."

"Will you let me split the fare with you?"

"If that'll make you feel better. But you're welcome either way."

She stared down the roadway. "I'm supposed to take my bridesmaids to breakfast in the morning, followed by a few hours at the spa." She looked at the hotel lights in the distance, then took a deep breath and smiled. "Getting out of here would be fantastic." She glanced back inside. "Can you wait three minutes?"

"Sure, but . . ." The green blob inched closer to the airport on the screen behind us.

"Sorry. Too much coffee. Was just trying to make it to the hotel. Figure the bathroom here is bigger than the one on that plane."

I laughed. "Chances are good."

Chapter Two

GROVER was sitting in the plane, headphones on, clicking buttons and turning dials in front of him. "You ready?"

"Grover, this is Ashley Knox. She's a writer from Atlanta. Getting married in forty-eight hours. Thought we could give her a lift."

"Be my pleasure."

He stowed our luggage behind the rear seat, and we climbed into the plane. Grover cranked the engine, while Ashley and I put on the headsets hanging above our seats. We rolled out of the hangar, where he sat flicking more switches, moving the stick between his knees, and adjusting knobs.

While he was going through his preflight, I dialed my voice mail. One message. I held the phone to my ear. "Hey . . . it's me." Her voice was low. Tired. Like she'd been sleeping. Or crying. I could hear the ocean in the background. "I don't like it when you leave." She took a deep breath. "I know you're worried. Don't be. It'll work out. You'll see. I'll wait up." She attempted a laugh. "We all will. Coffee on the beach. Hurry . . . And don't think for a minute I love you any less. I love you the same. Even more. Don't be angry. Trust me. We'll make it. Hurry home. Meet you on the beach."

I clicked the phone shut and stared out the window.

Grover gently pressed the stick forward, rolling us down the blacktop. He spoke over his shoulder. "You want to call her back?"

"What?"

He pointed at my cell phone. "You want to call her back?"

"No." I slid it into my pocket. "You've got pretty good ears."

He pointed at the microphone connected to my headset. "Your mike picked up her voice. Might as well have been listening to it myself." He pointed at Ashley. "There are no secrets in a plane this small."

She smiled, tapped her earphones, and nodded.

Grover slowed to a stop. "I can wait if you want."

I shook my head. "No . . . really, it's okay."

Grover spoke into his mike. "Control, this is one three eight bravo, request permission to take off."

A few seconds passed, and a voice spoke through our headphones. "One three eight bravo, you're cleared for takeoff."

Two minutes later we were airborne and climbing. Grover spoke over the microphone. "We'll climb to twelve thousand feet, then turn northeast, head across the High Uintas Wilderness Area, and descend to Denver. In-flight meal and entertainment service will begin immediately." He reached into the door pocket, passed two bags of smoked almonds over his shoulder, and began singing "I'll Fly Away." He cut the song mid-sentence. "Ben? How long you been married?"

"Got married fifteen years ago this week."

Ashley piped up. "Tell the truth. Is it still exciting or just ho-hum?"

Grover laughed. "I've been married almost fifty years, and trust me, it gets better. Not worse. Not dull. I love her more today than the day we married, and I thought that was impossible."

She looked at me. "How 'bout it? Got any plans?"

I nodded. "Thought I'd bring her some flowers. Open a bottle of wine and watch the waves roll up on the sand."

"You still bring her flowers?"

"Every week."

She turned sideways and lowered her head, raising one eyebrow. "You bring your wife flowers every week?"

"Yep."

The journalist in her surfaced. "What's her favorite flower?"

"Potted orchids."

"What does she do with all the orchids? Please don't tell me you just pitch them."

"I built her a greenhouse."

"A greenhouse? How many orchids do you have?"

I shrugged. "Last time I counted, two hundred and fifty-seven."

Grover laughed. "A true romantic." He spoke over his shoulder. "Ashley, how'd you meet your fiancé?"

"The courtroom. I was writing a story about a celebrity trial. He served as opposing counsel and invited me to dinner."

"Perfect. Where're you two going on your honeymoon?"

"Italy. Two weeks. Starting in Venice and ending in Florence."

Turbulence shook the plane. Ashley turned the questioning back to Grover. "Just curious, Mr. . . ." She snapped her fingers.

He waved her off. "Call me Grover."

"How many hours have you logged in the air?"

He dipped the plane hard right, then pulled back, shooting us upward and sending my stomach into my throat. "You mean, can I get you to Denver without dipping the nose into a mountain?"

"Yeah . . . something like that."

He rocked the wheel left, then right, dipping each wing. "Including or not including time spent in the military?"

I latched a death grip on the handle above my head.

Ashley did likewise and said, "Not."

He leveled out, smooth as a tabletop. " 'Bout fifteen thousand hours." I could hear the smile in his voice. "You two feel better now?"

His dog crawled out from under his seat, hopped up on his lap, and stared over his shoulder at us, snarling and twitching like a squirrel on steroids. His body was one massive, rippled muscle, but his legs were only four or five inches long.

Grover again, "You two, meet Tank. My copilot."

"How many hours has *he* got?" I asked.

Grover's head tilted. "Between three and four thousand."

The dog turned, hopped off Grover's lap, and curled back into his hole beneath the seat.

I leaned forward slightly to watch Grover's hands. Gnarled. Meaty. Dry skin. Big knuckles. Wedding ring thin around the edges. "How long will it take us to get there?"

He slid a silver pocket watch from his shirt, clicked it open. A woman's picture was taped to the inside of the cover. He then stared at his instruments. The GPS gave him estimated arrival time, but I got the feeling he was double-checking his instruments. "Given our crosswind . . . right at two hours."

The picture I'd glimpsed was tattered and cracked, but even faded she was beautiful. "You got kids?"

"Five, and thirteen grandchildren. Our youngest is probably older than you." He glanced over his shoulder. "Ben, how old are you?"

"Thirty-nine."

"And you, Ashley?"

"Don't you know you're never supposed to ask a lady her age?"

"Well, technically I'm not supposed to put two people in that backseat, but I'm old school and it's never stopped me."

Ashley smiled. "So this isn't legal? When

we land, are we going to the terminal or to jail?"

He laughed again. "Technically, they don't know you're on this plane, so I doubt they'll be waiting to arrest you. If they do, I'll tell them you kidnapped me and I'd like to press charges."

She looked at me. "I feel better."

He continued. "This plane is designed to fly low and slow. Because of that, I fly under visual flight rules, which means I don't have to file a flight plan as long as I plan to fly by sight. Which I am. Which means what they don't know won't hurt them. So?" He looked toward Ashley. "Your age?"

"Thirty-four."

He looked at his instrument panel and then eyed one of the GPS units. "Wind drift is killing us. This is a big storm coming in. It's a good thing I know where I'm going; otherwise, we'd be way off course." He laughed to himself. "Youngsters. Both of you. Your whole life before you. What I wouldn't do to be thirtysomething, knowing what I know now."

The two of us sat quietly. Ashley's disposition had changed. More pensive. I wasn't all that comfortable knowing I'd put her in a precarious position. Grover picked up on it. "Don't you two worry. It's only illegal if you get caught, and I've never been caught. In a couple hours, you'll be on the ground and on your way." He coughed, cleared his throat, and laughed some more.

The night sky shone through the Plexiglas above my head. The stars looked close enough to touch.

"All right, you two." Grover coughed again.

I'd heard it the first time, but it was the second time that caught my attention.

"Given that we're trying to outrun that storm, and given the wind drift, and given that I don't carry oxygen, we've got to stay below fifteen thousand feet or you'll land with a headache."

Ashley said, "I hear a 'so' coming."

"So," Grover continued, "hold on, because we're coming up on the Uintas."

Sounded like he said "you-in-tas." "The what-as?"

"The High Uintas Wilderness. Largest east-to-west mountain range on the continent, home to a million acres of uncivilized wilderness, gets five to seven hundred inches of snow a year, seven hundred lakes, some of the best fishing and hunting anywhere."

"Sounds remote."

"Ever see the movie *Jeremiah Johnson*?" He pointed down. Nodded longingly. "That's where they filmed it."

"No kidding? One of my favorites."

"No kidding."

The ride was starting to get bumpy. My stomach jumped into my throat.

Grover stared out the glass, and we did likewise. The dog jumped up on his lap. "In the middle is a national forest that's designated a wilderness, which means there are no motorized vehicles of any kind. Hence, it's one of the more remote places on the planet. More Mars than Earth. If you robbed a bank, it'd be a great place to hide." Another cough. Another laugh.

The wilderness spread out beneath us. "Grover?" Ashley raised an eyebrow. "How far can we see right now?"

He paused. "Maybe seventy miles, give or take."

There wasn't a single light in any direction.

"How many times have you made this run?"

He tilted his head. "A hundred or more."

"Good, 'cause if we get any closer to the snowcapped peaks, they'll scrape off the bottom of the plane."

"Naw . . ." He was playing with us. "We got a good hundred feet." He pulled a sleeve of Tums from his shirt pocket, popped two, started chewing, and coughed again. He tapped his chest.

I tapped him on the shoulder. "Tell me about your bum ticker. How long you been coughing and popping antacids?"

He pulled back on the stick, and we rose up over a plateau and skirted between two mountains. The moon appeared out the left glass, shining down on a world blanketed in white. He was quiet a minute, looking right, then left. "Beautiful, isn't it?"

Ashley answered for all of us. "Surreal."

"Doc," Grover started, "I saw my cardiologist last week. He's the one recommended the antacids."

"Did you have the cough then?"

"Yep. It's why my wife sent me."

"They run an EKG?"

"Yep. All clear."

"Do yourself a favor and go back. Might be nothing. But might be something, too. I think it'd be worth another look."

He nodded. "I live by a couple simple rules. One of those is that I stick to what I'm good at and I give people credit at sticking to what they're good at."

"So you'll go?"

"Probably can't tomorrow. Maybe the middle of the week."

I sat back. "Just get in this week. Deal?"

Ashley interrupted us. "Tell me about your wife."

We were rolling across mountaintops with precision. Grover was quiet a moment, then spoke. "A Midwest girl. She married me when I had nothing but love, dreams, and lust. Gave me children, stuck with me when I lost everything, believed me when I told her we'd be okay. She's the most beautiful woman on the planet."

"So, got any advice for a girl forty-eight hours from walking down the aisle?"

"When I wake up in the morning, she's holding my hand. I make the coffee, and then she sits with her knees touching mine while

we drink it." He shrugged. "We've been married a long time, seen a lot, but loving somebody gets better the more you do it. You
might think an old man like me doesn't get
fired up when she walks across the bedroom
in a faded flannel gown, but I do. Maybe she
ain't as perky as she was in her twenties.
Maybe she's got some wrinkles she don't like,
but I don't look like the man in our wedding
pictures either. I married a woman who fits
me. I'm one half of a two-piece puzzle."

Grover checked his instruments and continued. "You two walked into my hangar tonight and saw a blue-and-yellow plane piloted
by a crusty old man with a little dog at his
heels. A quick hop to Denver so you can get
on with your busy lives." He shook his head.
"I see an enclosed capsule that lifts you up
above the problems of the earth and gives you
a perspective you can't get on land. Where
you can see clearly. All of us spend our days
looking through lenses that are smudged,
scratched, and some broken. But this here"—
he tapped the stick—"this pulls you out from
behind the lenses and for a few brief seconds
gives you twenty-twenty vision."

Ashley's tone was quiet. "That why you love flying?"

He nodded. "Sometimes my wife and I will come up here and spend two or three hours. Not saying a word. And when we land, all the world seems right."

We were quiet several minutes. Then he coughed.

Grover grunted, something low and guttural. He grabbed his chest, leaned forward, and pushed off his headset, and his head slammed against the side of the glass. He arched his back, then grabbed his shirt and pulled, tearing the shirt and popping off the buttons. He lunged forward, jerked the stick hard right, and then dipped the wing ninety degrees toward the earth.

The mountain rose up to meet us. It felt like we were falling off a table. Just before we hit, he corrected her, pulled back on the stick, and the plane began to stall. Our speed slowed to almost nothing.

Then, as if he'd done it a thousand times, he pancaked the plane against the mountain.

The tail touched first, then the left wing, which hit something and snapped off. The weight of the right wing pulled on the plane, tilting us and making an anchor of sorts. Somewhere in there, Grover shut the engine. The last thing I remember was spinning, somersaulting, and the tail breaking off. Then I heard a loud crack. Ashley screamed and the dog barked and floated through the air. Snow peppered my face, followed by the sound of breaking tree limbs, followed by the impact.

The last image I remember seeing was the green blob inching across the bluish glow of the dash-mounted GPS.

HAVING just met Ashley, who reminds me a lot of you, I was thinking about the day we met.

After school. I was standing on the track. A good bit warmer then than I am now. We were running quarters when the cross-country team came across the field, clustered behind a break-away, single girl. You.

You were floating. Barely skimming the surface of the grass. A concert of arms over legs controlled by some unseen puppeteer. A sophomore on the team, I'd seen you before. You jumped the high hurdle next to me. Your breathing was deep, rhythmic, purposeful. Somewhere over the hurdle, you shot me a glance.

Your whipping arms slung sweat across my legs and stomach. I heard myself say, "Wow." I tripped over a hurdle, and in that single second, you broke your concentration. Or allowed it to be broken. Your eyes lit. Then your feet touched down, and you were gone.

I must have said "Wow" a second time, because my teammate Scott smacked me in the back of the head. "Don't even think about it."

"What?"

"Rachel Hunt. She's taken, and you don't stand a chance."

"Why not?"

"Two words. Nate Kelsey."

Nate Kelsey played middle linebacker. Had no neck. And set the state bench-press record.

"I can take him."

Scott smacked me in the head again. "Boy, you need a keeper."

But that was all it took.

Coach's wife worked in admissions. She was always trying to set me up. I asked her for your class schedule. Soon after, I discovered I had an insatiable desire to make a change in my third-period elective.

My adviser was not persuaded. "You want to take Latin? Why?"

" 'Cause I think it's cool when people speak it."

"People haven't spoken Latin since Rome fell."

"Rome fell?"

He was not impressed. "Ben, what's her name?"

"Rachel Hunt."

"Why didn't you just say that?" He signed my change form and smiled. "Good luck. You'll need it."

"Thanks."

I got to class early and watched you walk in. If I hadn't been seated, my knees would've buckled. You looked at me, smiled, and set your books on the table to my left. Then you spun and stuck out your hand. "I'm Rachel."

"Hi." Okay, okay. Maybe I stammered a bit.

I remember looking at your eyes and thinking I'd never seen green like that. Big, round.

You said, "You're Ben Payne."

My jaw fell open, and I nodded. "You know me?"

"Fast as you run, who doesn't?" You turned

your head sideways, half smiling. "Anyone ever told you you have a nice voice?"

My voice rose about eight octaves. "No." I cleared my throat. "I mean . . ." Lower this time. "No."

You opened a notebook. "Well, you do. It's . . . warm."

We spent the rest of the year as "friends," because I didn't have the you-know-whats to ask you out. Not to mention the fact that Mr. No-neck could break me in half—if he could catch me.

Junior year, I had just arrived at school, had about thirty minutes before the first bell rang, and we bumped into each other as you came out of the girls locker room. Your eyes were wet.

"You okay?"

You turned and began walking away from the school. "No!"

I took your pack, and together we walked out onto the track. "What's wrong?"

You were exasperated. "I'm not getting any faster, that's what."

"Well. I think I can help with that. Your arms. Too much lateral movement. And . . ." I waved my hand over your hip flexor. "You're

too tight here. Your feet are fast, but you need to cover more ground with each stride."

Your lips turned down. "And you can fix this?"

"Well . . . I can run alongside and maybe help you find a rhythm that will cause you to lengthen it. Run with someone who has a longer stride and your stride adjusts."

"And you'd do that?"

"Well . . . of course. Who wouldn't?"

You crossed your arms. "Until now? You! You're the only one who won't give me the time of day."

"What about number fifty-four? The guy with no neck."

"In case you haven't heard, Einstein, we stopped dating last year! You may be fast out here, but when it comes to this thing"—you tapped me in the chest—"I can run circles around you."

You still do.

Chapter Three

IT WAS dark, and the pain had worsened. I pressed the light button on my watch: 4:47 a.m. Maybe six hours had elapsed since the crash. Another two to daylight. But in this cold, I wasn't sure I'd last another fifteen minutes. I was shivering so hard, my teeth were clattering. Grover was covered in four inches of snow.

Ashley lay on my left. I touched her neck and the carotid artery. Her pulse was strong and elevated, but she was quiet. I couldn't see her in the dark. I felt around me. Snow and broken glass covered us. To my right, I found the compression sack strapped to the underside of Grover's seat. I pulled, and the sleeping bag came out slowly. I unzipped the side and spread it over us as much as I could. I could only move a little at a time, because the pain in my rib cage left me breathless. I tucked the bag around her, slipping her feet into the end. The unnatural cant of her leg told me she was in a bad way. The dog tucked himself in with me. Several feet in front of me, I saw the propeller stuck in the air. Caked in snow. Part of the blade was missing.

DAYLIGHT broke, and I woke to the dog standing on my chest, licking my nose. The sky was gray and still dumping snow. The down sleeping bag was warming me up. But with increasing blood flow came more pain in my ribs.

Ashley still lay next to me, silent and un-moving. I touched her neck. Her pulse was still strong and not as elevated. Meaning her body had burned through the adrenaline that flooded her system when we crashed. Her face was swollen and caked with blood due to the cuts above her eyes and on her scalp. I ran my hand along her shoulder. It was dislocated, hanging low from the socket. I slid my arm up her sleeve, pulled down, and let the tendons pull the bone back and snap it into the socket. Without undressing her and talking to her, I couldn't get a handle on whether she had any internal injuries. I ran my hands along her hips, then her legs. Her right was fine; her left was not. Her thigh was grossly swollen, maybe twice its normal size, and her pant leg was taut. Fortunately, the bone had not broken the skin.

I had to set it, but I needed space to work. Currently I felt like I was in an MRI ma-chine with all the sides too close to my face. I sat up and found that we were encased in a snow-and-plane-fuselage cave. Which, from a certain perspective, was good.

The impact, along with the storm, had buried us in a snowbank. That formed a snow cocoon, which meant that we were more or less maintaining thirty-two degrees, which was better than whatever the outside temperature was. The majority of the light was coming in through the Plexiglas atop the plane, filtering through the snow.

While I worked to dig away the snow to make room to get at her leg, the dog whined and spun in circles. Then he climbed up on Grover's lap and started licking the snow from his face. My hands got cold, so I dug around in front of Grover and found a plastic clipboard in the door pocket. I used it like a shovel to dig a shelf in the snow long enough for Ashley to lie in.

I pulled the bag off her, laid it flat inside the shelf, and slowly slid and lifted her body across the seat and onto the shelf. The effort exhausted me, so I fell back and sat there breathing, short and shallow, trying to lessen the pain in my chest. Thirty minutes passed before I had enough energy to return to her leg.

I spoke to her, but she didn't respond, which was good, because what I was about to do was going to hurt more than the initial break.

I took off my belt, wrapped it around her ankle and then my wrist, giving me an anchor to pull on. Then I took off my left hiking boot and slowly placed my foot between her legs. I straightened my leg against her, then tightened the belt and grabbed her foot with both hands. I took four or five deep breaths and felt her hand slide onto my foot. She patted it and mumbled, "Pull . . . hard."

I pulled, pushed with my leg, and arched my back, all at the same time. The pain shot through her, her head rocked back, and she uttered a muffled scream before losing consciousness. The leg popped loose; I turned it, let it straighten naturally, and then let go. The leg hung to the side in a mostly natural position that mirrored the right.

With the leg set, I began looking for a brace. Above my head hung two mangled wing supports, both more than three feet long and about as big around as my index finger. I began working them back and forth, weakening the metal, and they eventually snapped off.

My backpack lay behind us in the snowbank. Only a corner was visible. I pulled away some snow, found the zipper, and slid my hand inside until I found my Swiss Army knife. I slit Ashley's pant leg up to her hip. The leg was swollen, and much of the thigh was a deep purple.

The belt restraints on both seats were comprised of an over-the-shoulder harness system with a typical quick-release buckle. I loosened them and used both pieces of one harness to secure the "poles" around her leg, tightened the straps, and placed the buckle directly above her femoral artery. Then I took a T-shirt from my suitcase, cut it in two, and wound each piece into a taut tubelike piece, which I placed beneath either side of the buckle, taking pressure off the artery and giving her leg ample blood flow. Lastly, I packed the area around the break in snow to bring down the swelling.

I reached into my backpack and pulled out a pair of polypro long underwear and a wool sweater lined with a Windstopper fabric that's warm even when it's wet. I pulled off her down jacket, her suit coat, her blouse, her bra, and checked her chest and ribs for any evidence of internal injuries. No bruises had surfaced. I slid her into my long underwear and sweater, then back into her down jacket. I pulled the sleeping bag beneath her, wrapped her up like a mummy with only her left leg hanging out, then elevated and covered her left foot. I pulled a wool beanie from my pack and slid it down over her ears.

Once she was dry and warm, I realized how shallow my breathing and elevated my pulse had become. The pain in my ribs had intensified. I pushed my arms into my jacket and lay down next to her to get warm. When I did, the dog walked across my legs, walked in two circles while his nose stretched to find his tail, and burrowed between us. He looked like he'd done that before. I stared across at Grover's snow-covered body.

The fingers on Ashley's left hand extended through her jacket and touched my arm. I sat up in time to see her lips move, but I couldn't understand. I leaned closer. Her lips moved again.

"Thank you."

IT'S DAYLIGHT. THE SNOW *is still falling heavily, and it's really quiet, like somebody hit the mute button on the world.*

Ashley is not doing too well. I set her leg and her shoulder, but she'll need surgery on her leg when we get out of here. She passed out when I set it. She's been talking some in her sleep.

Grover, the pilot—he didn't make it. Did I already tell you that? He landed the plane after his heart had stopped. I don't know how. Putting it down without killing us was nothing short of heroic.

Me? I broke a few ribs. Maybe three. The pain on inhaling is piercing. And I may have a collapsed lung. Course, the elevation is above eleven thousand feet, so breathing isn't easy anyway.

I can't think of any reason why we should expect a rescue. Grover wasn't required to file a flight plan. He never told anyone he had passengers, so the tower had no idea we were on the plane.

From the side, Grover sort of looked like Dad. Although kinder.

Some said Dad was a jerk. Others said I was lucky to have such a committed father. Course, they wouldn't have lasted a day in my house.

Mom didn't. He abused her; she crawled inside a bottle, and he kept her hopping from one rehab to the next, stripped her of parental rights. I don't know the whole story. He let me talk to her by phone.

From the moment he clicked on the light at four fifty-five a.m., I had five minutes to be standing at the back door. Dressed. Two pairs of sweats, running shorts, and shoes. Most nights I slept dressed.

Six miles to the lifeguard station and back. I don't know why he chose six, but I think it had more to do with the doughnut shop than anything else. Cheating was impossible, because he'd drive to the shop, sit next to the glass, coffee in one hand, doughnut in the other, checking my time as I trudged up the beach and slapped the lifeguard's chair. If I was up a few seconds, he'd beat me home and say nothing. But if I was slow, he'd run out and shout across the sand, "Down seven!" or "Down twenty!"

I learned how to run within myself, monitoring and gauging output and speed. Fear does that.

When I got home, he'd meet me on the beach, where I was allowed to pull off both pairs of sweats before I started my speed work. Mondays *we ran twelve 660s. As in six hundred and sixty meters. Tuesdays were 550s, and so on. Sunday was my only free day, but it was a mixed pleasure because Monday was just around the corner.*

We always finished with a speed rope, sit-ups, crunches, push-ups, and whatever other pain-inducing thing he could dream up.

He'd say softly, "Pain is weakness leaving your body."

I'd stand there thinking, Good . . . Why don't we let some out of your body. I'm about out. I lost a lot of pain in his house.

By seven a.m., I'd have run seven to ten miles. I'd go to school, try not to fall asleep in class, and then go to track practice, which seemed mundane in comparison.

Dad was managing his firm, fifty traders, and because the stock market closed at four, he'd appear about four fifteen, loosened tie, stopwatch in hand, staring at me over the fence.

Yeah, he was committed all right.

My freshman year I won the four-hundred-meter dash in 50.9 seconds, anchored the 4x400 meter relay, and won the mile in 4:28. That made me state champion in three events. Dad drove me home in silence. No celebration. No day off. He parked the car. "If you're going to break four minutes, you've got work to do." Somewhere in there it occurred to me that, to my dad, I was only as good as my last time, and in truth, no time was ever good enough.

I had few friends, and if I wasn't in school, I was either running or sleeping. Then came my sophomore year. You entered the picture and lit my world with laughter and light and wonder. You ran by me, flicking sweat off your fingertips, and I wanted to take a shower, wash off Dad, and bathe in you.

So much of what I am, he made. Forged it in me. I know that. But Dad used pain to rid me of pain. Leaving me empty and hurting.

You gave me the one thing he never did. Love, absent a stopwatch.

IT WAS dark when I woke. I pressed the light button on my watch: 12:01 a.m. An entire day had passed. Then I checked the date. Make that two days. We'd slept thirty-six hours straight.

A billion stars stared down on me. Close enough to touch. The moon had appeared over my left shoulder. Big as Christmas.

As sleep pressed in, I made a mental

list, which included two things—food and water—and we needed both soon. With emphasis on water. If Ashley was fighting infection, I needed to get her kidneys working and I needed to get her hydrated. Shock has a way of burning up your fluids, and while I may not have been conscious of it, I had been in shock and running on adrenalin since the crash. Tomorrow, if I could get the GPS working, I'd try to figure out where we were, 'cause I knew better than to expect a rescue.

DAYLIGHT lit a blue sky. I tried to move, but I was so stiff it hurt to pick up my head. I sat up and leaned against a large boulder protruding from the snowbank.

Daylight and some clarity allowed me to see what had happened to the plane and us. Bad news first. While Grover's plane was bright blue and yellow, all but the left wing was buried in a ten-foot snowdrift. Needle in a haystack came to mind.

The only good news was that this "burial" gave us a measure of protection from the elements. Thirty-two degrees above zero is better than thirty-two below.

Ashley lay sleeping, and her face was flushed. I rolled to my backpack, pulled out my Jetboil, and filled the canister with fresh powder from just outside the cave. I clicked it on. The blue flame erupted, and as the snow melted, I added more. Either the noise of the burner or my movement woke Ashley. Her face was puffy, and her eyes were slits.

I held a cup of warm water to her lips. "Drink this."

She sipped. I had a bottle of Advil somewhere in my pack. I desperately wanted to down about four, but I knew she was in more pain and would need them more than I in the days to come. I found them in a side pocket, dumped four into my hand, and held one to her lips. "Can you swallow this?"

She nodded. I placed it on her tongue, and she swallowed. We repeated this three times. Slowly. The snow around her leg had long since melted, so the swelling, while it might have gone down, was back. And swelling brought pain. If I could reduce it, I could help reduce the pain. The Advil worked from the inside; snow would work on the outside.

I repacked her leg and felt for the pulse around her ankle. She was getting good circulation. I held the cup to her lips until she finished the whole thing. That meant eight ounces. My goal for the day would be five more of those.

I refilled the cup and the Jetboil, taking some fluid myself. Ashley forced her eyes open as much as the swelling would allow. She scanned the cave, what was left of the plane, her torn clothing, the brace on her leg. Her eyes settled on Grover's body. "Is he . . . ?"

"He was gone before the plane touched down. Heart, I guess. I don't know how he landed it."

She reached up, walking her fingertips across her face and head. Her expression changed.

Slowly I pulled her hand down. "I need to stitch you up."

Her voice was hoarse. "What day is it?"

I gave her the short version. When I finished, she didn't say anything.

I dug through Grover's fly-fishing vest and found some fine monofilament. I stripped one of the flies off the vest and removed all the stuff that made it look like a fly, exposing a single barbless hook. I needed to straighten the hook to more of a ninety-degree angle, but I needed a tool. Grover's belt. I dug through the snow around his waist and found the Leatherman. I straightened the hook and threaded the monofilament through the eye. When I looked back at Ashley, tears were rolling down her face.

She said, "I'm sure his wife is worried about him."

I dug out a second shelf in the snow, lower than the shelf on which she lay. I pulled my sleeping bag out of my pack and spread it on the shelf next to her. I wiped a tear from her face. "What hurts?"

She glanced at Grover's body. "Him."

"How about on your body?"

"Everything."

"I'm not finished hurting you. I need to sew a few stitches."

She nodded.

Three places. The first required two stitches in her scalp, which were relatively painless. The second was along the top of her right eye, running through the middle of her eyebrow. I pierced the skin with the hook and said, "There's an older scar here."

"Nationals. I was eighteen. Kid caught me with a roundhouse."

I tied the first stitch. "Knock you out?"

"No. Made me mad. I caught him with a spinning back kick followed by a double round, which cockroached him."

"Cockroached?"

"We had names for the positions people fell in when we knocked them out. The porpoise, the white man's dance, the cockroach."

I tied another knot and cut the line. "What I've done is good enough to hold you until we can get to a hospital."

"What about my pretty two-poled brace? My leg is killing me."

"It's the best I can do without an X-ray. When we get to a hospital, if it's not aligned, I'll recommend that they rebreak it and give you a few presents that will set off the metal detector when you pass through security. Either way, you'll be good as new."

"You've just said, 'get to a hospital' twice,

but do you really think anybody is coming?"

As we looked up at the blue sky through the hole created between the leaning wing and the snow wall, we saw a commercial airliner cruising at what looked like thirty thousand feet. I shook my head.

"We can see them just fine, but I'm pretty certain they can't see us. Any evidence of our disappearance lies under three feet of snow."

"Maybe you should crawl out and wave your shirt or something."

I chuckled. Which hurt. I clutched my side.

Her eyes narrowed. "What's up?"

"Couple of broken ribs."

"Let me see."

I pulled up my shirt. The whole left side of my rib cage was a deep purple. "Only hurts when I breathe."

We laughed.

I turned my attention to the side of her arm. Either the rock or a branch had cut the skin on her non-dislocated shoulder, about four inches in length. Fortunately for her, when the plane came to a stop, she was unconscious and pressed up against the snow.

Pressure mixed with snow stopped the bleeding. It would need twelve or more stitches.

She watched me work and spoke without looking at me. "What do you think our chances are?"

"You don't beat around the bush, do you?"

"What's the use? Sugarcoating it won't get us out of here any faster."

"Good point." I shrugged. "Let me ask you a few questions. Did you tell anyone you were getting on this plane?"

She shook her head.

"No e-mail? Phone call? No nothing?"

Another slow shake.

"So nobody on planet earth knows you stepped in a charter plane and attempted to fly to Denver? Me, either."

She whispered, "I imagine everyone thought I was still in Salt Lake. Now they'd be looking for me, but where would they look?"

I nodded and tied off another stitch. "Based on the way Grover was talking, there's no official record that we flew. And we never told a single soul we were going." I paused. "It's as if this flight never existed."

"It existed all right." She stared at Grover. "I just thought it'd be a quick hop to Denver and life would continue."

I cut the line. "Ashley, I'm really sorry." I shook my head. "You should be somewhere getting a manicure or something."

"Don't beat yourself up over good intentions. I was glad you offered. Not so much now, but I was then." She laid her head back. "I was scheduled for a massage. You know, one of those hot-rocks deals? Instead, I'm lying on ice with only one rock." She shook her head. "You have any idea how much I paid for that dress?"

"It'll be waiting when you get there." I held the cup to her lips, and she sipped, finishing off twenty-four ounces. "Your sense of humor is a gift."

"Well . . . would you think it funny if I told you I had to pee?"

"From a certain point of view, that's good." I looked at the bag and her immobility. "From another, it's not."

"Which way are we looking at it?"

"Whatever way lets you go without putting pressure on that leg." I looked around. "What I wouldn't give for a catheter."

"Oh, no, let's don't. Those things give me the creeps."

I grabbed a Nalgene bottle out of my pack and laid it next to her. "All right, here's the deal."

"I'm not going to go like this, am I?"

"It's better than the alternative, and you get to stay right there, but I've got to help. I'm going to finish slitting your pants up to your hip. That way, while you're lying there, you can lay them over you. Then I'm going to dig a hole in the snow beneath you big enough for this bottle. Then we're going to ease your underwear out of the way, and you're gonna go in the bottle."

"You're right; I don't like this."

"We need to measure your urine output, and I need to see if there's any blood in it."

"Blood?"

"Internal injuries."

I slit her pants, dug out the snow, and held the bottle in place, and she used her one healthy arm to lift herself slightly, without changing the position of her leg. She looked at me. "Can I go?"

I nodded. She went.

She shook her head. "This has got to be

one of the more embarrassing moments I've ever shared with another human being."

"Given that I blend orthopedics and emergency medicine, there are few days that go by that I don't study people's urine. Most of the folks I see in the ER have suffered some substantial impact, which means internal injuries, which can mean blood in their urine."

She looked at me. "Are you trying to make me feel better?"

I pulled up on the bottle and studied the color. "Yep. And the color's good."

I helped her dress, slid the sleeping bag underneath her, and then covered her up. The process of doing so brought her skin into contact with mine. And while I was acting as her doctor, her nakedness, her total vulnerability, was not lost on me. I thought of Rachel.

By the time we got it all finished, I felt like someone had stabbed me with a stiletto in the ribs. I lay down, breathing heavily.

She spoke down at me. "You taken anything for the pain?"

I shook my head. "No."

"Why not?"

"To be honest, if you think you're hurting now, just give it three or four days. I've only got enough Advil to get you through a week. I've got a few prescription-strength narcotics somewhere in that pack, but I thought I'd save them for tonight when you can't sleep."

She eyed my pack. "Got any red wine in there?"

"No, but I could make you a gin and tonic if you'd like."

"Great. My leg's throbbing like somebody hit it with a hammer."

I lifted the top of the sleeping bag and repacked the snow around her leg. "I'm going to keep doing this for several days. It'll speed recovery and help anesthetize the pain. Only problem is, you're going to be cold."

"Going to be?"

I screwed the cap on the Nalgene bottle and started crawling toward daylight. "I'm going to take a look around and empty this bottle."

"Good. I'm going to clean up a bit around here, maybe order a pizza or something."

"I like pepperoni."

"Got it."

I crawled out of the fuselage—or what was left of it—under the wing, and into the sunlight. The temperature was probably in the single digits, but I'd expected worse. I took one step off the packed snow where the plane had landed, and my foot submerged all the way to my groin. The impact shook my chest. I tried not to scream in pain, but I wasn't very successful.

Ashley's voice rose up out of the plane. "You okay?"

"Yeah. Just wishing I had some snowshoes."

I dumped the bottle and looked around as best I could. Nothing but snow and mountains. We seemed to be on some sort of plateau, with a few higher peaks to my left, but most everything else spread out below and before us.

I crawled back in and collapsed on the shelf next to her.

"Well?" she asked.

"Nothing. Grover was right. More Mars than Earth."

"Really, you can tell me the truth. I can handle it."

I stared up at her where she sat, eyes closed. Waiting. "It's . . . beautiful. The view is . . . panoramic. Unlike anything you've ever seen. I've got two lawn chairs set up, and a little guy with umbrella drinks will be back around in a few minutes."

She relaxed and laid her head back. The first ear-to-ear grin I'd seen since we'd been in the snow. "Glad to hear it's not as bad as I thought."

Somewhere in there it struck me that Ashley Knox was one of the stronger human beings I'd ever met. Here she lay, half dead, in the process of missing her own wedding, not to mention the fact that we had no probable chance of rescue—if we got out of here, it'd be up to us. Most people would be panicked, despondent. But somehow she could laugh. What's more, she made *me* laugh. And that's something I actually hadn't done in a long while.

I was spent. I needed food and I needed rest, but I couldn't get food without rest. I put together a plan.

"We need food, but I'm in no shape to go find it. Right now I'm going to keep feeding us both warm water and try and conserve my energy. We're breathing half the oxygen we're used to, and we need it to heal. I'm going to start thinking about getting to a lower elevation. Right now"—I turned the mounting screws for the GPS and unplugged it from the dash—"I'm going to try and get a fix on where we are while this thing still has life in it."

She stared at me. "How do you know to do all this?"

"When I was a kid, my dad realized I could run faster than most. He took that ability and turned it into his passion. But once Rachel and I were on our own, we gravitated to the mountains. We bought up gear and spent the weekends in the mountains. Maybe I learned a thing or two. Course . . . there was Boy Scouts, too."

"You're a Boy Scout?"

I nodded. "The one freedom my dad gave me away from him. Figured it was training I needed that he didn't have to give me."

"How far'd you get?"

I shrugged.

She lowered her head, gave me a disbelieving look. "You're one of those Hawks, or Ospreys or . . . Come on, what's it called?"

"Eagle." I got the sense that talking took her mind off the pain.

"Yeah . . . that's it. Eagle Scout. Guess we're about to find out if you really earned all those patches."

"Yep." I hit the power button, and the GPS unit flickered.

"Did they offer an electronics badge?"

I tapped the unit. "No, but I think cold interferes with their circuits. You mind warming it up inside your bag?"

She pulled back the sleeping bag, and I set it gently on her lap. "Vince—my fiancé— wouldn't know the first thing about all this. If he had been in this plane, he'd be looking for the nearest Starbucks and cussing the fact that there was no cell service." She lay back and closed her eyes. "What I wouldn't give for a cup of coffee."

"I can help with that."

"Don't tell me you have coffee."

"I have three addictions. Running. Mountains. And good, hot coffee. And not necessarily in that order."

"I'll pay you a thousand dollars for one cup."

The Jetboil is one of the greatest advancements in hiking technology, next to the compass. I scooped snow into it and clicked it on while I dug through my pack for my Ziploc bag of coffee. There wasn't much left, maybe a few days at best.

Ashley saw the bag. "Ben Payne, will you take a credit card?"

"It's amazing what we value when we're at our lowest." Jetboil makes an accessory that allows me to convert the canister into a French press. The water boiled. I measured and dumped in the coffee, let it steep, and poured her a cup. She cradled it in her good hand.

She smiled. "It's amazing the moment a cup of coffee will allow you." She passed the cup. I sipped. She was right. It was good.

She nodded at her attaché. "If you reach in there, you'll find a bag of snack mix I bought in the terminal."

Filled with dried pineapple, apricots, and nuts, it probably weighed a pound. We both poured a handful and chewed slowly.

I nodded. "I believe this is the best snack mix I've ever tasted."

I gave the dog a handful. He sniffed it,

then inhaled it, wagging his tail and begging for more. He put his paws on my chest, sniffing the air. "How do you tell a dog that he's not getting any more?"

She laughed. "Good luck with that."

I gave him one more small handful, and when he returned a third time, I pushed him off me and said, "No." Dejected, he turned his back on me and curled up at the foot of Ashley's sleeping bag.

We sat in the silence for a long time, drinking the entire pot. When we finished, she said, "Save the grounds. We can use them twice, and then, if we're desperate, we can chew on them."

"You're serious about your coffee." I touched the power button, and the GPS flickered to life. "You got paper in your briefcase?"

She nodded. "Should be right in front."

I pulled out a yellow legal pad and a pencil, found the screen that showed our location, and copied the map as best I could. Once I had a relatively detailed drawing, I said, "Be right back."

I climbed up and out of our hole and compared the picture on the screen with that before my eyes, marking mountains and making mental notes of mountain crests and where they landed on the compass. I knew the batteries wouldn't last forever, and whatever I could copy now would pay dividends in the days ahead. But the more our predicament sank in, the more concerned I became. Things were bad all around.

"You want the good news or the bad?"

"Good."

"I know where we are."

"And the bad?"

"Our elevation is eleven thousand six hundred fifty-two feet, give or take, and the nearest logging road is over thirty miles and something like five mountain passes"—I pointed—"that way. We're nearly fifty miles from the nearest thing that looks like a hard road. And most of the snow out there is higher than I am tall."

She bit her lip, and her eyes wandered the white-walled cave. She crossed her arms. "You're going to have to leave me."

"I'm not leaving anybody."

"You can't get me out. You have a better chance alone. Give me the coffee, put those legs to work, and take my coordinates with you. Bring a helicopter on your way back."

"Ashley . . . drink your coffee."

"Okay, but you've got to recognize that it's a distinct possibility."

"Look, we need a fire, we need food, and we need to lose a few thousand feet in elevation; then we'll talk about what's next. One crisis at a time."

"But . . ." She was strong. She had toughness that matters. "Let's keep the truth on the table. It is a possibility."

"I'm not leaving anybody."

The dog noticed my change in tone. He stood, walked up to Ashley, and dug his head beneath her hand. She scratched his ears, and his stomach growled. He looked over his shoulder at me.

"I know you're hungry."

We sat listening to the wind rattle my tarp. I looked at her. "Do you do that with all your friends? Prepare them for the worst?"

She nodded. "If the worst is a possibility. If and when it does happen, you need to have thought about it ahead of time. That way, you're not crushed when your worst thought becomes your reality."

I Jetboiled more snow and made us both sip. We napped on and off through the afternoon. The trail mix had taken the edge off our hunger, but food was a real problem, and I needed energy to trudge through waist-deep snow to find it. And the pain in my chest was spreading.

Night fell, as did the cold. I crawled out, shimmied beneath the lower limbs of a pudgy evergreen, gathered handfuls of dead pine needles, twigs, and branches, and piled them up beneath the wing. Doing this took three trips and left me gasping. Ashley watched me with narrowed eyes.

Grover's door was a single piece of some sort of sheet metal hanging by a single hinge. Probably didn't weigh ten pounds. I pried it up, laid it flat beneath the wing, and piled pine needles and twigs atop it. The problem with a fire in our current location was melting the more or less protective wall around us—not to mention the supportive base below it. The door would keep the fire out of the melting snow it created, and the cold air outside would keep our cave intact overnight.

I needed a light. I could use the Jetboil, but I needed to save its butane. Then I remembered Grover's lighter. I brushed the snow from his pocket, fingered out the brass Zippo, clicked it open, and thumbed the wheel. It lit.

I lit the end of a twig, let the flame climb toward my finger, and then fed it beneath the pine needles. Dead and dry, they caught quickly. I fed the fire, adding larger sticks as the fire grew in size.

The dog sensed the warmth, walked down to the end of Ashley's bag, and curled up in a puffy spot some four feet from the flame. The fire was a welcome addition. It improved our general disposition. We stared at it, letting our eyes grow lazy.

Ashley broke the silence. "I've been thinking about what to get Vince for a wedding gift. I'm coming up blank. Got any ideas?"

"First anniversary. A cabin in the Colorado Rockies. Snowed in." I forced a laugh. "A little like this. We were paying off school loans and, like our wedding, had agreed on a no-present anniversary."

She laughed. "What'd you get her?"

"A purple orchid."

She nodded. "Ah . . . hence the orchid and greenhouse thing."

I nodded.

"I like the way you talk about your wife. Sounds like you 'do' life together." She laid her head back. "I work with a lot of people who don't. Who treat their spouse like a roommate. Somebody they cross paths with, split the mortgage with, maybe have kids with. How'd you two meet?"

I rubbed my eyes. "Tomorrow. We need to try and get some sleep." I extended my hand. "Here, take this Percocet."

"How many do you have?"

"Three after this."

"Why don't you take one?"

"I'm not in that much pain. Go ahead. It'll help you sleep. And up here—where the air is thin—taking one is like taking two."

"Will it help my headache?"

"Probably not. That's the altitude mixed with the crash impact."

She swallowed, and her eyes fell to Grover. He sat, frozen, about five feet from her bag. "Can we do anything about him?"

"I need to bury him, but moving is tough right now."

"One favor? I need to go again."

"No worries."

This time was faster, still no red tint and a good bit of fluid. I repacked snow around her leg, and she said, "You know, you can stop doing that anytime you want. I'm freezing."

"If I let your leg warm up too much, we'll fall behind the pain curve." I dug out some snow on her good side, creating a flat spot, and laid my bag down alongside hers. "If we can share body heat, we'll both sleep better and live longer."

She nodded. "What time is it?"

"A little after six."

She lay down, staring up. "I should be walking down the aisle."

I knelt next to her. "Ever been married before?"

She shook her head, her eyes tearing up.

I held out my sleeve, and she leaned forward, wiping her tears. I checked the stitches on her head and eye. Her face was not quite as swollen. "We're going to get off this mountain, and you're going to have your wedding—just a little later than you planned."

She smiled and closed her eyes.

"You'll look beautiful in white."

"How do you know?"

"We had a small wedding . . ."

"How small?"

"Me, Rachel, and her folks. But the moment that door opened and she stood there, that white dress sweeping the ground . . . It's a picture a groom never forgets."

She turned her head.

"Sorry. Thought I was helping."

An hour later, when her breathing had slowed, I crawled out and pulled the recorder from my pocket. The dog followed me out. He was light enough to walk on top of the frozen snow, but he didn't like it. He walked a few circles, lifted his leg next to a small tree, kicked some snow behind him like a charging bull, and then disappeared back down the hole to curl up with Ashley.

I pressed RECORD.

LONG *day here. End of day three, I think. We're alive, but staying that way is another thing. Ashley is hanging in there, but I don't know how. If I had all the breaks and pains she had, I'd be begging somebody to thump me over the head or shoot me with morphine.*

We're a long way from anywhere, in terrain that's tough even with two good legs. Nearly improbable with one bad one.

I don't really know how we're going to get out of here. I can make some sort of stretcher, but how far can I drag her on that? We need to find someplace lower to rest up until help comes, which it's not, or until I can walk us out of here. And we need food.

I think I upset Ashley. I was trying to cheer her up. Maybe I'm out of practice.

Speaking of practice . . . you ever add up all the miles we ran together? Me neither. Seems like every time we ran, you'd ask me about your stride, and I'd act like I was really paying attention, but in truth, I couldn't take my eyes off your legs. I figure you knew that, too. I loved running behind you.

When I look back on us and our beginnings, I am reminded that we did something we loved and shared it. We never had to think of a reason to hang out. And nothing ever divided us.

Once you got your license, you'd drive to the beach, tap on my window at four a.m., and we'd take off running down the beach. Long runs. Where time didn't matter. No stopwatch. If we didn't run on the beach, I'd pick you up at the end of your drive and we'd run the bridges downtown. If one of us was tired or needed a break, we'd drive through Dunkin' Donuts, order two coffees, and tour the town with the top down.

There was that Saturday morning. We were coming back up the beach after a long run. This kid on a surfboard caught a wave. The nose of his board dipped, and he started tumbling. He washed up in front of us. The pieces of his board surfaced a moment later. His forehead was cut, his shoulder was out of socket, and he was disoriented and nauseous. I sat him down and put pressure on his head. He pointed to his house, and you ran to get his folks while I set his shoulder. When you returned, he was laughing, talking about getting a new board. His folks thanked us, walked him home, and you turned to me and said, like you'd known it all your life, "You're going to make a great doctor someday."

I'd never thought about doing anything other than getting out of my dad's house. But something clicked. "How do you know?"

"Your bedside manner. Something about the way you talk soothes people."

"It does?"

A nod. "I should know."

That was the first time I clued in to the fact that you saw potential in the mundane. The insignificant. The ordinary.

The second time occurred when I came to see you at work. Volunteering after school at the children's hospital. Bald, sickly kids. Oxygen tanks. Wheelchairs. When I found you, you were rubber-gloved, holding a bedpan, laughing with the little girl who, moments before, sat on top of it. You were all smiles. So was she.

I saw sickness and misery in every room. Not you. You saw possibility and promise. Even in the improbable.

Somewhere in my junior year, I looked around and you had become my best friend. You taught me what it meant to smile. To live with a heart that felt alive. With every mile, you chipped away at the rocks piled up around my soul. You put together the pieces of me. When it came to love, you taught me to crawl, walk, run, and then, somewhere on the beach, beneath the moon and running into a headwind, clipping away five-minute miles, you turned to me, cut the ties that held my wings, and taught me to fly.

Staring out across this ice-capped landscape with nothing but the impossible staring back at me, I am reminded.

I see what is. You see what could be. I miss you.

Chapter Four

TWICE during the night, I repacked snow around Ashley's leg. She moaned a lot in her sleep. I had been up a few hours by the time she woke. Her eyes were slits.

"How do you feel?"

Her voice sounded thick. "Like I've been hit by a Mack truck." With that, she rolled on her side and vomited for several minutes. It was mostly dry heaves and stomach acid. Finally she sat back. Trying to catch her breath. She was in a lot of pain.

I wiped her mouth and held the cup while she sipped. "I've got to get some Advil in you, but I doubt your empty stomach is going to like it."

Eyes closed, she nodded.

I added fuel to the fire and clicked on the Jetboil.

The smell of coffee opened her eyes. She eyed the contraptions to my left. "You make those?"

I'd taken the netting off the backs of the seats and disassembled the wire and metal frames using Grover's Leatherman. I had double-folded the netting, stretched it over the frames, and attached the squares using Grover's fly line. I held them up. "Snow-shoes."

"If you say so."

I poured coffee and handed it to her. "I'm going to leave you for a couple of hours. Walk around a bit."

I dug Grover's flare gun out of the box in the back where he kept his fishing tackle. I loaded it and handed it to Ashley. "If you need me, cock this and squeeze this. And when you do, make sure it's pointed out that hole. If I'm not back at dark, don't worry. I'm taking my sleeping bag and emergency blanket. Out here, conditions change quickly, and I might have to wait them out. I'm going to try and find some sort of food and an alternate shelter."

I unstrapped Grover's bow from its case in the tail of the plane, along with a fly rod, his vest, and one of the reels stuffed in it.

"You can fly-fish?"

"I've done it once. Didn't catch anything."

"I was afraid you were going to say that." She eyed the compound bow. "How about that contraption?"

"This I've actually done."

"Before you go, will you help me with something?"

Ashley went to the bathroom, and then I got her covered up. "Will you hand me my case?" She pulled out her cell phone. "Just for kicks." She turned it on, but the cold had killed it. "Got any books?"

A shrug. "Not much of a reader. Guess you're alone with your thoughts—and the dog." I scratched his ears. He had grown comfortable with us. "Can you remember his name?"

She shook her head. "No."

"Me, either. I think we should call him Napoleon."

"Why?"

"Just look at him. If ever an animal had a Napoleon complex, it's him. He's got the attitude of an angry bullmastiff shoved into a package the size of a loaf of bread."

She nodded and smiled.

I held out my hand. "The GPS."

She slid it from within her sleeping bag, and I tucked it into the inside pocket in my jacket. I unzipped a small pocket on the side of my backpack, grabbed my compass, and hung it around my neck. It's lensatic, or fluid-filled. Rachel gave it to me years ago.

I shouldered my backpack, zipped up my jacket, pulled on my gloves, and lifted the bow. "Remember, when it starts getting dark, remind yourself that I am coming back. It may be tomorrow morning, but I'll be here. Coffee date, you and me. Deal?"

She nodded.

I pulled out the Advil bottle. "Take four every six hours. And don't forget to feed the fire." I crawled out of our den and knelt to strap on the snowshoes. Then I turned and began walking up the mountain.

My senior year, state championships. You watched me win the four hundred in a new state record. I'd won the two mile just seconds off a national record, and I was standing at the start line of the mile. Somebody had started a rumor that I could run four minutes. At last count, I had twenty Division I scholarship offers. Full rides.

You had two offers. I was more proud of yours than mine.

I had my piles, and Dad had his. His prized pile centered around MBAs in finance. "They'll pay for five years of education. Get your BA in two and a half. Then your MBA. Once you're out of school, you can write your own ticket. You could run my agency."

I wanted nothing to do with his agency. I just never told him.

I could see his face out of the corner of my eye. Sweat was pouring off him. I'd run 4:04 several mornings on the beach, but that was on sand. He was sure I could run 3:58. You hung on the fence. The gun sounded.

After the first lap, we were still a tight group. By the start of the third lap, I was all alone. And I knew I had it.

People in the stands were on their feet. Screaming. Dad was stone-faced. A hundred meters to go and I was looking at 3:57. And it struck me that no matter what time I turned in, it wouldn't be good enough for him. He'd assume I hadn't tried hard enough.

Something about his Rushmore face cut something loose in me. I eased up. Slowed. I watched the clock roll through 3:53. Then 3:57. My official time would be 4:00:37. The place went crazy. I'd done something no Florida runner had ever done. Four-year state champion in twelve events headed to the national championships.

I stood on the track, swarmed by my teammates. But the only face I wanted to see was yours. And then you found me.

I never saw my dad.

We were going out. The whole team. To celebrate. I came home to change. We walked in. He was sitting in his chair. An empty crystal glass on his thigh. The bottle half empty next to him. He never drank. Considered it something weak people did.

You peered around me. "Mr. Payne, did you see?"

He stood, pointed his finger in my face. "Nobody ever gave me nothing. You son of a . . ." He shook his head, balled his fist, and swung. The blow broke my nose. By then, I was six two, two inches taller than him, and I knew if I swung back, I might never stop, but when I stood up, he was raising his hand over you.

I caught his hand and spun him into the sliding glass door. It shattered into a million pieces. He lay on the deck, staring at me.

You drove me to the hospital, where they set my nose. Around midnight, we drove to a twenty-four-hour pancake place and ordered one piece of French silk pie and two forks. Our celebration. Then I drove you home, where your mom met us, and we all sat at the kitchen table talking through the meet. You sat, sleep in your eyes, wrapped in a terry-cloth robe and your leg touching mine.

I got home around one. A few hours later, four fifty-five a.m. arrived, and Dad did not. He never woke me again. I lay awake. Wondering what to do. Who to be. I couldn't answer that, so I dressed and went for a walk on the beach, watching the sun come up. I walked through lunch. On toward dinner. The sun was falling when I quit walking some twenty miles north. I climbed out toward the end of a jetty.

Your voice sounded behind me. "What're you running from?"

"How'd you get out here?"

"Walked. Followed the footprints."

You climbed up and pulled me to you. You lifted your sunglasses. Your eyes were red. You stared out across the water, hands inside the long gray sleeves of your sweatshirt. "You think they'll care that we cut class?"

"I don't. You've been crying. Why?"

You pounded my chest. " 'Cause I don't want it to end."

"What?"

Your eyes welled again. "Us, dummy. Seeing you . . . every day."

Maybe that's what had me walking up the beach. And in twenty miles, I'd found no answer. We were both about to hurt a whole lot.

High school love was one thing, but choosing your college because of that love was something everyone cautioned us against. Remember? Sometimes I wish we'd listened to them. Then I shake my head and think. Not so. I don't blame us. I'd do it again.

I remember calling the track coach and asking him to look at your tapes and your times. He didn't skip a beat. "Would that influence your decision to attend this institution?"

"Yes . . . it would."

I heard some papers shuffling. "Funny, I just happen to have an extra scholarship lying on my desk."

Just like that.

THE storm had dumped three feet of snow. All fresh powder. Without the shoes, I'd have been thigh-deep, wet, and the cold would be stinging my legs. Given that, I stopped, cut two tethers, and tied one end to the back of each snowshoe and the other end around each ankle. Sort of like a surfer's leash.

Despite the fact that we needed to lose elevation, I needed to gain it to get a bird's-eye view of where we were. The air was thin, and I was much weaker than I expected. I climbed into the late afternoon before I summited a small ridgeline that rose up over the plateau, maybe a thousand feet above the crash site.

It was a desolate landscape, etched with jagged peaks and impossible routes that stretched sixty or seventy miles in every direction. I turned on the GPS and oriented myself, using the compass to confirm the directions and degrees the electronic unit was telling me. The only surprise was the number of lakes and streams showing on the screen. I was noting the few that were closest when the GPS flickered to black. I tapped it, but it was dead. The cold had drained the battery. I closed my eyes, tried to remember everything on the screen, and added that to the sketch I'd made yesterday.

I started back after dark. It was midnight by the time I got to the plane. Napoleon heard me and poked out his head. The temperature had dropped to single digits, which meant my pant legs were frozen. I was cold down to my bones. The snow was starting again. I'd only peed once the entire day, and even then not much. I watched Napoleon disappear, his feet making small indentations in the snow. Only then did I notice the larger tracks leading to and from our cave. My first thought was mountain lion. The tracks came out of some rocks above us, wound down a snowdrift and up to the entrance. I also noticed an area where it looked like something had been lying down. As in "lying in wait." Didn't take long to make sense of it. Even frozen dead people smell. So do injured people and little dogs.

I snapped off some dead limbs and carried

them into the hole. I stoked the fire, stripped, spread out my wet clothes, and climbed naked but for my underwear inside my bag. I was shivering, and my fingers were stiff, as though they'd been dipped in wax. I dropped some snow in the Jetboil and clicked it on. Ashley watched me. I curled up and let myself shiver, trying to create some heat. "Hey."

She was suffering, and it showed in her eyes. "Hi."

"Taken anything lately?"

She shook her head.

I placed a Percocet on her tongue, and she sipped the last of her water. "You don't look too good," she offered. "Why don't you take some of the Advil?"

I knew if I didn't, I might not get out of my bag tomorrow. "Okay. Two." She poured them into my hand, and I swallowed.

"What'd you see?"

"There's a level-one trauma center. The EMTs are pulling a gurney here now. I talked to the administrator and secured a private room for you. Should have you showered, warm, and pumped full of pain medication in ten minutes or less."

"That bad, huh?"

I slid down farther into my bag. "Nothing but snow, ice, rock, and mountain as far as I can see."

"And the GPS?"

I poured some warm water and started sipping. "Same picture."

She lay back and let out a deep breath. The one she'd been holding all day. "Got any ideas?"

"There are some lakes down below us. A few streams. I'm sure they're all frozen, but I thought I'd see if I could make my way down tomorrow and find some fish. How's the leg feeling?"

She closed her eyes. "Hurts."

I slid over, packed snow around it, and saw that while the swelling had gone down, her skin was a deep purple from the top of her knee to the side of her hip. I clicked on my flashlight and checked her stitches. I felt her toes. They were cold. Which was bad. By treating the leg with constant ice, I was compromising the toes. I had to get some blood flow in that foot.

I turned so we were face to toes. I unzipped my bag and pressed my chest and stomach to the bottom of her foot. Then I wrapped us both in the bag and wrapped my palm across the top of her foot. "When we get out of here, please don't sue me for putting you in danger the day before your wedding."

"Funny you should mention that. I've been lying here drafting my attorney's opening argument. If I were you, I'd hire a very good lawyer."

"That bad?"

"Let's see. . . . You started with good intentions, saved my life, and despite the fact that I've seen you cough up blood at least twice, you set my leg and really haven't left my side."

"You saw that?"

"Blood on snow . . . Hard to miss."

"We'll both get better when we lose a few thousand feet."

Ashley stared at the compass hanging from my neck. "When did she give you that?"

"Loggerhead turtles lay their eggs along our beach, leaving big mounds up in the dunes. Rachel would circle them with stakes and tape and then mark off the days on a calendar. She was amazed every time the turtles hatched and knew, somehow, to head for the water. She gave it to me one year after a particular nest hatched."

"How does a compass know which way to point?"

"Actually, it only points one way. Magnetic north. We find what we need off of that. The Earth is magnetized, and the source of that is up near the North Pole. I use the compass mainly to walk point to point."

"Point to point?"

"A compass can't tell you where you are, only the direction you are headed or have come from. A right-handed person, like me, will walk in a right-turning circle if given enough time without a compass. To walk in a straight line, you pick a direction, a degree on the compass—say, a hundred and ten degrees—then pick a visual marker in front of you that lines up with that point on the compass. A tree, a lake, whatever. Once you get there, you pick another, but this time you also use the point behind you as a reference point—double-checking yourself. Not difficult, but takes patience."

"Will that compass help us get out of here?" Her tone suggested something I'd not heard. The first outward sign of fear.

"Yes."

"Make sure you don't lose it."

REMEMBER *how elated we were to get that job offer in Jacksonville? We jumped at it. Back to the beach. The ocean. We were moving back home, closer to your parents. Dad had moved to Connecticut to run another firm but had kept the condo for residency. We had it to ourselves.*

But you were the activities coordinator at the children's hospital and couldn't stand the thought of leaving a week before your replacement arrived. So driving the moving truck—Denver to Jacksonville, from the Rockies to the beach—fell to me. All 1,919 miles.

I told you I'd buy you a condo, any house you wanted, but you said you liked the one I already had.

You hung on the truck door and pointed. "I left you a present. But you can't open it until you get out of the driveway."

On the passenger seat sat a silver handheld tape recorder. Attached to it was a piece of paper that read "Press play."

I backed out, put the stick into drive, and pressed PLAY. *Your voice rose up out of the machine.*

"Hey, it's me. Thought you'd like some company." You licked your lips like you do when you're nervous or being mischievous. "Here's the deal. I'm . . . I'm worried about losing you to the hospital. About being a doctor's widow, sitting on the couch, a spoonful of Rocky Road in one hand, the remote in the other. I gave you this thing so I can be with you even when I'm not. Because I miss the sound of your voice when you're away. And . . . I want you to miss mine. Miss me. I'll keep it a day or two, tell you what I'm thinking, then give it to you. We can pass it back and forth. Sort of like a baton. Deal?"

I nodded in the rearview mirror. "Deal."

IT'S *snowing again. Ashley's in a lot of pain and starting to show the effects of elevation. I've got to get her down or she's going to die up here. I know . . . but if I don't try, we'll both die.*

Grover? I need to bury him, but I'm not sure I have the strength. Plus, there's something up in the rocks that's got me a bit worried.

I've been studying the compass, trying to find a way out, but it's mountains all around. Tough to know which way to go. If I choose the wrong degree . . . well, things are bad here. Real bad.

I want to tell people that Ashley was trying to get home. I wish they knew. But chances are good they never will.

Chapter Five

I WOKE on day five with the sun, groggy and sore. Rolled over, pulled the bag up over my face, and woke again around lunch. No matter how hard I tried, I could not get out of bed.

Ashley seldom stirred. Elevation, mixed with starvation, mixed with a plane crash, mixed with a lot of pain had taken its toll on both of us. I hurt everywhere and could barely move.

Daylight on day six, the fire had long since died out, but my clothes were dry, so I pulled them on, forced myself to pack my backpack, rekindled the fire to keep Ashley warm, and dropped a few handfuls of snow in the Jetboil for her.

We needed food.

I shouldered my backpack, tied the bow onto the back of it, and stepped out as the sun was just coming up. The air was crisp and dry, with ice crystals floating on my breath. I threw fresh snow across the tracks at the entrance. It would let me know if anything visited while I was away. I tied on the snowshoes, pulled out my compass, took a reading, and set off.

For three hours, I picked points and plowed through the dry, frozen snow. I walked the first lake's frozen perimeter until I found the creek that spilled out of it. The water was clear and tasted almost sweet. It was cold, and I risked dropping my core temperature, but I was moving, so I kept forcing myself to drink.

A mile later, the creek made a hard turn, creating a deep pool below a rock overhang. I didn't put too much faith in my ability to work that fly rod with my hands. They were too cut up and cold to do anything effectively. Grover had a small bottle of synthetic salmon eggs. I slid one over a hook, threaded line through the hook, and dropped it into the water.

Twenty minutes later, no bites. I packed up and looked for a bigger pool. A mile later, I found one. Same routine. Same outcome.

Only this time, I could see little black shadows darting in and out beneath the rock into
the swirling current. Lots of black shadows.
I knew there were fish here. Why wouldn't
they bite?

Thirty minutes later, I packed up and continued trudging through the snow looking
for another pool. I was tired, cold, and hungry. I had to climb a small rise and then descend to another stream. I was expending
calories I couldn't afford. This stream was
wider but more shallow and running with a
good volume of water.

The black shadows reappeared. A good
number, too.

I brushed away the snow and lay on a
rock, a facedown snow angel, salivating at
the sight of mountain trout. This time, I
lowered Grover's hand net slowly into the
water below the bait. The problem with this
method was that it submerged one hand
into water that was probably twenty-eight
degrees. The pain was excruciating until it
went numb—which didn't take long.

The shadows disappeared, then slowly returned. Swimming closer. Slowly they approached the egg and began to nibble. Maybe

it was the cold water, but they, too, were sluggish. I slowly raised the net and caught seven finger-size trout. I dumped them in the snow and buried my cold hand into the pocket of my down jacket. With the hatchet, I cut a limb, lashed it to the net, and submerged both it and the egg, catching a couple more.

I ate everything but the heads.

When they were gone, I crept back to the bank and kept "fishing." When the sun started casting my shadow on the snow, I counted my catch. Forty-seven. Enough for tonight and tomorrow. I packed up and followed my tracks home. On the way back, I pulled an arrow from the quiver, nocked it, took a deep breath, and drew hard on the string. It resisted, then gave and released all the way to my face. The pain in my ribs was sharp, but I had the bow at full draw. I set the top pin on the base of a wrist-size evergreen some twenty yards away and released. The arrow missed the base by about two inches and disappeared in the snow on the right. I dug around a few minutes and retrieved it. Although I had not hit the tree, I was close. And at that distance, close was good enough.

It was plenty light when I climbed back onto our plateau. I approached slowly, keeping my eyes peeled for anything moving. I saw nothing, but the entrance to our cave told a different story. The tracks were closer, parked right at the entrance, with a rounded indentation between them where something had lain down. Chances were good that it was lying here as I walked up.

ASHLEY was weak, and her eyes hurt. Classic altitude sickness mixed with a concussion and lack of food. I found some more wood, stoked the fire, gutted several trout, and fed them onto a long, slender stick. I cooked them and made coffee at the same time. Caffeine would help her digest and absorb the nutrients. She drank and ate slowly as I held the cup to her lips and then held a fish while she chewed. She ate fourteen like that before she shook her head. Napoleon sat quietly licking his face. I laid out six fish on the snow and said, "Go ahead." He stood, wiggled his nose, and devoured them.

I gave Ashley a Percocet, packed and elevated her leg, and checked the circulation in her foot. She was asleep before I realized we hadn't said two words since I'd returned. I sat up a few more hours feeding the fire, making myself eat and watching the color return to her skin. Just before midnight, I walked outside. As I did, a long shadow disappeared up a rock face and into some trees. Napoleon stood next to me, snarling.

CAUGHT some fish today. And I shot the bow. If it came to a pinch, I think I could hit what I shoot at, inside twenty yards.

I gave Ashley a Percocet, hoping she'll get some sleep. I'm going to bury Grover tomorrow. Get him someplace where he can see the sun come up and set. Where he can count the stars at night.

You remember that cabin in the mountains? Our daytime hikes, nighttime fires, watching snow stick to the windows as a mountaintop wind whistled atop the chimney. Our honeymoon.

The second night . . . we'd finished dinner and were sitting in front of the fire. Between our student loans and the cost of life, we didn't have two pennies to rub together. Drinking a cheap bottle of cabernet. You were wearing your robe . . . and my sweat. The firelight was dancing across your skin as you handed me the box.

"I thought we'd agreed no presents."

"This isn't a wedding present. It's something you need if we're going to stay married for seventy years."

"Seventy years?"

You nodded. And then asked, "You sure you're going to love me when I'm old, wrinkly, and can't hear a word you're saying?"

"Probably more."

You smiled. "The way I look at it, there's Eastern Standard Time and then there's Ben Time. And Ben Time can be anywhere from fifteen minutes to an hour behind. This could help that little problem."

You were right. I'm sorry I was ever late for anything.

I peeled away the paper, and there sat a Timex Ironman. You pointed at the face. "To help you out, I set it thirty minutes fast."

You crossed your right leg over your left, and the split in your robe climbed halfway up your thigh. I remember marveling at how comfortable you were with me. Your smile. Flushed cheeks. I remember closing my eyes for a brief second and burning the image onto the back of my eyelids because I wanted to take it with me.

And I did. Rachel, you're still the measuring stick. No one else holds a candle.

NAPOLEON'S growling woke me up. Low and different. His tone told me he wasn't kidding. I opened my eyes. Ashley lay quietly. Napoleon stood between us, staring at the entrance. Bright moonlight filtered in. Napoleon lowered his head and took two slow steps toward the entrance. Two eyes stared back at us. They looked like two pieces of red glass. I sat up on an elbow, and Napoleon's growl grew deeper, louder. I put my hand on his back and said, "Easy."

Evidently, he didn't understand that. As if shot out of a cannon, he launched himself toward the thing staring back at us. The two collided, spun in an angry ball. A loud cat-like roar erupted and then disappeared, leaving Napoleon standing at the entrance, barking and jumping two feet straight into the air.

I crawled toward him and pulled him back. "Easy, boy. It's gone. Easy." He was shaking, and his shoulder was wet.

Ashley clicked on the flashlight. My palm was sticky, and the snow was splattered red beneath us.

Didn't take me long to find the cut. It was deep, from the side of his shoulder to the top of his back. I grabbed my needle and thread, and Ashley held him still. I closed it with four stitches. He turned in a few circles, stared at the entrance, then licked me on the face.

"Yeah . . . you did good."

Ashley cleared her throat. "What was it?"

"Mountain lion."

"Is it coming back?"

"I think so."

She closed her eyes and didn't say anything.

We slept in fits the rest of the night. I perched the bow next to my bag, nocked an arrow, and propped myself against the tail of the plane. Only when the sun came up did I finally drift off.

IT WAS weird owning the place that was the source of so many bad memories. You shook your head and smiled. "Let me remodel and I'll give *you new memories. Besides, 'paid for' and 'oceanfront' are both really cool."*

So we gutted walls, repainted, retiled. Cool blues, soft tans, sliding glass doors cracked so the sound filtered through, wave upon wave. How many nights has the sea sung us to sleep?

You remember the night of that crash? I'd worked late because the ER was slammed. I'd stayed until we had everybody stable. I was tired. Thinking about life and how short it is. How we're always just a breath away from overturned in a ditch with a fireman cutting you out with the jaws of life. It was one of those moments where I knew, really knew, that life is not guaranteed.

It was maybe three a.m. The ocean was angry ahead of a storm. I was standing at the glass, wrestling with life's impermanence, staring out over the beach. You appeared and said, "You okay?"

I told you what happened. What I was thinking. You tucked your shoulder under mine, wrapped your arms around my waist. Minutes passed. Lightning spiderwebbed the sky.

"You owe me something, and I want to collect."

Seemed a strange way to start a conversation when I was sharing my deepest thoughts. Sort of irritated me. I guess my voice betrayed this. "What?"

I don't know how long you'd been wanting to bring this up. Looking back, you'd been firing shots across my bow for months, and I was too wrapped up in work to pick up on them. I'd kept telling you, "Just let me get through medical school."

I guess you figured it was time to ramp up your efforts. You stepped aside, untied your robe, let it slip to the floor, and started walking to our room. At the doorway, you turned. "I want to make a baby. Right now."

I remember watching you disappear, the flash of a shadow across the small of your back. I remember kneeling next to our bed and saying, "Forgive me?" I remember you smiling, nodding, and pulling me toward you. A while later, I remember you lying on my stomach, your tears trickling onto my chest. And I remember that moment, when I knew. That you'd broken loose in me the stuff that only love breaks loose. That you'd given me all of you. Unselfishly. Unreservedly.

Something about the enormity of that gift

touched me down where words don't live. Where expression fails. Where there are no secrets. Where there's just you and me and everything that's us.

And I remember crying like a baby.

That's when I knew for the first time what love was. Not how it made me feel. Not what I hoped it was. But what it was.

You showed me. It'd been there all along, but something about that night, those people, the sense of gain, loss, heartbreak, and joy, all those things swirled into that moment and . . . I'd lived my whole life wanting to love but never able to do so apart from the pain I'd carried. The pain of my dad. Of my mom's absence. Of running but never being fast enough. Of never measuring up.

All of my life I'd struggled in the waves— tossed, turned, screaming for air. But in that moment, you held back the waves, lifted me above the surface, and filled me.

GROVER was stiff when I tried to move him. Frozen in a sitting position. One hand still holding the stick. His eyes were closed.

Ashley turned her head.

I popped off a section of the wing, laid

him on top of it, and slid-pushed him out
the entrance. I pulled him across the snow to
a boulder covered in lion tracks. I brushed
the snow off, sat him on the rock, and leaned
him backward.

I backtracked, counting. Eighteen steps.

I nocked an arrow, aimed at the snowdrift
a few feet from Grover, and released. This
time I didn't shoot over. The distance was
not so far away that I couldn't hit what I was
aiming at.

Napoleon kept running back and forth
between Grover and me. He'd started limping, and his circles had developed a hitch.
He looked up at me.

"I won't let anything happen to him."

Napoleon walked back into our cave; then
I crawled in.

Ashley's face was wet. She was breaking
down. "What're you doing?"

"Hunting."

"Are you using Grover as bait?"

"Yes, but if it works the way I'm thinking,
nothing will happen to him."

"Not to point out the obvious, but nothing has worked out the way you'd hoped since
we met in Salt Lake."

She was right. I had no response.

We didn't say much the rest of the day. Or that night. Or the next day. By the time the second night came around, I hadn't slept soundly in forty-eight hours and was running on fumes. So was Ashley.

The cold had intensified. I couldn't say for sure, but it was crisp and painful, suggesting that it had fallen into the negatives. Clouds moved in, blocking out the moon, and that was bad. I needed the moon. Without it, I couldn't see the sight pin.

Midnight came and brought snow. I was sleepy. Fading in and out. I could see the outline of Grover. Based on the layer covering him, we'd had another three inches.

I must have fallen asleep, because I jerked when I woke. Napoleon lay next to me. Crouched. His eyes were focused on Grover.

Something was leaning on him. And the thing was big. Six plus feet in length. My hands were nearly frozen, but I drew the bow and tried to find the pin. There was no way to see it in the dark. "Come on. Just a glimmer of light."

Still nothing. I swung the bow, knowing I only had another second or two. My arms were cramping, and my chest felt like some-body had stuck me with a spike. I coughed, tasting blood. Next to me, something brushed my leg. Then I heard a click, and a roman candle shot out the entrance. The light from the flare showered down. The cat had both his paws on Grover's shirt, like they were dancing. I found the pin, leveled it on the cat's shoulder, and pressed the release. I never saw the arrow.

I dropped the bow, clutched my side, coughed, and spat on the snow. Ashley lay to my right, staring out. "It's gone."

"Did I hit it?" I had hunched over, nursing my rib cage.

"Don't know. It left in a hurry."

Somewhere in the darkness, my hand found hers.

We lay there, catching our breath. I was too tired to carry her back to her bag, so I pulled her to my chest and wrapped us in my bag. Within minutes, her head fell to one side and her pulse slowed.

MORNING woke us. Napoleon lay curled between us. I climbed out of my bag and saw what Ashley had done last night. Drag marks in the snow told the story.

I needed to check Ashley's leg, so I lifted the bag and ran my hand gently along the skin. It was dark, and the swelling had returned. The hair was stubbly. Ten days overgrown. The pulse in her ankle was good. The problem was the swelling. She'd set herself back. The pain would be intense, and I only had one Percocet left.

I tilted her head and placed the pill on her tongue. She sipped and swallowed.

I propped her head on my bag, dressed, nocked an arrow, and stepped toward Grover. He'd fallen over and looked like he was asleep on his side. A trail of blood led away up the rocks.

It'd been several hours. If the mountain lion was mortally wounded, those hours would have given it time to die. If it was just sort of wounded, they would have given it plenty of time to get angry.

I climbed the rocks and followed the blood. It thinned; a thin blood trail means a bad hit and an angry lion. After a hundred yards, I was following a drop here and there.

But at a large outcropping, the drops increased in number. After another hundred yards, a large puddle suggested the thing had stopped there. The trail continued another two hundred yards up through some smaller rocks. I saw the tail first, the black tip lying flat across the snow, sticking out from beneath the limbs of some squatty trees. I took a deep breath and drew the bow. Eight feet away, I set the front pin on the cat's head and released the arrow. It sliced through the neck. The cat never moved.

I retrieved the arrow, hung it in the quiver, and sat on the rock, staring at the cat. She was not big. Probably five feet from head to rump and maybe a hundred pounds. I held her paw in my hand.

Small or not, she'd have ripped me to shreds. I checked her teeth. They were worn, which explained why she'd hunted easy targets.

I retraced my steps and found Ashley shivering and on the verge of going into shock. I stripped to my underwear, unzipped her bag, and pulled mine alongside. I climbed in, pressed my chest to hers, and wrapped my arms around her. She shook for close to an hour.

When she was asleep, I climbed out, wrapped both bags around her, stoked the fire, fed it fuel, and returned to the cat. I cut off the hide and then gutted it. That left me dragging maybe fifteen pounds of eatable meat through the snow. I cut several green limbs, built a frame around the fire, and began hanging strips of meat.

The smell woke Ashley. She picked up her head and sniffed the air. I tore off a piece, blew on it, and held it to her lips.

She chewed slowly, eating the entire thing. Dark circles shrouded her eyes. I tore off another piece and held it while she took small bites. "I just had the worst dream. You would never believe."

"Try me."

"I dreamed my flight out of Salt Lake was canceled, but then this stranger, kind of homely looking but nice, invited me to ride this charter flight to Denver. And somewhere over this interminable forest, the pilot had a heart attack and crashed our plane. I broke my leg, and after a week, all we'd had to eat was some trail mix, coffee grounds, and the mountain lion that had tried to eat us."

"Homely? Nice?"

She chewed slowly. "The strange part was that I agreed to get on a charter with a total stranger. Two, actually. What was I thinking? I need to reexamine my decision-making paradigm."

I laughed. "Let me know how that works out."

I rechecked her leg. She was afraid to look.

"You're lucky you didn't rebreak it. The bone ends are just now getting tacky enough to hold it in place, and there you go pulling some stunt with a flare gun. The swelling came back with a vengeance." Her skin was pale, and she looked clammy. I repacked the snow, adjusted the braces, then pressed her foot to my stomach.

For the rest of the day, we ate barbecued mountain lion and sipped warm water. I kept the snow packed around her leg and monitored the amount of fluid she was both drinking and expelling. She'd been lying still for ten days, breathing less than half the oxygen she was used to. I was worried about atrophy.

And if she got an infection, I wasn't sure her body could fight it.

Once the protein hit my system, I rubbed down her good leg, forcing the blood flow through it, and stretched it as much as I could without jolting her broken leg. Throughout the day, I continued cutting long strips of meat and suspending them above the fire. When I'd finished late in the afternoon, the color had returned to her face and cheeks.

With two hours of daylight remaining, I looked out the entrance, and my eyes fell on Grover, lying on his side like a toppled statue. I strapped up my boots. "I'll be right outside."

She nodded. As I passed by, she reached out and grabbed me by the coat. She pulled my forehead to her lips. "Thank you."

I nodded. This close to her face, I noticed how thin her cheeks had become. "I don't know how you managed what you did last night. It's a deep-down kind of strength"—I looked away—"I've seen only one other time." I pressed my palm to her forehead, checking for fever. "Tomorrow morning we're getting out of here. I'm not sure where we're going, but we're leaving this place."

She let go of my hand and smiled. "First flight out?"

"Yeah. First class, too."

I crawled out. My stomach was full, and for the first time in ten days, I was neither hungry nor cold. I looked around and scratched my head. Something was strange. Something I'd not noticed in a long time. I scratched my chin, and it hit me. I was smiling.

YOU remember the turtles? I wonder how they're doing. Where they are. Did they make it to Australia? Especially your little friend.

Seems we found the female just as she was starting to build her nest. She was digging the hole. We climbed the dune, lay down, and watched her. She was huge and dug a long time. Then she started laying eggs. Like she went into a trance or something. Must have laid a hundred eggs. When she finished, she covered the hole, crawled to the water's edge, and disappeared into the black water.

We slid down the dune to the mound, carefully drove the spikes in, and hung a line of pink surveyor's tape. You made me cut little flags to make sure every beachcomber for a mile could see it.

Then you started counting the days like a kid at Christmas, and at fifty-five days, we started camping out.

"Well, they don't know they're supposed to hatch at sixty days. What if they come early?"

We spread a blanket atop the dune and lay there. The beach was warm that night. A cool breeze came out of the southwest, so the ocean was more a lake than a raging torrent. Then came the fifty-ninth day. You were asleep. Drooling on your sleeping bag. I tapped you on the shoulder, and we hung over the edge and watched the first baby shake sand off his back and trek to the water. Wasn't long before the beach was crawling with loggerheads.

You were so excited. Counting quietly. Pointing at each one like you knew them by name. I remember you shaking your head. "How do they know which way to go? How come they don't get lost?"

"They have this internal compass. Tells them where the water is."

Then came our little friend. He crawled out, but unlike his one hundred and seventeen brothers and sisters, he headed the wrong way. Up the dune, toward us. He made it a few feet, then bogged down. Burrowing. The wrinkle grew on your forehead as you watched him dig his own grave.

You slid down the dune, scooped him up, carried him to the water's edge, and set him down. He found his sea legs, and the first wave scooped him up. "There you go, little guy. All the way to Australia." You were smiling. I think we stood there a long time, just watching him, a floating black diamond, swim out to sea.

That was when you saw it. You turned around, stared at the dune where we'd been hiding, and the scrub oaks and wire grass. At the "For Sale" sign. You said, "How much do you think they want?"

"Probably a good bit. It's been for sale a while."

"It's a strange size lot. The area where you can build is small, while the protected dunes are big."

"Yep. And you're surrounded by state park, so there are probably restrictions on what kind of house you can build."

"Must be ten nests right here. Why doesn't the state buy it?"

I shrugged. "Money, I suppose."

You nodded. "We should buy it."

"What?"

You began walking up the dune. "We could put a beach house right over here, back off the ocean. And we could build it with big glass windows where we could sit at night and watch the nests."

I pointed back down the beach. "Honey, we have a perfectly good condo right there. We can walk down here anytime we like."

"I know, but the next person to come along might not like the turtles digging up their front yard. We do. We should buy it."

A week passed. I walked in and threw my stuff on the couch and saw that the sliding glass door was open. The sun had gone down. It was my favorite time. That cool bluish light that falls before the darkness comes. You were standing on the beach, a white sarong blowing in the breeze. You waved.

I put on some shorts, grabbed my folder, and walked out. You were holding a small wrapped box. The breeze was pulling at your hair again. When I kissed you, you pulled it aside with your finger.

You handed me the box. I opened the card. It read: "So you can find your way back to me." I opened the box. It was a lensatic compass. I turned it over. It was engraved. MY TRUE NORTH. *You hung it around my neck and whispered, "Without you, I'd be lost."*

"I got you something, too." I handed you the folder.

You opened it, riffled through the pages. Looked like you were reading Greek. Your eyes narrowed. "Honey . . . what is this?"

"That is a land survey. And this is a contract on a piece of property."

"What piece? We don't have . . ." You stopped, stared at the survey, turned it sideways, and stared down the beach. "You didn't."

"It's just an offer. Doesn't mean they accept. I low-balled them."

You tackled me. Laughing and screaming. "I can't believe you did that!"

"Well, there's a lot we can't put there."

"Can we build a small house with a glass front?"

I nodded. "But we won't be able to build right away."

"I can wait."

GROVER deserved a proper burial. I studied the landscape. Just above him sat a rock outcropping. I climbed it, and the view stretched out for miles. He'd have liked it. I kicked away the snow, went back to the plane, pulled off a piece of the tail flap, and used it like a shovel. I dug a hole, which was more pushing stuff out of the way than digging through the frozen ground. I climbed back down, lifted Grover over my shoulder, and wound back up. I laid him in the hole and began collecting rocks.

I emptied his pockets and tried to take off his wedding ring, but it wouldn't budge. I unhooked his pocket watch and zipped all of that loose stuff into the pocket inside my jacket. Then I unlaced his boots, putting the laces in my pocket, pulled off his wool socks, and slid his belt out of the loops in his pants.

I stacked rocks under a cold sun that fell and turned a deep orange and then crimson. When finished, I stood back. It was a good place. The wind had picked up. I suppose it would always be breezy up here. Maybe that was good. Maybe he'd feel like he was flying.

I took the wool beanie off my head. "Grover . . . I'm sorry I got you into this mess. Guess if I hadn't hired you to fly me out here, you'd be home with your wife. If and when we get out of here, I'll go tell her what happened."

The wind blew hard against my face. "Unless God wants two more dead people up here, we're going to need a change in the weather. And some help as to where we're going. Maybe you could put in a word for us. I think Ashley would like to walk the aisle, get married. She's young. She deserves to wear white."

The light faded, giving way to a cloudless, cold sky. Overhead, maybe forty thousand feet in the air, a jet airliner flew southeast. "If that's your sense of humor, I don't think it's all that funny right now." A second plane crisscrossed the trail of the first. "Or that. By the way . . . won't take much to kill us out here. We're circling the drain now. I'm asking for that girl in there with the broken leg and the slowly breaking spirit. She thinks she's hiding it, but she's not. Up here . . . this'll break anybody. This is a tough place. It'll strip your hope fast." My lip trembled. "You and I, we never really finished our conversation, but I can tell you this. . . . Living with a broken heart is living half dead. And that's no way to live."

The mountains rose up around us, jagged, cold, unforgiving. "Once a heart breaks . . . it doesn't just grow back. It's not a lizard's tail. It's more like a huge stained-glass window that shattered into a million pieces, and it's not going back together. A pile of broken colored glass. And I know that when half dies, the whole thing still hurts. So you get twice the pain and half of everything else."

I pulled on my hat. "That's all I wanted to say." I held the compass, letting the needle spin and settle. "I need to know which way to go." The two planes crossed and disappeared. Their exhaust caught my eye. The intersection of the two created an arrow, pointing southeast. One hundred and twenty-five degrees.

"Given that I don't have a better option . . . that'll do."

I WALKED back into the cave and slipped Grover's socks on Ashley's feet. She looked at me with suspicion. "Where'd you get those?"

"Walmart."

"That's good to know. I thought you were going to say they belonged to Grover, and that, well . . . that might just gross me out."

She drifted off. Somewhere near midnight, she caught me staring at the compass face. The tritium dots on the dial glowed neon green. "What if you choose the wrong direction?"

"You, me, and Napoleon will be the only ones who ever know it."

She pulled the bag up over her shoulders. "Take your time . . . and choose wisely."

"Thanks. That's very helpful."

Chapter Six

ASHLEY was grinding her teeth when I shook her. "You ready?"

She nodded, sat up. "Any coffee?"

I handed her a mug of fluid that looked more like weak tea. "Go easy. That's the last of it."

"It's already a bad day, and we haven't even started yet."

We took care of the whole bathroom thing and got her dressed. She grabbed my arm.

"I'm going to ask you a question, and I want an honest answer. Can you get us out of here?"

"Honestly? No idea."

She lay back. "Phew. That's good to know. I thought you were going to say 'no idea,' and then we'd really be in a pickle. And I'm not even going to ask you about the direction we're headed, 'cause I know you've got that figured out. Right?"

"Right."

"Seriously?"

"No."

Her eyes narrowed. "We've got to work on our communication. I'm not asking you this stuff because I want honest answers. I want you to lie your butt off. Tell me we've only got a mile to go when there might be a hundred ahead of us."

I laughed. "Okay. Listen. There's a helicopter waiting just beyond that first rise out there. They've got orange juice, couple of egg sandwiches, sausage, muffins, raspberry Danish, and a dozen glazed donuts. And Starbucks."

She patted me on the back. "Now you're getting the hang of it."

IDEALLY, I'D HAVE BUILT a sled of some sort. Something that would glide and not beat her to death. Problem was, that'd work great on the flat parts, but from what I could see, there weren't a lot of those. And given the angles we'd be traversing, I knew I couldn't handle a sled. If I got caught off balance, it could get away from me. She'd survive the plane crash only to die on the stretcher.

I decided on a hybrid between a sled and stretcher. I started with the wing that had been ripped off. Given that its surface was cloth and plastic, it was light and slick. Its internal structure was metal. So I cut a woman-size cavity lengthwise and re-inforced the bottom with a piece of sheet metal from the engine. I eyed my creation. It might work. Given what I had to work with, it had to.

I packed everything I could find into my backpack and tied it crosswise over the wing where it could elevate Ashley's leg. I palmed four Advil and held the water to her lips. She sipped quietly as I explained my idea. "North-west, behind us, the mountains rise up. That way"—I pointed—"the plateau rolls away southeast. We need to get lower, and that's the only way down. So we're going to pick our way downhill. I'll have my hands on you all the time. When it's flat, I'll fix a harness that will allow me to use the straps and waist belt from my backpack to pull you. Any questions?"

She shook her head. I checked her leg, wrapped her warmly, zipped up her bag, and pulled the wool beanie down over her ears. "For the first time, your leg is down below your heart. It's going to swell. That's going to cause you some discomfort. But nothing is going to hurt like getting you out of here."

She gritted her teeth. I put my hands beneath her arms and pulled her gently toward the stretcher. The sleeping bag slid rather easily over the snow and ice until it hooked on a rock or root, and when I pulled, it jerked her leg.

She screamed at the top of her lungs, turned her head away from me, and threw up. Everything she had eaten, including the Advil, splattered the snow. I wiped her mouth and then her forehead, where she'd broken out in a sweat.

"Sorry."

She nodded and said nothing. She was grinding her teeth.

I got her to the wing, slid her and her sleeping bag onto it, and then laid Napoleon next to her. She put an arm around him but didn't open her eyes. She looked clammy.

I propped her head up with Grover's bag. I secured the bow and Grover's fly rods. It was ridiculously overloaded, but I was operating on the principle that it was better to have it and not need it than need it and not have it.

WE SAID little. The snow was knee-deep most places. Deeper in others. Couple of times I fell to mid-chest and had to crawl out. I focused on my breathing, and my grip on the makeshift handles. The pain in my ribs was considerable.

I didn't know how much fuel we had left, but it had to be running low. At sea level, the Jetboil would boil water in about seventy-five seconds. Up here, it was taking three to four times that long. The fuel in Grover's lighter had nearly evaporated, and we needed fire. I needed to keep my eyes peeled for wood I could use to make a bow drill.

After about an hour, Ashley said, "Excuse me, Doc, but we're not going very fast. You need to giddyup."

I collapsed in the snow next to her, breathing heavily in the thin air. My legs were screaming.

She tapped my forehead. "You know what I was thinking?"

I felt the sweat trickling down my neck. "There's no telling."

"I was thinking how great a cheeseburger would be right now. Maybe two patties. Extra cheese, of course."

I nodded. "Of course."

"Tomato. Got to be a good tomato. Onion. Preferably Vidalia. Ketchup. Mustard. Mayo."

White cottony clouds drifted overhead. Another commercial airliner streaked through the sky.

"And extra pickles," she added.

"And two orders of fries on the side."

"I think I could eat that whole thing twice right now." She looked through the trees in the direction I'd been walking. "You'd better get pulling. This thing's not battery-powered, you know."

"Funny, I figured that out about an hour ago." I took a few steps. "I need you to do me a favor."

"Don't push your luck with me."

I handed her a clean Nalgene bottle. "We need to drink. A lot. If, while I'm pulling, you could pack this thing with snow, then slip it inside your bag and let your body warmth melt it, it'll help."

She took the bottle.

I raised my watch and couldn't see anything on the face. I pressed the light button. Nothing happened. I pushed it again. Harder. Still nothing. I shook it and held it up to the daylight. A deep spider-webbing crack spread across the glass from the bottom left corner to top right. Condensation had gathered beneath.

She noticed the watch. "That important?"

"Rachel gave it to me. Years ago."

"Sorry." She was quiet a minute. Her voice was softer. "Can I ask you something?"

The temperature was probably in the single digits, yet sweat was pouring off my forehead. I'd pulled off my jacket, but my body was drenched. "Sure. Fire away."

"The voice mail you were listening to as we were taking off. What's the deal?"

"We had a disagreement."

"About what?"

I shrugged.

She smirked. "Is she right?"

I nodded. "Yes."

"That's refreshing. A man who admits when his wife is right." She watched me a minute. "What are you not telling me?"

I took a deep breath that did not fill me.

"Silence does not qualify as an answer."

Another shallow breath. "Rachel and I are . . . separated."

"You're what?"

"We had a fight. Kind of a big one, and we're working through an issue or two."

"She doesn't sound like she wants to be separated."

"It's complicated. I said some words I can't take back."

Cold filtered through my wet clothes, clung to me. We'd stayed too long. I backed up to the stretcher, lifted it, and began pulling.

"So . . . where does she live?"

"Just down the beach. I built her a house.

I see her and the kids most every day. We—"

"Kids! You have kids?"

"Two."

"You have two kids and you're just now telling me? How old?"

"Four. They're twins. Michael and Hannah."

She nodded. "Good names."

"Good kids."

"I'll bet they keep you busy."

I didn't respond.

She frowned. "You must've really screwed up. In my experience, it's usually the guy. Always thinking with your plumbing."

"It's not that."

She didn't look convinced. She nodded, closed her eyes, and laid back.

I turned and began pulling. From behind me, I heard, "You still haven't answered my question."

"I know."

AFTER another hour, we'd come maybe five hundred meters, dropping maybe a hundred feet in elevation. Every three steps was followed by several seconds of rest. But it was progress.

She was not impressed. "Seriously"—she took a sip of water—"how long do you think you can do this?"

"Don't know." I watched her out of the corner of my eye.

"We can't do this. You can't. We're in the middle of nowhere."

I stopped, sweat dripping off me, breathing deeply. "We can't stay up there. If we do, we'll die. And I can't leave you. If I do, you'll die. So we're walking out."

Her frustration at being helpless bubbled over. She screamed, "It's been eleven damn days and not a soul has come looking. What's your plan? How do you plan to get us out of here?"

"One step at a time."

"And how long do you think you can keep that up?"

"As long as it takes."

"And what if you can't?"

"I can. What's my choice?"

She closed her eyes. I pulled out the compass, took a reading of 125 degrees, picked a small ridgeline in the distance as a marker, and started putting one foot in front of the other.

We didn't speak for several hours.

My course took us slightly downhill and through the trees. I took my time. If I started to get overheated, I'd take more breaths between steps. In a little over six hours, we came what I judged to be a little more than a mile. It was nearly dark when I stopped.

I was soaking wet with sweat and exhausted, but I knew if I didn't start making my fire bow, I'd regret it. I slid Ashley beneath the limbs of an evergreen and up alongside a rock. The ground beneath her had been protected from the snow, so it was actually dirt and dry pine needles. I pulled off my sweaty shirt, hung it on a limb, gathered several handfuls of needles along with some twigs, and made a small fire. When I clicked the Jetboil and started it, it hiccupped. We had maybe a day left in the tank. I gathered more sticks, laid them in a pile next to her, and said, "Tend this. Don't let it die. I'll be within shouting distance."

I started looking for two pieces of wood. One piece, maybe three feet long with a bit of an arc, and then a straight piece out of which I could cut a spindle. Took me about thirty minutes to find both.

I slipped through the trees, the snow crunching under my makeshift snowshoes. I stopped at a distance. She was sitting up, tending the fire. The glow of the fire on her face. Even there, even then, she was beautiful. There was no denying that.

The difficulty of our situation was always on my mind. But I hadn't seen us through her eyes. Her sitting with nothing to do but tend the fire and scratch Napoleon's head. Dependent on me for movement, food, water, going to the bathroom. If I'd had to be as dependent on someone else, I'd have been much more difficult to live with.

I returned to the fire, slid into my bag, chewed on some meat, and made myself drink water. While the Jetboil was failing, I could still use the upper piece that we cooked in, sort of a small coffee can. It was aluminum and would stand up to heat. So I filled it with snow and leaned it against the coals.

We drank and ate for the next hour while I worked on my bow. Grover's laces were about to come in handy. I pulled out one lace, tied a knot in one end, threaded it through the groove on one end of the bow, pulled it tight, slid it through the groove on the other end, and secured it with a few loops and a knot. Tight enough so that there would be enough tension on the string to spin the spindle. I cut the spindle to about ten inches, carved both ends into points, and cut a groove in the middle to hold the shoelace in place.

That finished, I drank the last of my water and looked up for the first time in a long time.

Ashley was staring at me, her arms crossed. "I need an update."

"I think we made it about a mile. Tomorrow I'm going to climb that rise over there and see what's on the other side. We've probably got enough meat for several more days. So I think we just keep going. Stay as hydrated as you can, and tell me when I jar you too much. I'm sorry when I do. I know today was rough."

She let out a deep breath. "I'm sorry I jumped at you this morning."

I shook my head. "You're in a tough place. You can't do much of anything without my help. That'd be difficult for anyone."

I placed more wood on the fire, slid close enough to be warm but not set myself aflame, and closed my eyes. Sleep was falling on me fast. Then I thought of Ashley. I forced my eyes open. She was staring at me again. "You need anything?"

She shook her head. Tried to smile. "No."

She was asleep in seconds.

Chapter Seven

IT WAS difficult to wake up knowing we'd been doing this almost two weeks. I shook off sleep and was dressed before daylight. The fire was out, but a few coals remained. I blew on it, fanned a flame, and fed it. I scratched Napoleon and then headed up the rise.

I took my time, studying every indentation, every seam in the mountain. I kept asking myself, Does anything look man-made?

The answer was a resounding "No." Everything was pristine and untouched. A nature lover's paradise. I loved nature as much as the next guy, but this was ridiculous.

I steadied the compass, let the needle settle, and took a reading, then stared at the mountains in the distance. To get to them, we'd have to travel all day, maybe two, through tall trees and deep snow. Wouldn't be easy. Never make it without the compass. In the trees, I'd lose all sense of perspective. Direction. Maybe life is like that.

When I returned, Ashley was sitting up, stirring the fire. She started on me before I had a chance to say good morning. "How'd you know you wanted to marry your wife?"

"Good morning."

"Yeah, yeah. Good morning yourself. Seriously. I want to know."

I stuffed my bag into its compression sack. "I wanted to spend every second with her. Wanted to laugh with her, cry with her, grow old with her, hold her hand, and since we'd been hanging out a couple years, I really wanted to have sex with her. A lot of it."

She laughed. "Were you still pretty active before you separated?"

"The best-kept secret about the whole marriage thing is that the loving part gets better. You lose all the 'I've got to prove something' or whatever it is. I guess us guys get our ideas of what it ought to be through movies. When, in fact, it's nothing like that. It's more of a sharing than a taking. Movies show the hot, sweaty side. And that's great; I'm not knocking it. I'm just exposing the myth that that's as good as it gets."

"What about when one wants to and one doesn't?"

I laughed. "Rachel liked to call that 'mercy loving'—and it's ninety-nine percent of the time her having mercy on me."

"So . . . how's that work in the separation?"

"It doesn't." I began strapping stuff to the sled. "Listen, I need to get you to stand up, start bearing weight on the good leg. Forcing circulation."

She held out her hands. I unzipped the bag, she braced her good foot on mine, and I lifted her slowly. She wobbled and then finally stood up straight. "That feels good. Almost human."

"How's the bad leg?"

"Tender. More of a dull pain than sharp."

I readjusted the straps on the brace. She put her arms on my shoulders, balancing on me. I steadied her by the hips. "Let's just give this a few minutes. The change in blood pressure will be good for your heart."

She stared up into the trees, smiling. "You know, when I was in middle school, this was how we danced if we were going with someone. Vince hates to dance."

"Can't say I'm much of a fan, either."

"Okay, I've had enough. Put me down." I settled her in her bag and zipped her up. She pointed. "Come on. Let me see. Show me what you've got."

"What? Dance? You've lost your mind."

She swirled her finger at the ground. "Go ahead. I'm waiting."

I turned, did my best *Staying Alive* imitation, followed by YMCA and a Michael Jackson moonwalk, spin, and hat tilt. When I finished, she was laughing so hard she couldn't talk. Finally, she held out a hand. "Stop. . . . Don't. . . . I think I just peed a little."

The laughter felt good. Real good. And as much as I wanted a satellite phone, a helicopter ride out of there, and a surgical suite to fix her leg, the laughter was worth all of that put together. Napoleon looked at us like we were nuts. Especially me.

She lay back, breathing. Half laughing.

I zipped up my jacket. "Rachel made us take lessons. Swing. Tango. Waltz. Viennese Waltz. Jitterbug. Foxtrot. Even a line dance. Some of the most fun we ever had on dates."

"So you really can dance?"

"With her. I learned that I like dancing with my wife. Once I learned what to do, it wasn't so bad. Course, after that, she wanted to dance at every party we ever attended."

"And did you?"

I nodded. "I called it mercy dancing, and ninety-nine percent of the time it had to do with me having mercy on her. But it had its trade-off." I raised my eyebrows.

"You need to talk to Vince when we get out of here."

"I'll see what I can do." I gave her my jacket to stuff into her bag and stepped into the harness. "Come on, we're burning daylight."

"I've heard that before." She snapped her fingers. "Where's that come from?"

"John Wayne. *The Cowboys.*"

She slid down in her bag. "You are getting more interesting with every day that passes."

"Trust me, my rabbit's hat is just about empty." I strapped on my snowshoes and leaned into the sled, and it gave way across the frozen snow. I took two steps, and she called to me.

"Can I see that little dance move one more time?"

I shook my hips, mopped the floor, tossed the pizza, spun the Q-tip, and spelled YMCA. She was howling, gently kicking her one good leg. We pulled out through the trees, bathed in the smell of evergreen and the sound of her laughter.

BY LUNCHTIME, we'd walked a mile and a half and I was toast. My left foot was frozen, a bad sign, and because the last half mile was slightly uphill, the straps had been cutting into my shoulders, making my fingers numb.

We stopped for an hour alongside a small creek. I pulled Ashley up beneath a tree, pulled off my wet shirt, and hung it to dry.

Letting the shirt freeze was actually good, because it was easier to shake off ice than wring out sweat in this temperature.

The tree's branches canopied out over the ground, protecting it from snow. I slid Ashley down inside; then I climbed into my bag, where, warm and quiet, I slept for an hour. When I woke, I dressed, nibbled on some jerky, stepped back into the harness, and stamped my foot five or six times. It felt wet. Wet meant cold. And cold was bad. Especially for toes. I'd need to watch this.

Late in the afternoon, the sun poked through and heated things up slightly, which turned the snow to mush. I'd take two or three steps, fall, bury myself in snow, climb out, take two or three more steps, bury myself again . . . This went on for a couple of hours.

By nightfall, we'd come maybe two and a half miles. A total of three and a half or four from the crash site. I was cold and wet, but I didn't have the energy to make a fire. The little voice inside my head was telling me I couldn't keep this up for long. I needed to find a place to hole up tomorrow and rest a day.

We camped at a rock outcropping. A ledge that made somewhat of a cave. Good protection from the wind and snow while also offering a one-in-a-million view. I propped Ashley up against the wall, gave her the full effect. She said, "Wow. Never seen anything like that."

"Me, either" was all I could mutter. I sat down. Totally zonked. "Would it be all right with you if we didn't have a fire tonight?"

She nodded. I stripped out of my wet clothes and tried to hang what I could along the rock. My inner layer of Capilene was dripping with sweat. I pulled on my only pair of boxer shorts, slipped into my bag, and only then thought of my boots. If I didn't get my boots dry, tomorrow would be a miserable day.

I climbed out, grabbed handfuls of dead pine needles and twigs, and built a teepee about a foot tall. I stacked the dry needles inside, along with a few branches that were still holding on to their dead needles. I knew I would get only one shot at this.

I took out Grover's lighter, stuck it inside the teepee, and struck it. It sparked, but no

flame. I shook it. "Come on, just one time."
I struck it again. Nothing. "Last time." I
struck it, a flame appeared, grabbed the pine
needles, and was gone. The flame didn't last
more than a second, but it was long enough
to light the needles. I slowly fed more twigs
into it, blowing lightly at the base. Once I
felt like the fire had caught, I searched for
larger sticks.

Dead on my feet, I found enough wood to
feed the fire for a few hours and stacked rocks
along the edge. I set my boots close enough
to dry but not melt the rubber. Then I
climbed into my bag and fell asleep seconds
after my head hit the ground.

My last thought was knowing that Grover's lighter was finished. Conditions continued to worsen. Wet clothes, wet feet, blisters,
and little energy. We had the cooked mountain lion, but even at our current rate of eating it sparingly, we might have two days left.
That included Napoleon. If we didn't feed
him, maybe three.

Problem was, I couldn't not feed him.
Every time I looked at him, he licked my face
and wagged his tail, and every time the wind

blew, he stood up, facing into it, and growled. Anything with that tough a spirit deserves a chance. Others might have already carved him into dog steaks, but I just couldn't. He was probably tough as old shoe leather, anyway. But, to be honest, every time I looked at him, I saw Grover. Maybe that's reason enough.

SIX or seven hours later, with the first hint of daylight crawling across the gray-and-white mountains before us, my eyes opened to the unexpected sound of a hot crackling fire.

Ashley had been tending it for hours. My clothes were warm, dry, and, oddly enough, folded on top of a rock. Anything within arm's reach had been thrown into the fire. Now she was using the last of the sticks I'd gathered. My boots had been turned, and the leather was dry. As were my socks.

I rubbed my eyes. "I'd like some coffee, a cinnamon bun, six eggs over medium, a New York strip, some hash browns, more coffee, some orange juice, a piece of key lime pie, and peach cobbler."

"Can I have some?"

I sat up. "You didn't sleep much, did you?"

She shrugged. "Couldn't. You were pretty tired. And your clothes were dripping wet. I can't do much, but this I can do."

"Thanks. Really." I dressed, pulled on warm boots, which brought a smile to my face, and grabbed the hatchet. "I'll be back."

I returned a half hour later, arms full. I made three more trips. I'd heard wives and mothers in African tribes spend three to ten hours a day searching for water and firewood. Now I understood why.

I melted some snow, heated up some jerky, and fed Ashley and Napoleon. We were quiet a while. The fire felt good.

"How's the leg?"

She shrugged.

I unzipped her bag and ran my hand along her thigh. The swelling had decreased, and the purple had quit spreading. Both good signs. I stared at the stitches in her face. "I need to pull those out."

She nodded. I pulled out my Swiss Army knife, snipped each stitch, and then began the rather painful and unpleasant experience of pulling them out. She winced but never cried out.

When I'd finished, she asked, "How do I look?"

"Nothing a good plastic surgeon can't fix."

"That bad?" She changed the subject. "What's the plan?"

"Shelter and food." I unconsciously looked at my watch, forgetting it was dead, and said, "We're on a bit of a plateau. It continues another mile or so, then drops off, if I remember right. I'd like to get there tonight. If it drops off, it drops off to something. I'm thinking a water source. Lake, stream, something. Maybe we can hole up there a few days and give me a chance to find food."

She eyed Grover's bow, strapped to the top of the sled. "Are six arrows enough?"

"Don't have much choice." I stared out at the dark clouds rolling in across the peaks. "Looks like snow. I'd like to get through those trees before the worst of that drops on us."

She nodded. "I'm game."

We packed quickly, and I was back in the harness before I had time to dread it.

Quarter-size flakes began dropping in the first hour. Walking the mile through the trees took us more than three hours. We emerged where a steep slope seemed to fall off into a valley of sorts. Given total whiteout conditions, I had no real idea.

We pulled up under the limbs of an evergreen, and I pulled out the sketch I'd made. I guessed we were some eight miles from the crash site. I'd knew we'd walked down a 125-degree line, but we were also dodging to the right and left to skirt around rocks, ledges, small peaks, downed trees. We were probably two to three miles off our original line. People experienced with reading compasses can overcome the side-to-side adjustments required by conditions and return to a straight line, allowing them to arrive at an actual predetermined point. I wasn't that good. While we were now eight to nine miles from the crash site, we'd probably walked twice that, given the back and forth that the conditions forced upon us. My sketch suggested we were fifteen or twenty miles yet from the single line I'd seen on the GPS that might have been a logging road.

With the hatchet, I cut into the tree that

hid us and pulled down some limbs, then laid those limbs on the windward side to give us more protection. I was dreading what came next. The bow drill.

I gathered tinder, needles, and small twigs. I strung the bow and slowly began turning the spindle on the hearth board. Once I'd developed the hole and cut the notch, I gave myself to fully working the bow. At this altitude, it took several minutes to get smoke, but once I got it, I kept tugging. Five minutes in, I had a lot of smoke and felt like I might have enough to make a coal. I set down the bow and spindle, picked up my hearth board, and studied my coal. I blew gently, and a small red ember appeared. I blew again, too hard. It scattered like dust.

I started over. This time I pulled on the bow for eight or nine minutes, making sure I had ample dust to create a coal. I set down the bow, lifted the hearth, blew gently, blew again, and this time smoke curled up. I blew some more, then placed the red coal gently inside my handful of tinder. I blew some more. Blew some more. Blew some more.

Finally, a small flame. I blew into it, the flame spread, and I set the handful inside my teepee of sticks and twigs. We had a fire.

Ashley shook her head. "You're better than Robinson Crusoe." She lay back, closing her eyes.

Quiet settled around us. Our evergreen shelter was warm and comfortable, and the limbs above did a good job of providing shelter while also drawing the smoke out. But with two hours of daylight left, I pulled on my jacket, tied on my snowshoes, and grabbed Grover's bow. "I'm going to take a look about." I looked at Napoleon. "Keep her company."

He turned in a circle and hid himself in Ashley's sleeping bag.

I climbed up a small ridge. The lee side was sheltered from the wind, so the snow cover was less. Sprigs of dead grass and ice-covered rock spotted the snow. My lungs told me we were still above ten thousand feet. The snow had quit. The sky was gray, but the ceiling was high and I could see a large valley below me. Maybe ten to fifteen square miles. Frozen creeks and small streams creased between the trees. Except for the occasional roll and pitch of a hill, it was mostly flat. Certainly better than where we'd been.

A couple hundred yards from our shelter, I reached a small ledge, sat down, cupped my hands around my eyes, and scanned every square acre, asking myself if anything I saw hinted at the possibility that it might be man-made.

Just as the last light was fading, I caught a flash of something brown. It was horizontal, near the treetops. I squinted. It was hard to make out but worth a second look. I opened my compass, took a reading of ninety-seven degrees, and started back to camp. Twenty yards in front of me, something white flashed across my trail. I nocked an arrow and waited for any sign of movement. A small hop. Followed by another. There, a small white rabbit. Big ears, big feet, hunched over and hopping beneath the trees.

I drew, settled the first pin in the middle of the rabbit, let out half a breath, and squeezed the release. Just as the arrow left the bow, the rabbit hopped maybe six inches. My arrow sailed by harmlessly, and the rabbit disappeared.

I searched for my arrow, but digging in the snow was painful on my blistered hands. I decided to leave it until tomorrow.

ASHLEY had the fire crackling when I returned. She'd even managed to boil some water and heat up what was close to the last of our meat. Maybe a day left. She eyed the bow and the single arrow missing. "What happened?"

"It hopped."

"And if it hadn't?"

"I'm pretty sure we'd be eating rabbit tonight."

"Maybe from now on, you should let me hold them still while you shoot."

"If you can catch them, I'm game for anything. Say, do you feel like taking a walk?"

She raised both eyebrows. "Seriously?"

"Yeah. If you can lean on me, I think we could make our way up to this ridge. I need your eyes."

"See something?"

"Maybe. It's a horizontal line in a sea of verticals. I'm not willing to risk it unless both of us look at it."

"What are we risking?"

"I'd thought we'd keep trying to lose elevation, but this thing I'm looking at would keep us up on the plateau for a few miles. It's a two- or three-day change in direction, followed by another three or four if I'm wrong." I didn't need to tell her we were flirting with the edge as it was.

"Is it safe for me to walk?"

"No, but the sled would never make it. We'll take it slow, one step at a time. At first light. The rising sun may be our best chance."

We climbed into our bags and watched the flame light the underside of the tree limbs. It was the first time I'd been overly warm and had to unzip my bag. Once I got some food in me, I moved my attention to Ashley's leg. Swelling was down, and knotting and scar tissue were discernible around the break. All good signs.

I sat opposite her, placed her good foot on my lap, and began rubbing deep into her arch, then her calf, and finally her hamstring and quadriceps to force the circulation.

She looked up at me. "You sure you didn't study massage?"

"You've been lying prostrate for two weeks.

You try to stand on these things and liable to look like a Weeble."

"A what?"

"You know, 'Weebles wobble but they don't fall down.' " Ashley was all muscle. Long, lean, limber muscle. Which probably saved her life. I moved to her left foot, careful not to torque her leg. "I'd hate for you to get angry and kick me when your leg heals. You're nothing but one big muscle."

"Don't feel like much of one lying here." She flinched as I worked deep in her calf. "When we get back, you've got to teach Vince how to do this."

"Vince doesn't rub your feet?"

"Not even if I gave him rubber gloves."

"I better talk to that man."

"That's a good idea. And while you're making a list, add that little thing you did with the stick and making the fire."

I shook my head and smiled. "Nope. I think I'd convince him to do something else first."

"What's that?"

"Buy a satellite phone."

I'm not sure which was better, the fire or the sound of her giggling.

Chapter Eight

WARMED by the fire, I lay awake, staring at the ironic sight of another jetliner at thirty thousand feet. Ashley was out. Slightly snoring. A gentle breeze filtered through our tree, pulled on the limbs above us, and added extra twinkle to a sky lit by ten billion stars. Tomorrow's decision was worrying me. Had I really seen something, or had I wanted to so badly that my mind convinced my eyes that I had?

The sound woke me. Feet crunching snow. Packing it hard. I climbed out of my bag, grabbed the bow, and crouched between Ashley and the door. Then heard the knock of antlers rubbing against tree limbs. The thing snorted, then took off running.

"Ben, you mind sleeping over here?" Ashley said.

"Sure." I picked up my bag and slid it over. We both drifted off.

Sometime later, I woke again. There was hair in my face. Human hair. And it smelled of woman. My first tendency was to move. Respect Ashley's space.

But I did not. I lay there, breathing in. Stealing the aroma. Slow inhales followed by long, quiet exhales. Remembering what a woman smelled like.

After a while, she turned her head, pressing her forehead to mine. Her breath on my face. I pressed in, careful not to wake her. Then I drifted off again, feeling guilty and filled with longing.

IT WAS dark when I woke. The moon was high and bright through the evergreen limbs. The fire had died, but I blew on the coals, added tinder, and had a flame in seconds.

Ashley stirred. I dressed, helped her do the same, and once I had her bundled, slid her out the entrance. I could only pull the sled about a hundred yards before the angle grew too steep and I had to lift her to a standing position. She wrapped an arm around my neck. I put her on my right side so her bad leg was between us.

We took our time. One step, then another. Napoleon trailed behind, hopping in our footsteps. Happy to be out. What had taken me twenty minutes took us nearly an hour, but we made it without incident. I sat her on the ledge, the view spread out before us, and she scanned the sixty or seventy square miles looking back at us.

I leveled the compass on my leg, let the needle settle, then pointed across the carpet of evergreens toward a distant ridge. "See that brown-looking thing? Sort of flat, stretched left to right, sitting on top of the trees, just left of that white-capped ridge-line." I waited while she studied the horizon. We were looking at a speck eight to ten miles distant. The proverbial needle. "See it?"

She nodded. "Yeah." She was quiet a minute. "How in the world did you see that in the first place? It's hard to make out."

"Give it ten minutes. When direct sunlight starts coming over the ridges, it'll light on whatever that is. If it's man-made, we'll get some sort of reflection that's unnatural."

So we waited. Sunlight crawled down the mountain, uncovering what lay before us. An immense valley, hemmed on three sides by steep and jagged mountains. In the middle floated an evergreen sea crisscrossed by streams and small frozen lakes and ponds.

Just before the sun grew too bright and the reflection off the snow obscured the image we were looking at, the brown thing glimmered. Or shimmered.

I asked without turning my head. "You see that?"

"Yeah. I'm not sure whether it was a reflection off ice and snow or something else."

"Okay, look right. See that clearing? Could be a frozen lake."

"What's your point?"

"Well . . . if I was to build a mountain house, I'd build preferably near a lake." The glare grew painful, obscuring our view. "What do you think?" I pointed down our original line, which would take us out of the valley we were looking into. "Going that way is lower elevation. Probably warmer. Certainly breathe easier. I just don't know where it leads." I swung a wide arc left, toward the image in the distance. "Across the valley is a lot of deep snow, frozen creeks hidden beneath the surface that could swallow me. If that thing over there is nothing, it's going to cost us."

"How much food do we have?"

"If we stretch it? Day and a half."

"How long can you make it after that runs out?"

"I can keep breathing for maybe a week, but if I'm pulling the sled . . ." I shrugged. "I'm not sure."

"Sounds to me like we've got enough energy to get across the valley on what's stored up inside you right now. And if we make it to the other side without finding food, then it might be a good place to curl up and go to sleep for a long time. What if you left me here and scouted it out on your own?"

"I've thought about that. Granted, I could get there a lot quicker, but there's no guarantee I can do it safely or get back to you. If I fall, get hurt, get eaten by a mountain lion, then we'll both die alone with a lot of unanswered questions. I'm not willing to risk that."

She closed her eyes. "We've been at this for fifteen days. If you can go farther without me, then you've got to try it. One of us making it is better than both of us dying."

"That's where you're wrong. I won't do it."

We sat side by side. Staring out over a painful future. She hooked her arm inside mine. "Why are you doing this?"

"I have my reasons."

"One of these days, you've got to help me understand them, because they don't make any sense."

I stood and pulled her up on two feet. "That depends on whether you're looking at this through my eyes or yours."

We began walking back. Gingerly she set one foot in front of the other. Halfway back, I let her rest while I dug out my arrow.

"We look like two people in a potato sack race," she said through a running nose. "If Vince and I had tried walking to that ledge, we'd have ended up on our backs with me in a lot of pain, trying to shove snow down his throat for letting me fall."

"Not to pry, but every time you talk about him, you tell me how you two are different, not alike. What's up with that?"

"We're different, all right. But I enjoy him. He makes me laugh. And we have a lot in common."

"People go to the rescue shelter and choose dogs for similar reasons. Not seventy-year soul mates."

"Okay, Dr. Phil, what reason would you choose?"

"Love."

She shook her head. "That only happens to the select few. The rest of us better get what we can while we can; otherwise, we end up waiting on a fairy tale that never comes true."

"What if you could have the fairy tale, but getting it meant waiting for it?"

"I've waited, tried to be selective, but all the good ones are taken. Guys like Grover, and you . . . I've never had much luck finding one of them."

"I'm just saying I think you're selling yourself short if you settle for a marriage that is less than what you'd hoped for. I think you're quite remarkable, and if Vince isn't and he doesn't light you up, then, with all due respect to him, don't marry him."

"Easy for you to say. You've been married fifteen years and don't have to look at shopping in a market where demand is high and supply is low. And it's not that Vince doesn't light me up . . ."

"I never said it's easy. I just think you deserve someone stellar."

She smiled. "Thank you. I'll remember that."

We reached the shelter. I packed the sled, got her settled back in her bag, and strapped in.

WE LEFT the shelter and set out. The snow was frozen, hard on top, making my pulling easy. Ashley was quiet. She didn't look good. Gaunt. Hollow. She needed nutrients. Her body was working double-time trying to survive and feed the wounds inside her.

Toward lunchtime, we'd made maybe two miles. A good distance, but it had taken its toll on me.

Ashley broke the silence. "Hey, why don't you rest awhile?"

I stopped, hands on my knees, breathing down into my belly, and nodded. "Sounds good." I unbuckled myself and pushed the sled to a small flat area beneath two trees.

I stepped and had no time to react. The false top gave way, bent both snowshoes nearly in two, and swallowed me to my neck. The impact knocked the wind out of me, jolting my ribs. Water rushed over my knees. Reflexively, I grabbed for anything to stop my fall. I caught the sled. Doing so turned it on its side and threw Ashley and Napoleon out of it, screaming and whimpering.

I pulled, dragging myself from the sucking hole and the stream beneath. Every foothold gave way, and whenever I pulled with my right side, the pain sent spasms through me. I paused, gathered myself, and pulled once. Then again. Then again. Slowly inching myself from the hole, I pulled my body up on top of the snow.

Ashley lay several feet away, breathing deeply, knuckles white. I crawled to study her pupils. Shock would show up there first.

She darted a glance, then returned her attention to some speck in the sky she'd focused on. Something she learned in tae kwon do.

I was drenched. We were hurt, had no fire, I couldn't get dry, and we couldn't get across this valley of hell for at least another day. I could walk in wet clothes, but wet boots were another thing. And there was a hole in the sled. When I'd grabbed it, it had caught on something that tore a large hole just beneath Ashley's shoulders.

I propped her head up, unzipped her bag, and carefully studied her leg. The throw had not rebroken it, but it had torqued all the tender attachments and tacky bones that had slowly been resettling and regrowing. It was swelling right before my eyes.

I sunk my head in my hands. If our situation had been bad an hour ago, even dire, it was now circling the bowl of unimaginable.

I didn't have a solution, but I knew we had to get moving. My teeth were starting to chatter. I sat up, pulled off my gaiters, then my boots and socks. "I know you probably don't feel like talking to me right now, but can I borrow your socks?"

She nodded. I slipped them off her feet, wrapped her feet in my jacket, and zipped her gently back inside her bag.

Both sleeping bags came inside what are called stuff sacks. It's paramount to keep down bags dry, so most good bags come with waterproof sacks. I pulled both sacks out of my pack, stuffed my sleeping bag into the backpack, slid on Ashley's socks, and slid my feet into the dry sacks. I tightened the compression straps, slid into and laced up my boots, and then put my gaiters on beneath my pant legs. A poor solution, but the only one I could think of. I took a few steps. It felt like I was walking in moon boots.

The sled was a much larger problem. I needed to patch the hole. I had nothing but two bent snowshoes. The nets I'd used as their base had been double folded to support my weight. If I unfolded them . . .

I did and fastened the sides to either side of the sled. Doing so prevented Ashley from slipping through the hole, but it didn't prevent snow from gushing through. My only option was to lift one end of the sled and tie it to me via the harness. This lifted Ashley's head and shoulders off the snow and meant I dragged the back end. Compared to sliding the sled, this was several times harder. And it was harsh and bumpy for Ashley and slower by a large margin.

I didn't see any other way.

I pulled out the last of our food and split it with her. "Here, this might take your mind off the pain. But go easy. This is the last of it." I ate my three pieces, which only made me more hungry. I strapped the sled higher on the harness, buckled myself in, and put one foot in front of the other. Then did it again. And again.

I didn't stop until I could go no farther.

I WOKE UP FACEDOWN in the snow. It was pitch-dark, no moon, no stars. My hands had cramped from holding on to the front of the sled behind me, trying to prevent Ashley's head from beating about. The straps were cutting into my shoulders, and I couldn't really feel my legs.

I stood, pushed into the snow, and sank for the ten thousandth time up to my thighs. I could move no more, and my core was cold. Ashley was either asleep or unconscious. I unbuckled, lifted the harness over my head, crawled beneath an evergreen, kicked away the snow, and pulled Ashley in. I rolled out my bag, stripped, and climbed inside.

I realized that I did not expect to wake up.

Chapter Nine

THE sun was high when I cracked open my eyes. I was sore in places I'd forgotten were part of my body. I wasn't hungry, but I was so weak that I didn't want to move.

I rolled over and took a look around. Ashley was looking at me. Her eyes spoke two things: compassion and resolution. As in, resolved to the fate we faced. Even Napoleon looked weak.

The reality of last night returned in a wave of hopelessness. Ashley leaned over me, a strip of meat in her hand. "Eat."

Spread across her lap lay several strips of meat. My thinking was cloudy. It didn't register. "Where'd you get it?"

She tapped my lip. "Eat."

I opened my mouth; she set a small bite on my tongue, and I began to chew. It was tough, cold, mostly sinew, and may have been the best thing I'd ever put in my mouth. I swallowed, and she tapped my lip again. We didn't have that much food yesterday. "Where'd you . . ."

Clarity came with a rush. I shook my head.

She tapped me again. "Eat this and don't argue with me."

"You first."

"You need this. You still have a chance."

"We've had this discussion." I pulled myself up on one elbow.

"Why!" She threw the gnarly piece of meat at me. It ricocheted off my shoulder and landed on the snow. Napoleon jumped up and devoured it. Her voice echoed off the mountains rising up around us. "Why are you doing this? We're not going to make it!"

"I don't know if we're going to or not, but either *we* are or *we* are not. Ashley, I will not live the rest of my life staring at your face every time I close my eyes."

She curled up, crying. I sat up, staring at my frozen clothes. The only thing dry was my jacket. I needed to figure out where we were. I pulled on my long underwear, then my pants. Sliding my badly blistered feet into my boots was painful, but not as painful as those first few steps. I pulled my jacket on over my bare skin.

We'd slept in the open and were lucky it hadn't snowed. I knelt next to her and touched her shoulder. Her face was buried in her bag. "I'm going to look around."

One unique thing about the trees around us was the limbs. They were straight, started near the ground, and were spaced like ladder rungs. I found one I thought I could climb, slipped off my boots, and started up, my arms telling me I weighed a thousand pounds.

At thirty feet, I took a look around. I was amazed at how far we'd come since the evergreen shelter of yesterday. The ridgeline off which we'd seen the valley lay maybe eight to ten miles behind us. That meant we had to be close. I cupped my hands around my eyes. "Come on. Please be something."

Being down in the valley changed our perspective, which was part of the reason it took me a few minutes to find it. Once I did, I actually laughed. I checked my compass reading, turned the bezel to mark the degree, and climbed down.

Ashley was weak and wouldn't look at me. I stuffed my bag into the backpack, strapped everything onto the sled, and buckled myself into the harness.

The snow was wet and thick, and I felt more like a plow than a man walking. The trees obscured my view. Every few feet I'd stop, check my bearing, pick a tree, walk to it, pick another, and so on. That continued for two or three hours.

When we finally broke through the tree line, the snow started in earnest. The frozen lake spread out before us, stretching an oval mile toward the mountains behind it. The snow obscured my vision, but the sight at the other end was one of the more beautiful things I'd ever seen. I collapsed, hit my knees, and tried to catch my breath. My wheezing was deep, and my ribs were throbbing.

I crawled around and spun the sled. Ashley's eyes were closed. I tapped her on the shoulder. "Hey? You awake?"

She stared at me. "Ben . . . I'm sorry . . ."

I put my fingers to her lips and pointed across the lake.

She craned her eyes, staring through the thickening snow. When she tilted her head and the picture made sense, she started crying.

IT WAS late afternoon. Four-seventeen to be exact. I'd just finished in surgery when my nurse said, "Your wife's waiting on you."

You never just appeared. I walked into my office, and you were looking at a color wheel. One of those things that look like a fan, covered with rows of every color in the spectrum. "Hey," you said.

"What're you doing here?"

You held the fan thing up to the wall. "I like this blue. What do you think?"

I scratched my head. "You like it better than this sixty-seven-dollars-a-square-yard paper we picked out last year?"

You picked up a catalogue off my desk. "And I like this color wood. It's not too dark. It's something we can grow with."

I looked around at the six thousand dollars of swanky office furniture. I said nothing.

Then you pulled out a large portfolio and started flipping through prints. You tapped one. "This reminds me of Norman Rockwell. And here are a few Ford Rileys and even a Campay. I just don't know if we have wall space for all of them."

"Honey?"

You looked at me. Eyebrows raised.

"What in the world are you talking about?"

You said it so matter-of-factly. "The nursery."

Your words echoed in slow motion. Nurrrr- serrrr-ieeee. Maybe a dumb look crossed my face. You took my hand, slid it beneath your shirt, and pressed my palm to your stomach. "The nursery."

In that moment, my hand pressed to your

stomach, your butterflies fluttering beneath my palm. . . . You took my breath away.

I COULDN'T risk walking across the middle. I had a pretty good feeling the lake was frozen several feet deep, but I had no way of knowing, so I kept to the shoreline. It was the easiest walking to date. It felt like we were speeding. The distance to the far shore was nearly a mile. We crossed it in a little over thirty minutes.

I pulled Ashley up the small incline and into the trees that lined the bank. Again I turned her so we could both look.

The A-frame construction rose up some forty feet in the air. Its front was entirely glass. A few roof shingles were missing, but on the whole, the building was doing fairly well. The front door faced the lake and had been painted yellow. Because the prevailing winds came from behind the building, it was only half covered with snow.

I pulled the sled to the door and spent several minutes pulling away snow. I pushed on the door, and it swung open.

The supports for the A-frame were built of lodgepole pine, the floor was concrete, and the inside of the building was one huge room. On the sides, the roof went all the way to the floor, and the only windows were at either end. A fireplace—big enough for two people to sleep in—sat off to our right. A huge iron grate filled the middle. Stacked ten feet high in the corner sat six or seven truckloads of wood. Beyond that, two dozen worn pews were mounded on top of one another. Several silver canoes lay atop them, awaiting summer. Off to the left was a kitchen area, and at the far end, a set of stairs rose to a second floor that was open to the area above the fireplace. There were fifty or sixty bunk beds, all covered with pencil drawings and lettering detailing who loved whom. Dust covered most everything, and there were no lights.

Napoleon hopped off the sled, ran into the room, barked, barked again, then turned in four circles and returned to me, wagging his tail and snotting all over my leg.

Slowly I pulled the sled onto the concrete floor. We stared, awestruck. I pulled Ashley over to the fireplace and began stacking wood for a fire. I started laughing when I found a box of fat lighter next to the pile of wood. I built the fire, small sticks on the bottom, larger pieces on top. Off on a side shelf, a can of lighter fluid sat next to a box of strike-anywhere matches. I grabbed the can, doused the wood, struck a match, and threw it on.

We sat, mesmerized. Neither of us spoke. I pulled off my wet jacket, sat next to Ashley, put my arms around her shoulders, and hugged her.

We'd caught a break, and doing so had pushed back the hopelessness that was crowding in, choking the life out of us.

AFTER the fire bled out the cold, I climbed the stairs. A single twin foam mattress lay wedged and half folded in a corner. I beat it against the railing, dragged it downstairs, and laid it in front of the fire. Napoleon immediately took his place at the end closest to the fire and curled into a ball.

I laid my bag on the mattress, then unzipped Ashley's bag and helped her slowly lift herself to mine. She was weak and needed help to get across. I propped her head on my pack, unbuckled the brace, helped her out of her clothes, and hung them across a pew.

With Ashley dry and warm, I pulled off my clothes and spread them across the pew. I dug in my pack and pulled on my only dry clothing, a pair of athletic underwear. Then I eyed the kitchen.

It contained two large black cast-iron wood-burning stoves and several long preparation tables. A long stainless-steel sink lined a wall ending in a gas hot-water heater. The whole thing looked effective at serving large amounts of food for lots of people.

I tried the faucet, but the water had been turned off. I tried to shake the hot water heater, but it was full and wouldn't budge. I turned on the gas, smelled propane, and lit the pilot light. I stacked the stove with wood, lit it, and adjusted the damper. I filled a huge pot with snow, then placed it atop the stove.

On one wall stood a rather menacing-looking door with large hinges and a padlock. I grabbed the steel poker from the fireplace, wedged it in, broke the hinge, and opened the door. On the left side, there were paper napkins, plates, and cups. On the right, a box of decaffeinated tea bags and one two-gallon can of vegetable soup. That was it.

An hour later, slowly chewing each piece of potato and savoring each bite, Ashley looked at me, soup dripping off her chin, and mumbled, "What is this place?"

I'd given Napoleon a bowl of soup, which he'd inhaled. He now lay at my feet, contentment on his face. "Some sort of high alpine camp. Boy Scouts, maybe."

She took a sip of tea and turned up her lip. "Who would make, much less drink, de-caffeinated tea? I mean, what is the use?" She shook her head. "How do you think they get up here?"

"Don't know. I'm pretty sure they didn't stick those iron stoves on their backs and just pack them up here. When my clothes dry, I'll see if there are any other buildings. Maybe find something."

She took another bite. "Yeah, like more food."

Two bowls later, we lay in front of the fire, not hungry for the first time in days. I stared out the window. The snow was falling thick, a total whiteout. I rolled up my jacket and placed it behind her head.

She grabbed my hand. "Ben?"

"Yeah."

"Can I have this dance?"

"If I move, I'll throw up all over you."

She laughed. "You can lean on me."

I hooked my arms beneath her shoulders and lifted her gently. She wasn't too steady, so she hung on me.

I'd lost so much weight that my underwear was hanging low on my hips. She was wearing a baggy T-shirt that needed to be burned, and her underwear sagged where her butt used to be. I held her waist, and we stood without moving. Her leg was badly swollen, nearly half again the size of her right leg.

Eyes closed, she was swaying. She put her arms around my neck, humming a tune I couldn't understand. She sounded drunk.

I whispered, "Let's not hear any more of this nonsense about me going on alone. Deal?"

She stopped swaying and was quiet for several minutes. "Deal."

When she grew tired, I laid her on her bag and poured her some more tea. I elevated the broken leg. It needed ice. I laid my bag out across the concrete, patted Napoleon, who was snoring, and lay back. I was dozing off when it hit me that during all that dancing, when Ashley's body leaned against mine, when the feeling of her as friend and woman warmed me, I hadn't once thought of my wife.

Chapter Ten

DAWN outside. Day seventeen. New snow piled high. Pulling on dry clothes was worth its weight in gold. Ashley lay sleeping. Her face was flushed, and she was muttering in her sleep, but she looked warm and, for the first time in weeks, not uncomfortable. I found the lever on the wall that supplied the hot-water heater with water, broke it loose, and turned it on. Brown rusty water spilled into the sink. I ran it until it turned clear, then turned up the heat. A bath sounded like a good idea.

I slid the hatchet into my belt, grabbed the bow, and set out in search of other buildings. Napoleon beat me to the door, jumped out into the snow, sank to his belly, and lay there grounded. I picked him up and cradled him. He growled at the snow as we walked. Flakes landed on his face, and he snapped at them.

I scratched his stomach and told him, "I like your attitude."

It turned out there were seven buildings in all. One was a bathroom. I found a few bars of soap and rolls of toilet paper. Five were cabins, one-room A-frames, each with a wood-burning stove, carpet on the floor, and a loft. One even had a reclining chair.

The seventh was a two-room cabin. Maybe the scoutmaster's. The back room had three bunks. Green wool blankets lay folded at the end of each. One bed even had a pillow. In a closet, I found three towels and a thousand-piece jigsaw puzzle. In the front room sat two chairs, a wood-burning stove, and an empty desk.

It took three trips to haul everything we needed—including the reclining chair. I was closing the door on the third trip when I noticed the most important piece.

A bas-relief map hung thumbtacked to the wall, a 3-D map with raised white-capped plastic mountains. It didn't give distances. Across the top it read HIGH UINTAS WILDERNESS. Along one side it read WASATCH NATIONAL FOREST. And in the right-hand corner were the words ASHLEY NATIONAL FOREST.

Fitting, I thought.

A small dialogue balloon with an arrow pointed to the center of the Ashley. It read FOOT AND HORSE TRAFFIC ONLY. NO MOTORIZED VEHICLES ALLOWED AT ANY TIME.

Evanston, Wyoming, sat in the top left-hand corner, with Highway 150 leading due south. Small letters across the highway read CLOSED IN WINTER. Interstate 80 bordered the top of the map, running west to east from Evanston to Rock Springs, where Highway 191 led south to Vernal. Highway 40 led west out of Vernal and intersected Highway 150, which ran north to Evanston.

Somewhere in the middle of that plastic-capped mess, someone had stuck a thumb-tack, marked an X, and written "We are here."

I pulled the map off the wall, and Napoleon and I returned to the A-frame. As we were coming into the building, Napoleon spotted something and ran off, snarling, his feet spewing snow. Ashley was still sleeping, so I dumped my goods and slid the chair in close to the fire. I checked the door for Napoleon, but all I could hear was a distant bark. I figured I didn't need to worry. Of the three of us, he was probably the most able to take care of himself.

I returned to the kitchen and built a fire in one of the cast-iron stoves. The sink was deep and big enough to sit in. I washed it out and filled it with water as hot as I could stand. When I sat in it, steam was rising off the top. It was one of the more magnificent moments I'd had in the last few weeks.

After I bathed, I plunged our clothes into the water, scrubbed each piece, and then hung them over the pew. I poured two mugs of tea and returned to Ashley, who had just begun to stir. I helped her sit up, and she sipped.

After her third sip, she sniffed the air. "You smell better."

"Found some soap."

"You bathed?" She set down her mug. "Take me to it."

"Okay, but the hot water will increase the swelling, so we'll need to ice it when you get out. Okay?"

"Agreed."

I helped her hobble to the sink. She caught sight of her legs and shook her head. "You didn't happen to find a razor, did you?"

I helped her sit on the edge and lowered her in. Slowly she bent her left knee, laying it flat across the prep area of the sink. She leaned her head back on the built-in dish drainer, closed her eyes, and held out her hand, her finger hooked where the mug would be. I brought her tea, and she said, "I'll be with you in a little while."

It's amazing how a bath can improve your disposition.

I walked off, then turned. "Oh, and you'll never believe the name of the forest we're in. It's called the Ashley National Forest."

She was laughing as I stepped out the door.

You were four and a half months. You were lying on the table. The nurse squeezed the goo, as you liked to call it, on your stomach and started rubbing it with the wand.

I handed her an envelope and said, "We'd rather you not tell us right now. If you don't mind, just write whether it's a boy or a girl, then seal it. We'll open it at dinner."

She nodded and began showing us the head, the legs, even a hand. It was the most magical thing.

Then she started laughing.

We should have picked up on it, but we didn't. She shook her head, wrote on the card, and handed me the envelope, saying, "Congrats. Mom and baby are healthy."

I drove you home. You kept asking, "What do you think? Boy or girl?"

I laughed. "I don't care. I'll take whatever comes out of the oven."

Our favorite restaurant. Matthew's. They seated us in a booth in the back. You were glowing. I don't remember what we ordered. Matthew came out of the back, said hello, and sent us some champagne. We sat there, champagne bubbles bubbling, candlelight flickering off your eyes, and the envelope lying on the table. You pushed it to me. I pushed it back to you and kept my hand on top. "You do it. Honey, you've earned it."

You pulled out the note and pressed it to your chest. Laughing. Neither one of us could talk. Then you read it. You read it two or three times before you said anything to me.

"Well . . . what is it?"

You grabbed my hands. "It's both."

"Come on. Quit kidding. It can only be one."

Then it hit me. I stared at your tears streaming down. "Really? Twins?"

You nodded and buried your face in your napkin.

We bought champagne for the entire restaurant.

Driving home, you didn't say a word. Your head was spinning with colors, a second crib, a second everything. We walked in the door, and you said, "You thought about names?"

"Not really. Still getting over the sticker shock."

"Michael and Hannah."

The moment you said it, it clicked. Like pieces of a puzzle snapping together. From then on, it became the four of us.

Maybe that was the moment. Maybe if I could go back and start over, bathed in the crazy thought of laughter, warmth, and two of every-thing, I'd go there.

Because I'm pretty sure I wouldn't go much beyond that.

NAPOLEON had been gone a while. When my clothes dried, I grabbed the bow, zipped up my jacket, and stepped outside. I whistled but heard nothing. I followed his zigzag footprints up a hill, then along a ridgeline. They were hard to follow, as snow was filling them. I crossed a second hill and saw him down near the lake, hunkered over what looked like a red ball of fuzz. When I got close enough for him to hear me, he growled. Part of a rabbit lay beneath him. "Hey, boy. Good job. How would you feel about finding two more and dropping them off at the big house up there?"

He looked at me, ripped, chewed, and swallowed. Then he picked up what was left and carried it farther from me.

"Suit yourself."

I took a different route back. Several times I crossed moose and rabbit tracks. I needed practice with the bow, but if I missed the target, the arrow could penetrate several feet into the snow and I'd never find it. Wouldn't take long to lose all the arrows.

I returned to the A-frame, stoked the fire, and checked on Ashley, who was frolicking about like a dolphin and told me to go away. I went to one of the other cabins and pulled up a piece of carpet. Back at our place, I laid it over a pew and tacked a paper plate to its center. In the center of the plate, I cut a hole the size of a dime.

The A-frame was more than forty yards long. I only needed about fifteen. I counted off the steps and drew a line in the dust with my toe. I nocked an arrow, drew, settled the sight, told myself, "Front sight, front sight, front sight," and then, "Press." I gently squeezed the release. The arrow struck the paper three inches above the hole. I nocked another, and it struck just a hair to the right of the first.

I needed to make an adjustment, so I pushed down the peep sight, the little circle inside the string through which your eye looks. Pushing it down would bring the arrow's impact down.

It did. Just not far enough. I adjusted it again, bringing the impact too far. I readjusted, and within thirty minutes, I could hit the hole every third or fourth shot if I held true and still.

Ashley heard the commotion. "What's all that racket?"

"Just me trying to improve our chances at getting some dinner."

"How about helping me out of here."

She'd washed her T-shirt and underwear and spread them across the dish-drainer grooves. She reached out her hands, and I helped her climb out. She wrapped a towel around herself. "I'm told guys are visual. So how're you doing with all this?" she asked.

"I'm still your doctor."

"Doctors are human, too." She was smiling. Acknowledging the elephant in the room. "I can't get much more naked."

I got her to the reclining chair, which would elevate her leg, taking the pressure off it. "Ashley, I'm not blind. You're beautiful, but I still love my wife. The part of my heart that needs to be filled with that has been filled. And I want to get home and be able to look a guy named Vince in the eye and hide nothing." I stared at her. "I'm separated from my wife because of something I did. Anything that furthered that separation . . ."

She was quiet a minute. "I envy her."

"You remind me of her."

"How so?"

"Well . . . physically, you're lean, athletic, muscular. Emotionally, you don't hide from anything. You put stuff on the table rather than dance around it. And you have a deep reservoir of strength, evidenced by your sense of humor."

"What's her greatest weakness?"

I didn't want to answer.

"Okay, what was her greatest weakness prior to the separation?"

"The thing that's also her greatest strength. Her love for me and the twins. She put us first. Always. Making herself a distant third."

"And that's a weakness?"

"Can be."

"What would you prefer?"

"I'd prefer she was selfish like me." I dusted off a piece of plywood, laid it flat across her lap, and handed her the jigsaw puzzle. "Found this. The picture's worn off the box, but . . ."

She wiggled off the lid, dumped out the pieces, and immediately started separating those with straight edges. "You want to help?"

"Not a chance. Makes me dizzy just looking at it."

"It's not that bad." Her fingers flipped the

pieces. "Just take your time. Eventually it'll come together."

I stared at the mess in front of her. "I don't have the patience."

"I doubt that."

I shook my head. "No, thanks."

GIVEN the continuing snow, the light outside stayed dim and gray. The size of Ashley's leg did not encourage me. I carried our large pot outside and made a dozen tightly packed snowballs. I then folded a towel, set it beneath her leg, and began rubbing one snowball at a time in circles around the break. She squirmed.

"Just give it a few minutes. Once it turns numb, it'll be better."

Four snowballs later, she lay back and turned her head, staring up through the window. I iced her leg for close to thirty minutes. Other than turning her skin bright red, the effect was minimal.

"Every hour on the hour. Got it?"

She nodded. "Any idea where we are?"

I spread the map and showed her the X that marked our spot. About then, Napoleon pushed his way through the door and sauntered over like he owned the place. He walked to his corner of the mattress, circled it, then flopped down, tucked his face beneath one paw, and closed his eyes. The sides of his muzzle were red, and his stomach was rounded.

"Where's he been?"

"Eating breakfast."

"He save any for us?"

"I talked to him about that, but he wasn't having any."

She rubbed his tummy. "So . . . what's the plan?"

"I'm going to see if I can't find us some dinner."

"And then?"

"Well . . . we'll eat until we can't eat anymore, then head out."

"Where are we going?"

"Hadn't gotten there yet. I'm tackling one crisis at a time."

She laid her head back and closed her eyes. "Let me know when you get it all figured out. I'll be right here."

I made more snowballs, set them on the far side of the chair, and grabbed the bow. "If I'm not back in an hour, ice that leg."

She nodded.

"And keep drinking."

"Yes, sir."

"I'm not kidding. Thirty on, sixty off."

"You sound just like my doctor."

"Good."

THE wind had picked up, swirling the snow, sending miniature twisters through the trees where they rattled the limbs and played out. I climbed up the hill behind the camp. The ridgeline circled the lake. Lake on one side, another valley on the other.

I stared at the layout of the camp. People, Boy Scouts—somebody had to get here on something. It was conceivable that they got here only via foot or horseback, but where were those trails? If we were in fact inside the Ashley and they allowed only foot and horse traffic, we couldn't be too far inside it. Otherwise, they'd never get up here.

I circled south, and it didn't take me long to find it: a winding footpath, wide enough for two horses abreast, that led down from the lake through the notch in the valley behind us.

I was getting cold. I needed to get back.

Ashley slept on and off most of the day. I continued to ice her leg. Sometimes she woke, sometimes not. Sleep was the best thing she could do. Every minute spent sleeping was like a deposit in the bank that she'd have to draw on when we pulled out of here.

Late in the afternoon, I slipped out with the bow and returned to the ridgeline where I'd seen the majority of the tracks. I pulled myself up into the arms of an aspen. The cold made it difficult to sit real still. Toward dark, I saw a white flash out of the corner of my eye. I studied the snow. When it moved again, the picture came into focus.

Six rabbits sat within fifteen yards of me. I drew slowly, aiming at the closest. I came to full draw, let out half a breath, focused on my front sight, and pressed the release. The arrow caught the rabbit between the shoulders. When the others didn't move, I nocked a second arrow and let it fly.

I walked in with two rabbits' bodies skewered on a green aspen limb and hung it over the fire.

Ashley sat with the jigsaw across her lap. "Just two?"

"One moved."

I slow-cooked the rabbit and even happened to find some salt in the pantry.

Ashley hovered over a leg, her lips greasy, rabbit in one hand, a bowl of soup in the other, a smile from ear to ear. "You know, it doesn't really taste like chicken."

"Who told you it did?"

"Nobody. It's just that everything tastes like chicken." She pulled out a small bone. "Nope. That's not entirely true. Since I've been hanging around with you, nothing really tastes like chicken."

"Thanks."

A WEEK later, we were back at the doctor's office. Twins required more ultrasounds, and your doctor wanted to make sure we were on track. And given my place at the hospital, they were, in a sense, taking care of one of their own. A nice perk.

They called us back. Another wand smearing goo across your tummy. They strapped the monitor around your stomach, and we could hear both heartbeats. Dueling echoes. Everything normal. Right?

The technician paused, ran the wand over

you a second time, and said, "Be right back."

Your doc, Steve, strode through the door. He studied the picture, nodded, swallowed, and patted you on the leg. "Sheila here is going to run a few tests. When you finish, come see me in my office."

I spoke up. "Steve . . . what's up?"

"Maybe nothing. Let's run the tests."

I'd have said the same thing if I was trying to figure out how to communicate bad news. I followed him into the hall.

He turned. "Just let her run the tests. I'll see you in my office."

I didn't need to. His face told me plenty.

We sat down opposite him. He was in pain. He stood up, walked around his desk, and pulled up a chair. "Rachel . . . Ben . . ." He didn't know who to look at. "You have a partial abruption."

Rachel looked at me. "What's that mean?"

He spoke for me. "It means your placenta has torn away from the uterine wall. I've seen larger tears, but it's not small, either."

"So you're saying . . ."

"Total bed rest. Let's give it time. If we can slow it down or even stop it, everybody will be fine. No need to panic."

On the ride home, you put your hand on my shoulder. "So what's this really mean, Doc?"

"You need to take up needlepoint and find about a hundred movies you've been wanting to see. Maybe read several dozen books."

"Will we make it?"

"If it doesn't tear any more."

"And if it does?"

"We're not there, honey, so . . . one hurdle at a time, okay?"

Chapter Eleven

DAYLIGHT found me slipping along the ridge-line. The snowfall had not lessened. We were approaching three feet of fresh powder. Moving was difficult. I walked an hour but saw nothing. Returning, I approached the back of the A-frame and spotted a building I'd not seen before. The only thing showing was the top of a pipe chimney. The rest of the building was buried.

I circled it, trying to decide where the door would be, and then started pulling at the snow. I found a window. I dug it out, tried to lift it, and couldn't. I kicked it, and the single pane shattered. I knocked off the sharp edges with the hatchet and crawled in.

It was a storage room of sorts. Old saddles hung on one wall. Fishing reels with no line, some tools, jars of rusty nails. On the other wall hung old tires that looked like they could fit a four-wheeler. Some tubes, even a chain. I scratched my head. If they brought four-wheelers up here, we had to be on the outside border of the Ashley, which meant we were closer to a road than I'd thought.

Part of me wanted to get excited. To let my heart race. To run down the rabbit trail of all the possibilities. But if I did, and if Ashley read it on my face and none of my hopes were true, then . . . false hope was worse than no hope at all.

I kept looking. What actually carried all the stuff up here? Pots, pans, food, supplies. Then I looked up.

Above my head, in the rafters, lay blue plastic sleds made for hauling equipment behind a snowmobile or a horse. I pulled one down. It was about seven feet long, plenty wide enough to lie in, had runners along the bottom, and didn't weigh fifteen pounds.

I slid it out the window and was in the

process of climbing out when I looked up a final time. There, lying on top of the other sleds, were several sets of snowshoes. This time my heart did race. Someone had put them there, which meant that someone might have used them to walk up here, and if they could do it, well . . .

They were old, and the bindings were stiff and cracking, but the frames were strong. And they were light. I found a pair that fit, strapped them on, and returned to the A-frame, pulling the sled.

Ashley stirred, stared over her shoulder. "What's that?"

"Your blue chariot." I pulled the harness off the old sled and anchored it to the new one. Between the wool blankets and sleeping bags, I felt I could make Ashley a good bit more comfortable. "You get to ride forward in this one."

"That means I've got to look at your back-side the entire time. If you ain't the lead dog, the view never changes."

It was good to hear the humor return.

An hour before dark, I set the puzzle in her lap and said, "I'll be back." I strapped on

the snowshoes and slipped along the ridgeline in search of something to eat. The snow
wasn't falling as heavily, but it was still falling. The entire world was muted.

After maybe a mile, I found a lot of tracks
merging into a ravine. The snow was all
torn up. I set up under an aspen and waited.
Didn't take long. A fox ran through the ravine and disappeared before I could draw.
A doe soon followed, but it winded me,
threw its tail in the air, and took off at light
speed. That's about when I figured my hide
wasn't all that great, given the prevailing
wind. This hunting stuff wasn't as easy as it
looked on TV.

I stayed put five more minutes. One rabbit
appeared and hopped down into the ravine
and up the other side. It stopped, and I let
the arrow fly. Fortunately for us, I did not
miss.

I retraced my steps, returning to Ashley.
Napoleon was gone again, and she was asleep
in the chair. I boiled some water, steeped tea
bags, and sat alongside her while I turned
the rabbit above the fire.

When I'd sufficiently burned it, she
woke, and we ate slowly. Chewing every

bite longer than normal. Savoring what we could. It was barely enough to feed one, much less two.

Napoleon returned shortly thereafter. He walked, licking his red muzzle, to his section of mattress, circled, rolled over, and stuck his feet in the air. I rubbed his tummy, and he started involuntarily kicking one leg.

When I leaned over, my recorder slipped out of my shirt pocket.

Ashley asked, "How are the batteries holding up?"

"Thanks to the airport, batteries are not a problem."

"So . . . what are you telling her?"

I didn't respond.

"Is that too personal?"

"No. . . . I described the snow and the crappy situation in which we find ourselves."

"You saying you don't like having me as a traveling companion?"

"No. Other than having to haul you halfway across Utah, you're a great traveling companion."

She laughed. "Why don't you tell her what you miss about her?"

The moon must have been shining behind the clouds, because an eerie and bright light shone. "I've done that. I've told her a good bit. Why don't you tell me what you miss about Vince?"

"Let's see. . . . I miss his cappuccino maker, and the smell of his Mercedes, and the sparse cleanliness of his penthouse—the view off the balcony at night is really something. If the Braves are playing, you can see the lights of Turner Field. Boy . . . a hot dog would be good right now. What else? I miss his laughter and the way he checks on me. He's very good at calling me even when he's busy."

After she fell asleep, I lay awake a long time, thinking. She had told me very little about Vince.

A MONTH passed. You were ready to climb the walls. Couldn't wait for the next ultrasound. We got to the hospital, and Steve met us in the room. The attendant squirted the goo, and Steve squinted, watching the screen.

The attendant stopped circling and looked at him. A blank stare. You said, "Somebody better start talking to me."

Steve handed you a towel, and the technician left. I helped you wipe the goo off and sat you up.

Steve leaned against the wall. "The tear has worsened. A lot." He fumbled with his hands. "This doesn't mean you can't have more kids, Rachel. You're healthy. You can have more children."

You looked at me, so I translated. "Honey, the abruption has . . . worsened. Sort of hanging by a thread."

You looked at Steve. "Are my babies okay?"

"For the moment, but . . ."

You held up your hands. "But what? What else is there to talk about? I stay on bed rest. I rent a room in the hospital. I do something. Anything."

Steve shook his head. "Rachel . . . if it tears . . ."

You shook your head. "But as of this moment, it hasn't."

"If you were in OR right now and I was scrubbed for surgery and it tore, I'm not sure I'd have enough time to get them out and stop the bleeding before you bled to death. Your life is in danger. I need to take the babies."

You looked at him like he'd lost his mind.

"I'm not letting you do any such thing."

"If you don't, none of you will make it."

"What chance do I have? I mean, in percent."

"If I wheel you into surgery right now, real good. Beyond that, the numbers fall off a cliff. Even if we monitor you, we won't know it until it's too late. Once it tears, the internal bleeding will—"

"But it is conceivable that if I can lie real still for the next four weeks, then I can have a C-section?"

"It is conceivable, but you have better odds in Vegas."

You held a finger in the air. "Is there a chance we could make it?"

"Technically, yes, but . . ."

You pointed at the screen. "I've seen their faces. You showed them to me with your fancy television. I'll not sleep the rest of my life looking at their faces on the backs of my eyelids. Wondering what if you were wrong and if they'd have made it."

I piped in. "How long do we have to make this decision?"

Steve shrugged. "I can push it to first thing tomorrow morning." He looked at you. "You can have more children. This is not something you will incur again. It's a fluke. An accident of nature."

"Steve . . . we didn't have an accident."

The ride home was quiet.

I parked and met you on the porch. The breeze was tugging at your hair. We sat staring out across the waves. The ocean was choppy. The silence was thick.

I spoke first. "Hey . . . your chances aren't real good."

"Like, what are they?"

"I'd say less than ten percent. Steve doesn't think it's that much."

"Seventy-five years ago this wasn't even an issue. People didn't have this much information."

I nodded. "You're right. Now technology is giving us a choice."

"Ben . . . we made our choice. That night, about five months ago. It's the risk we took then, and it's the one we're taking now."

I bit my lip.

You placed my palm on your stomach. "I can see their faces. Michael has your eyes, and Hannah has my nose. . . . I know which side of their lips turn up when they smile, whether or *not their earlobes are connected, the wrinkles in their fingers. They are a part of me. Of us."*

"This is selfish. Ten percent is nothing. It's a death sentence."

"It's a sliver of hope. A possibility."

"You're willing to bet on a sliver?"

"Ben, I will not play God."

"I'm not asking you to play God. I'm asking you to let Him work it out. Let God be God."

You shook your head. Touched my face. "There's always hope."

I was angry. I couldn't change your mind. The very thing I loved about you—your laser-beamed focus, anchored strength—was the very thing I was fighting. "Rachel, you're playing God."

"I love you, Ben Payne."

"You don't love me. And you don't even love them. You just love the idea of them. If you did, then you'd be in surgery right now."

"It's because of you that I love them."

"Forget them. I don't want them. We'll make more."

"Are you absolutely certain it'll tear loose?"

"Rachel . . . I've spent the last fifteen years of my life studying medicine. I come at this with some credibility. This will kill you. You will die

and leave me alone. Why are you being so stubborn? Think about someone other than yourself for a minute."

You turned, amazement in your eyes. "Ben . . . I'm not thinking about me. One day you'll see that."

"Well, you're certainly not thinking about me."

I laced up my shoes and took off running. A half mile down the beach, I turned. You were on the porch, leaning against the railing. Watching me.

When I close my eyes, I can still see you.

And whenever I get to this point in our story, I never quite know how to talk about what comes next.

SEVERAL days passed. Three weeks since the crash. One moment, it seemed like a year. At another, like a day.

In the last couple of days, we'd eaten rabbit and two ground squirrels, but nothing bigger. We weren't wasting away as quickly, but we weren't putting much in the bank, either. We needed several days' worth of stored food because of the simple fact that I couldn't pull, take care of Ashley, and hunt. I needed to hunt now and freeze the meat, preferably seven days' worth. To set out before was to invite a cold, hungry death.

Ashley woke, stretched, and said, "I keep hoping to crack open my eyes and find that you've hauled us out of this place, back to where the smell of Starbucks lures me on my way to my office, and my biggest struggle is road rage, and where Advil exists, and"—she laughed—"disposable razors and shaving cream are found."

I had grown used to that laugh. "Amen to that."

I massaged Ashley's legs and was encouraged by both the healthy blood flow and lack of swelling. I got her settled in the recliner.

Ashley was chatty. I was not. She picked up on it. "You don't want to talk, do you?"

"Sorry. Guess I don't multitask very well."

"What is it?"

"Are you interviewing me for an article?"

She raised both eyebrows. Universal women's body language for *I'm waiting.*

I sat on my bed, legs crossed. "We're at a bit of a crossroads."

"We've been at one since our plane went down."

"True, but this one is a bit different."

"How so?"

I shrugged. "Stay or go. We've got shelter here, warmth, maybe somebody will stumble upon us, but it's likely that'd be two or three months off. If we head out, we're taking our chances on shelter and food. If we increase our food stores, we could probably last a week or two out there. But we're left with one big unknown."

"Which is?"

"How far. We don't know if we're twenty miles or fifty or more. There's four feet of fresh powder, and avalanches will be a constant concern. And what if I walk you into that mess only to get us both killed—while if we stayed here, we might get lucky and hold out."

"Sounds like you're in a pickle." She lay back. "Let's sleep on it. You can give me your decision in the morning."

"Me? I'm not deciding for us. We are."

She pulled Napoleon up under her arm

and pulled the bag around her shoulders. It was dark except for the fire. "Let me know when you get around to voicing what's really bothering you."

I scratched my head. "I just did."

"Nope. You did not. It's still in there." She pointed toward the door. "Why don't you go for a walk. And take your recorder. By the time you get back, you'll have figured it out."

"You . . . are annoying."

She nodded. "I'm trying to be more than just annoying. Now go for a walk. We'll be here when you get back."

Did you have something to do with this? I don't know how you did it, but I'd bet you put her next to me on the plane. I don't know what she's talking about. Well, maybe I do a little, but that doesn't make her right. Okay, it makes her right.

But what am I supposed to do? I haven't hunted seriously since Granddaddy took me. Well, we were just hanging out. Granddaddy took me hunting because he should've taken Dad when he was a boy but didn't, and Dad grew up a jerk. I was the consolation prize. Which was fine with me; I loved him, he loved me, and we became pals, and it got me out from under Dad's thumb. But if we didn't shoot anything, neither of us died. It was a social thing. Not a life-or-death thing.

Out here, if I miss, we die. Out here, it matters. A lot. I just didn't know when I got on Grover's plane that I was going to have to hunt my way out of this eternal wilderness. A lot of people have survived much worse conditions, but it's not like I have any idea what I'm doing, and I'm scared that if I don't get it figured out, that girl in there is going to die a slow, painful death.

There. I said it. I feel responsible. How can I not? She should be back at her office racing to meet a deadline, e-mailing her friends, glowing in post-wedding bliss. Not lying helpless in the middle of nowhere with a bumbling idiot who's slowly starving her.

I've got nothing to offer her. And I've got nothing to offer you. What is it with you women? Can't us guys not have the answer? Can't we not know what's going to happen next? Can't we be incapable and broken and worn down and disheartened?

But I'm not telling you anything you don't already know.

I'm sorry for yelling at you. This time . . . and the last.

Guess I needed to get this off my chest. But I'm not telling her that.

Okay, I heard you. I'll tell her. I know she's lying there with a broken leg, dependent upon a total stranger. Although we're not as much strangers now as we once were. And no, it's not what you're thinking. Well, of course, I find her attractive. She's incredible. Honey, she's getting married, and I'm trying to get her home to her fiancé. I don't know if she likes him or not.

I'm not having this conversation with you.

No, I'm not having a tough time with all this. I'm missing you.

Okay, maybe it's a little tough. There. I said it. It's not easy. . . .

I will say her sense of humor is rare. Something I've found myself leaning on. Needing. It's a strength thing. Like yours. Comes from way down deep. She's tough. I think she'll make it. Provided I don't kill her first from starvation.

Will I? I don't know. . . . I didn't think I'd make it this far. Could it get worse? Sure. This is not the worst thing. The worst thing is being separated from you. That's ten times tougher than being stuck out here.

I'm going to bed now. I'm sorry for raising my voice at you.

Both now . . . and then.

THE following day, I was out early. I circled the lake. When I reached the other end, I found the snow torn up and moose tracks everywhere. Standing-around-eating tracks. Wasn't hard to figure out. The cow moose stood on the lake and ate the tree limbs extending out over what, during summertime, was water. I got settled in an aspen tree and sat three hours before I saw anything. A young moose, followed closely by its mother, came waltzing onto the lake. It ran out a few feet, then ran back to the trees and began feeding. It might have been eight months old. Its mother was huge, probably eight feet at the shoulders. She could have fed us for a year. But we didn't need a year. If I took the calf, the cow would make it. If I took the cow, chances were good the calf would die anyway.

They fed to within forty yards, and my heart started beating pretty fast. The cow moose moved to within twenty yards. The calf didn't let her get too far away and moved in closer. Getting within ten yards of me. Any closer and they'd hear my heart beating.

I drew slowly, and the mother popped her head up. One big eye looking at me. Or rather, at the tree. She knew something was in here. She just didn't know what.

I settled the pin on the calf's chest, took a deep breath, let out half, and whispered, "Front sight, front sight, front sight . . . *press.*"

The arrow disappeared into the chest of the calf. It hopped, bucked, spun in a circle, and took off running out across the lake, followed closely by the cow. The mother's head and ears were held high. Full alert. Pounding through the snow.

I caught my breath and allowed my nerves to settle. I'd intended to hit the calf in the heart area—causing it to die quickly—but I'd flinched and pulled the shot right. That meant the arrow had pierced the lungs, which meant that the calf, afraid and in pain, would run. It would bleed to death, but in the process, it might run a mile. The mother would follow. Once the calf ran into cover, it would stop and listen for her. Seeing her and feeling safe, it would lie down and bleed to death. If I stepped out of my hide and traipsed off after it, I would scare it some more and push it farther away.

I waited almost an hour, nocked another arrow, and stepped out. The blood trail was a red brick road. The calf had run a straight path into the trees. I followed slowly, keeping a lookout for the mother.

It quit snowing, a breeze pushed out the clouds, and the moon shone above me. It was the brightest night I'd seen in a long time. My shadow followed me into the trees. The only sound was my breathing and the sound of snowshoes crunching snow.

An hour later, I found them. The calf had begun climbing up a ridgeline and, too weak to continue, had toppled and rolled down. The mother stood over it, nudging it. It lay unmoving.

The cow was standing straight up, as was her tail. I hollered, raised the bow, and tried to look bigger than I was. She looked at me, then back over her shoulder. While its nose is quite good, a moose's eyesight is poor. I walked within forty yards, approaching downwind, arrow nocked. I didn't want to shoot her, but if she charged me, I wasn't sure I'd have much choice.

At twenty yards, she charged as if she was shot out of a cannon and caught me with her head and chest, launching me into the limbs of an aspen. I slammed against the trunk. She snorted, made a deep bellowing sound, then stood over the calf again.

I stayed underneath the tree, lay on my belly, and watched. The cow stood in the moonlight, breathing heavily, nudging the calf with her muzzle. Every few minutes she'd fill her stomach with air and sound a deep bellow.

In the hours that followed, the cow stood over the calf, shielding it from the snow that had returned. At daylight, when the calf was little more than a white mound, she bellowed one last time and wandered into the trees.

Quietly I pulled the calf into the trees. I cut out the backstraps, pulled as much meat as I could off the tops of the shoulders and the tenderloins from between the shoulder blades. Doing so gave me enough to feed us for a week to ten days. Or more.

I tied it down in my pack and went to retrieve the bow where I'd dropped it during the charge. It lay in pieces, and all the arrows had snapped where the cow had stepped on it. I left it.

I strapped on the snowshoes and walked back to the lake. At the far end, I could see the A-frame, the fire glowing bright through the glass. I doubted Ashley had slept.

I reached the red brick road and stopped. In the distance, the cow bellowed. She'd probably do that all day and into tomorrow. I wasn't sad for killing the calf. We needed to eat. I wasn't sad that the cow was lonely. She'd have another calf. Most had twins or triplets when they gave birth. The thing that had my stomach in knots was the sight of the mother standing over her young.

I sank my hand into the snow, ran my fingers through the clumps of red. Fresh snow had covered most of it. Only a dim outline remained. In an hour, there would be no reminder.

I fell forward on my knees, my pack driving me into the snow. I scooped my hand beneath a red clump the size of my fist, lifted it to my nose, and breathed.

To my left stood a tall pine. I unbuckled my pack, pulled the hatchet from my belt, and crawled to the tree. With several good swings, I cut a band, maybe two feet long, three inches wide, and an inch or two deep, around the base. Come summer, when the heat rose, the sap would ooze and trickle out of the scar like tears.

Chances are, it would do that for years.

You were right. . . . You were right all along.

Chapter Twelve

I SHUFFLED in and put down my pack. I didn't realize how drained I was until I tried to speak. "I tried to call, but the line was busy."

Ashley smiled and fingered me closer. I knelt next to her. She raised her hand to my left eye. "You've been cut. Deep, too. You okay?"

Next to her, the puzzle lay complete, a panoramic view of snow-capped mountains and a sun behind. I turned my head, squinted my eyes. "Is it a sunrise or sunset?"

She lay back, closed her eyes. "I think that depends on the eyes of the viewer."

I SPENT the day cutting strips of meat and slow-cooking them over the fire. Ashley held up a small mirror and flinched while I sewed up the skin above my eye. We ate off and on. Napoleon, too. We didn't gorge, but by night-time, we were content. All three of us.

She asked me to run her a bath, which I did. While she bathed, I packed the sled. We didn't have much left. My pack, our bags, the blankets, the hatchet, the meat. I helped Ashley out of the bath, got her tucked into bed, then bathed myself.

I was asleep by nightfall and slept until just before daylight. I didn't want to leave. I wanted to stay by that warm fire and hope somebody stumbled upon us.

I cut the foam pad to fit into the sled, laid two blankets atop it, then dressed Ashley, zipped her up in her bag, slid her onto the sled, and lifted her head onto a folded blan-ket. I tied the tarp across her and tucked Napoleon alongside her. He must have been worried, because he licked her face more than usual.

I strapped on my gaiters, grabbed the matches and lighter fluid, buckled myself into the harness, took one last look at the warm fire, and pulled her out the door and back into the never-ending snow.

Surprisingly, I felt good. Not strong, but not tired and not as weak. If I had to guess, I'd say I'd lost more than twenty pounds since the crash. A lot of that was muscle. Meaning, I'd lost strength as well. The good news was that, with the snowshoes, I was a bit lighter now on my feet.

I tied a long tether from the harness around my shoulders and handed her the loose end. "If you need me, just tug that."

She nodded, looped the tether over her wrist, and tucked the tarp up under her chin.

Within minutes, we were climbing up the ridgeline en route to the trail leading out of the valley and through the notch. I seldom felt much tension on the harness, because the sled glided well, but the snow was blowing into my face, landing on my eyelashes, blurring my vision. Our path took us down small hills and up short rises, but on the whole, I could tell we were losing elevation, and thankfully the path was mostly clear.

By lunch, I calculated we'd walked three miles. By midafternoon, we'd covered six. Toward dusk, the trail came down off a small hill and flattened out. I'd pushed it, and hard. I looked behind us, thinking back through each turn. Maybe we'd covered ten miles.

WE SPENT the night beneath a makeshift shelter using our tarp and some limbs I cut to help shed the snow. Ashley lay snug on the sled.

A blanket and my bag separated me from the snow. "I miss our fire."

"Me, too."

Napoleon was shivering. I pulled him up close. He sniffed me and my bag, then hopped across the snow and dug himself in with Ashley. She laughed. I rolled over and closed my eyes. "Suit yourself."

BY MID-MORNING, we'd come down another four or so miles, and the temperature was warmer. Maybe just around freezing—the warmest it'd been since the crash. On the hillsides, small shoots shot up through the snow, suggesting that the ground rested only a few feet beneath us rather than eight or ten. While we had lost elevation, down as much as nine thousand feet, the snow was wet and pulled at the sled, increasing the workload.

Around mile five, the trail dropped down, widened, and straightened. Almost unnaturally. I stopped and scratched my head.

Ashley spoke up. "What's wrong?"

"This thing is wide enough to drive a truck down." That's about when it hit me. "We're on a road. There's a road beneath us."

To our right, I saw something flat, green, and shiny sticking up through the snow. I brushed away the snow. Took me a minute to figure out what it was.

I started laughing. "It's a road sign." It said EVANSTON 62.

"What's it say?"

I stepped back into my harness. "It says Evanston, this way."

"How far?"

I shook my head. "You really want to know?"

A pause. "Not really."

I leaned into the harness. "That's what I thought."

"Can you pull this thing as far as it says we need to?"

"Yes."

"You sure? 'Cause if you can't, just tell me. Now would be a good time to come clean if you don't think—"

"Ashley?"

"Yes."

"Shut up. Please."

We walked five miles, most of which sloped downhill. It was relatively blissful walking. Night came, but with colder temperatures, the sled slid easier, so I walked a few hours more. Putting ten miles on the road. Twenty-five since the A-frame.

Sometime after midnight, I saw an odd shape to my right. I unbuckled and investigated. A building, eight feet square, with a roof and a concrete floor. I dug out the door and slid the sled down into it. A laminated sign hung on the wall. I lit a match. It read THIS IS AN EMERGENCY WARMING HUT. IF THIS IS AN EMERGENCY, WELCOME. IF IT'S NOT, THEN YOU SHOULD NOT BE IN HERE.

Ashley's hand found mine in the darkness. "Are we okay?"

"Yeah, we're good." I unrolled my bag and climbed in. The floor was hard. "How's the leg?" I asked.

"Still hurts."

"Differently or the same?"

"Same."

"Let me know if it starts feeling different."

"And when it does, just what will you do about it?"

I rolled over, closed my eyes. "Probably amputate. That way it'll quit hurting."

"That's not funny."

"Your leg is fine. It's healing nicely."

"I want to ask you a question, and I want an honest answer. If we needed to, could we get back to the A-frame? Is it still an option?"

I thought back through the miles since the A-frame. Most had been slowly losing elevation. I was pretty sure I could not make it back. "Yeah . . . it's an option."

"Are you lying to me?"

"Maybe."

"So there's no going back? We'll never see the A-frame again?"

"Something like that." I stretched out flat, staring up at the ceiling. It felt like we were in a hole, which, given the eight feet of snow banked against the walls, we were. After a few minutes, she quietly slid her hand inside my bag and placed it flat across my chest.

It stayed there all night.

I know.

WE STARTED again at daylight. I was feeling the effects of yesterday, not to mention the fact that our road was slowly turning upward. Gradual at first, it turned ugly four miles into the morning, snaking and twisting its way up the mountain I'd been staring at for the past two days. Given the incline and the wet, sticky snow, pulling the sled became a lot harder. By lunch, we'd made five miles total and probably regained a thousand feet in elevation. And the road was still going up.

By dusk, we'd made a total of seven miles, but I was spent and my legs were cramping. I needed several seconds' rest between steps. I kept hoping we'd find another warming hut, but we didn't.

We camped next to an aspen. I tied the

tarp around it, anchored it to the end of the sled, rolled out a blanket, and was asleep before my head hit the ground.

I woke in the middle of the night. Snow was falling heavily. I pushed the tarp up from underneath and dumped off the snow. I ate a bite of cold meat, sipped some water, and poked my head out. To the north, the clouds were clearing. I slipped on my boots, strapped on the snowshoes, and went for a walk. The road was winding tighter toward the summit. It turned left sharply, and I bent over, catching my breath.

Standing straight, I stared out across the darkness. The clouds were low, tucked down into the mountains. Cotton on a wound.

Beyond that, maybe thirty or forty miles, it cleared. I squinted. It took me a second to realize what I was looking at.

I UNTIED the tarp and startled Ashley. She jerked. "What? What's going on?"

"I want you to see something."

"Right now?"

"Yep."

I buckled up and began pulling. What had taken me fifteen minutes alone now took an hour. My stomach and neck muscles were sore, I was winded, and the straps were cutting into my shoulders.

We rounded the corner, and I pulled her up to the ledge. After a few minutes, the clouds rolled off and the view cleared. I pointed.

A single lightbulb sparkled some forty miles in the distance. Beyond that, farther to the north, was a single trail of smoke.

She clutched my hand, and neither of us said a word. I took a reading on the compass, careful to let the needle settle and get an exact reading.

She said, "What're you doing?"

"Just in case."

We stared at it for the rest of the night. The sun rose. I needed to sleep but knew I couldn't. I was too excited. We trudged across the snow quietly, thinking about a world out there with electricity, running hot water, microwavable food, and coffee baristas.

The mountain plateaued. We walked several miles across what felt like the top of the world. The wind was steady, straight on. It burned my face, and the snow stung

my cheeks. I leaned into it, numb, counting the miles in my head. Maybe forty-five
to go.

I walked, counting backward to myself.
"Forty-two to the lightbulb . . . forty-one to
the lightbulb . . ."

When I got to forty, we came down into a
saddle atop the mountain, a bowl protected
from the wind. Halfway through it, we discovered another warming hut with the same
laminated sign.

Given the lighter fluid we'd stolen from
the A-frame, getting a fire going was easy.
I pulled out of my wet clothes and hung
everything on the bunks. I got Ashley situ-
ated, fell into bed, and don't remember
falling asleep.

SHE shook me. "Ben . . . you in there?"

"Yeah."

The day was full. Overcast but not snowing. Not yet. I didn't know what time it was,
but it had to be close to lunch.

"You slept a long time."

I looked around, trying to remember where
we were.

My legs were sore. My feet felt like

hamburger. In truth, all of me was sore. I sat up, but my legs and stomach muscles quickly cramped. I stretched, easing the knots out. Ashley handed me a bottle of body-temp warm water. It felt good going down my throat.

I ate, sipped, and wondered how far we could get today. Thirty minutes later, I was leaning into the harness, pulling.

The road turned right and started descending. Every few minutes, the clouds would blow over, and I could see the road winding down below us for what looked like eight or ten miles. We were soon going to lose several thousand feet of elevation. The problem with such a drastic elevation change meant steep pitches and the possibility of the sled getting away from me.

I took it slow, winding my way, so the sled wouldn't pick up speed. After four or five miles, the road turned right in a huge horseshoe that curved some ten miles in the distance. It bent around a valley off to our right. The hillsides were steep, but the valley was only a half mile across.

I weighed the difference—ten miles versus a half mile. If I worked us slowly down the steep incline, lowering Ashley with a rope before me, anchoring on a tree, moving tree to tree, we could be across the valley before nightfall and cut ten miles out of our trip. With luck, we could make the lightbulb tomorrow.

I turned to Ashley and explained. She eyed the steep quarter mile to the valley below. "You think we can get down that?"

We'd been down steeper when we left the crash site but had yet to traverse anything this steep that was this long. "If we take it slow."

She nodded. "I'm game if you are."

There was a little voice inside my head, whispering, "Shorter is not always better."

I should've listened to it.

I CHECKED the harness ropes. The sled was secure. I tied the snowshoes to the sled and began easing down the incline. My boots cut into the snow, giving me leverage to hold the sled back. I lowered Ashley over the ledge, and she slowly slid down, pulling the harness tight. Then I began picking my way downhill, using the trees as my anchors.

It actually worked quite well. I'd step

down, dig a foot thigh-deep into the snow, and grab a tree or branch. We'd move forward, and then I'd do it again. In ten minutes, we were halfway down. Napoleon was sitting on Ashley's chest, staring at me. He didn't like it at all.

Two weeks of constant snow meant at times I was waist-deep, with another ten feet below me. It didn't take much to set it loose.

I don't remember it letting go. I don't remember tumbling and rolling. I don't remember the harness snapping. And I don't remember coming to an abrupt stop where, even though my eyes were open, all the world went black.

The blood was rushing to my head, so I knew I was upside down, and the snow was pressing in on me, allowing only shallow breaths. The only part of me free of the snow was my right foot.

I tried to clench my fists. Pulling in. Pushing out. I tried moving my head back and forth. I wasn't getting much air, and I knew I didn't have long. I began shoving. Jerking. Above me, along my torso, I could see a faint light. I worked myself into a frenzy, but I was stuck, and chances were good I was going to die upside down, frozen and suffocating in the snow.

Something with really sharp teeth began biting my ankle. I heard snarling and began kicking at it, but it wouldn't let go. Finally I kicked it loose. Seconds later, I felt a hand on my foot. Then I felt snow being pulled away from my legs, then from my chest.

Her hand shot in, pulled out the snow around my mouth, and I sucked in the sweetest, largest breath of air I'd ever known. She worked out one arm, and with it I righted myself, pulled myself out of that snowy grave, and rolled on my side. Napoleon jumped onto my chest and licked my face.

It was almost dark. Ashley lay to my right. She was off the sled, out of her bag, and lying facedown on the snow. Her hands were cut and bloody. Her cheek was swollen. And then I saw her leg.

We didn't have long, and I knew I couldn't move her.

THE avalanche had carried us down to the base of the hillside. The harness had evidently saved my life, because while the sled surfed the topside, it kept me, albeit only for seconds, from being totally swallowed by the snow. When the ropes broke, Ashley shot off like a missile and collided with a huge boulder.

She'd worked her way back up to me, crawling. Her leg had rebroken, and this time the bone had pierced the skin. It was poking up underneath her pants. She was in shock, and any movement, absent drugs, would send her back into unconsciousness.

"I'm going to turn you."

She nodded.

I did, and she screamed louder than I'd ever heard a woman scream.

I crawled out across the snow and found the sled. Her sleeping bag lay crumpled where she left it when she climbed out of it. One blanket lay twisted around it. Everything else was gone. No pack, no food, no tarp, no water bottles, no snowshoes, no bow drill, and no fire.

I unzipped her bag and laid her in it. Blood had soaked through her pants and painted the snow. I pulled the sled up next to her, laid the wool blanket across the bottom, slid her on top, and wrapped the blanket over her. I wanted to cut away her pants and look at her leg, but she shook her head and managed a whisper.

"Don't."

She lay still, unmoving. Her bottom lip was shaking. I'd kill her trying to set the leg in place. She'd lost blood, but not much. The bone had come out the top, outside her thigh. If it had gone the other way, through the femoral artery, she'd have been dead. As would I.

Snow returned, hastening the return of darkness.

I knelt, whispering, "I'm going for help."

She shook her head. "Don't leave me."

I tucked the bag around her. "You've been trying to get rid of me since we started this trip, so I'm finally doing what you asked." I leaned in. She turned to me. The pain was riffling through her. "I can't move you, so I'm leaving Napoleon with you and going for help, but I'm coming back."

She gripped my hand, squeezed it tightly, and whispered, "Promise?"

"Promise."

She closed her eyes and let go of my hand. I kissed her on the forehead, then the lips. They were warm and trembling, and both blood and tears had puddled there.

I tucked Napoleon in with her, stood, and stared off down the road. Clouds were thick, and I could not see where it went.

I'VE spent my life running. One thing I've learned is to look ahead no more than four or five steps. It helps in long distance; breaking it into small, doable pieces is about all you can handle. Others will tell you to keep your eyes up, focus on the finish line, but I can only focus on what's in front of me. If I do that, the finish line will come to me.

So I put one foot in front of the other. The road wound down toward the valley in which we'd seen the light and single smokestack. I figured I had twenty-five to thirty miles to go, and if I was lucky, I was averaging two miles an hour. All I had to do was run until the sun rose over my right shoulder.

I could do that. Couldn't I?

Yes. Unless I came to the end of myself first.

That wouldn't be so bad.

What about Ashley?

I closed my eyes, and Ashley was all I could see.

IT WAS day twenty-eight, I think. I'd fallen a thousand times and pulled myself up a thousand and one. The snow had turned to sand. I could smell and taste salt. I heard a seagull somewhere. My dad was standing at the guard shack, a scowl on his face. I slapped the lifeguard's chair, cussed him beneath my breath, turned, and picked up the pace. The beach stretched out before me, and every time I thought I was getting close to the house, it would fade, reset; the beach would lengthen, and another moment would take its place. The past played before me like a movie.

I remember falling, pulling with my hands, standing, and falling, again and again.

Many times I wanted to quit, lie down, and sleep. When I did, I'd close my eyes, and Ashley was still there. Lying quietly in the snow, laughing over a leg of rabbit, chatting from the sled, shooting the flare gun, sipping coffee, pulling me out of the snow . . .

Maybe it was those thoughts that got me up and helped me put one foot back in front of the other. Somewhere under the moon, I fell, eyes wide open. The picture changed. I saw her.

Rachel.

Standing in the road. Running shoes on. Sweat on her top lip. She held out her hand and whispered, "Run with me?"

I reached, pulled, took a step, and fell. Then again. And again. Soon I was running. Chasing Rachel. Her toes were barely touching the ground, and I was back on the track with the girl I'd met in high school.

She ran with me, up the hill, toward the sunlight, and when it cleared the mountaintop, I fell. Face forward for the last time. My body would not go. I could run no more. I had done something I'd never done. Reached the end of myself.

She whispered. "Ben . . ."

I lifted my head, but she was gone. I heard her again. "Ben . . . Get up, Ben."

In the distance, a few hundred yards away, a single column of smoke spiraled above the trees.

IT WAS a log cabin. Several snowmobiles parked out front. Snowboards against the porch railing. Lights inside. Deep voices. Laughter. The smell of coffee. I crawled up the drive and pushed open the door. All I could muster was a cracking whisper. "Help . . ."

MOMENTS later, we were screaming across the snow. My driver was wiry, on the short side, and his snowmobile was not slow. With one hand, I held on for dear life. With the other, I pointed up the road. We made it to the valley, and Ashley's blue sleeping bag lay flat against the snow on the far side. She was not moving. Napoleon barked at us and spun Tasmanian-devil circles in the snow. The kid cut the engine. In the distance, I could hear the helicopter.

When I made it to her, Napoleon was licking

her face and looking at me. He was whining. I knelt. "Ashley?"

She cracked open an eye.

THE kid popped a handheld flare, and LifeFlight landed in the road. I briefed the medics. They got Ashley breathing oxygen, injected her with painkillers, loaded her onto a stretcher, started an IV, and slid her into the helicopter. I backed out, and she reached for my hand and slid something into it. The helicopter lifted and shot across the mountains, blinking red lights fading in its wake.

I opened my hand. The recorder. It was warm where she'd held it close to her. I must have lost it in the avalanche. I pushed the power button, but it would not play. The red warning light for low battery was flashing, keeping time with the one on the tail of the helicopter.

Chapter Thirteen

SHE lay sleeping beneath a fog of sedation. Her vitals were good. Strong. Blue lights and numbers flickered above her. I sat, her hand resting in mine. Her color had returned.

LifeFlight had bypassed Evanston and rerouted her to Salt Lake, where in two hours, the ER docs put in a few bars and pins. When I arrived at Evanston atop a snowmobile, I was loaded into an ambulance and started on an IV. By the time we arrived in Salt Lake, camera crews were everywhere.

I asked for the chief of surgery. His name was Bart Hampton, and we'd met on more than one occasion at conferences around the country. He led me to a viewing room above the OR, where we observed the last hour of Ashley's surgery. The intercom allowed the doctors to talk me through what they were doing. She was in good hands. My body was trashed, and my hands were little more than raw meat. I was in no condition to be a doctor.

They rolled her into her room. I walked in, flipped the switch on the light, and viewed her pre- and post-op X-rays. I could have done no better. She'd make a full recovery.

I turned. Blue light lit her forehead, showered the sheets. I pushed her hair back and gently placed my lips to her cheek. She smelled like soap, and her skin was soft.

I whispered in her ear, "Ashley, we did it."

All I wanted to do now was sleep.

THE next thing I knew, it was daylight and I was in a bed with white sheets, in a room filled with the aroma of fresh coffee. Bart stood over me holding a Styrofoam cup. The perspective was odd. I was used to standing in his shoes. "That for me?"

It was good coffee. We talked a while. I gave him more of the details. When I finished, he said, "What can I do for you?"

"My dog. Actually, he's not mine, but I've fallen in love with the little guy, and—"

"He's in my office. Sleeping. Fed him some steak. Happy as can be."

"I need a rental car. And I need for you to protect us from the media until she's ready to talk to them."

"You know, when the details of this get out, they're going to want you two on every talk show in the country. You could be an inspiration to a lot of people."

I stared out the window, at the white-capped mountains in the distance. It was strange, looking at them from the other side. A month ago I had stood in the Salt

Lake City Airport and wondered what was on the other side. Now I knew. I imagine prison bars are the same way. Maybe a grave.

"I just put one foot in front of the other."

"I called your people at Baptist in Jacksonville. They were elated, to say the least. What else? Seems I could do more to help you."

"In my hospital, we know our best nurses. If you could . . ."

He nodded. "She's got them now and will, around the clock."

LATE morning, she stirred. I went down the hall, bought what I needed, and came back. When she cracked an eye, I leaned in and whispered, "Hey." She turned slowly. "I talked with Vince. He's on his way."

Her nose twitched. One eyebrow lifted. "Do I smell coffee? Can you just drip it into my IV?"

I held the cup to her lips, and she sipped. "Second best cup of coffee I've ever had."

She laid her head back, tasting the beans.

Out the window, a jetliner was taking off from the airport in the distance. We watched it gain altitude, turn, and bank across our mountains.

She shook her head. "I'm never flying again."

I laughed. "They'll have you up and walking in hours. Good as new."

She smiled. "It's about time you gave me some good news. I mean, how long have we been hanging out and all you've had for me is one bad bit of news after another."

"Very true."

She stared at the ceiling. "I really want to take a bath and shave my legs."

I went to the door and motioned for the nurse. She followed me in. "This kind lady is Jennifer. I've explained to her where you've been the last month. She'll help you in the shower." I patted her hand. "I'll check on you later. Vince lands in two hours."

She pushed back the sheet, reached for my hand. How do you explain to other people what we'd been through? We'd just walked through hell, a hell that had frozen over, and survived. Together. I didn't have the words. Neither did she.

"I know. It takes some getting used to. I'll be back."

She squeezed my hand tighter. "You okay?"

I nodded and walked downstairs to the Grille. It was typical hospital short-order, but it would have to do. I stepped to the counter. "I'd like a loaded double cheeseburger with a double order of fries. Can you please have someone deliver it to room three sixteen in an hour?"

The cashier nodded. I paid and then walked to my rental car and typed the address into the dash-mounted GPS.

It was a simple house. White with green shutters. Sitting up on a hill. Flowers all around.

She was sitting on the porch. Rocking. Snapping beans. A tall, handsome woman. I stepped out of the car. Napoleon jumped onto the ground, sniffed the curb, then tore up the sidewalk, flew up the stairs, and jumped into her lap. She laughed, hugged him while he licked her face, and said, "Tank, where on earth have you been?"

Tank. . . . So that's his name.

I climbed the steps. "Ma'am, I'm Ben Payne. I'm a doctor from Jacksonville. I was with your husband when his plane crashed—"

She shook her head. "He didn't crash. He was too good a pilot."

"Yes, ma'am. He had a heart attack. Landed the plane up in the mountains. Saved our lives." I opened a box and set it next to her. In it sat his watch, his wallet, his pipe, and his lighter. She touched each item. Her lip trembled, and tears dripped off her face.

We talked for several hours. I told her everything I could remember, even where I'd buried him and what the view was like. She liked that. Said he would have, too.

She told me their story. It was filled with tenderness. Hearing it hurt.

Several hours later, I stood to leave. What else could I say? I fumbled with the car keys. "Ma'am . . . I want to . . ."

She shook her head and inched forward on the rocker. Tank hopped off her lap, and she stood slowly and smiled.

I knelt. "Tank, you're the best. I'll miss you." He slobbered my face, then ran down into his yard and began peeing on every tree he could find. "I know, you'll miss me, too."

I gave her my card for if and when she ever needed me. I was unsure how to leave. I mean, what's protocol for saying good-bye to the wife of the pilot who died saving your life? Not to mention that if I hadn't hired him to charter me to Denver, he'd have been home with her when he died, and I imagine she'd thought of that, too.

"Young man, thank you." Her eyes shone a clear bright blue. "Grover didn't fly just anybody in that plane. He was picky. Turned away more clients than he accepted. If he took you flying . . . he had a reason. It was his gift to you."

"Yes, ma'am."

She hugged me and squeezed my arms. I kissed her on the cheek. When I drove away, I glanced in the rearview mirror. Napoleon was standing on the top step of the porch, chest out, barking at the wind.

VINCE was sitting with Ashley when I walked in. He stood. A warm smile, warm handshake. Even a stiff hug. "Ashley is telling me what you did." He shook his head. "I can't thank you enough."

"Remember, I'm the one who invited her

onto the plane. You might want to consider pressing charges."

He laughed. I liked him. She'd chosen well. They'd be happy. He'd marry above himself—as would any man who married Ashley.

Three empty coffee cups sat on the bedside table. Her new cell phone was ringing off the hook. Media crews had called. Everyone wanted the exclusive.

She asked, "What are you going to tell them?"

"Nothing. I'm ducking out the back door, going home." I looked at the clock on the wall. "Leave in ninety minutes. Just came to say good-bye."

Her expression changed.

I walked to the bed. "I'm sure we'll be in touch."

She crossed her arms. "You called your wife yet?"

"No." I shook my head. "I'm going to go see her as soon as I get home."

She nodded. "I hope it works out." She squeezed my hand. I kissed her forehead and turned to go. She held on and smiled. "Ben?"

Vince patted her on the shoulder. "Be right back. I'm going to get some coffee." He put his hand on my shoulder. "Thank you. For everything."

He walked out. She was still holding on to my hand. I sat on the edge of the bed. Something was tugging at my insides. It most closely resembled an ache. I tried to smile.

"Can I ask you something?" she said.

"You've earned the right to ask me anything."

"Would you ever hit on a married or almost married woman?"

"I've only hit on one woman in my life."

She smiled. "Just checking. Can I ask you something else?"

"Yes."

"Why'd you ask me to get on the plane with you?"

I stared out the window, thinking back. "Seems like a long time ago, doesn't it?"

"It does. Then sometimes it feels like yesterday."

"Our wedding was one of the happier days either of us ever knew. It was a launching out. A beginning. We were free to love each other without interference. I think when two people really love each other—way down deep, like where their soul sleeps and dreams happen, where pain can't live 'cause there's nothing for it to feed on—then a wedding is a bleeding together of those two souls. Like two rivers running together.

"When I met you, I saw in your face the hope that yours might be that, too. I guess meeting you was a reminder that I knew a precious, tender love at one time. And I think if I'm honest, I wanted to brush up alongside that. In doing so, I thought maybe I could remember because . . . I don't want to forget."

She reached up and thumbed the tear off my face.

"I think that's why I invited you. And for that selfishness, I'm both eternally sorry and eternally grateful. Those twenty-eight days in the mountains with you reminded me that love is worth doing. No matter how much it hurts."

I stood, kissed her on the lips, and walked out.

THE plane landed in Jacksonville just after two p.m. Media crews were waiting. My picture had circulated. Problem was, they were looking for a guy thirty pounds heavier.

I had no bags, so I skirted the frenzy and walked to my car, which after a month and a half was still sitting there, covered in yellow pollen. The lady at the ticket booth told me with little or no facial expression, "Three hundred eighty-seven dollars."

I had a feeling that arguing with her would have little effect. I handed her my American Express, grateful for the chance to pay my bill and go home.

The change in my environment was strange. Most striking were the things I was not doing: not pulling a sled, not staring out across snow, not starting fire with a bow drill, not skinning a rabbit, not dependent upon shooting an arrow to eat, not listening for the sound of Ashley's voice . . . not hearing the sound of Ashley's voice.

I drove south down I-95 and passed the hospital where I live most of my life. I drove through San Marco, then stopped at a flower shop. I bought a purple orchid with a white stripe down the middle. The stem must have had thirty blooms. Rachel would love it.

I stopped at the liquor store and bought a

bottle of wine. I drove past my condo at South Ponte Vedra, then to Rachel's house. I'd fenced the property with a tall wrought-iron fence. I grabbed the orchid, walked beneath the towering live oak and up the stone steps, dug in the rocks for the hide-a-key, and unlocked the door. I pulled on the squeaking door and stepped inside.

I TALKED to Rachel through the night. I poured the wine, pressed PLAY on the recorder, and stared out through the glass, watching the waves crawl up and down the beach. I think parts were hard for her to hear, but she heard every word.

I gave her the orchid, placing it on a shelf by the glass where it would draw the morning sun. It'd be happy there.

It was four in the morning when my last recording finished. I was tired and had drifted off. The silence woke me. Funny how that works. I was rising to leave when I noticed the recorder. The face plate was flashing blue. One file remained unplayed.

I always recorded in the same file. For the first time, I noticed a file I'd not created. I pushed PLAY.

A faint whisper. There was wind in the background. A dog whining. I turned up the volume.

RACHEL, *it's Ashley. We were caught in an avalanche. Ben went for help. I don't know if I'll make it. I'm really cold.*

I wanted to tell you—actually, I wanted to thank you. . . . I write a column about love. Relationships. Which is ironic, because I've had my share of bad ones. I'm headed home to marry a man who is well off, good-looking, gives me nice things . . . but after twenty-eight days with your husband in this cold, white-capped world, I'm left wondering if that's enough. . . . What about love? Is it possible? Can I have it? Are there other Bens out there? I've been hurt—I imagine we all have—and I think somewhere in that pain, we convince ourselves that if we don't love again, we don't have to hurt again. Take the Mercedes and the two-carat ring. Give him what he wants and everybody's happy. Right?

But when I met him, I was attracted to this man I now know as Ben Payne. Sure, he's good-looking, but what attracted me was something else. Something . . . tender and warm and whole.

I don't know what to call it, but I know it when I hear it . . . and I hear it when he speaks to you in this recorder. I've listened many nights when he thought I was sleeping. I've never had anyone talk to me like that. My fiancé's kind, but in Ben, there's this palpable thing that is rich, and I just want to bathe in it. I know I'm talking about your husband, so you need to know that he's treated me like a gentleman. Truly. And I saw it had to do with this thing I'm talking about, with you . . . and it's deep-wired into his DNA, like you'd have to kill him to get it out. It's the truest thing I've ever sensed. I have lain awake at night, listening to him talk to you, share his heart, apologize for what I don't know, and found myself aching for a man to hold me in his heart the way Ben holds you.

He says you two are separated. . . . I guess I'm just wanting to go on record to say he can't love you any more than he already does. He said you two argued. Said he said some things. What terrible words could he possibly have said that caused this? What did he do to lose your love? If a love like Ben's can be had, if it's real, then . . . I'm left wondering. What can't be forgiven?

THE recording ended, and I rose, ready to leave, but Rachel beckoned me to stay. She had never wanted me to leave in the first place. I told her that many times I'd wanted to return to her, but forgiving myself had turned out to be easier said than done.

Maybe there was something different in me. Maybe something different in her. I'm not really sure, but for the first time since our argument, I lay down, my tears dripping onto her face, and slept with my wife.

I TIGHTENED my cummerbund, straightened my bow tie, then walked around the back of the country club. One of Atlanta's finest and most private. I showed the guard my invitation, he opened the gate, and I walked up the winding walk. A throng of people stood inside. Sparkly women. Powerful men. Laughter. Drinks. The rehearsal dinner. The night before the wedding. A happy occasion.

It had been three months. I had returned to work, put on a few pounds, told bits and pieces of the story, and deflected the attention. I had not contacted Ashley. Figured it best. But it seemed strange to be so close for a month, so dependent upon one another, and then, in a second's time, end that. It seemed unnatural.

I fell back into a routine, working my way through the separation. Up before the sun, a long run on the beach, breakfast with Rachel and the kids, work, sometimes dinner with Rachel and the kids, then home, maybe another run. Putting one foot in front of the other.

Ashley stood on the far side of the room. The invitation had included a handwritten note, along with a gift. The note read, "Please come. We'd love to see you. Both of you." She went on to say that her leg had mended well and she was teaching youth classes in tae kwon do, though she was only kicking at about 75 percent. The gift was a watch made by Suunto. Called the Core. Her note continued, "The guys at the store said this is what all the climbers wear. Gives you temperature, barometric pressure, elevation. Even has a compass. You deserve it more than any."

I stood staring from a distance. Her posture

said her confidence had returned and that the pain was gone. She was beautiful.

Vince stood alongside. Seemed happy. In the wilderness, I'd conjured my own idea of what he looked like, how he held himself. I was off by a good bit. Were it not for her, Vince and I could have been friends.

I stood in the shadows, just outside, staring in the windows. Nervous, I turned the plastic package in my hands. I'd bought two new recorders. One for her. One for me. I removed one from the packaging, inserted the batteries, and clicked it on.

Hey, it's me. I received your invitation. Thanks for including me . . . uh, us. I know you've been busy. It's good to see you on your feet. Looks like the leg healed well. I'm glad.

Just so you'll know, I went to see Rachel. Took her an orchid, number two fifty-eight, and a bottle of wine. Talked long into the night. I played her the tape. The whole thing. I slept with her. It'd been a long time.

It was also the last time.

I had to let her go. She's not coming back. The distance is too great. The mountain between us is the one mountain I cannot climb.

I thought you should know.

I've been spending a lot of time lately trying to figure out how to start over. The single life is different than I thought. And it's tough. Rachel was my first love. My only love. I've never dated anyone else. Never been with anyone else.

I never told you this, because it just felt wrong, but . . . even at your worst—broken leg, stitches lining your face—well, being lost with you is better than being found and alone.

I wanted to thank you for that.

If Vince doesn't tell you that, call me and I'll remind him. I'm an expert on what a husband should have said.

After Rachel . . . I didn't know what to do, how to live, so I gathered all the broken pieces of me, shoved them into a bag, and hefted it over my shoulder like a bag of rocks. Years passed, dragging myself around in a bag behind me, buckled into my harness and leaning into the weight, the history of me slicing into my shoulders.

Then I went to this conference, found myself in Salt Lake, and for reasons I don't understand, you sat down. I heard the sound of your voice, and something emptied the bag, scattering the

*pieces of me. Laid bare and broken. Now here I
am, hidden in the trees. The pieces of me no
longer fit together.*

*Funny, I have loved two women in my life,
and now I can't have either. Wonder what that
says about me? I wanted to give you a gift, but
what could I give you that would equal what
you have given me?*

*Ashley, for that alone, I wish you every
happiness.*

I STARED around the dogwood tree and
through the glass. She was laughing. A single
diamond hanging around her neck. She
looked good in diamonds. She looked good
in anything.

I left the recorder running, recording,
emptied my pockets of my last two batteries, put all that in the box, tied the bow, left
no card, slipped through the back doors,
and slid it beneath the mound of a hundred
other gifts. In thirty-six hours, they'd be on
a plane for Italy. She'd find my gift upon
their return.

I walked out through the unlit garden,
started my car, and pointed the wheel south.

The night was warm, and I drove home with the windows down. Sweating. Which was okay with me.

When I got home, I changed clothes, grabbed the second of my new recorders, and walked out onto the beach, stopping at the ocean's edge. I stood there a long time. Linus and his blanket. While the waves and foam washed over my feet, I turned the thing in my hands and wrestled with what to say, where to begin.

With the sun breaking the horizon, I clicked RECORD, took three steps, and threw the recorder as far as I could. It spun through the air and disappeared into the daylight and the foam of a receding wave and an out-going tide.

I WOKE to the sound of cats on my porch. They had returned in force. Bringing friends. A beautiful black cat with white feet. I named him Socks. The second was playful, always purring in my face. Long tail, long whiskers, quick ears. I named her Ashley.

I took the day off. Spent it at home. Leaning on the railing, cupping a warm mug, staring out over the ocean, listening to the waves, talking to the cats. Listening for the sound of laughter. Ashley was never far away. Neither the cat nor the memory. I thought back through the wilderness and drifted off to sleep sometime after dark. I dreamed of her sitting in a gondola with Vince beneath an afternoon sun in Venice. They were tan, and she looked happy.

I didn't like the picture.

I crawled off the couch a few hours before daylight. The moon was full and hung low on the horizon, glittering on the crest of each wave, casting my shadow across the beach. I laced up my shoes beneath a warm breeze.

I turned into the wind, taking me south. Low tide. I had the beach to myself. I ran an hour, then two. A single path of turtle tracks led from the water to the dunes. She was laying her eggs. When St. Augustine came into view, I turned for home. The sun was coming up.

Halfway back, I intersected the mother turtle. Exhausted from her night's work. She was big, old, cutting deep grooves in her push to the water. The first wave reached her; she submerged, then floated and skimmed the surface, her shell glistening.

After a few minutes, she was gone. Logger-heads can live to be nearly two hundred years old. I let myself think she was the same one.

I passed the park, and the condo came into view. I slowed, jogged, and finally walked. The July sun had climbed, harsh and bright. The water was blue, rolling glass. A few bottlenose dolphins were trolling near shore, but there was no sign of the mother loggerhead. But there would be. In the weeks ahead, the beach would be crawling with signs.

I DID not hear the footsteps. Only felt the hand on my shoulder. I recognized the veins, the freckles where she did not wear a watch.

I turned, and Ashley stood facing me. A Windbreaker, running shorts, Nikes. Her eyes were red, wet. She looked as though she hadn't slept. She shook her head.

"I was hopeful you would show, but when you didn't, I . . . I couldn't sleep, so I started picking through our presents. Anything to take my mind off . . . today." She held my hands in hers, then pounded me softly in the chest with her fist. Her left hand was naked.

No ring. "My doctor says I should start running again."

"Be a good idea."

"I don't like running alone."

"Me, either."

She picked at the sand with the toe of her shoe. She folded her arms, squinted against the rising sun, and said, "I'd like to meet Rachel. Will you introduce me?"

I nodded.

"Now?"

We turned and walked down the beach. Two miles. The house I'd built her sat up on the dunes, framed in scrub oaks and wire grass.

We wound up through the dune and up the walkway. The sand was soft. A lot like snow.

I unlocked the door. To combat the summer heat, the entire house, walls, floor— everything—was lined with or made of marble. In the solarium, many of the orchids were in bloom.

I led Ashley through the door.

Rachel lay on my left. Michael and Hannah on my right.

Ashley put her hands to her mouth.

I waved my hand, "Ashley, meet Rachel. Rachel, meet Ashley."

Ashley knelt. She ran her fingers through the grooves of Rachel's name and the dates. On top of the marble lid, about where Rachel's hands would be folded atop her chest, sat seven digital recorders. All covered in dust. All but one. The one I'd carried in the mountains. Ashley touched it, turned it in her hand, and then returned it to its place. On top, about where Rachel's face would be, lay my jacket, rolled up like a pillow.

I sat down, my back against Rachel, my feet resting against the twins. I stared up through the blooms and the glass above.

"Rachel was pregnant with the twins. She had what's called a partial abruption, when the placenta tears away from the uterine wall. We put her on bed rest for a month, hoping we could stop it, but it worsened. She was a walking time bomb.

"I tried to reason with her, telling her that when it ruptured completely, it would kill the twins and her. Her doctor and I wanted to take the twins. She stared at us like we'd lost our minds. I wanted Rachel, and if it meant the kids had to go to keep her, then the kids had to go. I wanted us to grow old, laugh at our wrinkles. She wanted that, too, but because there was a chance . . . she took a chance on the twins. I questioned her love, screamed, yelled. She said, 'Ben, I love you, but I'm not living the rest of my life looking at Michael and Hannah on the backs of my eyelids. Knowing they might have made it.' "

"So I tied on my shoes and ran out the door. A midnight run on the beach to clear my head. When my cell phone rang, I sent it to voice mail. I can't tell you the number of times I . . ."

I ran my fingertips along the lettering of Michael's name. Then Hannah's.

"As best I can piece together, moments after I left, she ruptured. She managed to dial nine one one, but they were too late. Not that they could have done anything. Two hours later, I returned. Flashing lights. Police in my kitchen, a call from the hospital. Strange people drove me to the morgue to identify her. In trying to save Rachel, they'd performed an emergency C-section. They'd laid the kids out next to her, tucked them alongside her. The voice mail you heard on the plane is the one she left me. I've sent it to myself most every day. To remind me that despite myself, she loved me."

I looked at Ashley. Tears were streaming down her face.

"You asked once, 'What can't be forgiven?' " I nodded. "It's words. Words you can't take back because the person you spoke them to took them to their grave four and a half years ago."

I waved my hand across the marble sarcophagus. "A simple tombstone didn't seem right, so I built them this. I put the solarium up there so she can see the orchids. And at night, the stars.

"Many nights I have come here, leaning against her, my fingertips resting on the twins, tracing their names, and listened to myself tell her our story." I pointed at the recorders. "I've told it many times, but the end is always the same."

Ashley's lip was trembling. She held my hand between both of hers. Her tears had dripped onto the marble. Alongside ten thousand of mine. "You should've told me. Why didn't you tell me?"

"So many times I wanted to stop dragging

that sled, turn around, and spill it, tell you everything, but . . . you have so much in front of you. So much to look forward to."

"You should have. You owe me that."

"I do now. I didn't then."

She placed her hand flat across my chest, then placed both palms on my face and shook her head. "Ben?"

No answer.

"Ben?"

I opened my mouth, my eyes on Rachel, and pushed out the words. A whisper: "I'm . . . so sorry."

She smiled, shook her head. "She forgave you . . . the moment you said it."

Forgiveness is a tough thing. Both in the offering . . . and the accepting.

We sat there a long time. Through the glass above, I watched an osprey fly over. Beyond the breakers, bottlenose dolphins were feeding south, rolling in groups of six and eight.

Ashley finally wiped her eyes, pressed her ear to my chest, and whispered, "Give me all the pieces."

"There are a lot of them, and I'm not sure they'll ever go back together again."

She kissed me. "Let me try."

"You would be better off to leave me and—"

"I'm not leaving you. Not going it alone." She shook her head. "Not looking at the memory of you every time I close my eyes."

Something deep inside me needed to hear that. Needed to know I was worth that. That despite myself, love might snatch me back. Lift me from the fire.

I stood and kissed the stone above Rachel's face. The twins, too. There were no tears this time. It wasn't good-bye.

We walked out, locked the door, and wound through the dunes. I held her naked left hand in mine. She stopped me, a wrinkle between her eyes. "I gave Vince back his ring. Told him that I liked him very much, but . . ." She wiped her nose. "I think he was relieved to know the truth."

We stood atop the last dune, staring out over the beach. South, to our right, one of the nests had hatched. Hundreds of tiny tracks led to the water. The waves and foam were filling them. Far out, beyond the breakers and waves, shiny black circles of onyx floated atop the water's surface. Glittering black diamonds.

I placed her hand flat across mine. "Start slow. It's been a long time since I've run with anyone."

She kissed me. Her lips were warm, wet, and trembling. Then she laughed and took off running. Her arms swung side to side, causing too much lateral movement. And her stride was too short by maybe three inches. And she favored her left leg. And . . .

But she was a quick study. We could fix all that. Broken people just need piecing back together.

For so long, I'd carried the pieces of me. Every now and then, I'd drop one like a breadcrumb. So I could find my way home. Then Ashley came along and gathered the pieces, and somewhere between eleven thousand feet and sea level, the picture began taking shape. Dim at first, then clearer. Not yet clear. But these things take time.

It's risky for both of us. You must hope in an image you can't see, and I must trust you with me.

That's the piecing.

Ashley ran up the beach, the sun spilling down her back. Fresh footprints in the sand. Sweat shining on her thighs.

I could see them both. Rachel in the dunes, Ashley on the beach. I shook my head. I can't make sense of that. I don't know how.

Ashley returned. Breathing heavily, laughing, smiling. She raised her eyebrows, pulled on my hand. "Ben Payne?"

More tears I could not explain. I did not try. "Yes?"

"When you laugh, I want to smile. And when you cry"—she brushed the tear off my face—"I want the tears to roll down my cheeks." She whispered, "I'm not leaving you . . . won't."

I swallowed. How, then, does one live? A memory echoed from beyond the dunes. *Put one foot in front of the other.*

Maybe piecing is continual. Maybe the glue takes time to dry. Maybe bones take time to mend. Maybe it's okay that the mess I call me is in process. Maybe it's a long, hard walk out of the crash site. Maybe the distance is different for each of us. Maybe love is bigger than my mess.

My voice was slow in coming. "Can we . . . walk a bit first?"

She nodded, and we did. First a mile, then two. A gentle breeze in our face. We reached the lifeguard chair and turned around.

She tugged on me, the breeze now at our backs. "You ready?"

So we picked up a jog. Wasn't long and we were running.

And we ran a long time.

Somewhere in the miles that followed, sweat flinging off my fingertips, salt stinging my eyes, my breath deep, rhythmic, and clean, my feet barely touching the ground, I looked down and found the pieces of me melting into one.

LEAVING UNKNOWN

KERRY REICHS

WHEN her car breaks down outside Unknown, Arizona, Maeve Connelly makes an unexpected rest stop that just might change her life.

Prologue

I CAN honestly say I didn't *intend* to be bad. It's just that I have rotten luck. I was nine and on a camping trip. It was very "after school special": four suburban families with expensive tents that didn't get out of the garage much and Coleman stoves that the fathers couldn't really figure out but that required hours of happy tinkering while the women gossiped and made burger patties. A dozen kids charged about in OshKosh B'gosh brand overalls.

We were marshaling forces for the day's excursion. I was instructed to stay put while the adults debated Grandfather Mountain versus Blowing Rock. A nearby trailhead tantalized. I begged to explore. My father gave me permission to go for ten minutes, not a minute more.

But the lure of each new bend of the trail was too much for me. I *had* to see what was around the corner. And the next. And the next. By the time my father caught up with me an hour later, my punishment was to sit in the tent and "think about things." What I thought about was how great that trail had been and how I wished I'd gotten to the end. Back then, I was different. Back then, I was fearless. It was much later that the death of my best friend made me dread things I couldn't see coming.

I've always been restless. I can't seem to settle on anything. That's probably why it took me seven and a half years to finish college. I finally graduated at the ripe old age of twenty-five with a major in Anthropology and a minor in Film Studies. I had no idea what I wanted to do and a lot of time on my hands. That was the situation four weeks ago. That's when the trouble began. That's when I discovered Facebook.com.

Chapter One

Getting Fired from My Job; Getting Fired from My Family

THE day had started with no indication that I was headed for life in a cardboard refrigerator box under an I-85 overpass. I'd savored the arrival of spring during my three-

mile run and returned to my apartment looking for diversion.

"Are you thinner?" squawked my cockatiel Oliver, as he did at least once a day. One
of my more successful projects. I grinned as
I settled down to start screwing around on
Facebook.

Today it was the Cities I've Visited appli-
cation. It involved sticking virtual pins into a
world map of all the exotic locations you'd
been to. Unless Frying Pan Landing, North
Carolina, counted as exotic, it was going to
be a short diversion.

I was distracted by an e-mail from Laura
Mills. Laura had lived across the street and
been my best friend when I was eight. But
then her family had moved to Texas when I
was eleven, and I never saw her again. After
I'd joined Facebook, I'd received a friend request from eleven-year-old Laura looking
out from behind the glamorous makeup of a
woman living in Los Angeles. I'd accepted,
and she'd been sending me delicious details
of her life in Los Angeles ever since. I wished
I had the money to take her up on her repeated invitations. The fantasy was delicious.
It was whimsy, of course, but if I did go to

California, no telling what I could accomplish. Look at Laura, living at the beach and working as something called a First AD, which meant she worked on the Fox Studios lot, met all kinds of famous people, and got to see movies before they were released.

Reality was the picture on Facebook of an old boyfriend, arm slung around the shoulders of a petite redhead, matching happy smiles. His change of status to "engaged" was a Facebook bomb.

I frowned, then immediately stopped and rubbed my forehead. A wrinkle between your eyes is so unattractive, and our family was prone to the Connelly divot. I glanced at my watch, knowing the cure for a foul mood. I had plenty of time.

"Road trip. Don't forget the bird," chirped Oliver as I put him in his cage.

"Next time, pal," I promised.

My car, Elsie, grudgingly started after gentle coaxing. She was an ancient 1970 Plymouth Road Runner, sunshine yellow with a black stripe across her hood. Elsie had over 150,000 miles and was limping through her golden years. I loved her.

Twenty minutes later, I was happily browsing Nordstrom's shoe section. From forty feet away, I felt the jolt you get when you first lay eyes on the boots you know will shortly be yours. I sprang toward them like a lioness on an antelope, canvassing the room for a salesperson as I moved.

"Size eight, please." I waved the red suede boot at a clerk.

As he glided off, I glanced at the $225 price tag. Ouch. I wrestled with myself briefly. Maybe I shouldn't.

"This is your lucky day," said the shoe salesman when he returned. "They're an additional twenty percent off."

"Fantastic." I grinned as I reached for the box. God did love me.

Fifteen minutes later, back in Elsie, I was at a standstill. I gripped the steering wheel as if my übercontrol of the car would make traffic move. Four twenty-three. I should be at work.

I spotted red and blue lights flashing and groaned. An accident was narrowing traffic to one lane. I banged the steering wheel. Elsie responded with an ominous rattle.

"I'm sorry, Elsie." I patted the console. "Please don't die." I glanced at the gas gauge. Elsie liked to play fun games where needles plummet from half full to below empty in the course of one mile. The last thing I needed was to run out of gas.

I ran out of gas. I leaned forward in my seat, as if shifting my five-foot-nine, 140-pound frame would give the 4,000-pound car momentum, and willed Elsie to coast. Still pissed about the steering-wheel thing, she rolled to a stop a mile from the Texaco.

"How much bad luck can one person have?" I moaned, reaching for my cell phone. My boss, Joe, was going to be furious.

My phone had no service. I looked at it blankly. How come I had no service in the middle of town? I had a text message, so I opened it curiously as I stepped out of Elsie. I froze. "Your Sprint mobile phone service has been suspended for nonpayment."

I couldn't believe it. I was *sure* I'd paid the bill. I recalled the stack of bills on my counter. Hadn't I? I frowned, then smoothed the groove between my eyes. I blew out my bangs. Nothing for it but to trudge to the gas station.

It was close to six when I walked into the Gin Mill. The place was packed. I mean, *really* packed. I could see Jules's long, dark ponytail flying as she whirled to grab bottles of beer. Next to her, Joe was sloshing something pink into shot glasses. My heart plummeted. Today was our inaugural Young Professionals happy hour.

I dashed to the bar. The look Joe gave me would have made a frailer woman faint, but now wasn't the time to explain. I started taking orders and slinging beer.

By eight, most of the crowd had moved on and we could draw a breath. Joe was back in the office. "That was crazy, daisy!" I said.

"You should have seen it earlier." Jules leaned her tall frame against the back counter. "Wall-to-wall Wall Streets."

"Jules, I'm so sorry. I ran out of gas." When she laughed, I protested. "No, really, I did!"

Jules shook her head. "You don't have to convince me, girl." We'd been friends since junior high. She was used to forgiving me. "Joe was pissed, though."

I hesitated. "How pissed?"

"Well—"

"Maeve!" Joe's holler cut her off. "Get in here."

"Good luck, little camper." Jules patted my shoulder. I tapped the photo of me taped on the wall as I passed, for luck. It was a fetching shot, and you can't see them in the picture, but I was wearing my favorite polka-dot kneesocks.

Joe's look was black. "Shut the door," he instructed. I did and sat in the uncomfortable chair that wobbled.

"Today was unacceptable—" Joe began.

"Joe, there was an accident, and then I ran out of gas. . . ." I hung my head, long blond braids drooping penitently.

Joe sighed. "I'm sorry, Maeve. But I gotta let you go."

"But—"

Joe held up his hand. "The bottom line is that you're regularly late and other people aren't." His gaze softened. "I know you're sorting things out. . . ."

I sprang from my seat. I didn't want his pity. "Mail me my check," I directed. I strode out with a wave and a chipper, "Thanks, Joe."

Behind the bar, I hugged Jules and practi-

cally skipped to my car to show how carefree
I was. It was only when the door was shut and
locked that the weepies threatened to win.

I pulled myself together. I needed spaghetti. If my mother was cooking spaghetti,
my luck would change, I told myself. I could
already taste the meatballs as I started the
car. Good news was just around the corner.

MY FATHER'S face lit up when I walked into
the kitchen. He was leafing through the mail,
still in his suit. "Joining us for dinner?"

"Yep." I received one of his excellent hugs.
I was feeling better already.

"Hello, dear." My mother popped up
from behind the counter. "You're in luck.
I'm trying something new tonight. A curry
chicken."

I wobbled, but rallied.

"Hey." My attention returned to my father.
"You're looking at your mail." My father only
looked at mail on Sunday, when it was guaranteed no more would arrive while he was
sorting.

He gave me a rueful look. "Your mother
has insisted on some *reforms* since she finished the Spirit Square project." He shot

me a grin as he headed upstairs to change.

My mother, a sculptor, alternated between periods of complete oblivion, when she was immersed in a project, and ruthless organization, when she emerged and tried to make up for lost time. That explained the new recipe.

When we were alone, my mother looked undecided for a minute, then said, "Speaking of mail, there's a letter for you. It's from Cameron's parents. I believe they plan to do something to commemorate her birthday. A memorial."

I met her eyes. "I don't think I can," I said.

She opened her mouth to say something more, then thought better of it. "No need to decide right now." She sat at the table. "Have you given any thought to what you'd like to do now that you've graduated?" Her tone was careful.

"I don't know." I hesitated. "I don't know what I'm good at."

My mom squeezed my hand. "You're good at so many things."

"You have to say that. You're my mother."

"It's the truth. Look at what a good bartender you are!"

I grimaced.

"You're good with people." She looked thoughtful. "What about something in health care? You . . ."

I blanched at the thought. I hated hospitals. "No way."

She sighed. "What about photography? You did a remarkable job taking pictures of my sculptures and updating my portfolio."

"I don't think you can make a living—"

"Maeve!" My father's bellow echoed down the hallway. He strode into the room, deep crease between his eyebrows, waving a sheaf of papers. "What the hell is this?" He thrust the sheets under my eyes, and I winced. The country-club bill had arrived. I couldn't believe it. The one day this month I needed to be far away from home happened to be the day I got fired, dropped in unexpectedly, and Dad uncharacteristically opened his mail before Sunday.

"Um . . ." I looked at the bill. Had I really eaten at the club *nine* times?

"We don't begrudge you the occasional meal, Maeve," my father chastened. "But massages? A new tennis racket?"

"I . . ."

Dad's outrage deflated at the sight of my hunched frame. "Your mother and I understand that you've had a hard time. We've been allowing you time to figure things out. But now you must take responsibility for your life. You're a bright girl; you've got your degree. You need to start thinking about your future."

I stared at them, aghast. My future loomed impossibly large and intimidating. I had no idea how I'd fill the chasm.

"You can't buy something every time you're upset," my father lectured in a gentle voice. He paused, as if afraid of his own words, then plunged in. "I'm going to require you to repay us. You need to learn responsibility. The way you live now is"—he waved his hands in the air—"flitterdegibbety," he pronounced.

"Flitterdegibbety?" My voice rose an octave. It was an unfair categorization. It's not like my parents were perpetually rescuing me. I had a *job*. Well, I did yesterday.

"Flighty," my mother affirmed.

"I am *not* flighty." I adopted a haughty tone. "I graduated with a three-point-five.

I take excellent care of Oliver." I wanted to say more, but the fact that I never missed an episode of *Bones* didn't seem quite right.

"I'll help you work out a payment plan." My father seemed happy to sidestep the debate. "We'll look at your shifts at the Gin Mill and your expenses and create a budget."

My stomach turned. "Um . . . I sort of lost my job . . ." I mumbled.

"What was that?"

"I'm not working at the Gin Mill anymore," I said. "I ran out of gas, so I was really late to work."

"Joe fired you for being late?" My father looked confused.

"It wasn't just the once," I confessed.

My mother rubbed her face tiredly. We sat there for a moment; then my parents' eyes met, and my father voiced a decision I suspected they'd prearranged. "Maeve, you cannot be dependent on your mother and me any longer. We've been happy to help you get on your feet, but now you're on your own. It's for the best."

"How is it whenever someone tells me they are doing what's best, it ends up hurting me?" I was *not* some basket case. I had a wicked bad-luck curse. Something was out of kilter in the universe, but it wasn't me. I had a vision of palm trees. "I am *not* a flake," I squeezed out as I grabbed my purse. "And I'll prove it."

I made it to Elsie and leaped in, praying for once that she would start right up. My stomach was roiling. I'd already gone for a run, but I needed more, like a hit.

I steered Elsie toward the track. I parked and slipped on sweatpants. I stretched for only a nanosecond before I was sprinting. My feet pounded rhythmically along the track in a steady alternation, wind rushing by my ears, blocking all other sound. I lost myself in the physical exertion of repetitive motion. Of my body obeying me. Of the rare moment when I was in total control.

I was not someone to be pitied. I would prove them wrong. I would elude my rotten luck if I had to go all the way across the country to do it. In fact, that sounded like just the trick. I was ready for Hollywood.

Chapter Two
Fired Up

To: LALola@neticom.net
Subject: LA Here I Come!

Laura, guess what? You've talked me into it. I've decided to come to California. I'm still working out the details, but I'm thinking sooner rather than later. Why wait for Paradise, right? Give me a call to talk about details.

Can't wait to see you in person!

Later gater, M

"ARE you sure about this?" my older sister Vi asked me.

"Never more." I used my shoulder to hold the phone in place while I reached for a carrot.

"It's an awfully big move without a *plan*," Vi pressed.

"I have a *plan*, Stan." I mimicked her tone. I was in high spirits.

Vi snorted. "What, drive west until the ocean stops you?"

"Laura invited me. Remember Laura Mills?"

"Laura Mills from when you were ten?"

"We reconnected." Laura was the unknown variable in the plan. I was counting on being able to crash with my old friend while I got sorted.

"A marathon, huh?"

"Yep. The Los Angeles Marathon." The first step toward a new me was a personal goal. I would train over the summer, and the fall marathon would literally be the starting gun for my new life.

"A marathon is twenty-six-point-two miles because that's when the first to run it dropped dead."

"Are you saying I can't?" I bristled.

"Of course not. You can do anything you put your mind to. It just seems so . . . far. From all of us. If anything happened . . ."

"Nothing's going to happen. And I need to make a change. Here, I don't know, I feel trapped in, well, in *before*. I want to prove that I am a completely responsible and capable person."

She sighed. "I know. But let me help. I'm sending you a check."

I wanted to say no, but I was stone-cold broke. "Not much," I capitulated after embarrassingly little inner struggle.

"Trust me." She laughed. "I'm buying peace of mind that you won't end up stranded in the middle of the desert in a town named Skeleton Junction with a population of four people and one tooth. Promise you'll call before you leave?" It made my departure sound so definite I caught my breath. I almost recanted it all as a big joke. Instead, I assured Vi I'd call her and hung up.

I explored my instinct to retract from the trip. Was I doing this because I wanted to or because I wanted to prove people wrong?

No, I *did* want to make a real change. I'd been living down to everyone's (low) expectations of me. I'd lazily adopted the Maeve-is-a-slacker notion as my own. But not anymore. If I went far enough away, I could be anyone.

I assembled my morning vitamin regimen as I pondered, absently lining up vitamins A through D, a woman's multi, ginkgo bi-loba, manganese, flax oil, selenium, and the other dailies. I made a note to pick up ginseng and coenzyme Q10 to counteract the increased stress of travel. My eye fell on a Post-it that read *Before you can arrive where you want to be, you have to know where you are going.*

I SPEND hours studying maps. They fascinate me. Riding back from the beach one weekend with Jules, studying a map, I'd noticed a nearby town called Half Hell, North Carolina. I'd insisted she detour, and my passion had been born. I'd organized day trips all over the state to visit Toast, Erect, and Whynot. I loved capturing the curves of the road and the quirks of the towns on film. For me, it was like that trail when I was nine. I liked to snap an Elsie centerfold at each destination and developed quite a collection of my car in front of one-of-a-kind town signs. I wanted to photograph America from the inside out.

Elsie couldn't handle the high speeds of the interstate, so I happily planned a backroads course wending from one alluring destination to the next. I was in no hurry. The marathon wasn't for months. Only, the longer the trip, the more money I'd need. That *was* a problem, since I didn't have any.

Affordable camping would figure heavily in my trip, and I'd chosen the southwestern route because southern states not only had some crazy town names, but also the warm, dry weather would be best for camping. Food would be a bigger problem. I pondered. Hard-boiled eggs keep well, travel easily, and are a good source of protein. I'd throw in trail mix and cheese sticks for variety. And oranges. I lived in constant fear of scurvy, so oranges were essential. I'd reserve my cash for necessities, like Diet Coke and water. You want to take lots of water when you drive through the desert.

That left the last hurdle. Cold, hard cash.

The phone rang. It was Jules.

"Can I borrow your ladder?" she asked without preamble.

A year ago in a fit of DIY that petered out almost before I got home from Lowe's, I'd blown $300 on a ladder. It now served as the world's most expensive drying rack for my delicates. The only time the poor emasculated ladder was used for its intended purpose was when I loaned it to friends.

"For a hundred dollars you can keep it," I joked.

"For real?" she demanded. " 'Cause if you mean it, you're on."

"Really?" I was surprised. A hundred bucks was a lot for something as boring as a ladder.

"Hell, yeah. Save myself the hassle of driving to your place and back every month. And that's over half off."

My eye fell on my new, troublemaking tennis racket, tag still on. An idea was forming. "You know my turquoise BCBG pumps you love?" Jules and I wore the same size shoe.

"Of course."

"I'll sell them to you for another hundred dollars." I held my breath. The shoes had cost me $160, and I'd worn them in only two battles before the pain in my toes won the war. Jules wore them much more often—she has a commendable tolerance for pain when it comes to shoes. She'd survive the siege of Stalingrad in spikes as long as she looked good.

"Seriously? Hell, yes! I love those shoes." Jules jumped at my offer. I couldn't believe it. I'd made $200 just like that. My brain raced.

"Jules, if you help me organize a yard sale, I'll give you an employee discount on all my shoes." My eyes flicked from item to item around the room: treadmill, bowling ball, tennis racket, chess set, television, sofa, yoga ball, juicer, waffle maker. I was going to California for a fresh start. I'd sell it all.

"Sure. I'd help anyway." She was quiet for a moment. "So I guess you're really leaving. I'll miss you."

I thought of her bright eyes and easy laugh. I wanted to say something in return, but it was hard for me. I said, "When I leave, I'm giving you my yellow suede Fiorinas as a memento, pimento."

"Girl, I can't get you out of town fast enough." Jules laughed.

When I hung up, I hoped she knew I'd really been trying to say thanks for being a friend.

I WAS fidgeting anxiously as I stared at my possessions arrayed in an eclectic fire sale. Rollerblades next to a paint easel, an ice-cream maker sitting atop empty photo

albums, a fishing rod leaning against a cro-
quet set.

"Do you think we're charging enough for
the dartboard?" I asked Jules.

"Yes." She ignored me as a girl wearing a
purple scarf over an orange sweater picked
up one of my silver Marc Jacobs peep-toes.
Oh no. She could *not* have those shoes.

"Maeve!" my mother exclaimed, quick
eyes taking in the scene. My father, crowding in behind her, was beaming. When I'd
told them about my plan, they'd been delighted, proud of my sacrificial initiative.
In return, they'd been more than generous
in discharging my debts. Dad had even
given me a gas card with $200 to get me
started.

"We've come to help!" bellowed my
father.

"Great!" Jules beamed. "Here—wear
this." She produced a sticker that said "Ask
me for help!" and handed it to my dad.

My gaze returned to Tacky Girl. She'd
slipped on the Marc Jacobs. They fit. I
jumped. "I have to . . ." I started toward
her.

"Actually"—my mother looped her arm

through mine—"your father's going to stay and help so that you and I can spend some time together. We thought you'd need a little break."

"I don't think . . ." Tacky now had the box tucked under her arm. "Oh." I reflexively reached an arm toward the shoes, but my mother was herding me helplessly toward the door.

"Don't you worry, dear. Your dad's happy to help!"

Jules and my father waved as if I was off to my first day of school, and just like that, I went from a person who had everything to a girl with a moderate wad of cash and only ten pairs of shoes.

WHILE my ownership of material possessions was being decimated, my mother distracted me with lunch.

"We're quite proud of you," my mother said as we shook out our napkins. "It's very brave to start over like this."

"Thanks." My voice was a little choked.

She reached across the table to touch my hand. "I know it's been tough, Maeve. Would you like to talk about anything?"

I instinctively hunched as I shook my head.

"It's not too late for you to reconsider postponing your departure a few weeks for Cameron's memorial service. Her parents would love to see you." My best friend's birthday was approaching. She would have been twenty-eight.

"I can't," I said. "They don't mean it. Seeing me only reminds them. Best to leave it and move forward."

"Sometimes you have to move through something before you can move forward," she ventured.

"Mom, I'm leaving soon, and who knows when I'll be able to come back. Can we make this about me and *not* Cameron?"

A flicker crossed her face, but all she said was, "Of course. Tell me more about this marathon."

We talked about everything and nothing. The bill came, and I reverted to a child, not even pretending I'd contribute.

"Before we go, I have one last thing for you. A kind of Connelly road map," she said, extracting a bundle from her bag.

JULES AND I WERE collapsed on folding chairs in my barren living room, Oliver hopping about the apartment in an agitated manner, cataloguing empty space. Jules had sold almost everything. Anything left in the apartment would either go home with her or be packed in my car bound for Los Angeles.

We were studying the seven small statues perched on an empty box in front of us. Oliver danced along the box, approaching then retreating from them, not sure if they were friend or foe.

"So what are they again?" Jules asked.

"My mom made them for my trip. She called them *kachinas*." The seven figures were partially anthropomorphized, happy, round, animal-Buddha-type figures, each about the size of a pool ball, incorporating a combination of animals, or animal and human. "I'm supposed to spend time getting to know each one and identifying it with . . . something. Whatever I feel when I contemplate the kachina is its chakra. When that chakra is evoked, either because of how I'm personally feeling or because of how a place makes me feel, I'm supposed to commit the kachina to that place."

"Sounds complicated."

"See, like this one, it's a knot of intertwined leaves and stems, like new shoots, and what looks like a hummingbird in there. It makes me think of new growth. So maybe I'd take it to my first day of my new job or leave it in the yard of my new apartment or something."

"It sounds pretty cool, letting go of things," mused Jules. "You can make them mean anything—fear, loss, a bad guy, a bad time— and then you leave them behind. Because you can't really get attached to something you already know you're going to leave somewhere. So maybe it's more for—"

"Maybe." I cut her off. I was feeling good and forward-looking. I didn't want to dwell on past missteps. It didn't help that the first kachina was a girl intertwined with a crab, looking backward. I had a good idea what that one meant. "I'm supposed to keep the last one."

"That one?" Jules gestured toward a statue.

"Yes." It was a combination of a plump

female mother figure and an owl that re-sembled my favorite stuffed animal. My protectors.

Jules looked at me. "Well, I guess it's time to say good-bye."

I nodded. "Take care of the bar," I said. "And make sure Joe doesn't have a heart at-tack." Translation: I'm going to miss you and Joe, but I can't admit it and I refuse to cry.

"You, too, girl. We're going to miss the hell out of you."

She hugged me so hard I thought my ribs would crack. We were both blinking.

"You call me, kid." She didn't look at me as she gathered her bags of my former stuff. We both knew I wouldn't call often. It wasn't really my thing. But, for her, I would, once in a while.

Jules stopped at the door. "You know, bad luck isn't really a thing. It's like weather. It happens, but it doesn't follow you around specifically. But frame of mind, now that stays with you forever."

And she was gone. Seconds ticked by. Then adrenaline and the voice clamoring in my heart won over my inertia. I ran to the back of the room, then whirled to dash after her.

Her car was pulling out when I hit the sidewalk. "Jules," I screamed. She hit the brakes, and I ran to the driver's-side window.

"I forgot to give you these." I offered the box.

Jules looked confused. She took the brand-new pair of prized red suede boots that didn't hurt my feet even a little bit.

"You didn't have to"—she smiled—"but I'll take them. Love you." She paused, then smiled more broadly. "And I know you love me back." And she drove off, one hand fluttering out the window.

I waved back, good-bye to my friend, good-bye to my boots, and good-bye to the small kachina I'd tucked into the box. It was one of an egg intertwined with what looked like a tadpole, and it was the first one I'd had an immediate reaction to. My reaction had been gratitude. To Jules, for putting up with me, for understanding me. And most of all, for being around to say good-bye to me. My journey had begun. I went to bed, ready for my new adventures to arrive.

Chapter Three

Road Trip, Don't Forget the Bird

THE trip started out fine. Our routine was set from our first night camped outside Sweet Lips, Tennessee, I in my tent, Oliver cozy in a little birdie fleece-lined Snuggle Hut that hung from a hook at the peak of my tent. We'd followed back roads, snapping stylish pictures of Elsie in front of landmarks. I ate a lot of boiled eggs.

I tapped my pencil against my teeth now as I studied the map. I could go the lower Arizona route, entering at Portal and passing through Paradise to Greaterville and Tombstone, before reaching pinprick-tiny Unknown. Beyond the irresistible Unknown was the equally alluring Why, Arizona, on the Tohono O'odham Indian reservation.

My other option was the northerly route, through Superior, Carefree, Surprise, and Nothing. There was also the appeal of a little town named Brenda near the California border. I wondered if the whole town dressed in dowdy clothes and was secretly resentful of a prettier older sister town somewhere named Betty.

It was a difficult choice. I called my sister.

"It's early, cruel wench," Vi mumbled into the phone.

I looked at my watch. Oops. "Sorry. I've driven across three time zones in two weeks, including states and Native American reservations that don't observe daylight savings. The actual time can ricochet wildly within sixty miles, so my understanding of it has devolved to 'diner open' or 'diner closed.' I'm in a diner."

"Diners allow birds?" Oliver was talking up a storm, wooing me for some pancakes.

"This one does." I explained my dilemma.

"Brenda is tempting," she agreed. "But Superior, Carefree, Surprise, and Nothing denote a negative emotional trend from vain purposeless to unanticipated emptiness. In contrast, Tombstone, Portal, Paradise, Greaterville, Unknown, and Why all tap into the fundamental questions of life, the afterlife, and why we're here. That sounds more interesting. Besides, I've been to Surprise, and the surprise is that it's a boring suburb of Phoenix."

"There's an Eden around there, too."

She laughed. "Call me if you find the Fountain of Youth."

IT MIGHT not be heaven on earth, but the drive from Tombstone toward Unknown was gorgeous. The sky was blue and impossibly large, the road a ribbon of asphalt snaking across the wide golden prairie. In the distance the grasslands met sloping brown hills.

As I headed south, the distant hills became more pronounced, pushing upward to fully fledged mountains and jutting cliffs. Cattle and the occasional cluster of deer roamed the high-desert scrublands. I felt like I'd stepped back in time to the cowboy era.

"Howdy, pardner," I said to Oliver as we cruised past the occasional ranch with gates proclaiming Circle Z or Lazy Bar.

"Carrot," said Oliver.

"Howdy, pardner," I repeated, waiting for him to catch on.

"Carrot. *Squaaawk*. Are you thinner?"

A few miles ahead, a road traveled off to the east. I consulted the map. It looked to be the turnoff for Unknown. I took it, looking at the sky to assess the time. I'd learned that the sun dropped fast in the west. From about four, the sun's rays slanted noticeably with a day-is-ending feeling. When it began to set in earnest, you had about an hour before it dropped like a stone and everything became as dark as ink. At that point you wanted your tent up for the night.

As I was mentally counting my remaining pairs of clean socks, Elsie emitted an ominous clunk and rattle. A horrible grinding noise came from under the hood, and the car bucked once before all momentum ceased. We coasted to a stop on an unnamed road in the least populated place I'd ever been.

For a moment I sat there, my mind not grasping our predicament. Stupidly I looked at the gas gauge, but I wasn't out of fuel. Next most stupidly, I looked at my phone. I hadn't had a signal since this morning. Besides, who would I call? This bad-luck curse was getting out of hand. I looked at Oliver. He looked at me.

"Howdy, pardner," I said.

"Oh crap," Oliver said.

I opened the door and stepped out. I looked up the road, which stretched without variation to the east. I looked down the road, which stretched without variation to the west. I felt the impending presence of bad news, as in a long-ago waiting room. Cameron had not been doing well. Her family had asked me to wait outside her room for a bit. A white-coated doctor stepped out. He conferred with a nurse, and she pointed. They both looked at me. He started in my direction, shoulders weighted with news I didn't want. The room pressed around me, and I wanted to escape, to run away from that white coat that was going to ruin things.

"Dirty rotten luck, you won't always win," I shouted at a sky that calmly absorbed my rage into its wide, unwavering depths.

Calmer, I realized I had to figure out what to do.

First, ascertain the level of hopelessness. I slid behind the wheel and tried the ignition. Nothing. I shifted the car into neutral and got out, then put my shoulder into it and pushed. It was slow, sweaty, exhausting going, but I eased the car over to the side of the road.

Next, I considered Oliver. Who knew when I'd get back tomorrow? I'd have to take him with me. Thank God I'd had his wings clipped right before we left.

"Want to go for a walk, buddy?" I extracted him from his cage.

"Road trip. Don't forget the bird!" he chirped happily.

"Yeah, this is all fun and games to you," I chided as I secured a loop around his right leg that connected by a long cord to a bracelet on my wrist. I perched him on my shoulder. He promptly clambered up my braid like a rope ladder to settle down on top of my head. I slipped his Snuggle Hut inside my jacket. When it got cold, he could nestle in it.

I removed extra socks from my overnight backpack and replaced them with my sleeping bag, my current book, and essentials from my purse. I tied my tent to the bottom loops. I tested my headlamp: no telling how far I'd be walking in the dark. Finally I grabbed two large bottles of water and stuck a boiled egg in my pocket.

With a last pat for Elsie, I locked the door and started walking.

"I'm a girl with a bird on her head, destination Unknown," I said to no one in particular. The landscape was unchanged when the sun abandoned me. Soon after, the darkness was impenetrable and I was dependent on my headlamp.

I sat down after a while to rest and put on an extra sweater. Oliver clambered down my arm to my wrist, not liking the cold either. I tucked him into his Snuggle Hut and put both into my jacket as he gave a happy *tut*. I resumed walking. I hadn't seen a single car in three hours. It was only around nine, but I was getting tired.

After half an hour, the road did something funny. I swept my headlamp from side to side, but the night gobbled its puny effort. As far as I could tell, the road split around an island of land. I stepped off the road and advanced cautiously. After picking my way several hundred yards, my headlamp caught a picnic table. I wilted in relief. It must be some kind of roadside facility. I would stay here.

I pitched my tent beyond the picnic table, moving carefully so as not to jostle Oliver. I hung his hideaway from the hook on the tent ceiling and undid my braids, combing my fingers through my long hair. It was cold. I alternated between worrying about Oliver and my conviction that my own glands were swelling with the onset of a sore throat. I would double my Emergen-C intake tomorrow.

I slid into my sleeping bag. "Tomorrow will be a better day, pal," I murmured to my sleeping bird before I dropped off myself.

I WAS being abducted by aliens. Bright lights were flooding the tent in a swirl of colors. Some red, some blue, but most of all a penetrating white light. My brain struggled to understand.

A car door slammed. I heard booted footsteps crunching toward my tent, accompanied by another beam of bobbing light. Oh God. I was going to be murdered by some isolation-deranged cowboy.

"Knock, knock," drawled a pleasant,

twangy voice. "Care to come on out here, lil' camper?" The voice sounded amused.

"Howdy, pardner!" my bird introduced himself.

There was a disembodied chuckle. "Howdy back atcha. Whadda ya say ya come on out and make our acquaintance properlike?"

I unzipped my bag and crawled out of the safety of my tent. I stood blinking at the light shining on my face.

"Wall now, ya are a young thing, ain't cha?" the amused speaker pronounced. "And prettier than ya sound."

"Road trip, don't forget the bird!" Oliver chirped, anxious at being left alone. The beam left my face and shone on the tent.

"That a 'tiel in there?" My assailant's question surprised me. "My ex-wife had one a them."

I squinted, trying to make out my extraordinary visitor while his beam was directed toward Oliver. I could only distinguish impressive height and breadth before the light returned to me. I winced.

"Sorry." The light went out. "Guess you musta been sleepin'."

I faced him again, but he was backlit by

the headlights of what I guessed was a size-able dual-wheel SUV, and all I could ascertain was his considerable bulk.

"My name's Lawrence Oscar Fenter Ashburn Perry. I'm the sheriff here in Unknown. People mostly call me Bruce." The light clicked on again, this time shining at a bronze star on his chest. The beam then angled up, revealing a thick dark mustache, round cheeks, and deep eyes surrounded by appealing crinkles. "An' you?"

"Maeve," I said. "Maeve Connelly." It registered that I might be saved. This man could take me to civilization.

"Wall, Maeve Con'ley, what're you doin' camping in the middle of my town square?" were his astonishing next words. My jaw must have dropped wide open because Lawrence Oscar Fenter Ashburn Perry chuckled. I looked around, and sure enough I could make out faint building outlines in the truck headlights.

"Is it . . ." I hesitated. "Is it a . . . ghost town?"

His chuckle turned into a guffaw. "That'd make my job easier. No, Unknown's a full-on thrivin' little town with enough colorful characters for a serial TV show."

"How many people?" I asked.

" 'Bout eight hundred or so, give or take."

"But I didn't even know it was there. There are no lights."

"Wall now, you're right there. You picked quite a night to visit. Ronnie Two Shoes was being a doofus as usual when trimmin' his old cottonwood, and one of the branches snapped the power lines clean through. It's a miracle he didn't fry hisself up like a chicken nugget."

"I thought I was in the middle of the woods."

"A hundred more feet and you'd be bunking in the community center," he said. "That your Plymouth Road Runner 'bout ten, twelve miles back?"

I nodded.

"You walk all that way in the dark? With a bird?"

Another nod.

"Wall, I can't let ya stay in the square, I'm 'fraid. And I can't put ya in the jail without ya bein' under arrest. But I might be able to help. You break down your little campin' site while I make a call."

I did as he said. I was perched on the picnic table with all my worldly goods in a backpack and a Snuggle Hut when Bruce returned.

"Looks like you're in luck. Follow me." When we got to the truck, it was "Climb on up." I was too tired to ask where we were going. In the cab of the truck, blessed heat seeped into my bones.

"Lawrence," I said. "Why do they call you Bruce?"

"Wall, I reckon it's because I like Monty Python so much," he answered obligingly, leaving me as mystified as before.

After a short trip, we pulled up to a long, low adobe house. The truck headlights lit up attractive pink walls and a doorway framed by some kind of flowering tree. Bruce ignored the front door and followed a path to the left through an archway cut into the long wall. Beyond it appeared to be a courtyard garden. I could see candlelight flickering through double glass doors to the right. Bruce went through them, and I followed him into a beautiful and spacious kitchen. A welcoming fire flickered in the hearth.

"Hello, Bruce. How you doin', Bruce? All right there, Bruce?" squawked a voice from beyond a darkened doorway to the left.

Oliver, on my shoulder now, began hopping agitatedly, lifting one foot then the other, a cockatiel sign of anxiety.

"Lulabell, hush your beak," said Bruce.

"Quiet, Lulabell," mimicked the squawk.

It was too much for Oliver. He released a torrent of sounds. "*Squawk*. Carrot. Are you thinner? Howdy, pardner. Oh crap."

A tiny woman hurried into the room. She wore her graying hair in two long braids. "Don't you mind Lulabell," she said. It clicked that this was Bruce's ex-wife. It was hard to make out detail by candlelight, but she was clearly no more than five feet tall. At five foot nine, I towered over her. And Bruce towered over me. I didn't realize I was transfixed until she demanded, "Well, are you two going to sit, or am I going to need neck surgery from looking up at you?"

We sat. Bruce cleared his throat. "Maeve,

this here is Ruby. Ruby, this is the gal I was tellin' you about," he said.

"It would be a remarkable feat if you managed to come up with a substitute stray girl in the fifteen minutes since you called, Lawrence," Ruby said. She examined me in the candlelight.

"I'm Maeve Connelly," I said. "This is Oliver."

"Howdy, pardner." He focused on Ruby, on his best behavior.

"Howdy yourself." Ruby's level gaze returned to me. "I'm Ruby Ransome. I understand you've had car trouble."

There was another squawk. We all looked confused, because it emanated from the vicinity of Bruce's stomach.

"Bruce? Bruce, you there?" It was a walkie-talkie.

Ruby rose fluidly. "Lawrence, you're needed. Go back to the station. I'll handle it from here. Call me tomorrow at ten o'clock with information on PIGS and Barney's schedule." I had no idea what she was talking about, but I knew that when she said ten o'clock, she meant ten precisely. From Bruce's look, he knew it, too. He bent and kissed her cheek.

"You're a good woman, Ruby." To my surprise, Ruby blushed. To me he said, "I'll be seein' about your car." Then he was gone.

"Maeve, you'll sleep in room number one." I didn't question her choice to identify her rooms by number rather than function. "Oliver can bunk with Lulabell."

I froze, panic blooming. "No. I'm sorry, it's just . . ." My voice trailed away. How to explain that I couldn't be parted from my bird? "He might get scared," I finally said.

"I don't want bird poop all over my bedroom."

"I have this Snuggle Hut, see." I held it up. "I can wrap him in it. He won't be roaming free. And he was just clipped."

Ruby relented. "Keep him in his tent. Follow me."

She lifted a candle, and I followed her outside and down a covered adobe walk. We stopped in front of a door with a brass numeral affixed. Room number one. Ruby opened the door.

"I trust you'll be comfortable. There are towels in the bathroom. I'll expect you for breakfast at eight thirty." She took my hand and gave it a squeeze. "Sleep well. Everything will sort itself out. Or we'll get it sorted."

I BOLTED upright in the sickening way you do when you've had a sudden, horrifying realization. My eyes leaped to the clock. I wilted in relief when I saw it was only eight and I hadn't missed meeting Ruby. I rubbed my temples and surveyed the room.

Coral adobe walls met ochre tiles, accented by sage-green window trim. White curtains flanked windows on both sides of the room. I pushed back thick, feather-filled covers and stepped out of bed. My dusty backpack was on an antique dressing table that matched a wardrobe and bedside table. Ruby must have brought it in. I retrieved a clean sweater and underwear. After some deliberation, I decided on my favorite parrot-adorned kneesocks. I hoped Ruby would like them.

Showered and dressed, I collected Oliver and left the room. My door opened onto a passage flanking a square courtyard garden. To my right, the corridor passed doors numbered to six. To my left was the door we'd exited last night. I went through it. Daylight revealed a beautifully decorated house with a Native American motif. Through an arched doorway on the left was a sunken living room, with more doors beyond. On the right I could see a comfortable social room with a number of small tables and a television. I turned into the kitchen, pulse accelerating out of nervousness.

Ruby Ransome was sitting at the long table, red reading glasses studded with rhinestones perched on her nose, perusing a paper. She didn't look up when she said, "There's coffee."

I helped myself to a cup from the carafe on the sideboard, loading it with milk, and listened absently to the low murmur of voices coming from the room opposite.

I sat across from Ruby, curious. Three minutes passed; then, with meticulous movements, she folded the paper and placed it aside. "Good morning." She assessed me. "Did you sleep well?"

"Yes, ma'am, thank you," I said.

"No more ma'am," she said.

"Sure," I said. There was a burst of laughter from the other room. "Is this a hotel?" I worried about paying her.

"More of a boarding house," she said. "Tell me your plans."

"I'm driving to California," I said. "Or I was. I'm going to Los Angeles. To start over." I mentally groaned. Why had I said that last bit?

"What are you starting over from?" Ruby pounced.

"I needed a change," was all I said. What else was there to say?

She nodded. "You're going to have some setbacks, I'm afraid. Unknown's mechanic, Barney, is out of town for a bit. You just missed him."

Could my luck have been worse? "A bit?"

"Yes. You never know with Barney and these trips. Sort of depends on his luck at the tables. Simon Bear will drive over from Sierra Vista with the tow truck and bring your car to PIGS in a few days, but Barney could be gone anywhere from a week to a month."

"PIGS?"

"Politically Incorrect Gas Station."

My mind raced. I had no idea how I was going to pay for the repair . . .

"I don't have the money to stay here," I confessed. "I just have my tent and enough gas money to get to California."

She regarded me some more. It was like she could see everything. "You seem healthy." I was, but I felt irrationally guilty and furtive, as if a remainder of every sick day was germinating within me.

"Yes." My answer was breathless. "I am."

"Then I see no reason why we can't work out an arrangement." She folded her hands, neat on the tabletop. "For some time I've been chafing at the demands of the boarding house, as I've wanted to spend more time on other pursuits. You can manage those requirements for me, in exchange for room and board. Number one is empty."

I was speechless. She was offering to let me stay in this oasis. I wondered if it was too much charity to accept.

"It isn't charity, mind you." Ruby read my thoughts. "You'll do what's needed when it's supposed to be done. I won't be paying you, so you'll have to discover other ways to earn the money you need to pay Barney. The schedule here is plenty flexible to allow for that, and I suspect you are a resourceful girl."

"What on earth makes you think I'm a resourceful girl when I'm broke and stranded in the middle of nowhere?"

"Unknown, Maeve. You're in Unknown. Nowhere is in Oklahoma," Ruby admonished. "A young lady who gets herself this close to California on a shoestring and boiled eggs in a 1970s relic while taking care of her bird is resourceful in my book. Not to mention walking twelve miles in the dark and managing to pitch a tent in the middle of the town square during a blackout."

I said the only thing there was to say. "I accept your offer, Ruby. Thanks. Um, how did you know about the eggs?"

"Your things are in the common room. We retrieved the keys from your rucksack, and Lawrence brought them by this morning. I took the liberty of discarding the last egg. It looked a little forlorn." She stood and eyed Oliver, who had been docilely sitting on my head the whole time. "Now follow me. I expect it's about time we introduced your young man to Lulabell."

I followed Ruby through the door to the left of the hearth into a large common room. A collection of tables was arrayed in front of double French doors opening onto the courtyard. Two women were having breakfast at one, the source of the chatter I'd heard earlier. In the corner was a kitchenette. A large rolltop desk hugged the far left wall, along with a sofa and armchair grouping centered around a television. Crowded bookshelves filled the space between.

Next to the door was a palatial birdcage. Inside was an inquisitive-looking pearl cockatiel. Oliver came to attention. I scooped him down to my hand as a precaution.

"This is Lulabell," Ruby pronounced. "She's very friendly. Normally she's free to wander, but since your man is human-bonded, I thought we'd see how they got on for a bit first."

Oliver's cage had been set adjacent on the cabinet. I slipped him inside, and we both stepped back to watch. Lulabell didn't move, affecting an uninterested air, though following Oliver's every move with her eyes. Oliver hopped from one perch to another in a constant cycle of movement, muttering to himself.

"Great hair," he finally squawked. "Are you thinner?"

Lulabell tilted her head.

"Pretty," Oliver tried again.

Lulabell was won over, and the two of them began madly chirping back and forth.

"There'll be no peace now," growled one of the ladies.

Ruby smiled. "Maeve, let me introduce you to the Cowbelles." We walked over to the two women who could have been a hundred and looked to have another hundred in them each. "April War Bonnet." Ruby gestured to a tiny Native American woman with long, still-dark hair and a brown face as wizened as a crab apple. "And Busy Parker." Busy's skin was powdery pale, every wrinkle emanating the essence of smiling, and framing snapping blue eyes. "This is Maeve. She's going to be staying for a while."

April considered me. Busy stood and embraced me.

"Welcome, welcome," Busy fluttered, all

bonnets and tea services. "Don't mind April. That's just her way. She's a total bitch."

I was surprised into a belt of laughter.

"Better that than a stranger-hugging nincompoop," April retorted in a gravelly voice. She shook my hand in a firm clasp.

"What's a Cowbelle?" I gave in to my curiosity.

"Back in the forties, a group of ranch women was organized to foster social interaction among women living on isolated ranches. They called themselves the Cowbelles. April and I are the last founding charter members of the Santa Cruz County Cowbelles," Busy explained. "We still have regular meetings."

"At eight o'clock here for breakfast, at noon over there for lunch, and at five on the sofa for sherry." Ruby's tone was dry.

"Bite your tongue, Ruby," April growled. "Sherry my foot. It's Scotch. And mind we don't run out. The bottle's light."

"That's Maeve's job now," Ruby said. "I'm about to show her the ropes."

And just like that, I became a boardinghouse manager.

Chapter Four
The Girl Who Could

MY JOB was to clean the common areas and Ruby's kitchen, do dishes, laundry, and keep the cupboards full of clean sheets and towels. Ruby provided breakfast supplies and household basics, so I was in charge of stocking those things. It was definitely a good deal, but I had to figure out how to make some cash to pay for the tow and repair of Elsie.

I scribbled "throat lozenges" on the grocery list, as my throat was sore and scratchy after my nocturnal adventures, and stepped outside. I promptly had a sneezing fit. I hoped I wasn't becoming one of those people allergic to sunshine. I followed Ruby's directions to the center of town. It wasn't far. Unknown consisted of a handful of streets, named after the colors of the rainbow. No stoplight. All of the commerce existed on Main Street and Red Road, which flanked the center square. It was an eclectic mix. There were several local artisan craft stores, the Guess Who's Coming to Diner, and two clothing stores. The Wagon

Wheel Saloon boasted that it was Unknown's original cowboy bar, serving cold beer and pool. The Velvet Elvis offered pizza, several doors down from a shuttered PIGS, sign proclaiming "Back in a few." Up Market was your only bet for groceries and sundries.

"So it's fancy stuff, then?" I'd asked Ruby.

"No, it's quite normal. It's owned by Patrick and Jenny Up."

I was heading in that direction when I was arrested by a store called The Little Read Book. The sign featured a grass-skirted Hawaiian dancer and Chairman Mao, both reading red tomes as they swayed to the hula. Unable to resist a bookstore, I pushed open the door. It was perfect. The hardwood floors creaked just right. There was a table for staff picks and favorites. Comfy chairs occupied sunny nooks, and café tables invited people to linger over coffee. The sound of grinding beans drew me to a small café within the store, where a beautiful woman worked an espresso machine. She was exotically unique, with almond eyes and long dark hair.

"Aloha!" A beatific smile accompanied her greeting. "What can I do for you?" Her wide smile made you want to know her.

"I'm Maeve," I said.

"Tuesday," she said, in response to my non-answer, smile widening.

I frowned. It was Thursday, I was pretty sure.

"Coffee in five days?" I asked.

She giggled as if I'd told the funniest joke in the world. "No, silly. Tuesday's my name. You're funny."

"I just got here," was my inane response.

"Cool." Her nod supported my decision. "I live on Purple Street. My car is the one with the bumper sticker saying 'I'd Rather Be Doing the Hula.'"

"Mine is the one sitting outside PIGS waiting for Barney to get back to town and fix it."

"Ah. A compulsory visit." Tuesday laughed.

"Kind of," I admitted. "That's why I came in. I'm looking for work."

"Oh, yay!" Tuesday beamed at me. "I need more time off."

My heart burst. I'd found a job. In a book-store! "I love your shop," I gushed.

"Yeah, it's good. But it isn't mine. I teach

hula and dance. I only help out when Noah's in a bind. Grouchy owner extraordinaire."

"Want to be my best friend?"

"Sure!" Her laugh was rich. "Where are you staying?"

"Ruby Ransome's boarding house."

"Tuesday!" A bellow interrupted us. "Tuesday!"

A man appeared from around a bookshelf. He was tall, very tall, maybe six foot four, with dark-brown hair and startling green eyes. And a frown. I'd never allow a furrow that depth on my forehead.

"Did you see where I put the receipts from the Decatur Book Festival?" As he spoke, he sighted me and did an unexplained double take before refocusing on Tuesday.

"Nope," she said with a wide smile. He looked perplexed.

"I swear I put them somewhere special."

"I'll bet you did!" Tuesday chirped. "Remember the Monkey Flower special orders? You put them on the top shelf of the cookbook section." She winked at me. "We found them two years later."

His forehead remained creased. "But I never lose things."

"Only when you put them in special places," Tuesday agreed. "You're the most organized person I know."

"Apparently not." He gave a rueful laugh, then turned distractedly to me, extending a hand. "Sorry. I'm Noah. Glad to have you here. Traveling in the area? Anything I can help you find?"

I took his hand. It was strong and knew how to shake properly. In fact, all of him was fit. Long and lean, with defined features. I'm a sucker for killer cheekbones, and Noah had them like razors.

"Maeve Connelly." I felt a little fluttery. "In town temporarily."

"Nice socks," he said. "I like socks with birds on them." I gripped the coffee-bar counter to keep upright. His attention returned to Tuesday. "Well, crap," he said. "So I've lost them."

"I'm very organized," I piped up. They both looked at me. "I keep great track of things." It was true. I might not always deal with my paperwork, but the stacks were meticulous.

"Maeve's looking for work," Tuesday said.

Noah's green eyes evaluated me. "Do you have bookstore experience?"

I hated answering. "No."

"And you're looking for a temp position?"

I wanted to lie, but it was true, so I nodded.

He shook his head. "I'm sorry. This is a bookstore, not a summer job fair. My staff has to be knowledgeable about books, and intend to stick around more than three weeks."

"I've spent legions of time in bookstores, as an avid customer."

"I'm sorry. People come here because we know literature. You look more like a . . . a . . . model, or something, than a book geek."

He was pissing me off. "You don't look like a creepy, evil child-toucher, but I'm reserving judgment."

"Don't take it the wrong way. I take matching people to books seriously." Pause. Frown. "And I'm not a child molester."

"Well, not a good one, at any rate," I snorted. "You don't have any kind of children's section to speak of." I pointed. "If you had a genius like me working here, I'd shift those shelves over and turn that corner into a kid-friendly section called the Little Read Picture Book, and offer Saturday story time."

"Noah." Tuesday's eyes widened at my suggestions. "She isn't Gina." I caught her eye, and she mouthed, "Tell you later."

"It wouldn't be responsible to hire an un-qualified person," Noah resisted. "I've hired walk-ins before. It doesn't work—even if they have charming braids and funky kneesocks. I'm being realistic."

"Try me. You're the customer; I work here. Ask me a literary question I can't answer. If I can answer five toughies, I get the job."

"What are you reading now?"

Easy. "*The Bean Trees*, Barbara Kingsolver. I'm being regional." *The Bean Trees* was set in Tucson.

"Who wrote *Dubliners*?"

I fought back my eye roll. This was almost insulting. "James Augustine Aloysius Joyce. Who also wrote *Ulysses, A Portrait of the Artist as a Young Man, Finnegans Wake,* and some mediocre poetry."

"Okay." Noah squinted. I knew it was going to get harder. "I like the classics. I've read most of them. I'm looking for something I haven't yet discovered. What do you recommend?"

I racked my brains. "*I Capture the Castle* by Dodie Smith or *Good Behaviour* by Molly Keane are excellent choices."

He shifted his feet. "I like thrillers but don't want garbage. What's an intelligent new release?"

"The new Jack Reacher novel by Lee Child," I said. I'd spied it on the bestseller shelf when I'd walked in.

"I'd like something for my son," Noah persisted. "He's thirteen."

I paused. I didn't want to give the obvious Harry Potter answer. I pondered a moment, then nailed it. *"The Boy Who Could Fly,"* I announced. "It's not that well known, but it's a wonderful book, where a boy who loses his father escapes into his imagination as a superhero while he struggles to take care of his mother and sibling."

"You are *so* hired." Tuesday burst out laughing.

Noah looked uncomfortable. And oddly distressed. They exchanged glances. She nodded.

Finally, "Fine." His tone was terse. "You can help out a few days a week. Come on Monday at ten. Tuesday, you'll train her."

"Sure." Tuesday's head bobbed.

Noah walked away, then paused. "But we don't recommend *The Boy Who Could Fly* around here," he said, before disappearing through a door at the back of the room.

I was confused, especially as Tuesday's giggles amplified.

"He wrote it," she said. "He wrote the whole series. He's N. E. Case." And my jaw hit the floor just like that.

I WAS bubbling over when I talked to Oliver as I tidied the breakfast area. "And I met the guy who wrote *The Boy Who Could Fly*, and *The Boy Who Could Walk Through Walls*, and *The Boy Who Could Stop Time*. All of them—he's my new boss! And I have a new best friend. Well, besides you. Her name is Tuesday. She's half Hawaiian, half Chinese."

After Noah had conceded to hiring me, Tuesday had explained his odd behavior. "You're blond and she was brunette, but, otherwise, the resemblance is strong. Gina wore long braids and had this great smile. The problem was that she was a *criminal*."

"What'd she do?" I marveled.

"She told Noah she wanted temp work to be near a grandmother who'd broken a hip, so of course he couldn't say no. He's a big old softy. After a few weeks, I went to Tucson at the same time Noah flew to New York for a meeting, and we left her in charge. When we got back, the register had been cleaned out."

"She was a con artist?" I was shocked.

"Totally. Noah was heartbroken. It wasn't the financial loss—he makes his money from his books. He was wounded to the core that a person could be so calculating and callous. Plus she pinched his favorite stuffed monkey." I didn't ask. Tuesday sighed. "He feels things too deeply. He hasn't hired anyone since."

A violent sneezing fit yanked me back to the present. I'd been sneezing quite a bit since arriving in Unknown, and my sore throat hadn't improved. With my luck it wasn't just a cold.

"Oh my God," I said to Oliver. "I have pneumonitis."

"Better go see Dr. Samuel Looking Horse," growled April War Bonnet. I jumped. She'd been silent, her diminutive frame completely concealed by the large armchair she occupied.

"What?"

"Dr. Looking Horse, over at the clinic on Blue Street. He'll put you right." April's eyes had a gleam, and I wondered if she was setting me up for trouble. I'd already endured a near heart attack over the dried llama fetus she'd left on my bed, a good-luck token from a Bolivian witch doctor.

"Is he a real doctor? Not like your witch-doctor friend." I hadn't been able to get rid of my "lucky charm" fast enough.

"Phffft. Native Americans can be real doctors, you know. Plus, he's the only doctor in town."

That sealed it. I was going.

"And when you go, steal the lobby magazines for me."

An hour later, I was sitting in a paper gown, my backpack stuffed with clinic magazines. I'd been delighted to find a cheery little health center, rather than a larger, impersonal hospital. I didn't like hospitals. Waiting for Dr. Samuel Looking Horse, I envisioned a kindly, wizened old Native American. That's not who walked in.

Dr. Looking Horse was in his early thirties, well over six feet tall, and chiseled like the dusky-skinned shirtless lothario sweeping up a feisty beauty on the cover of a book called something like *Savage Native Love*. In this case, he wore a white lab coat and his gleaming black hair was pulled into a ponytail. April's twinkle became understandable. I was ready for my exam.

"I have my charts." I handed him a sheaf of folders.

"You carry your charts around?"

"Mmm-hmmm." I was noncommittal.

His eyes met mine after he scanned the first file.

"I had a sneezing fit, and my lungs feel a little swollen."

"A sneezing fit?"

"It could be spores. I'm new to the area. Not adapted."

It took less than twenty minutes for Dr. Looking Horse to pronounce me perfectly healthy. "There's absolutely nothing wrong with you. I'll write you a prescription for a multivitamin if that will make you feel better about acclimating to our spores."

I squinted at him. "Uh, no thanks. I have loads."

"Ms. Connelly, there's no reason for a woman of your health to worry about such minor discomforts. It's very unlikely—"

"Are there things a newcomer to the area would need to be concerned about?" I persisted, this time with a new agenda. Why take home a prescription if you could take home the doctor? "Contaminants in the water, poison oak? Maybe you should give me a primer. Over dinner."

"I—"

The door opened, and a nurse with violent pink lipstick popped her head in. "Dr. Looking Horse? Liz Goldberg is here—it's an emergency. Tommy fell out of a tree and broke his arm."

"I'm sorry," he said to me. His regret looked genuine. "I must go." Then he smiled. "I imagine you'll survive any Unknown hazards just fine." And with that he was gone.

ON MONDAY morning, I bounced down Red Road to The Little Read Book, eager to embrace my new job. I'd already done my chores for Ruby and gone for my run. No one was in the shop when I entered, and all the lights were off.

"Hello," I called, walking to the register. A note on the counter read "IOU. I got that book. Ronnie Two Shoes."

"Hello?" I repeated. I flipped on the lights. I walked toward where Noah had disappeared on my first visit. I found him in his office, but hesitated in the doorway.

N. E. Case was playing with dolls. Specifically, he was sitting on the floor, swimming an action figure through a tub of water, muttering to himself. He looked up, confused, a thousand-mile stare.

"I'm Maeve," I reminded. "I'm starting work today?"

"Oh." He seemed torn between the toys and me.

"Nice dolls." I couldn't resist.

His expression became haughty. "They are *not* dolls. They are creative visualization devices. They help me when I'm blocked. Anyway, I need—"

"You need a shower, no more coffee, and some sleep." Tuesday bustled in and cut him off. Noah looked back at his tub.

"I'm close. I think. I mean . . ."

"I didn't see your car all weekend, which means you've been here and are probably sugar-deprived, which makes you cranky, which makes me cranky. It is therefore in my self-interest to feed you and send you home. Up, up, up." Her hands under his armpits were firm as she lifted him to his feet and propelled him out into the café. I trailed after them.

"I have to finish ten chapters of *The Boy Who Could Breathe Underwater* by Friday," he protested. "How does he get back? Does he—"

"Noah, you were playing with your toys, which means you're stumped. I'm making you breakfast, then sending you home."

He capitulated. "I could use some sleep. Will you be okay?"

"I'll be fine," she assured him. "I've got Maeve."

"Sorry." Noah looked at me, tugging a hand through his nest of hair. "Not much of a welcome. I've been working all weekend."

"When I have a hard time focusing, I find that picking the right socks can help." He looked dubious, so I rushed on. "I mean, organizing your thoughts to choose the right pair can put you in the proper mind-set." I hitched my jeans and showed him my favorite bookworm socks. "I wore these to start my new job."

"I appreciate the effort," he said. "Those are nice socks."

"Eat this." Tuesday dropped a plate of scrambled eggs and a sliced tomato in front of Noah. "Then go home. Maeve, let's get this place operational. Can you please fire up the register while I try to figure out which book Ronnie Two Shoes walked off with?"

I didn't see Noah until the next day. I showed up promptly at 9:45 a.m., key in my hot little hand. Tuesday had a performance in Tucson, so she wasn't coming in for two days. I'd gotten up early to run, eager to start work on time. I hoped I remembered everything she'd showed me.

"When Noah's on deadline, he doesn't do anything but write," Tuesday had explained to me. "And I mean anything—he can forget to eat, sleep, change clothes. Forget about helping you in the store. You'll probably want to bring him a sandwich around lunch. It might seem like the secretary fetching coffee, but, trust me, low blood sugar equals cranky equals not fun. It's in your best interest."

I was feeling confident. It was nothing I hadn't done in past jobs. Traffic was light. In the absence of customers, I busied myself dusting the front table. Then I busied myself changing it. No one was going to buy *War and Peace* unless they already intended to, no matter how prominently it was displayed. It was a waste of prime real estate. I replaced it with *Eat, Pray, Love* by Elizabeth Gilbert.

At 11:38 exactly, I could resist no longer. It was *almost* noon. I sidled into Noah's office. He was sitting at a large desk drumming his fingers. He looked less demented. And very attractive.

"Knock, knock, J. Alfred Prufrock," I called.

He looked up, surprised. "Oh, hello." Back to drumming.

"I was wondering if there's anything you don't like on your sandwich?"

"Hmmm?" Absently. "Oh, whatever." He didn't move.

I hesitated. "What's got you blocked?"

His office was tasteful wood and leather; only the numerous "creative visualization devices" belied the perfect image of a gentleman's study. A polar bear, a male action figure, and what looked like Nemo the fish lay on the desk. I bit my lip.

"I don't know how to balance underwater time and land time."

I pondered. "Maybe he can breathe both water and air, but to preserve his ability, he has to return to an aquatic environment at various intervals. It would add a race-against-the-clock element. And show his ingenuity— like the length of time he can spend on land can be prolonged if he goes somewhere with lots of humidity."

Noah's jaw dropped. He turned his back without a word and started typing madly into his laptop. I slipped out to fix the most delicious sandwich ever. When I slid it onto the desk, he didn't look up from his rapid key pounding. He was still doing it when I left for the day, locking him inside at six o'clock.

SHORTLY BEFORE closing the next day, I surveyed the new arrangement of shelves in the rear-left corner, wiping my brow. A voice in my ear made me jump out of my skin.

"The boy has universal consciousness of, and can communicate with, all sea life. How would it apply to animals that spend time on land *and* water, like sea lions and polar bears?"

I thought. He waited, stare intense.

"Can he push his telepathic powers to the higher land creatures by finding that element of their brain that dates to their ancestors' time in the ocean? Whether you believe in the Bible or Darwin or Native legends, at one point the earth was entirely covered in water and our genetic origin was aquatic."

"I like it. It's a good way to slip in some science as well." He turned toward the office. I was buoyant. He paused. "What do your socks look like today?" was his surprising question.

I tugged my jeans to show him the fish, sea horses, and aquatic creatures decorating my favorite undersea kneesocks.

"Interesting." He gave a thoughtful smile, then was gone.

I WAS brewing coffee when Tuesday came in the next morning.

"You're early! How'd it go yesterday?"

"It was divine." I glowed. Tuesday did a double take.

"I rearranged the Religion section," I covered. I didn't want to disappoint her yet by telling her that soon I'd be spending all my time huddled in the back office collaborating with Noah, inspiring kids everywhere. "How was the show?"

"It was good, but I wish I'd had someone take pictures. People kept asking me."

"I'm pretty handy with a camera," I offered. It was the one hobby I'd stuck with. I loved the permanence of pinning something as fleeting as an expression or a shadow to paper.

The bells on the door sounded before Tuesday could answer. Her expression plummeted. "Back in a sec." She disappeared.

I looked up to see a human Jersey barrier in front of me. The woman's short stature combined with her gray wool coat created the impression of a cement postbox. It also begged the question of why she was wearing a gray wool coat when it was seventy degrees.

She marched over to me. "Helen Rausch. I need a book on poisons."

"Oh. Okay. I'm Maeve." I blinked. "Do you want a history of poisons, an encyclopedia of poisons, an Agatha Christie novel . . ."

"I want to know how to cause death by poison."

Use your face, I thought. "Plants, then? Or pests?"

"Liz Goldberg."

Two blinks this time. "Um."

"Are you developmentally challenged? I. Want. To. Poison. Liz. Goldberg."

"Helen, how lovely you're looking today." Noah, at my side, was the epitome of gallant. "Now, I understand you're looking for a book." He placed a hand on her shoulder and guided her to the gardening section, head bent.

"Is she gone?" Tuesday hissed from where she was crouched below the counter. I nodded. "Sorry I had to dash, but Noah has strict orders that he handles Helen. What did she want?"

"To poison Liz Goldberg," I marveled.

I admired the way Noah rang up a Thai

cookbook for Helen only ten minutes later, and saw her out before returning to his office.

Tuesday snorted. "Those two have been feuding since a ranch-boundary dispute between their great-great-great-granddads. Oh!" She bounced back to me. "Can you really photograph my student recital on Thursday? If you do it, I'll treat you to dinner."

"Will do, cockatoo."

A tall blond woman entered the store, having just stepped from the Lacoste advertisement where she lived. I'd never seen a more perfect embodiment of pink-cheeked Midwestern beauty. The only thing keeping her out of the Colgate tooth-paste annex to her Izod home was the lack of smile.

"Hey, Beth," Tuesday greeted her.

"Is he here?" Beth dispensed with hello.

"Yeah, you know."

Beth rolled her eyes. Apparently she did know. She turned to me. "Hi, I'm Beth Watson, Noah's girlfriend."

I shot the coffeepot I was gripping out of its cradle, and hot liquid ran down the back of my hand. "Damn!" I jerked my burned appendage out of harm's way. "Sorry! I'm Maeve."

"Are you okay?" asked Beth.

"Sure, sure. It barely got me." My hand was throbbing.

"Listen." Beth turned to Tuesday. "Can you remind Noah that I'm going up to Tucson for work? I'll be back Friday. Oh, and remind him we have dinner with my brother and his wife on Saturday."

"I'll try!" Tuesday's cheerful reply sounded forced.

Beth turned back to me. "You should be more careful. I think there's aloe vera cream in the bathroom for that burn." And with that, Becky Thatcher's doppelgänger left to do whatever it was perfect blondes did in their spare time.

I didn't know why I was disappointed. Had I really thought I'd become writing partners with Noah and spend the rest of my life in Unknown, Arizona?

"I think Beth is right." Tuesday pulled me from my thoughts, with a sly grin. "You should do something about that hand." I looked at it. It was angry red and hurt like hell. "But I don't think aloe vera's gonna do it." She winked. "You'd better see a doctor."

"You know," I responded, "I think you may be right."

Chapter Five

Getting Incorporated

I LOOKED around the Velvet Elvis pizzeria. It didn't disappoint—in addition to velvet Elvises depicting every stage of his career, there was no shortage of poker-playing dogs.

"Early Elvis or late Elvis?" I asked my companion.

Samuel looked thoughtful. "Early Elvis." He flashed his white grin. "I'm a sucker for 'Hound Dog.' "

"Uh-oh," I said. "I'm late Elvis all the way. I love the idea of the comeback. And 'A Little Less Conversation.' "

"We'll have to see if we can overcome this seemingly insurmountable obstacle," Samuel said. His off-duty hair was down, a shiny curtain. I didn't think we'd have a problem.

"Thanks for fixing me up this afternoon." I waggled my bandaged hand.

"Yes, well, before you continue a course of self-injury, you should tell April that she's perfectly able to subscribe to magazines herself. I had to put out my medical journals after your last visit, and self-diagnostic hysteria skyrocketed. Everyone thought they had lupus."

I blushed. "You noticed."

"Don't worry. Happens every time Busy comes in for her heart medication." His smile was warm. It was hard to imagine him being angry with anyone.

Samuel was a charming and attentive companion. We ate pizza, and I was fascinated by his stories from the reservation.

"I'd love to see it sometime. I really like Arizona," I said. "It's the opposite of anything I've known. North Carolina is lush and verdant. Maybe that's why I find the barrenness of the desert so striking. When I get my car back"—a wistful pause for Elsie—"I'd like to photograph more of it."

"You like photography?"

"Yep. I'm covering a recital for Tuesday on Thursday."

"The Bitty Bees Touch Their Knees? I'll be there, too. Last year Celia Sweet danced right off the bandstand, so now we have a doctor on call just in case." He was thoughtful. "My grandmother turns ninety next week. What do you think about coming to the party and taking pictures?"

"I'd love to."

"No one cooks like my grandmother and her sisters. None of them ever left the res."

"Did you grow up on the reservation?"

"Yes and no. My family home was there, but I went to an off-reservation boarding school. I always wanted to be either a doctor or a vet. I didn't get into vet school, but someone slipped up at the University of New Mexico medical school, so doctor it was."

"Did you ever think of moving back?"

"Not really. Health care on the res is terribly underfunded. I struggled with a sense of obligation to go back, but I had to pay off my med-school loans. My compromise was a split—private practice here, and one day a week I provide nonemergency medical services at an Indian Health Services clinic on the res. Mostly I treat diabetes management. Long-time residents aren't made to process the high-concentrated-sugar foods introduced from the outside. Speaking of sweets," he asked, "would you like dessert?"

What was sweet was when he covered my hand as we shared a sundae. He kept the hand as we strolled back to Ruby's.

"Well, thanks for walking me home," I babbled when we got to her door, suddenly shy. "You really need to come back in the daylight and see the garden. And you can meet Oliver. Though it's—"

Samuel interrupted, leaning close. "Maeve. How about a little less conversation?"

"Hound dog," I whispered, before I shut up and did something else with my mouth.

"WELL?" demanded Tuesday when I danced into work.

"Dr. Samuel has *excellent* bedside manners."

"Ay-yi-yi! I'm so jealous. He is soooo hot."

"I know," I said smugly. "We're going to your recital together tonight and out to dinner tomorrow."

"You should treat yourself to a new pair of socks. Go remind Noah he has to write you a check tomorrow."

I found Noah leaning back in his chair, crossed ankles propped on his desk, bouncing a ball against the wall. "Howdy," I said.

He turned and broke into a wide smile. "Hello, little muse!"

I had to stop from shuffling my feet and saying "Aw, shucks" like a country bumpkin. "Tuesday says to remind you to pay me."

"I sent ten chapters to my editor, so I've rejoined the living," he announced with satisfaction. "I'll write your check now. Look." He hitched up his trouser legs to reveal bright blue socks covered in polar bears. My laughter satisfied him. He swung his legs to the ground and wrote the check. He stood, but when I reached for my salary, he held it beyond my grasp. "First you have to agree to put *Grapes of Wrath* back on the front table."

He'd noticed. I groaned. "It's so *depressing*."

"It's also the book-club selection this month. Promise."

"Fine," I grumbled. "But only for the month. Then I'm replacing it with *The Coroner's Lunch*."

"To higher learning." He held up his hand

for a high five. I jumped to slap his palm, and toppled into him.

"If you wanted to dance, you only had to ask," he teased as he caught me. He spun me in a twirl. I was astonished at his rock-solid frame, considering he typed for a living. He led me in a little waltz around the office. Then, arms pointing, we tangoed cheek-to-cheek out into the store, where he dipped me dramatically. "Are you fond of dancing?" He looked down at me dangling over his arm.

It never failed that when I was the object of one guy's attention, others came out of the woodwork. What I said was, "Where do you go dancing?"

"Bitty Bees Touch Their Knees." He righted me. "Tuesday's having a recital tonight."

"I'm already going. I'm taking pictures for Tuesday."

"Great! We can go together and get something to eat after."

"Um. Actually, I'm going with Samuel. Dr. Looking Horse."

His smile vanished. "Ah. That was fast work."

I started to get mad. "I'd invite you *and*

Beth to join us, but it doesn't sound like you and Samuel get along." My tone was sharp.

Noah turned away. "Samuel's a great guy. I like him. I'm not sure about Beth tonight." I was pretty sure he meant that literally. He didn't know where Beth was.

"She's in Tucson," I said. "For work. She said to remind you that you're having dinner with her brother Saturday."

"Oh, right. Well, here's your check. I'll see you at the community center later." With that he disappeared.

Samuel and I headed to the town square. The site of my aborted campout was a pleasant rectangle filled with trees, picnic benches, and lawn. At one end was the community center, and at the other was a bandstand decorated with fairy lights and a rainbow of paper rosettes, surrounded by rows of folding chairs.

The park was crowded. The whole town had turned out. News of my arrival preceded me, and I was surprised at people's eagerness to get acquainted, and their warm reception.

"It's the most tasty salad—basically green

beans and peas," Liz Goldberg said as she scribbled a recipe for me.

As Liz moved on, Jenny Up wandered over and struck up a "casual conversation" about the sanitary (read: unsanitary) nature of pet birds visiting grocery stores. It was almost a relief when Helen Rausch approached, with muttered invective that I'd best watch out before eating anything Liz Goldberg recommended because "that hussy is pure poison."

When the music cued, Samuel went to claim our seats. I lurked around the bandstand as unobtrusively as possible, snapping shot after shot. The show was an unintended work of comic genius, as Tuesday tried to shepherd the children of Unknown through various routines. It was like herding cats. Little Bloom Tarquin stomped on Frieda Watson's foot when Frieda stepped upstage of her. Frieda ran off in tears, Tuesday scurrying after her, as Bloom pirouetted prettily alone center stage. But it was little William Up who stole the show when his lederhosen came undone and the short pants fell to his ankles, revealing Spider-Man Underoos.

I burned through film, but I was nervous. It'd been a long time since anyone depended on me. I didn't want to let Tuesday down.

Even once Celia Sweet had danced (safely) offstage after the last number, I continued to shoot. Liz Goldberg with Tommy, arm in a sling, telling the story of his fall to Jenny Up, with elaborate hand gestures. Helen scowling at them. *Click. Click.* I loved the sound the shutter made as I stole this part of Unknown. The permanence of photography left me in awe. *Click.* Tuesday flushing with pleasure as she accepted accolades. *Click.* The setting sun highlighting the planes of Samuel's throat as he laughed. *Click.*

"Aloha? Where are my people?" I heard Tuesday demand. "Maeve, Samuel! Let's go eat!" She waved us over, and it was my turn to flush. I was her people.

Later, stuffed with chile rellenos, Samuel and I meandered back to Ruby's. Inside, I noticed that Oliver had taken up residence with Lulabell. They were snuggled up on her perch.

"Look," I whispered to Samuel. "They're in the same cage."

"What an excellent idea," he murmured.

And without another word, I took his hand and led him to number one.

"You need to see Child," April rumbled. We were contemplating the pile of film on the table.

"My goodness, you took a lot of photos," Busy fluttered.

I was worried about the cost of developing. "What child is that?" I asked absently.

"Child Sugar. He develops the pictures here. In the back of the print shop."

"The octagonal building?" I'd seen it on my runs.

"Yep. You'll like Child. He's a lovely man."

A picture-perfect model for cardigan sweaters looked up when I walked into the print shop an hour later. When he saw me, he smiled, white teeth brilliant against his ebony skin. "I'm guessing you're Maeve Connelly," boomed his rich bass.

"How did you know?" We'd never met.

"Ruby mentioned that a young lady wearing kneesocks might be by today, most likely with a barter scheme at the ready."

I laid the eleven rolls of film on the counter. We eyed them.

"Will Noah let you work for me on Mondays from four to eight o'clock in the evening? I'll instruct you in the operation of the machines. You may develop your own film after the paying customer orders are complete. You will be required only to compensate me for the cost of the paper if you rely on your own labor."

"Absolutely," I said, with no idea what Noah would think.

"Let us be civilized." Child gestured to two armchairs and I sat. He pressed a button on an electric kettle, and in less than a minute loose tea was steeping in an Aurora Royal Patrician bone-china teapot. Child settled in his chair. "Tell me about yourself, Maeve."

"Not much to tell, really. My car broke down, and I'm earning the money to fix her up. Are you originally from Unknown?"

"My family comes from Pittsburgh. I am sorry for your car misfortunes. Where is your family?" He poured the tea.

"North Carolina. How long have you lived here?"

"I moved to Unknown in 1988. Did you attend university in North Carolina?" Most people can be conversationally diverted with ease. Child was unshakable.

"Mmmm-hmmm. I bet Unknown hasn't changed much. Is it pretty much the same as when you arrived?"

"They offer an excellent book on the history of Unknown at the artisan shop on Red Road. What did you study?" It was like fencing.

"Oh, lots of things. How did you get into prints?" The walls were hung with beautifully framed antique maps, posters from something called the Monkey Flower Festival, and intricate line drawings.

"I studied art history. What did you do after college?" *Riposte.*

"This and that. I haven't really decided on a career." *Parry.*

"When did you complete your studies?" His gaze was level.

"December. When did you open the shop?"

"Ten years ago. So photography is a career interest for you?"

"Career? I don't know. I like taking pictures." I decided to give him something.

"Tell me what you like about it."

"Capturing people as they really are. My goodness, is that the time? I have to get to work." I didn't have to do any such thing.

After agreeing to meet on Monday, I fled. The encounter left me unsettled, a feeling that stayed long after I was sprinting between grassy meadows. I ran hard, but I couldn't run off the feeling that something was following me.

"THESE are incredible, Maeve! A million mahalos!"

We were looking at the photos from Tuesday's recital.

"This one of Bloom Tarquin is precious!" I'd caught her mid-pirouette, tongue at the corner of her lip in concentration.

Child had carefully tutored me in operating the sensitive developing machines. After mastering the machines, I'd cleared the backlog of customer orders and had turned to my own film. My pile of rolls had grown as I continued to take images of Unknown and its citizens.

"I can totally use these for promotional cards." Tuesday fanned out pictures of herself dancing, and hugged me.

"What are those?" Noah pointed to another folder.

"Oh." I shrugged, embarrassed. "Nothing."

I reached for it, but he was quicker, flipping it open and spreading the candid photos. Tuesday doing the hula behind the coffee bar when she thought no one was watching. Child snoozing in his armchair. April War Bonnet whispering dirty words to Lulabell.

"Maeve, these are amazing." Tuesday's voice was hushed.

Noah paused at one of himself. Beth was talking to him, but he wasn't listening; he was looking past her, directly at the camera. He looked at me again now. "You've captured the town well."

I liked that he used the word *capture*. I was grabbing moments. "You can keep things from disappearing," I said.

"But you're not in any of them. Where are the pictures of you and Tuesday gossiping when you should be working? Or you running down the back roads, braids flying?" He tapped a photo of Ruby, Sheriff Bruce, Samuel and Tuesday walking over to the Wagon

Wheel Saloon. "You should be in this."

"How can I take the picture if I'm in it, silly?"

He gave me a look. "That's exactly it. Why were you behind taking the picture and not walking with everyone else?"

"I was catching up."

"Or hanging back?"

"I'm a tourist here," I said breezily. "Strictly observer status."

"Don't remind me." Tuesday groaned. "It feels like you've always been here in Unknown. I hate the idea that you'll leave."

Anxious tickle. California waited.

Noah considered me, then said, "We'll display your pictures in the store. You can sell prints for Elsie."

"No one'll want to *buy* my pictures," I protested.

"I think you'll be surprised. How much for this one?" He tapped a shot of him and Beth walking, heads bent together.

"Five dollars unframed." I named a ridiculous price.

"Fine."

"Kill me for vanity, but I'll take these

two." Tuesday waved two pictures of herself dancing. I felt guilty for overcharging.

They both handed me money, and just like that, I was Maeve Incorporated.

Chapter Six

Snapping

IT WAS my bad luck that Jenny Up decided to buy new cookbooks as soon as the store opened the day I was late. Noah smiled pleasantly at Jenny as he rang up her purchases, but his right eyebrow was drawn down, so I knew he was steaming. He didn't return to his office when the door closed behind her. "You're late."

"I'm sorry." I was still breathless.

"How am I supposed to finish ten chapters if I'm tending customers while you loll in bed? God help us if someone needs a doctor."

I was offended. "I was not lolling! I was in the darkroom."

The previous Monday, Child had led me around to the back of the octagonal building to a small room painted black, counters covered in trays, machines, filters, and bottles. "This is my darkroom. How would you like to learn to develop negatives and print by hand?"

"I'd love to." I breathed in a chemical smell that wasn't offensive.

Clipped to a clothesline were eight-by-ten-inch black-and-white prints of pueblo life. They were flawless, capturing snapping eyes in a wrinkled face, a profile half in shadow, colorfully garbed dancers.

"Did you take these?"

"My wife." His voice was heavy with sadness.

I remembered that Child was a widower.

Loss makes you selfish enough to think you alone know what it feels like. You don't. Child reminded me what we shared. "My best friend died," I surprised myself by offering. "She loved to draw. The last picture she gave me means the world to me now."

Child gave a brief nod. I was relieved he didn't ask *how* Cameron had died. I hated recalling my last images of her, stretched gaunt by an illness that didn't understand the rule that the young don't die.

Time disappeared as Child taught me the

process. For a week, I spent every free moment in the darkroom, and the rest of the time in a semi-daze, smelling faintly of chemicals. I saw everything through the frame of the lens.

Which brought me back to my present predicament. I'd been *working*. I'd popped into the darkroom to drop off film, but the need to see my dawn photo shoot had been too great. Then, I couldn't leave until the negatives were done.

"I'm sorry, Noah. I really am." I wasn't. The man could ring his own register once in a while. I was doing work people *valued*.

"Stock hasn't been put out, sales reports never got generated last week, and you put peanuts in the salad instead of walnuts. We're lucky no one went into anaphylactic shock."

"You're not an infant, you know," I snapped. "You own the shop. The buck does not stop with your minimum-wage slave. It stops with you. Your shop, your buck." I was angry.

"Yes, and I'm the one *paying you* to work for me. This place is a wreck with your half-finished projects. We have shelves in disarray for some imaginary future children's nook. We have half a vegetarian menu. And now we have only half the bestsellers in stock!"

"And the store is half again as appealing as it used to be. I've worked hard." I shouted over the little voice that said he was right.

"Until you lost interest."

"My career has no value? I'm supposed to tiptoe around your creative brilliance and not do anything for myself?"

"Interacting with humans wouldn't be a bad idea. It beats running away from everyone or hiding in a darkroom."

"I am not *hiding*." My protest felt oddly like a lie.

"Right. You're so focused on your *career* that you don't replace sold prints? There aren't any left. My store is naked."

That stopped me. "We sold them all?" I hadn't noticed.

He was yelling now. "You aren't doing even the basics of your job. You've become unreliable."

My bravado left me. He couldn't see me as that girl. I wasn't careless Maeve. I was reliable Maeve. Talented Maeve. Desirable Maeve. New Maeve. I needed Noah to see that. "I . . ."

At my expression, he stopped, his own face becoming stricken. He plowed a hand through his hair and dropped into a chair.

"Damn, I'm sorry. I should not be taking my stress out on you." He rested his forehead in his hands. He looked exhausted.

"Have you eaten?" was the closest I could come to "Sorry."

"Forgetting my morning coffee is no excuse to be rude. I'm a grown man. It's not your job to fill my bottle."

"We could both use some." I set about making a pot.

"I like having you around the shop," he said as he watched me. "And you have good ideas." I felt awful.

"I *am* sorry." This time it was easier to use the word. "I like being here. I'm not sure why I got so obsessed with the photography."

"Who am I to talk? You've seen me work. A lot of being able to create is stepping out of your life into someone else's. I love it, but I'm no good at straddling two worlds. When I'm in the not-real one, it makes me dependent. You make it easy to count on you."

"You *should* count on me," I protested. "As long as this is my job, I should be doing what I'm paid for."

"Your photography is beautiful, Maeve. I don't want you to stop that."

Squelching my flush of pride, I poured two cups of coffee and pulled up a chair. "Been playing with your toys?"

He rose to my bait. "They are *not* toys. They're—"

"I know—'creative visualization devices.' What's the problem?"

He sighed. "I think it's wrong to have an environment where everyone coexists happily. That doesn't happen. My setting is full of joyful sea creatures. There needs to be threat within the society."

"Make an evil sea creature." The answer seemed logical.

"It's not that simple. I'm afraid to characterize anything as a bad element. You should see the angry letters I received from third graders when I painted warthogs in a negative light." He grinned.

I thought a minute. "How about jellyfish? No one likes jellyfish."

We talked until the lunch crowd arrived. I spent the afternoon catching up. I was shamed when I saw how much I'd let slide. I had to put limits on my darkroom time.

"STILL no Barney?" my sister Vi asked. "How long has it been?"

"I don't know. A little while."

"A little while? It's been over two months!" Vi exclaimed. "How can you not notice? You're stuck in the sticks!"

"There's a lot going on," I defended. "I'm training for the marathon, taking hula lessons, and Tuesday and I started a book club. And I spend lots of time in the darkroom." But still. Two months?

"The pictures you sent are amazing, Maeve."

"It's hard to take a bad photo here." I went for casual. "I've been getting lots of jobs. I've got my first wedding in two weeks."

"I'm impressed," Vi said. "How's Samuel?"

"He's like a male version of you—he watches what I eat, he slathers me with sunscreen, he makes sure I don't train every day, and he turns on a light when I read. He takes good care of me."

"I like to hear that!" She paused. "Why don't you stay?"

"Because I'm going to California," I insisted. "Stopping halfway would definitely qualify as flaky. I'm making the best of a bad situation."

"Really? It sounds to me like you're having the time of your life."

I was seething.

"I couldn't resist," Beth had exclaimed. "Aren't they great?"

They were four framed prints depicting pastel scenes of Victorian children playing on beaches. They were *not* great. They were tacky and ugly.

"They'll be *perfect* in the children's nook." Her narcissistic rant continued. She paused and gave me an assessing look. "It's just that, Maeve, well, with your taste . . ." Her gaze swept from my Converse low-tops to my "That's How I Roll" T-shirt. "You're what, Maeve? Thirty? Thirty-one?"

"Twenty-six," I ground out.

"Oh." Delicate brows arched. With a bemused shake of her head, she walked out, French manicure smoothing a blond tress.

I tried to conceal my fuming, but couldn't help thumping books down harder than necessary as I muttered.

"The Little Read Picture Book is *mine*." Thump, thump. "*I'm* the one who dragged those heavy shelves all over. Who does she think she is, foisting ugly-ass mass-produced art on me?" Thump. The cheap prints were a far cry from the classic children's book covers I'd planned to frame. Slam.

"Hey, easy on the furniture." Noah appeared behind me after I banged the cabinet. "What's up?" His eye fell on the pictures. "And what in God's name are those awful things?"

My mood lightened a tad. I told him.

"Oh no. No. Those things are not hanging in my store."

I blew out my fringe in relief. "I thought we could use children's book covers. You know, framing the books in shadow boxes."

He was distracted by the pictures. "Is that boy wearing a dress?"

"I thought maybe used copies with the original cover art. I've been finding them on the Internet." I reached under the counter and pulled out some vintage copies. "I have a stack of them."

"How long have you been doing this?" He lifted an old copy of the first volume of the Hardy Boys series almost reverently.

"A while."

"Why didn't you go down to the used-book store in Nogales?"

His question sparked my ire over another sensitive subject. I turned my back on him. Slam. Thump. "I. Can't. Go. To. Nogales. Because. You. Don't. Give. Me. The. Six. Days. Off. I'd. Need. To. Walk. There." I bit out my words. Since Vi's call, I'd been chafing at my utter inability to leave Unknown's confines.

"You've been here, what, two months? And you haven't been out of town? You must be going stir crazy. Let's go. Road trip."

"Don't forget the bird," I said automatically.

"What?"

"Never mind. We can't just go in the middle of the day," I protested.

"Despite the way you fan about the place, last I checked, I still own it. Which gives me the authority to close it."

I was already halfway to the door.

Ten minutes later we were heading south. Only half an hour later we pulled into the good-sized city of Nogales, on the border of Arizona and Mexico. It was bustling with traffic and humans.

"Lunch first, or bookstore?" Noah asked.

After the sleepy tempo of Unknown, I was a little overwhelmed by the activity. "Um . . ."

Noah read my face. "Lunch," he pronounced. "With beer. Let's go to Mexico. The taqueria awaits."

It felt like I could follow him anywhere.

"I HAVE enough to decorate the whole nook now," I gloated as I hugged my bag. "That place was the mother lode!"

"Aha." Noah laughed. "A convert!" It was true; he had practically had to drag me back across the border. I'd *loved* Nogales, Sonora. Stepping through the gate had literally been a portal to another world. My mind was aswirl with the chaos and color of the town. I'd run out of film. In addition to my books, I boasted a fabulous turquoise ring, a brightly woven belt for Tuesday, pottery bowls decorated with chilies for Ruby, a deliciously full stomach, and a slightly sunburned nose. I was having a perfect day. I didn't want to go home.

"I don't want to go home," Noah said. "I'm having too much fun." He slung a casual arm over my shoulders.

"What's in mind, partner in crime?" I masked my overdelight with a bland tone.

He looked around. "How about we get inked?" he said. For a moment I thought he'd said "naked," and my pulse shot into my mouth. Then I spied the tattoo parlor next door and felt like an idiot.

"Got any?" Noah asked playfully. He pulled on my jeans' belt loop and pretended to peek down my backside. "Anywhere interesting?"

"No." I giggled, swatting him. "I always wanted one." I was serious. "I still do."

"Why haven't you gotten one? Afraid of the needle?"

"I couldn't decide what to get. It's so permanent. What would I love enough to live with for the rest of my life? I'm not exactly

great with commitment." Noah knew enough
of my history. I changed the topic. "Thanks
for a great day."

"The pleasure was mine." His look made
it the truth. "If I thought I had to crowbar
you out of Mexico, that was nothing compared to the bookstore."

"Books are my friends. A bookstore is kind
of like a reunion for me."

His look was dubious.

"It's true! I had a hermit period. I
dropped out of college and didn't know
what to do with myself. Books were better
than people."

"I know what you mean." He became
serious. "For me it was writing. After my
dad died, things were tough. Mom worried
all the time. It was like she was eroding
before my eyes. I was sure she'd disappear.
So I took care of my kid sister and escaped
into stories about a boy who could do
everything."

"Weren't you a kid, too? Who took care of
you?"

"I took care of myself." I opened my
mouth, but he beat me. "So who were your
best friends? Of the bound-page variety? If

you were stranded on a desert island, which three would you take?"

I mused. *"Pride and Prejudice,* because it's the greatest romance ever written. *Catch-22,* because its satire gives you perspective on what's really crazy. And *A Bear Called Paddington,* because no matter how many times I read it, it makes me laugh every time."

Noah waited, but I was done talking about books. Instead, I launched into one of my favorite games. "Would you rather only drink water for the rest of your life, or never see the ocean again?"

"Would you rather . . ." lasted us through the drive home. I was deciding whether I wanted to eat only hamburgers for the rest of my life or live for ten fewer years when we pulled up to Ruby's.

"Really?" Noah demanded. "Ten fewer years?"

"Of course! I love food. Living forever is overrated. Why cling to life when you can't eat or enjoy yourself?" I thought of how hard Cameron fought to live when she couldn't do either, and got flustered. Fortunately, Noah was getting out of the car and didn't notice. I slid out of the truck and looked up at him. His head blocked the porch light, giving him a halo and obscuring his features. He leaned toward me.

"Maeve." Ruby's voice cut the tableau. Noah stepped back, and I turned, refusing to wonder what he'd intended. "I have good news. Barney has returned. He will look at your car tomorrow."

"Oh." The news didn't feel like I'd thought it would.

"I can see you're pleased," Ruby said. I squinted at her unreadable expression. "Noah, Beth was looking for you. Something about tickets to the ballet. Maeve, come along. It's high time we discussed the Monkey Flower Festival. October is nigh upon us."

"I'm off," Noah said with a casual wave. "See you tomorrow, Maeve."

"Right." I matched him. "Hey, Ruby, what's the Monkey Flower Festival? We're still in June, right? I didn't miss a month, did I?" I followed her into the house, shutting the door firmly behind me.

AT MY approach, the man extracted himself from under Elsie's hood.

"Hi! You must be Barney. I'm Maeve." I stuck out a hand.

He shook with a filthy paw. "Barney." He was a bear of a man, in denim overalls, with bushy red facial hair. "Quite a car you got here." He patted Elsie and explained the problem.

"How much?" I asked him.

"If'n I get that part, be around twenty-seven hundred. If'n I don't, you'd need a whole new engine. At that price, be better to get a new car."

"Can you get the part?"

"Miss Elsie here's no spring chicken, so those parts aren't just lying around like one-legged beggars." I winced. Politically Incorrect Gas Station was right. "It's gonna be hard to find, but if'n anyone can, it's Carla. She's my parts gal over at Tucson Auto. But you'll need cash up front. She won't order till it's paid for."

"If she finds it, how much time will I have?"

"You don't want me to guess. Way my luck's going, I'd bet wrong." He pulled a face.

Despite the magnitude of Barney's bad

news, the prospect of more time in Unknown was not as distressing as it should have been. Still, I cursed myself for the money I'd blown on children's books, pizza with Tuesday, and photo paper. I'd forgotten my agenda. What on earth was I doing on a committee for the town festival the same month as my marathon? I needed to get back on plan. With that thought, I hurried back to work.

I was surprised to find Ruby at the bookstore's café when I arrived. "I brought you some lunch," she said. Bruce waved from a table set for three with chicken salad, fruit, and iced tea. "I suspected you might have received bad news."

My shoulders slumped. "It's going to be a lot of money."

"Howdy, gal!" Bruce beamed as we joined him. "I hear you're going to chair the publicity committee for the Monkey Flower Festival."

"Oh. I . . . I . . ." The festival was four months away. The marathon was four months away. I visualized LA in October but couldn't conjure the sandy beaches as clearly as I used to. "Tell me more about the festival," I said.

"Wall, it's 'bout the biggest thing that happens in Unknown all year. There's a parade and booths sellin' food and art, a stage for singin' and performances, and fireworks at night. There's drinkin' and dancin', too. Someone always ends up in the tank."

"It commemorates the first bloom of a flower the Navajo have relied upon for many purposes," Ruby said.

"Actually, it's not just one flower. There are hundreds of monkey flower varieties," Noah chimed in from behind me. My pulse jumped. "Ruby, is that your famous chicken salad? Who's sick?"

"No one's sick. I thought perhaps Maeve could use some cheering up after seeing Barney this morning."

"How did it go?" Noah pulled his chair close to mine.

"It's going to cost a ton, and it may take ages to find the parts."

"Bummer," Noah said cheerfully. "You know, the festival would be a great time to inaugurate The Little Read Picture Book."

"I could teach the hula!" Tuesday swooped in. "Ruby, is that your famous chicken salad? What's the occasion?"

"Maeve's stuck here," Noah announced. "The car repair will take forever and cost a ton!" He made it sound like I'd won the lottery.

"Yay!" Tuesday pulled up a chair. "I always do a performance at the festival. This year the Cowbelles want me to teach them to do something as well."

"I'll get some great pictures!" I said.

I couldn't remember when I'd been happier.

Chapter Seven
The L Word

THE sun slanted through the front window, highlighting the planes of Noah's face and the bulge of his forearm muscles below rolled-up sleeves. Forearms that were crossed in anger as he glared at me.

"Maeve, The Little Read Book is not that kind of store. We are a *book*store. My goal is not to make my customers dumber."

"That's the *Economist*." I pointed at the brand-new magazine rack at the front of the store, the cause of Noah's ire. "It makes you smarter."

"This is *Us Weekly*." He shook it at me. "I'm less intelligent just for holding it. I can't believe you did this behind my back. I take one day off, and this is what happens. We are a *book*store, not a newsstand. We do *not* sell magazines!"

"You've actually been selling them like crazy," Tuesday interrupted mildly from where she was arranging the staff picks.

We both stopped and looked at her.

"In one day, Barney bought *Popular Mechanics* and *Sports Illustrated*, Ruby bought *Traveler*, and Bruce bought *Cooking Light*. April War Bonnet picked up copies of *Oprah*, *Newsweek*, *Glamour*, *Cosmo*, *Self*, *Ebony*, *GQ*, *Road and Track*, *Men's Health*, and *Forbes*. She requested that next week you get in *Garden and Gun*."

We continued to stare. She shrugged.

"I didn't ask. In contrast, you only sold one book yesterday. Liz Goldberg bought the latest R. L. Stine *Goosebumps* for Tommy."

Noah's brow wrinkled. "We don't carry *Goosebumps*. Kids Tommy's age should be reading R. L. Stevenson, not R. L. Stine."

I looked away guiltily, to see Samuel coming through the door, and I welcomed the distraction. "Samuel!" I smiled and waved. He gave me a harried look as he came over.

"And what is this emergency that requires me to leave the clinic and run over here while actually sick patients are waiting for me?" Underneath his skeptical look was concern that something might truly be wrong.

I remembered the rash I'd discovered that morning. "Oh, see, look." I worriedly lifted my shirt and showed him the outbreak along my abdomen. He stared in disbelief. I started to feel foolish. "Um, it could be Omenn syndrome or Rickettsialpox . . ." My voice trailed off. Noah and Tuesday busied themselves stacking books and pretending not to eavesdrop.

"Maeve." Samuel looked at me kindly. "You don't have Omenn's. And I doubt you've been bitten by mice mites." That was how you got Rickettsialpox.

"Well, I'm not a doctor," I snapped. "How would I know? With my bad luck, if there was just one mite in the whole state of Arizona, it would be me that got bitten!"

"Maeve." He looked deep into my eyes. "It's not bad luck. And it's not the leukemia.

You're in remission. You're healthy now."

I felt like I'd been punched. I couldn't breathe. My eyes filled, and I couldn't see either. Tuesday gasped; then silence hit the room like a bomb. I stared at the blurry outline of Samuel, aghast. How could he? He'd said the L word out loud. No one did that around me. It was forbidden.

"What the hell?" said Noah. "Maeve?"

I blinked hard. The room spun. I felt Noah staring, mouth hanging open, while Tuesday gnawed at her lip. I felt dizzy and hot. The room was pressing in. The white coat was walking down the corridor toward me. Cameron was in a box. I was . . . I was . . .

"Maeve," Samuel beseeched. I shook my head and backed away. He reached for me, but I turned and dashed out the door. I broke into a run. I ran as if my life depended on it, past the post office, past the market, and up the hill. I ran and ran even after my side was stabbing with pain. Now that the word had been spoken, it permeated the air and I might breathe it in. It could catch me unless I stayed ahead of it. I kept running, until a stone caused me to roll my ankle and took me down hard. I lay gasping, face pressed into the warm grass at the side of the road, and my gasps turned to sobs.

I'd pretended to leave it behind. It was part of Charlotte. It was part of the past. But it wasn't. Leukemia was part of me, and it was constantly lurking, waiting for me to let my guard down.

STRONG hands on my shoulders brought me back. Samuel rolled me over and eased me up against his solid shoulder, brushing the tangled hair from my face. "It's going to be okay, Maeve." He placed a soft kiss on my forehead, then slid his arms under my knees and shoulders, carrying me to where Noah was waiting in his truck. I could only sniffle. I didn't even care that I looked a wreck. Now that everyone knew I was rotten on the inside, what did it matter what I looked like?

Samuel settled me onto his lap in the front seat. Noah started the truck and turned around on the dirt road, pausing once to encircle my ankle for a squeeze so brief and private I might have imagined it. Then he put the truck into drive and took us home.

RUBY WAS WAITING AT the door and led us to my room with her precise steps. I buried my face in Samuel's neck, ignoring everyone. He started to speak, but Ruby gave a shake of her head. He nodded, and after laying me down, gave me another gentle kiss and left the room. Noah followed Samuel. When we were alone, Ruby gently washed my face with a cold, wet washcloth.

"You'll sleep now." Her voice didn't invite contradiction. She pulled the shades on the afternoon sun, then faced me in the gloom. "A closet isn't scary in the daytime, Maeve. It holds clothes, not monsters. Whatever is scaring you, bring it into the light. Its strength will fade."

I figured Ruby wasn't talking about cancer itself being my monster in the closet, but its memory. It was a nice idea, but almost three years later, I still looked over my shoulder, fearful. Ruby pressed her palm gently on my forehead and held my eyes with hers. As if she'd drawn something out of me, I relaxed, lashes fluttering down, and sighed. Perhaps I could sleep, just for a bit.

When I woke, it was full dark. For a moment I was confused. Then memory flooded back. A part of me was relieved. It'd been getting harder and harder to hide my secrets.

At home, people knew I'd been sick, but by my dictate, no one talked about it. We pretended everyone took nine million vitamins. We pretended that eight years of college was average.

In Unknown, no one knew better. I'd refused to spoil their untainted image of me with the truth. I couldn't bear the pity creeping back into my life. But it had begun to chafe. How could I make new friends if I couldn't trust them enough to be myself? Samuel was like heaven. I'd cut him short when he'd tried to discuss my medical history, but he knew everything all the same. Maybe because he was a doctor, or maybe just because he was Samuel, he'd been perfect. Samuel made me feel human again.

"Cancer" is a word like "rape." Being told you have cancer alters everything. I used to think my body and I were partners, together against the world. We acted in sync. We were a team. With that word, our relationship broke. Who was this body, full of cells out to destroy me? We became two separate things, me and my body. I always worried what it was doing behind my back.

In the dim light, I saw that Ruby had laid clean jeans, a T-shirt, and my favorite Rainbow Brite striped kneesocks on the chair by the bed. I pushed back the bedcovers and sat up. My secret was out now, so no help for it but to face them. And maybe . . . I looked at the socks. Well, just maybe. I smiled as I pulled them on.

TUESDAY was sitting with Ruby at the kitchen table, talking over mugs of tea. I tensed walking in, but for once, the conversation didn't stop, replaced by guilty looks and fake, overbroad smiles, when I entered the room. Instead, Tuesday said, "Hey there, Sleeping Beauty. I brought over Season Three of *Bones.*" I remembered it was our night and felt guilty for assuming she was there to cluck over me. "I'll cook 'cause you've had a rough day," she continued matter-of-factly. "Do you want cereal, salad in a bag, or frozen pizza?" I laughed at my choices.

"Don't you want to hear about the cancer

first?" I surprised myself by saying. No one gasped; no glasses shattered.

"If you want," said Tuesday. "There's time." Her response astonished me more than my offer. There's time, so nonchalantly. The presumption that you could get to something later was novel. I turned it over in my mind. Could you be happy doing half a trail because you could go back and do the rest another time? The idea was like a green shoot poking through the dirt. The kettle whistled, and Ruby prepared more tea.

"You're good now?" Tuesday met my eyes straight on. It was alarming but pleasing.

"I am—about two and a half years."

Tuesday nodded. "That's excellent."

I stuck to the facts. "I was diagnosed with acute lymphocytic leukemia in the spring semester of my freshman year of college. I had chemo and radiation treatment for two years. I dropped out of school and moved home. I was pretty sick most of the time." I'd never spoken about it to someone who didn't already know.

"Did you lose your hair?"

"Every strand. But the treatment worked. After two years, I was in remission. My hair grew back; I returned to school. I was fine for a while." No point in being suspenseful about the hard part. "I relapsed a year and a half later."

"That must have been hard," Tuesday said.

"Mmm-hmm." I avoided eye contact. "It was tough for my family. I dreaded telling them more than I dreaded being sick again. I couldn't bear the fear returning to my father's eyes."

"Is it different when you relapse?" Tuesday asked.

"The second time, we caught it early. The treatment was nowhere near as bad. They'd made a lot of advances, and I needed a much less severe regimen."

We were quiet for a moment. Then Tuesday said, "Well, from now on I'll remember not to tug your braids so hard in case they fall off. So, what do you want to eat?" And I snorted tea out of my nose, I was laughing so hard.

WHEN Samuel came over later, we didn't talk.

"I'm sorry," he whispered as he settled me against him in bed.

"I'm sorry, too," I said, "for putting you in that position for so long. And I promise we can talk about it. But not now, okay?" I was worn out. I felt rather than saw him nod. He held me close, stroking my hair until I fell asleep.

Chapter Eight

The Girl Who Could, Part II

WHEN the knock came, I turned off the safelight and admitted Child to the darkroom.

"I thought I might find you here," Child said. No surprise there. For days I hadn't been anywhere else.

"I gave myself the week off work," I said.

Child examined the hanging prints. "Nice work."

"I'm not in any of them," I said. It wasn't self-pity; it was more like a question. I remembered Noah's earlier comment. How could I be expected to be in the picture if I was taking it? Was it strange to love being behind the camera?

Child didn't answer right away. "I think

you're in all of them," he said finally. "Your eye, your world, how you see things. Anyone looking at these is closer to you than to the subjects." He tapped a picture of Samuel sitting alone, eyes closed, meditating. "This is how you look at someone with affection." Then he tapped a picture of Bruce with Ruby. "This is how you look at someone with love."

I frowned.

"And this." He chuckled. "Well, don't let Beth see this."

"What do you mean?" It was just a picture of Beth sitting in the Wagon Wheel, looking like . . . Beth.

"Trust me." Again the chuckle. "I was thinking you could assist me in developing some prints. It's just one roll."

"Sure."

He turned out the lights. I heard him pop the film canister open.

"The night my wife died wasn't special." Child's disembodied voice prompted a jolt of adrenaline. "I'd cooked a pot roast. Janie did most of the cooking, but I chipped in where I could."

"Her name was Janie?"

"Janie Sugar, sweet as candy. I ate my dinner and put the rest away. I figured she'd got caught up in Tucson and could reheat something when she got home. I was watching *Prime Suspect* when the state trooper arrived. She loved that show."

"What happened?"

"She hit a deer. They gave me a box of her things. She never went anywhere without her camera. The lens was shattered in the crash, but the film was safe."

"What was on it?"

"We're about to find out."

I took in a breath. "Child, when did Janie die?"

"Six years ago. I was afraid to know the last thing she saw. What if she'd spent her last day immersed in disappointment or injustice? I wasn't ready for her final impressions of the world."

"Why now?"

"For six years no one's used this room. You unfroze things, Maeve. Watching you work images reminded me that no matter what's on this film, Janie loved her craft."

We were quiet. "No one talked to you about it?" I asked.

"Some of the widows tried, but I wasn't interested."

"When I had leukemia, I met this girl, Cameron. We were on the same treatment schedule. We became best friends. It was stupendous to have someone who understood. But then she got sicker, and I felt guilty because treatments working for me were failing her. My 'treatment twin' faded and died in front of me. After that, I put space between myself and other patients."

"Seems to me you keep the healthy world at arm's length as well."

"Once you tell people, they change toward you. My cousin told me I was unfairly lucky, because she'd been dieting for years and I lost tons of weight just like that. She said I looked like I'd been in a famine like it was a good thing. I told her she looked like she'd caused one. There should be a Miss Manners for cancer."

Child chuckled. "They need Miss Manners for loss, too. I had a fellow tell me I was lucky to be able to date again, that he was stuck with his old lady for the rest of his life. I remember thinking I'd trade half of my remaining days to have Janie back, and the other half to shove the guy into a sack and stow him on a plane to Uzbekistan."

"I detest the hijackers who turn your diagnosis into their drama. One aunt was so overcome with my news that she had an asthma attack and had to be rushed to the emergency room."

"I recall a widow who wanted to hold hands and weep together over our loss. I wanted to stuff her in a sack bound for Uzbekistan, too."

Janie's pictures were beautiful. She'd stumbled on a community picnic. Her camera caught women sharing mangos covered in hot sauce, children chasing one another, men squinting through cigar smoke. Each one drew you into Janie's eye, and I understood what Child had meant earlier when he said he could see me in my photos.

Child interrupted my thoughts. "You're not responsible for other people's happiness, Maeve, just as I wasn't responsible for Janie's last day. Let yourself believe that. Figure out what makes you tick. Don't wait as long as I have."

"I'm trying, I guess. It's like a split path. I used to love chasing a curved trail, and now

I'm stuck at a fork. My *It'll never happen to me* is gone forever. I can't go back, but I'm unsure how to go forward."

"All I can assure you is that nothing will happen if you spend your time alone in a darkroom. The sun is shining, Maeve. Let's go outside and share some lemonade. I love cold lemonade."

"If you'll let me give you something," I said. The second kachina was an organic twining of leaves, like new shoots rising around the hummingbird with its strong heart. Healing.

"It seems a fair bargain."

And so we did. "Child," I asked as we stepped into the light, "why do you dislike Uzbekistan so much?"

WHEN I got home, there was a large envelope with my name on it on the floor. I settled onto the bed to open it.

I extracted a slim volume, heavy pages bound between beautiful handmade covers. I turned it over gently. It was a children's picture book, each page framing its words in beautiful watercolor drawings filled with a boy, a girl, a bird, and lots of tall trees. It was inscribed to me. I began to read.

The Girl Who Could
for M.

Once upon a time, there lived a Boy and a Girl. They were about that age where they were curious and just starting to understand things—a little older than you and a little younger than me.

The best way to see curious things was to climb very high. The Girl was an excellent tree-climber. The trees were very tall. The Girl wore kneesocks to protect herself.

The Boy did not like to climb. He was afraid of heights. He would stay at the bottom and write down what the Girl saw. He had excellent penmanship.

One day the branch the Girl was sitting on broke. It wasn't her fault, but she fell a long way. Even though she was wearing kneesocks, she got a bad cut on her knee.

The Girl went to the best doctor, and she gave her a special bandage. Time went by, but she refused to take off the bandage.

"Does it hurt?" asked her mother.

"No," said the Girl.

"Are you bleeding?" asked her father.

"No," said the Girl.

"Why won't you take the bandage off?" they asked.

"I'm afraid," said the Girl. "The bandage stays."

The Girl decided to go where there were no trees. She walked a long way and came to a fence. On the other side was a vast open space with no trees. She went through the gate and walked to the middle. It was a very large space indeed.

"How large do you think this space is?" the Girl asked. No one answered her because she was alone. The Girl thought about writing it down, but she had forgotten a pencil. It didn't matter. No one could read her handwriting anyway.

The Girl sat down. "I'll be safe here." She sat for a long time. Nothing happened. There wasn't much to look at.

The Girl decided to go home. It wasn't any fun with no one to talk to. When she got to the fence, the gate was locked.

The Girl sat down. The moon kept

her company all night, even when the lights went out in the town.

In the morning, the Boy walked up to the gate. "What are you doing?" he asked.

"I'm stuck on this side of the gate," she answered.

"Why don't you climb over?" he asked.

"I can't," she said. "I might get hurt."

The Boy went away.

The next day the Boy came back. "I brought you some kneesocks," he said.

"I wore my kneesocks and I still got hurt," she said.

"These are special kneesocks," he said.

She took the socks. She was getting lonely and tired of the vast open space with no trees. She put on the right sock. It fit perfectly. She put on the left sock. It wouldn't fit over her bandage no matter how hard she tugged.

"Take off the bandage," said the Boy.

The Girl wanted to wear the kneesocks. She liked curious things better than vast open spaces. She took off the bandage.

They both looked at her knee. There was nothing there. Not even when they looked really close.

"I guess you can climb over now," said the Boy.

"I guess so," said the Girl.

And she did.

The next day, the Girl woke the Boy up early. They found a very tall tree.

"What do you see?" called the Boy. "Have you made a discovery?" There was no answer. "How can I know what's there if you don't tell me?" shouted the Boy.

Something floated down from the tree. It was a kneesock. A second one followed the first.

The Boy paced back and forth. Then he sat. Then he paced some more. There wasn't much to look at down there.

Maybe I'll just try the socks on, the Boy thought.

And just like that, the Boy and the Girl were sitting side by side on the highest branch, admiring the view.

NOAH LOOKED surprised when I walked into The Little Read Book. I was suddenly shy. "Hi," I said.

"Hi," he said. "That color looks pretty on you." I was wearing a ruffled lilac top with a deep-V neckline.

"Thanks. I love my book."

"I'm glad." He walked to a table and held out a chair. I sat. He sat. Without a word, he reached out and grasped my hand, hard. "You could have told me."

A minute passed. I fidgeted. He looked awkward. "A lot of having cancer"—I forced out the word—"is worrying about the people around you. There's an overwhelming need to take care of the recipient of your bad news. It's exhausting."

He nodded, holding my eyes.

The door tinkled, and I realized we were still holding hands. Embarrassed, I withdrew. Beth's arrival made me more flustered.

"Oh. Hello, Maeve! How. Are. You. Doing?" She spoke slowly and overenunciated. Did she think my illness had rendered me deaf and slow? Noah's frown matched mine.

"Fine." I stood. "Getting back to work. Things have piled up."

"I just came by to drop these off, honey. You left them on the counter." She handed Noah his sunglasses. "Gotta run." She bolted from the store.

I frowned. Noah mistook the cause.

"You're not going back to work. Let's get out of here," he commanded.

"Nogales?" I perked up.

"Wagon Wheel. I'm buying you a beer." He strode to the front, flipping the sign to CLOSED as he held the door for me. Twenty minutes later, we were the only patrons at the bar at one in the afternoon on a weekday. Imagine that.

"You from around here?" I teased, with the hackneyed pickup line.

"I grew up on the Gulf Coast of Florida."

"Really?" Noah didn't strike me as a beach-volleyball type.

"Yep. It was the winter training ground for the Ringling Brothers Circus. Every kid in the neighborhood spent every waking minute watching the clowns practice."

I was fascinated. "Were they creepy? Do they wear makeup when they practice? How do they all fit in that little car? Can you juggle?"

He held up his hands in surrender. "I can't tell you the tricks of the trade." He winked. "But I *can* juggle."

"Show me."

"Hey, Vic, throw me a couple of limes," Noah called. The bartender complied, and Noah expertly tossed the fruit.

I applauded. "All I can juggle is credit-card debt."

"You're falling behind." Noah indicated the full pint stacked up behind my half-finished one. I drained my glass and clutched the full one.

"Don't hug the glass!" Noah chided. "It's the first sign of alcoholism."

"I have a reputation for abuse." I laughed. "Half my college dorm thought I was on drugs. I was pale, not eating, losing weight, skipping class, and sleeping all the time."

"You stayed in school when you were sick?"

"Not long. I moved back in with my parents. They put everything on hold to take care of me, and I acted like a petulant teenager."

He squinted at me. "I'm trying to imagine you telling your dad to mind his own beeswax."

"Oh, I can tell you to mind your own bees-wax with the best, buster. I've perfected fifty inflections of sneer in English *and* Spanish." I did my best impression of a snotty teen-ager. " 'Where are you going?' 'Out.' 'Out where?' 'Out*side*.' "

"Scarily accurate."

"That's probably why the hospital sent me home."

He signaled the bartender. "Vic! Two more." I closed my eyes to check if my head was spinning. Not bad. Only mild spin.

Vic delivered our beers. And two shots. "Upgrade," he said.

I was dubious.

Noah tossed back his shot. "Chicken?"

Not a chance. "Prost!" I downed mine and slammed the glass upside down. My en-thusiastic gesture tipped me off the stool and onto Noah, pinning his beer between us. "Don't hug the glass," I sputtered.

"I'm too busy hugging you." He didn't hurry to put me aright. I didn't rush to pull myself off. When I did, our eyes caught.

Confused, I shoved my face in my beer. "How come you left Florida?"

He looked away. "My dad died in a plane

crash. His Cessna went down in the Florida Gulf during a storm. They never found a body. After that, I detested the sight of the ocean. As soon as my sister started college, I moved to the desert."

"How old were you when your dad died?"

"Eleven."

"Your first book was about a boy who could fly."

"My sister Lily was only eight when Dad died. Mom was working all the time, and Lily started getting in trouble. I made up stories to keep her in line. She wouldn't get to hear the next chapter if she didn't behave. I wrote about a boy who could fly, because I wanted her to know that just because something bad happened to Dad didn't mean that it would happen to everyone. It was rotten luck."

"Now you're writing about a boy who can survive underwater."

He shrugged. "Just because I occasionally escape into stories doesn't mean I don't try to tackle my demons."

"Just because I run doesn't mean I always run away," I offered. We smiled at each other. "Where is your sister now?"

"If you can believe it, Lily flies mail planes in Alaska. She's the one who sent *The Boy Who Could Fly* to an agent. It never occurred to me."

"I think it's great that you do what you love."

"What about you? What do you want?" Noah's smile was naughty.

"All I want is a warm bed, a kind word, and unlimited power."

"It's good to have goals."

"It's good to have beers!" I toasted.

"How're you guys doin'?" Vic called.

"No more." I shook my head. "I'm done. I'm Drunky Drunk, the mayor of Drunkville."

"We are in violent agreement." Noah nodded. He tossed Vic a credit card and waved off my effort to contribute. "The boss can pay for the company meeting."

We tumbled out of the Wagon Wheel into bright sunshine. We lingered, looking at each other. Noah had just opened his mouth when I ripped a loud hiccup. I fell apart into giggles.

"Good night, good night! Parting is such sweet sorrow," Noah said with a grin. "Now get thee to a nunnery."

412   Kerry Reichs

"To sleep, perchance to eat ice cream," I responded as I turned away. I carried his smile with me as I staggered home. I needed a serious nap to sleep it off before my date with Samuel.

"READY?" Samuel asked several hours later. Tonight's outing to an open-air movie was my first public appearance post-Cancergate. I didn't feel anxious, though. I felt floaty and happy.

"Yeppers." I giggled. He gave me an odd look. I wiped off my smile. Proper ladies didn't go boozing in the middle of the day. I concentrated on walking a straight line to the door. Thank God I'd managed a nap and a shower.

The square was a checkerboard of blankets on which picnics were being consumed. We saw Tuesday waving and headed in her direction. We weaved our way through the patchwork of quilts.

"Oh, Samuel," Liz called. "Tommy got into the poison oak. I was wondering . . ."

Samuel was already extracting a bag from his pocket. "Ruby mentioned it," he said. "I brought some samples. If this doesn't work, come see me." She accepted the package gratefully.

"And Maeve, thanks so much for agreeing to babysit next week." Liz looked so appreciative, I hid my wince. Minding Tommy was like caring for ten Ritalin-deprived demons.

"No problem," I lied.

"I imagine watching him will make cancer seem like a walk in the park." I started, then appreciated the casual acknowledgment.

"Don't be so sure," I joked.

We moved on.

"It's polite to arrive no later than six so that you don't trample over more considerate people's blankets," Helen Rausch sniped as we passed.

"But then you would have trampled on ours," was my logical retort. My tongue had a mind of its own.

"Don't think that just because you were sick you get special treatment, missy. You don't."

Samuel hustled me on. We were almost at our destination when we reached a seamless row of blankets. There was no way across without stepping on one. The dirtiest one, next to April and Busy's blanket, was unoccupied. I gingerly hopped toward the middle to vault to the other side, when I tumbled into a heap.

April doubled over in fits. Busy's breathy giggles accompanied her. Samuel reached down and helped me stand. I'd stepped into a hole, covered by the blanket.

"Haw, haw, haw." April's deep honk sounded over and over as she delighted in the success of her trap.

"Sleep with one eye open," I managed through gritted teeth.

We reached Tuesday's blanket as April reassembled her joke.

"Yay!" Tuesday smiled and wiggled when we arrived. "I got here super early so I could get all our blankets together. It's perfect!"

"Mahalo," I said, ready to sit. I was starting to feel a headache coming on, and I was famished. "Ruby, is that your chicken salad?"

She passed me a plate while Samuel poured us wine. I was scouting a place to dump some of my wine discreetly when April's guffaw sounded again, accompanied by an enraged shriek. We looked over to see Beth, hair askew, panties flashing, taking an unexpected tumble. Noah and Bruce skirted the trap and reached to help.

"Damn it, April," Beth screeched. "I could have been seriously injured." She turned on Noah. "Noah, *do something*."

"Like what? You want me to fight April?"

"No! Yes! Aaargh! You are so passive! It's like dating Gandhi!" She grabbed Noah's arm and hauled herself upright. "Drunk-in-the-middle-of-the-afternoon Gandhi, that is." I flushed at that. "I'm going home," Beth announced, and stomped out of the square.

"Beth."

Noah started after her but stopped when she snarled, "Don't follow me! I strongly suggest you give me some space for a good while." And off she went.

"Chicken salad, anyone?" Ruby asked.

Dark clattered down the way it did in southern Arizona, and we looked toward the screen set up against the back of the community center. I'd faced the town, and it hadn't been bad at all. They knew I'd had cancer, and it didn't change a thing.

Chapter Nine
Bell Pepper

EATING a fresh, cold bell pepper on a hot, sunny afternoon is like a religious experience. I'd spotted the smooth, golden vegetable in Ruby's fridge when I was putting away her groceries, and even though it was her only one, I couldn't resist its organic curves. I had decided to try an experiment. I settled onto the edge of the picnic table, legs dangling. I tore off the top of the pepper and crunched into it, loving the cool crispness exploding in my mouth, feeling the hot sun, the dusty planks under my butt. I was a girl sitting in the sun, enjoying a pepper. I took another bite.

"I remember this," rejoiced the inner voice that did the movie narration for my life. I caught my breath. This was the sort of thing I didn't think. I forced myself to relax. This was the experiment after all.

"Yes," I said out loud. "I remember this. I liked this. I *like* this." I felt a scary delight in articulating the words as if acknowledging my pleasure would alert someone to take it away from me. I took another bite.

"I wonder what else I can remember," I challenged the empty yard. The yard didn't do anything. "Well, if no one is going to stop me . . ." I wondered if I hoped someone was going to stop me. But of course no one did. No one ever had. Only me.

"Honeycomb cereal," I pronounced. "Eating an entire watermelon while reading a trashy novel. Watching a dog chase sticks. Finding money you didn't know you had in your pocket."

After a while I stopped speaking aloud. I let my mind wander wherever it wanted for a change, reacquainting itself with all the simple pleasures I'd walled off because to admit they mattered would be to suffer if I lost them, and apprehension slowly, slowly released its talons.

Holding hands. First dates. Clean sheets. As my thoughts roamed, I lightly held the kachina of the girl entwined with the crab, Cancer, warming it with my hands. I knew my mother had made it for the moment when I decided to let it go. I hadn't been in the grip of bad luck, but had myself been the crab, clutching the past tight with my claws. I rose and settled the third statue among the raspberry bushes. I sat back down to continue my musings, a fraction lighter. Relaxing outside on a sunny day.

I sat there a long time. A girl, just like any other girl. Enjoying her pepper. I had expelled cancer from my blood, but it continued its grip on my mind. When was it over? When did "remission" become "normal?" What "normal" would I go back to? I didn't know who cancer-free Maeve would have been. She didn't exist.

Except we both liked bell peppers.

"MAEVE, sweetheart, would you be a dear and pick up some sherry for me?" Busy intercepted me on my way out.

"Okeydokey, smoky. April?"

"Copy of *Family Handyman Magazine*." I stopped and faced her, hands on hips. No way was I putting ammunition for mayhem into her hands.

She glared, then huffed. "All right, all right. I promise not to tape the sink sprayer."

I didn't move. I wasn't falling for any more of April's practical jokes. "I'll get you a nice gardening magazine if you untie the lines around my desktop items by the time I get back." I'd been poised to pull out the chair when I'd spotted the fishing line strung between the legs and my desk set, prepared to tumble it all to the floor when the seat was pulled out. April's face fell as the sound of Busy's giggles followed me to the kitchen.

Oliver and Lulabell were in her cage on the table.

"Road trip! Don't forget the bird!" said Oliver.

I paused. I hadn't really had much Oliver time. He preferred Lulabell to my shoulder these days. "You want to come, buddy?" Jenny didn't really like it when he came to Up Market, but she'd get over it. Oliver hopped onto my finger, and I settled him on my shoulder. He ran up and down, excitedly tugging hair out of my braids.

"Carrots! Howdy, pardner." He looked expectantly at Lulabell. "Nice hair!"

Lulabell mirrored Oliver's movements back and forth across her perch, crest feather up and down. "Howdy there! Howdy!"

"You want to come, Lulabell?" I'd never taken her on an outing before, but I didn't see the harm. I was getting Jenny's dirty looks anyway. Lulabell hopped onto my other shoulder.

I walked toward the square, considering whether to stop by Barney's first. So far, he hadn't made any real progress on Elsie. We were still in limbo, waiting for that missing part. It was when Oliver bit my ear that I noticed the clouds. They were coming in fast. What had been a sunny day looked to be a humdinger of a storm. I knew enough to know that I'd better get inside. Oliver didn't like storms, so I'd hole up in the bookstore until it passed. He was pressed so close to my neck that he was practically in my ear. Lulabell was rocking anxiously. As I stepped into the square, thunder sounded like a crack. And Lulabell flew away.

My jaw dropped. Lulabell could fly. Cockatiels were clipped not to fly, but Lulabell could fly, and I had taken her outside. Did I have the worst luck on the planet?

"Lulabell!" I called, frantic. Thunder cracked again, and I saw the flutter of a terrified bird thrashing among the treetops. I was petrified she would hurt herself. I was also horror-struck at the possibility that she would fly away. "Lulabell!" I cried again, but my voice was drowned out by the commencement of falling hail.

I started shaking. My bird was freaking out, and Lulabell was flying farther and farther away. Think. How did you get a free-flight bird down from a fifty-foot tree in a hail storm?

"Maeve, what's the matter with you? I've been calling. Get inside!"

I didn't even look at Noah. "Take Oliver." I held out my hands.

"Are you crazy? Come inside!"

"I can't." My voice cracked. "Please. Look after my bird."

He stared. Without a word, he took Oliver and hurried back to the store. Within minutes he was back, shaking a jacket over my shoulders. Rain mixed with the hail. "What is it?"

"Lulabell." I pointed. "Give me your phone." Noah handed it to me and I dialed. "Bruce? I have an emergency, and I need you to do something." I forced my voice to be calm.

After giving him instructions, I hung up and focused on the bird. Lulabell fluttered agitatedly from branch to branch. I made clucking and calling noises. When Bruce arrived fifteen minutes later, Noah and I were both soaked to the bone. Bruce'd brought what I'd requested. Noah unloaded the ladder and rope, while Bruce extracted Lulabell's cage. I kept my eyes glued to the bird. When Noah started to climb, I shouted, "No! She knows me better."

I tied one end of the rope around the cage handle and the other into a thick knot. "Once I'm up there, throw me the knotted end of rope." I was already on the ladder. Bruce started to object, but I gave them both a look. They shut up.

I climbed past the top of the ladder into the branches, then turned to catch the rope. I caught it on the first try, then hefted the cage. I balanced it on a branch and began pulling myself from branch to branch, lugging the cage after me. When I'd climbed as high as I could go, I found a good branch and hung the cage, door open.

"Lulabell," I called. I almost cried with relief when the panic-stricken bird flew to the safety of her haven as soon as she saw it. I closed her inside and carefully reversed my course out of the tree.

Bruce shut Lulabell in the truck and squinted at the sky. "I don't like this storm. Too much rain too fast."

"I'll bring Oliver home," said Noah. "Ride with Bruce. Go get dry."

I shook my head. "I'd like to walk," I said. The rain had all but stopped, and I wanted to collect my thoughts.

"Don't tarry," Bruce advised. "Rain could start again anytime. Hard to say what this storm's got left in it."

I nodded, and set off on foot, one eye on the sky. I tried to prepare words for Ruby. I tried not to think about what I'd temporarily forgotten, that I was a girl who stung those close to her, even when I tried to do the right thing. I was too tired. Bad luck had won. All I wanted to do was give up and go to sleep.

I GATHERED my courage at the doorstep, then stepped into the kitchen to face Ruby. Her back was to me as she packed a bag at the kitchen table at a greater speed than her normal high efficiency. She sensed me enter and turned.

"There's been an accident. We'll need your help. Please gather as many extra blankets as you can find in the hall closet. Hurry now."

I did as I was told. I changed into a dry sweatshirt and rain jacket, and grabbed all the blankets I could carry. When I returned, she was loading her Volvo wagon with thermoses and jackets. She collected and tested an enormous flashlight with a radio and siren built in. We got into the car, and she turned west.

"Where are April and Busy?" I asked.

"The rain this afternoon flooded Harshaw Creek and weakened the banks at the bridge. The seniors were going on a trip to early-bird dinner in Sonoita in their bus when one of the banks gave out and the bridge collapsed. The bus is in danger of falling into the flooded water." Ruby's white knuckles on the steering wheel belied her even tone. "April, Busy, Helen Rausch, Elsa Morrow, Diane Wall, Lupe Ortiz, and Henrietta Mankiller are trapped on the bus, along with Liz Goldberg, who was driving."

A shiver ran down my spine as icy as floodwater. My knuckles were as white as Ruby's when we pulled up to the collection of flashing lights and vehicles clustered at the south end of the bridge.

It was a disaster scene in miniature. The creek wasn't wide, maybe thirty feet across, but it was wider than the bus was long. The bridge had failed on the north side, bank crumbled, and now angled from the south bank straight into the water. The bus was tilted, tail in the water, nose pointing up at a hypotenuse angle. The fierce current of the swollen creek was tugging at the tail and west-facing side of the bus. The immediate threat was obvious. The south bank sustaining the bridge, and the bus, looked dangerously un-stable. Ruby hurried over to where Samuel stood, a few feet back from the bank.

"Everyone is on the bus and seems un-harmed aside from bumps and bruises," he answered her unspoken question. "But Helen . . ." He pointed. I squinted. There were six frightened faces that I could see, sit-ting very still in the first two rows of the bus, and Liz in the driver's seat. Helen had tum-bled to the bottom of the bus and was cling-ing to one of the bench seats. From her knees down she was submerged in filthy water swirling around the rear door.

"Can we get blankets down to them?" Ruby's voice was tight.

"Too risky," Samuel said. "We don't want Liz to open the door in case the water rises. Also, we can't risk adding any weight or getting too close to the edge of the bank until Barney secures the tow rope to the front of the bus."

Bruce and Barney were deep in conversation. Barney was shaking his head. "The weight is likely to cause the whole bank to collapse. I'm afraid to get too close."

"Can we come at it from the other side?" asked Bruce.

"I called Simon Bear. He's driving in from the north with John Buell, but it'll take them twenty minutes to get here."

"What about the ladder from the extension fire truck over at County? Can we stretch it out over the bus and harness them ladies to safety? Forget the bus."

"Mebbe. Fire truck can be farther back."

Rain started to fall again as Noah and Tuesday pulled up. Right behind them came an ambulance and the county ladder truck. More people arrived, prepared to help however they could.

Barney took off his cap and smoothed his hair, then replaced it. "Mebbe we could extend the tow cable and get Ronnie to climb down. He's pretty nimble and the lightest. Not ideal with the tow back that far, but lower risk of stressin' the bank."

"I'll do it, Chief," Ronnie said.

"There are life jackets on the ladder truck," Ruby said. "Can you make a harness out of one with a rope? Then he's attached and has a life preserver on, just in case."

"Good idea, Ruby," Samuel agreed, as Bruce nodded.

Samuel and Noah fashioned a harness for Ronnie. Tuesday and I watched Barney back the tow truck within ten feet of the bank. We held our breath as Ronnie struggled with the tow cable toward the lip of the creek. He attained the front of the bus and rolled onto his back to hook the cable around the axle.

"I need more cable," he yelled.

Bruce nodded. Barney backed up inch by cautious inch.

"I got it!" Ronnie shouted, and everyone cheered, when there was a horrible grinding sound. A section on our side of the bank gave way, and the near-right lip of the bridge shuddered and slipped a foot, tilting precariously and causing the rear of the bus to fishtail downstream. Barney put his truck in drive, wheels spinning without traction. Under increased pressure, the collapsed cement piling on the far upstream side crumbled further. Without its support, the bottom of the bridge sank another three feet into the relentless current. The back door of the bus was torn open completely, and Helen Rausch lost her grip and was washed out, arms flailing against the torrents sweeping her away.

"Get the truck!"

"Get the ambulance!"

"Throw a life preserver!"

Voices cried all around me, but I knew there was no hope for that. Helen was bobbing away quickly. The fields were too rutted for any vehicle. I wasn't good at much. I couldn't even take care of a pet bird. But there was one thing I could do, and that was run. I grabbed a life preserver off the pile and started sprinting. I could sense people running after me, but I quickly outpaced them. I kept my eyes glued to Helen. My feet ate the ground, and soon I overtook her. I looked ahead to a bend in the creek and sighted my target entry. There was an S-curve in the creek leaving a shallow beach and protected spit on the far side. I launched over the lip of the bank, grabbing an overhanging tree branch with one hand and dangling above the water. For once, luck was on my side, and Helen passed the curved spit of land close enough for me to grab hold of her.

The weight of her body combined with the pressure of the water almost snapped my wrist. The one clutching the tree strained as well. I was strong, but both the water and Helen were fighting me.

"Stop thrashing!" I yelled, but she was like a wild animal. I wasn't going to be able to hold her with one hand. I let go of the branch. The freezing water took my breath away, but I didn't have time for shock. If I went into deeper water with Helen, we didn't stand a chance. The little peninsula was providing a limited barrier against the churning water. I thrust my feet into the silty bottom for traction and used both hands to haul Helen to my chest. Inch by inch, I used the creek bed, branches, anything I could, to move us farther into the lee of the spit. At last the water released its suction, and I heaved our bodies onto the beach. I lay gasping for air on my back, Helen crushed against me.

"Over here!"

People descended. Several hands rolled Helen from my chest. The scene was chaos.

"Bring the stretcher! We need blankets!"

"Are you insane?" Noah shouted. "You could have killed yourself!"

"Noah, hush. She saved Helen's life," Ruby chided. To me, "That was something, Maeve." She reached for my hand to help me up, and I cried out. Samuel was there in an instant.

"Let me see." His gentle fingers probed my wrist while Ruby helped me sit up. Someone wrapped a jacket around my shoulders.

"I'm fine." I used my other hand to push to my feet.

"Stretcher!" Samuel and Noah shouted at the same time.

"No, I can walk." I couldn't stop beaming. "I can *run!*"

"You sure can," Bruce voiced admiration.

My smile faded. "The bus . . ."

"It's secure on the cable. Firemen are getting everyone off."

"Let's get back." Noah's tone was impatient. "You'll catch your death."

We crossed the field back toward the road

behind EMTs porting Helen on a stretcher. "Her vitals are stable," Samuel said. "They'll take her to the hospital and keep her overnight to be sure. I need to get you to the clinic and X-ray that wrist."

We reached the road in time to see a fireman handing a cable-clipped Liz from the bus to a waiting fireman on the safety of the road. The rest of the seniors were bundled in blankets, clutching thermoses. Everyone looked shaken but unharmed.

"I think you're going to have to take them all in," Ruby said.

Samuel nodded. We piled into various wagons and trucks to be chauffeured to the clinic. Other than bruises and Busy's elevated blood pressure, my hairline wrist fracture was the only injury of note. Samuel wrapped it tightly. When he was done, we headed for the door. I was starving. To my surprise, the waiting area was packed with people. Everyone was there. They stood when they saw me and began to clap and cheer. I was surrounded by well-wishers, congratulating me and patting me on the back.

As one creature, we migrated out of the clinic and down to the Wagon Wheel. Within minutes, plates of potato skins and pitchers of beer appeared. Everyone chattered excitedly now that the danger had passed. Tuesday handed me a beer and cried, "To Maeve!"

"Hear! Hear!" everyone shouted.

I couldn't stop smiling. Noah appeared at my elbow. "I'm sorry I yelled," he apologized. "I thought I was going to have a heart attack when you jumped into the river. Breathing underwater is only for made-up people."

"Excuse me," a voice interrupted. I turned. "Chuck Hall." He introduced himself. "Are you Maeve Connelly?" At my nod, he said, "I'm with the *Daily Dispatch*." He named the regional paper. "We'd like an interview, if you're up for it."

We sat at the table surrounded by everyone, and I answered the reporter's questions, frequently interrupted by other witnesses.

When we were done, he said, "We'll need a picture. Didn't have time to bring someone down with me."

"I can do it!" Tuesday trilled. "Who's got a camera?" Someone handed her a digital camera. "What do I push?"

Chuck had me pose surrounded by everyone raising his or her beer. Tuesday snapped the shot and promised to e-mail it to Chuck.

A wave of tiredness hit me. Samuel saw it happen, and stood. "All right, folks. Time to get Wonder Woman home."

He insisted on driving me. When I headed to my room, I registered that Lulabell seemed no worse for wear and that Oliver had been returned and was sharing the safety of her cage.

WHEN I woke, I was sore all over. I groaned and swallowed two painkillers. Then I headed to the bookstore. It was early, but I couldn't wait to see the paper.

April called after me on my way out. "Hold up, Atalanta. We're coming, too." She, Ruby, and Busy fell in. I couldn't help but marvel at the bright blue of the sky. It was like the storm never happened. But I felt transformed by the events of the day before.

We arrived to find Bruce, Liz, and little Tommy chatting on the step. "Look, Tommy," Liz said. "Maeve has a wrap on her wrist, like you."

"Did you fall out of a tree?" Tommy asked.

"She saved Helen Rausch from drowning in the river yesterday."

Tommy looked baffled. "Why?"

By 9:30 a.m., there was a crowd sipping coffee. When it seemed like everyone in town was crammed into the store, Helen walked in. She marched up to the counter. "Half caf, half decaf vanilla cappuccino with two percent skimmed milk, and I want that milk piping hot." She looked around at everyone staring. "What?"

She swung back toward me. "If you think you get some kind of special treatment or thank-you from me, you've got another think coming," she snapped. Brushes with death do not, apparently, have the same effect on everyone.

The entrance tinkled again. The newspaper deliveryman dropped the bundle of papers on his foot in alarm when the crowd surged toward him. He staggered out in a hurry, leaving it to Bruce to cut the ties and disseminate papers.

The article wasn't hard to find. Right on the front page was the headline: LOCAL GIRL SAVES UNKNOWN WOMAN.

RUBY WAS IN THE kitchen having tea that night when I got home from work. I sat down. She set homemade coffee cake before me.

"Maeve, I owe you an apology. In all the excitement yesterday, I never acknowledged it."

My mouth dropped. Didn't *I* owe *her* the apology?

"I should have attended to clipping Lulabell's wings some time ago. She is not accustomed to free flight. I overlooked the proper care of my bird as I pursued my attempt at playwriting."

"You're writing a play?" It was the first I'd heard of it.

"One of the projects I've been able to undertake with your assistance around the house. It turns out, however, that I do not have a talent for playwriting. The world shall live in wonder over the founding mothers of Unknown."

It was hard to imagine Ruby not accomplishing whatever she set her mind to. "Ruby, do you believe in luck?"

"I believe that birds fly away because their wings have not been clipped, not because they are in the company of someone afflicted with bad luck. I also believe it is reasonable that girls who have had bad things happen might believe in bad luck."

I looked off. "When I first got sick, I walked around in a cloud of angry with a chance of rage. I, who had never done anything to anyone, was fighting for my life. What had I done to deserve it?"

"You could conjure a variety of explanations where you internalize responsibility for becoming ill, but they would all be incorrect. Our own worst enemy is often ourselves. I would hope that yesterday demonstrated to you your own capabilities."

"I'm good at one thing, at least," I said. "I can run."

"We all have the potential to be good at anything we choose. Have you heard of deliberate practice?" Ruby asked.

I shook my head.

"It's a way of thinking about achievement. Researchers suggest we've historically been incorrect in our belief that talent is integral to success. It's not that talent doesn't exist, but, rather, that it may be irrelevant."

"So what causes success?"

"Carefully designed hard work and always stretching beyond your abilities. Continually focusing on your weakest elements and trying to improve them. Those who persevere are high achievers. The key lies in knowing what you deeply want."

"So you make your own luck?" I liked the idea that if I figured out what I *wanted* to be, I didn't have to settle for the mess I had.

"Why not?"

"So what you're saying is, if I don't have any talent for playwriting but engage in deliberate practice of the craft, my community might be able to see the story of our founding mothers performed at the Monkey Flower Festival?" I said, smile sly.

Ruby looked surprised, then laughed. "I suppose I am."

THE candlelight played on the planes of Samuel's face. We were back at the Velvet Elvis. We'd made a special date to talk. We hadn't yet discussed what had happened. I'd needed a little time.

"I'm sorry, Maeve." He repeated his apology. "It wasn't my place to tell people."

"It's okay." I meant it. "Part of me was relieved."

"It was torture watching you torment yourself. The old folks say you can't kill emotion. You might squash it flat, but it doesn't lose mass—it will spread wide, seep through the cracks, find a way."

"Turn into rashes on my tummy?"

He smiled. "You're my favorite hypochondriac."

"Maybe I was trying to get face time with the hot doctor."

"You didn't have to work that hard. Ah, perfect timing!" He looked up to see the waitress approaching with a cake and candles. Behind her were three others. When they reached the table, they broke into a chorus of "Happy Birthday." Soon the entire pizza joint was singing.

I let them serenade me, blushing and sending Samuel filthy looks.

"Thank you! Thank you!" I waved to everyone as the entire restaurant clapped, and blew out my candles. "Just so you know," I hissed, "it's *not* my birthday!"

"It is for part of you. Healthy cells are being born by the hundreds as we speak. Today is their birthday. Instead of pretending nothing happened, why don't we celebrate what did happen. In many ways you're a miracle." His look got earnest. "Today could be your *re*birth day." He reached down and pulled out a thick folder and two oblong packages wrapped in bright paper.

"What is it?" I was curious.

"It's a rebirthday gift. It has three parts. This first." He flipped open the folder. "Here. This is a study about cancer recidivism. And see here, these are your last blood-test results. Now do you see how when you relapsed . . ."

I stared in wonder as Samuel patiently and carefully showed me just how healthy I was, with charts and diagrams and medical records. My heart constricted.

"So you see," he said at last, "there is no reason you won't live a long and healthy life. At this point you're no different from anyone else." He smiled. "Except your cells are younger and sexier."

"Are you getting fresh with my plasma?"

"Beauty is only skin deep." He pushed the first package toward me. I opened it. It was a beautifully framed image.

"Your last scan," he explained. "I had it

framed so you won't forget." It was oddly beautiful, the radioactive tracer injected in my veins lit up to provide a color-coded picture of my body. "Now this one." He pushed over the second package. It was a leatherbound *Taber's Cyclopedic Medical Dictionary*, like the ones in his office. This one was inscribed. It read: *A book full of things that don't apply to you. Trust me, I'm a doctor. Samuel.*

"Every day you're supposed to look up something you don't have. Go on, try it."

I flipped to a page near the beginning. "Ankylosing spondylitis. A form of chronic inflammation of the spine and the sacroiliac joints."

"Excellent choice." He beamed at me.

This was fun. "Can I do another?" I asked.

"There are only so many entries in the book, and you have a lot of mornings left," he answered. "Maybe you want to go slow."

I looked at the voluminous tome and thought about having more days than it had entries. What would I do with them all? It was a little terrifying. In that, I was no different from anyone else.

I looked across the table at Samuel,

blinking back tears. His thoughtfulness was overwhelming. I felt warmth. And affection. And that was all. "Samuel," I said.

He met my gaze, and nodded. Then he covered my hands.

"It's just . . ."

"We're friends." His eyes were sad.

That was it exactly. "I think you're wonderful. Thanks for taking such good care of me."

His smile was rueful. "I did too good a job, I'm afraid. I don't think you want someone taking care of you anymore."

"Maybe. I want more for both of us. Passion, crazy climbing-all-over-you need and joy. And we're . . . we're like a warm bath."

"I know."

"Thank you," I said. "For being you."

Chapter Ten

What You Take to a Desert Island

AFTER my morning run, I hurried into The Little Read Book, anxious to be there before Noah. I wanted to see his face when he came in. He'd flown to New York for a meeting with his publisher, and Tuesday and I had worked around the clock to finish the children's nook in his absence. The bookshelves were painted bright primary colors, there were kid-sized chairs and tables, and the café now offered juice boxes. I'd stayed until 2:00 a.m. to hang shadowbox frames displaying our collection of classic children's books. It was perfect.

By the time he walked in at 12:47, I was vibrating with impatience. The sight of him sent a jolt through my system.

"Oh, are you back already?" The most erect posture of my life belied my casual tone. Noah gave me an amused look.

He smiled. "Careful, or I'm going to think you missed me. You're wearing your favorite rainbow socks." He had me there. I was wearing my most happy socks. I was about to retort when he said, "I missed you." And there I was, mouth hanging open like a fish.

"Did I miss it? Am I late? Rats!" Tuesday's bracelets jangled as she bounded in. "Well?" She turned a shining face toward Noah.

"What?" He looked confused.

"Close your eyes." I smiled. He did. I led him to face the corner nook. "Okay, open."

He did. I waited. He didn't say anything. For a long, long time. I felt an anxious wiggle. Did he hate it? Was it too unserious? Noah was very serious about books.

He looked at me, tone controlled. "You did this?"

Oh God. He was upset. He hated it. I blinked so he couldn't see I was fighting not to cry. I managed a nod, looking down.

"This is . . . by far . . . the most . . ." I peeked up and noticed he was blinking, too. Kind of like me. He was staring at the mural on the far wall. "Is that . . . ?"

"Tuesday did it." I relaxed. He was looking at a large painted image of a girl with long braids and a boy wearing kneesocks sitting in a treetop. "There's even a shelf for your toys." I pointed. "*If* you feel like sharing."

"They are not toys," came his lofty refrain. "They are visualization facilitators." He ventured farther in. "It's amazing." His smile was huge. He tugged a braid. "I could get used to you being around."

I took an involuntary step backward. Part of me wanted to take care of Noah so badly I dreamed of snatching him under my arm and running far away to shove him in a warm nest and feed him soup. But with my luck, I'd trip and drop him into poison ivy, where he'd break an arm. I was still too unsure of myself.

"Hey, man, don't cry or anything. It's just a shop." I looked around for Tuesday, but she'd vanished. It was a trick she perfected when Noah and I bickered.

He caught my shoulder. "It's not just a shop. It's perfect. Thank you, Maeve." He hugged me tight. I didn't want him to let go, but this was exactly the problem. I was trying to be a new girl. One who could take care of herself. Certainly not one who over-hugged another girl's boyfriend.

I pulled back. For the first time, I was relieved to see Beth walk in. She was beaming. "Hello!" she sang. "Welcome back!" She flung her arms around Noah.

The smile he returned seemed forced.

"Have you got anything to say to me?" Her tone was coy.

His "Of course" was clipped. "Happy anniversary."

"You didn't forget!" She kissed him. Air left my lungs.

"I did not," he said. "We're going to Bella Mia in Nogales."

I realized I was staring and bolted for the café. What was the matter with me? I'd seen them kiss before. Samuel and I kissed in the store all the time. Or we had, I corrected.

I shoved napkins in the dispenser in irritation. As if I'd conjured him, Noah appeared. I registered Beth dancing out of the store. Noah sat at a café table and gestured to the chair opposite. "So, tell me what happened while I was gone." His smile was genuine.

"Not much." I shrugged, remaining behind the counter. "We had a good week in the café."

"The store stayed open, then?" he teased. "You didn't float off to take pictures of dust motes or something?"

How could he take a frosted tart like Beth seriously and treat me like a piece of fluff? I tossed my rag down and flung an arm toward the nook. "How much time do you think I took off, Noah?" I demanded. "You were only gone for three days. You think that Little Read Picture Book sign and the shelves all painted themselves?"

He looked startled. "Maeve, I . . ."

"And considering you forgot to pay me before you left, technically I've been working for free, so if I wanted to take off and photograph naked baby bottoms, I'd be perfectly entitled!"

His face was stricken. "I'm sorry. I'll pay you right now. I didn't mean . . . getting ready to leave . . . I was distracted . . . I just . . ."

"Forget it," I snapped. "Include it in next week's check. But try not to forget that most people don't have their jobs for kicks. And for the record, taking care of you is a lot more work than you think." I turned my back, hating myself but unable to stop my mouth. I sensed rather than saw him disappear into the office.

TWENTY minutes past closing time, the store was empty. I sat on a sofa watching the light change.

"Maeve?" Hesitant. I turned my head. He held out a check. "My New York trip went really well. So I'm giving you a raise. You deserve it." He looked away. "I know I'm a little difficult."

"No." I shook my head. "I don't know why I said that."

"Is everything okay?" He sat down next to me.

"It will be." I said the truth. "I think it just takes time."

"Why did we fight today, Maeve? Did I do something wrong?"

"No," I said. "You didn't. You're a good man, Noah. And an excellent friend. I'm grateful you put up with me. I can be a moody, bossy creature!" I forced a laugh.

His relief was evident. "I'm glad. I really value our friendship." He looked at his watch. "Are you okay to close up? I have to get Beth." He gave my shoulder a quick squeeze. "I love the nook. Every time I turn around, things get better here because of you."

I watched him walk out, knowing two things. I was in love with Noah Case, and I had to get the hell out of town because of it.

"CLAPP Cement."

"May I please speak with Clem Clapp?"

"You got him." The voice was brusque.

"Is this *the* Clem Clapp, editor and CEO of *Plymouth Road Runner: The (Good) Times*?" I poured all the admiration I could into my question.

His voice warmed. "That'd be me. Who am I speaking to?"

"Sir, it is an honor. You are speaking to Maeve Connelly, 1970 Plymouth Road Runner N96 Air Grabber coupe, 727 auto transmission, yellow black stripes."

"That's a rare beauty, that one. I have one of those myself: Moulin Rouge, no wheel covers." Satisfaction radiated from his voice.

"Three eighty-three CID rated at 335 bhp and 425 torque?" I carefully read Barney's notes.

"Four twenty-six CID Hemi rated at 425 bhp—that's 317 kW—and 490 torque." Perfect. It was engine-compatible.

"Is it true, Mr. Clapp, that you have *six* Plymouth Road Runners, sir?" Awe.

"Call me Clem. There's no better vehicle than the Road Runner. It's a personal privilege to ensure these American icons never become extinct. What would the road be without them?" Bingo. "And how can I help you, Miss Connelly?"

"Call me Maeve. Clem, I couldn't help but be impressed at *Plymouth Road Runner: The (Good) Times*. That's quite a publication for a man as busy as yourself." I had the latest issue up on the Internet. It looked like a third-grade newsletter. You could almost smell the Elmer's glue.

"Well, thank you kindly. It's a labor of love."

"I noticed you don't publish on a regular schedule. I wanted to find out when the next edition will be available."

"My wife doesn't quite share my passion, so I do most of the work myself. With running a company, my time is limited."

"Clem, I might be able to help you out." I laid out my proposal.

"So HE went for it?" my sister Vi asked.

"Uh-huh." I crunched a celery stick.

"And what exactly do you have to do?"

"I promised to help him modernize the newsletter and to write a regular column about my various road trips, and feature pictures of Elsie in all the small towns I've visited, the car troubles we've had, and how we fixed it. Car enthusiast stuff."

"That sounds like a pretty sweet deal."

"Not exactly." Clem hadn't been a total mark. "I also have to help him with his company newsletter, *Cement Times: Solid Facts*."

"In return you get the part."

"Yep. One of his six Road Runners will be Elsie's organ donor. I help him out until I've worked off my debt."

"Ingenious. But wouldn't it be easier to buy the part off Clem and avoid the newsletter business?"

I cleared my throat, with slight shame. "I don't think I could afford it."

"But you've been working for ages! And selling your pictures!"

"Yeah, well, there were things . . ."

"What kinds of things?"

"Oh, I put some money into projects for the store. And it was Ruby's birthday. Then there was the DVD player for the house, some hula skirts for Tuesday, a yoga mat for Samuel, some rabbit ears for my in-room TV, new running shoes. You know, *things*."

Vi was quiet. "Maeve, has it ever occurred to you that maybe you don't want to leave Unknown? Maybe there's a reason you're not saving more efficiently."

I opened my mouth. I closed it. I tried. "Have you ever stayed up all night picturing someone who wasn't there?"

She sighed. "Noah?" Somehow she knew

I was nodding over the phone. "Are you sure it's hopeless?"

"Yes."

"Are you sure it's hopeless because he has a girlfriend or because you don't think you're good enough?"

Her words were a shock. At my silence she went on. "I don't know if I'll say this just right, but you got a second chance, didn't you? And the thing about second chances is that they aren't worth beans if you don't do anything about them."

"But . . ."

"Get out of your own way, Maeve."

"Ay-yi, I can't believe you're leaving us!" Tuesday wailed.

True to his word, Clem had delivered the parts to PIGS, and Barney was performing the transplant. I was giving notice at the bookstore.

Noah's face was expressionless. "When do you expect to leave?"

"Next week." I had enough to pay Barney for his time and get to Los Angeles.

"Noooooo . . ." Tuesday ran around the counter and flung her arms around my neck. "But you'll be back for the Festival?"

"We'll see, Tuesday," I demurred. I didn't want to make promises I couldn't keep.

Noah cut in. "I don't suppose you can be any more specific than 'Next week,' can you? It's not very professional notice."

I might've laughed, if it wasn't so sad. There wasn't much about how we ran the store that constituted standard business practices. "I'm leaving Monday," I said gently. "Barney will be finished Friday. Sunday night Ruby's having a farewell dinner for me. I hope you'll both be there."

"You bet I will! I'm going to call Ruby right now. We'll send you off with a *mino'aka*—that's a smile." She twirled, dance infusing her movements. "We'll need fairy lights and paper flowers. . . ." She talked to herself all the way out the door, forgetting it was my day off and she was scheduled to work.

I turned back to Noah, *mino'aka* playing on my mouth as I pulled off my jacket. Looked like I was staying. The smile faded at his expression.

"Well?"

I was ready. "I've filled out the café and

stockroom order forms for the next four weeks. All you have to do is fax them in on Mondays. You'll have the books and food you need. I've also asked Beth to come by and help out for the next few Thursday mornings until you get into the new routine. She can put out the new stock."

"Beth?" He frowned. "The last book Beth read, the title began with 'CliffsNotes.' She has no idea . . . and . . . well . . . never mind."

"No problem," I soothed. "We'll ask Ruby. It only entails putting out new stock. I ordered the titles. Anyone can do it."

"So you're just anyone?" His anger dissipated.

"No. I'm the girl who spent the last seven years of her life in neutral, who needs to get back on course."

Noah sat heavily on the couch. I joined him.

"Careful," I mimicked. "Or I'll think you're going to miss me."

He stood abruptly. "I'm sorry, but I need to go through the office so I can prepare for this rather abrupt departure." He wasn't going to make this easy. He headed toward the back. "Oh, just curious." He turned, tone caustic. "What socks are you wearing today?"

We both looked at my naked toes in flip-flops for a moment, and then he strode to his office and shut the door without a word.

RUBY laid hands on my shoulders. "Come along. Everyone is here."

"Everyone?" I tried to sound casual. I hadn't seen Noah since I'd told him I was leaving.

Ruby sensed my question, but she also sensed I didn't want it acknowledged. "I'm sure there'll be stragglers," she reassured me. "But at the moment, your farewell party has quite a crowd already."

I followed Ruby to the yard. It was an enchanted place. There were lights and paper flowers Tuesday had strung along the walls and trees. Bruce, Child, Barney, and Ronnie Two Shoes were at the grill, preparing kabobs. Male imperative. April and Busy were tippling and bickering about sherry versus Scotch. Ruby laid silverware down in precise settings, as Tuesday was cluttering the table with scattered napkins. Liz prepared a salad, while Patrick and Jenny Up laid out pies. Samuel pressed a brown paper bag into my hands.

"It's vitamin samples. Obscure ones like bilberry extract and selenium."

I hugged him. He was a gift I'd miss.

When the kabobs were ready, we gathered for chicken, pineapple, onion, and tomato treats on sticks. Candlelight lit the faces of those who'd gathered. I laughed along as Samuel exaggerated stories of his favorite Maeve Hypochondriac Moments. April brayed a little *too* loudly at some. But I'd already unscrewed the top of the saltshaker closest to her. April liked salt on prickly pear pie, which we happened to be having for dessert. Heh.

I didn't dwell on the fact that Noah didn't appear. Beth didn't show either. I wanted to enjoy my own party, and Noah would have strained things. It was better that he didn't come. I took what he'd told me about missing me and put it in my vault.

We ate and laughed and drank for hours. April and I carried Busy to bed at midnight. Liz, Ronnie Two Shoes, Patrick, and Jenny faded away shortly after. Soon, it was down to the hardest. Child clasped my hands. "Maeve, it would be a privilege if you would continue to share your images." He hugged me. When he pulled away at the natural conclusion of the embrace, it was me who still clung.

"I'll treasure my carved memory," he whispered about the kachina I'd given him, "though it won't replace the giver." With that he was gone. I had more than a million words caught in my throat. I said nothing.

I was grabbed and squeezed tightly. "I can't," said Tuesday. It was the most distress I'd seen her demonstrate. "Breakfast?"

"Breakfast," I agreed. "Wagon Wheel?"

"No. I can't bear a public farewell. I'll cook."

I laughed. "Salad in a bag?"

"*I'll* cook," growled April. We all looked at her in fear.

"No, *I'll* cook," Ruby rescued. Everyone exhaled.

Tuesday sniffed. "Ruby, the dishes tonight . . . I can't . . ." She hugged me fiercely and fled.

To me April growled, "Sleep with one eye open," and departed. The salt trick had worked. I tried not to contemplate the repercussions.

"You look after yourself, gal." Bruce gave

me a bear hug. "No camping next to town hall in LA." Then he and Ruby followed April inside.

"Don't touch the dishes," Ruby ordered as she left. "They'll be there in the morning."

That left Samuel and me. We held hands companionably as we walked to the gate. "I'll miss you," he said.

"I'll miss you, too. And if you don't date Primrose Tarquin after I leave, you're a nincompoop," I teased, naming Bloom's attractive older sister.

As we approached the gateway, Samuel swung me close and hugged me tight. He kissed the top of my head. "Be good, Maeve. Believe in your capacity. You're not going to get sick again."

"Thank you, Samuel." I held on to his comfort. "You're the best thing that happened to me here." Even as I said it, my mind was a cheater.

Something caught my eye in the dark, and I fantasized it was Noah's shadow in the door archway. I squinted, but there was nothing.

Samuel cupped my face in his hands. "It's been a pleasure."

"I'll stay in touch," I said, hoping I would.

Kerry Reichs

And with an amicable hug, we said good-bye. And if I was weepy when I went to bed, it wasn't because I hadn't had the perfect parting from my friends. I had. It was because of the one that hadn't happened. Noah hadn't come at all.

"So you're really going?" he asked.

"No, I thought I'd load all my things into Elsie and then unload them for fun." I was being glib, but I was afraid if I looked at him I'd break down and cry or beg him to leave Beth or something equally foolish. Plus I was still angry he'd blown off my going-away dinner. I busied myself arranging things that didn't need arranging. When I peeked, his face looked grim.

"Well, that's about it." I backed out of the car. I'd be in LA the day after tomorrow.

Noah crossed his arms. "Do you know where you're going? You haven't been out of Unknown."

"I managed to get here; I guess I'll manage to get out." I hated being snarky, but if he was kind, I'd come unglued. My throat was tight as it was.

"Why this sudden rush to leave?"

"Elsie's ready; my debts are paid. Why would I stay?"

"What about The Little Read Picture Book? Forgetting your plans for story time and book events for kids? And the Monkey Flower Festival events?"

"It offends you that I'm pursuing my own projects rather than spending all my energy on yours?"

His eyes narrowed. "*You* begged *me* for your job."

"I'm releasing you from the burden of your charity."

"Are you being deliberately difficult?"

"Are you? Buy some more kneesocks—you won't even miss me."

"It's not about me; it's about you! You're always running. You're going to end up exhausted. What's there in LA for you?"

"What's there for me in this no-stoplight village?"

He flinched. "And how long before it's off to the next place? Are you capable of settling down?"

"Yes, I am!" I yelled. "But I'm not settling for less. You're a self-absorbed, high-strung prima donna who expects he can drop out of life whenever he wants and have a cadre of women cater to his every whim. I'm not interested in being a water-carrier."

"At least I finish what I start," he thundered, hitting my tender spot.

"I *am* finishing what I started. My trip to LA. I'm finishing it *right now!*" I yanked open Elsie's door to climb in.

Before I could, Noah grabbed my shoulders and turned me to face him. His face was contrite. "Wait, Maeve. I'm sorry. I'm sorry. I shouldn't have yelled."

I stepped away from his touch. He noticed. He dropped his hands.

"I'm sorry I missed the party last night. I thought I'd be back from Tucson in time."

"Oh? Weren't you there?"

"I have something for you." Abrupt. "It's the reason I went to Tucson. It wasn't ready, so I had to wait. By the time I stopped by Ruby's last night, it was too late." He looked off. "It was always too late." I frowned, not understanding. When had he come to Ruby's?

"Here." He handed me a small box. "You didn't give me much notice." I opened it. Inside was a chain and round silver locket.

Affixed to the front was a miniature silver Paddington Bear, in his duffle coat and hat, holding his suitcase. On the back was etched *Please look after this bear.* I opened it, and was confused.

"It's microfiche." Noah explained the negatives inside. "I had *A Bear Called Paddington* scanned onto microfiche, so if you ever get trapped on that desert island, you'll have it with you."

My throat closed entirely, my mouth forming a perfect *O.* This was no match for the kachina I'd hidden on his office shelf among the "toys." It was an ascending swirl of birds taking flight, a thing to lift your heart. To me it meant potential, attaining great heights. Noah's heights would not include me, but it meant a lot to know that a part of me remained with him, a potentially undiscovered talisman. But it didn't hold a candle to the talisman he'd just given me.

I struggled to make a sound, and failed. What could I say when all I wanted was for him to grab me, to kiss me. I wanted it badly.

"Maeve . . ." His voice was low, and he reached toward me.

Do it, I willed him. *Just do it. Tell me it's me you want.* I couldn't take my eyes off his mouth. I could almost feel his lips on mine. I swayed slightly. Then a burst of light caught my eye. We both glanced as Beth's silver BMW pulled onto Main, sunlight flashing off her windshield as she headed south. Shame and humiliation washed over me. What was I doing? It wasn't me he wanted.

"Take lots of pictures of the Monkey Flower Festival." I stepped away from Noah. I had to get away. Now.

His right eyebrow creased down, and his look darkened. "*You* should be taking the pictures."

"Hollywood calls." I affected a careless air.

"So this means nothing to you?" Angry now. "You don't care about Unknown or the people here counting on you?"

"Of course I care! But you knew I never intended to stay," I defended. He wasn't being fair. "What do you want from me?"

"I want you to tell me why you're leaving." His dark green eyes penetrated mine.

So I don't die inside when I see you look at Beth with those eyes, I thought. "Because I'd rather be there than here." I broke what was left of us with my answer. "I have to go."

This time he didn't try to stop me as I clambered into Elsie, blindly jamming the key into the ignition. I accelerated hard, kicking up a cloud of dust that surrounded the man standing in the middle of the road in the rearview mirror until I was too far away to see.

Chapter Eleven

Welcome to Your Water Stain

THE standstill traffic on I–10 should have been a clue, but it was the perfect round ball of the sun heading toward the sea that signified my arrival in Los Angeles. The jittery feeling I'd had since leaving Unknown abated for the first time, replaced by a blossoming euphoria. And disbelief. How had I, Maeve Connelly, gotten myself this far? I forgot about kachinas and a bookstore blocked from my mind and sat in wonder. I'd *done* something.

I called my mother. "Guess what I'm looking at?"

"I couldn't possibly know, dear. A cow's butt?"

"I'm in LA, Mom! I made it!" I was actually teary.

"I'm so happy for you, Maeve." Her voice was tender. "We never doubted you for a minute. Your father and I are so proud. I've always been in awe of your strength."

Her statement took my breath away. *My* strength? "But I . . ."

"I'm talking about your tenacity. I honestly don't know if I could have endured what you did. Maeve, you dug deep for resources many of us never need. I thank God every day you had enough. After it was over, perhaps your fields needed to lie fallow for a while. Now it's time to start using all the wealth you possess again."

"Thanks, Mom." I blinked back tears.

"If I could give you one gift, Maeve, it would be to see yourself as I see you. And if you could give me one gift, it would be a chunk of George's Clooney's lawn. But don't get arrested."

I hung up, images of verdant fields, sunny beaches, and palm trees swirling in a kaleidoscope of color behind my eyes.

It was four in the afternoon, and Laura wasn't expecting me until eight. We'd planned to meet at her place, but I knew she was at work. She wasn't answering her phone. I decided to head to Fox Studios. I knew she worked in Building 100, so I figured I could track her down. If the shoot was really demanding, maybe I could help. It might make getting a job easier if I could dive right in. My trip had proven that an ability to sell on my feet worked. My mother's words buoyed me with a new kind of confidence.

After consulting my map, I headed north. I knew from Laura I couldn't park on the lot, but I spotted a public park across the street from the studios. The weather was perfect—Oliver would be fine. In the rearview mirror, I glimpsed the box filled with crimson paper flowers Tuesday had given me to decorate my new home and smiled. It would do nicely.

"I'm sorry, girl, I don't see your name," the guard apologized.

"Well, hell's bells. What'm I supposed to do with five hundred paper flowers?" I find a Southern accent useful from time to time. I blew out my bangs for effect.

"You say Laura Mills? That the gal, with, you know, the *clothes?*"

"Sure is," I agreed, having no idea.

He gave a conspiratorial giggle. "Tell you what. I don't want that girl to lose her job 'cause a me. This ain't the first time she done forgot to send someone's name up." He tapped his keyboard, and a badge spat out of his printer. "Don' be stealin' no golf carts, hear?"

"Thanks, man." I stuck the badge on my T-shirt.

I consulted the map he'd given me. Building 100 was easy to find. I followed the map, distracted along the way by signs for *House, Bones, The Simpsons,* and *24.*

Building 100 was a squat white building, identical to Building 101 and Building 102. Its sign proclaimed *"Black Angus."* The unattended reception area fed into a hallway. I could hear activity. My choices were right or left. I hovered. The door opened and a Greek god walked in.

No, really. Colin Cantell had played a Greek god in *Athens.* And here he was, larger than life (at least his chest), three feet away. Sadly not in a toga. I vaguely remembered that he currently played a detective on a TV show. He hurried off to the right. Decision made, I followed, carrying my box of paper flowers.

"Joel!" he called in a surprisingly high-pitched whine. "I need to talk to you!"

"Oh joy," a disgruntled voice answered. "What now?" Colin Cantell followed the voice, and I almost trailed him right into the producer's office until I realized it and stopped short.

"It's the script. It needs to be rewritten. All those scenes need to be taken away from Kate and given to Angus. The show is called *Black Angus*. Like on page sixty-seven . . ."

"Hold on. Where's my script? Why the hell isn't the script ever where it's supposed to be?" His voice became a roar. "Lola! Lola!"

I stepped out of sight. A second later Laura Mills tottered down the hall looking like Cyndi Lauper and Posh Spice got into a fight and both lost. The tottering was due to bizarre heelless platform boots, requiring her to balance on the balls of her feet. These accompanied mesh tights and an extremely short, pleated kilt. She didn't notice me as she wobbled into the office. She looked almost green when she wobbled out. If someone had directed that language toward me, I'd be green, too. The only noninvective had been the word "intern."

The voices in the office dropped to murmurs. I tiptoed after Laura. The hallway drained into a large room filled with desks. Laura was nowhere to be seen.

"Excuse me," I asked that-guy-who-tries-too-hard-with-the-skinny-tie. "Did you see where Laura went?"

"Laura-Lola, Fashion Icon?" His signature was sarcasm, naturally. "Copy machine." He snickered at the paper flowers. "Those all the flowers you could afford?"

"That all the tie you could afford?"

I followed the sound of the copier. Laura was muttering over the machine, collecting pink sheets as it spit them out. "God, please let the final be pink."

"Hey, Laura," I ventured.

"For the last time, it's *LOLA*," she snarled as she turned. Then her mouth dropped open. "What are *you* doing here?"

"Surprise!" My announcement was weak. "I got in early."

A big smile replaced her shocked look,

and she gave a theatrical shriek before hugging me, box and all. "Maeve! Wow! How'd you find me?" She sounded genuinely glad. I relaxed.

"From your e-mails."

"Wow," she repeated. She gave a little hop, then regained her balance. "You're here! How fun! We're going to have all *kinds* of—"

"Scriiiiipt!" A bellow reverberated down the hall. Laura jumped.

"Damn. Hang on a sec." She grabbed the sheaf of pink pages and lurched off. I stayed where I was and studied the chart above the machine that indicated all final scripts were to be printed on green paper.

Laura returned shortly. Joel was either color-blind or just happy to have a script. She led me to an impossibly cluttered desk. "I have to share with the other in— I mean, another staffer."

"What does a First AD do?" I asked.

Laura looked shifty. "This and that," she hedged. Then you could almost see the lightbulb pop over her head. "But I'm so outta here. I've got a connection with this new cop drama, *Badge Attitude*." I was pretty sure I heard a snort from Skinny Tie.

Laura seemed to recall the golden halo she'd painted over her current job. "Not that this place is *bad*. I mean, I've learned *a lot*. But I've grown as much as I can here, and it's time to move on." Another snort. I was starting to forgive him. "*Badge Attitude* is totally going to be groundbreaking. They're tough cops, but they don't have guns. Just *badges* and *attitudes*." She opened her eyes really wide at me.

"Oh," I said. A tiny frown appeared. *"Amazing."* I ramped it up. She smiled, satisfied.

"Where's the intern?" a female voice called from an office somewhere out of sight. "Colin needs a ride back to Stage sixteen."

Laura gave an exaggerated sigh and addressed me in a martyred tone. "Oh, *I'll* do it. Colin and I are *so* close. Then I've *got* to focus on *my* work. So much to do! I'll see you tonight around nine?" It was a dismissal. "Listen, there's a café near my place called the Sidewalk Café. They'll let you sit there for hours. They don't mind. I'll call when I'm on my way home, 'kay? See ya."

I watched her wobbly departure, trying to check my disbelief. My excitement about LA threatened to come crashing down. A miniature, weepy me was inside my head somewhere, curled up in a ball, homesick for Unknown and—but I shut her down. That girl was pathetic. This one wasn't. I pulled myself up, clutching my box.

As I passed Skinny Tie, I paused. "What's a First AD?"

"An assistant director. She preps the episode, oversees the shooting schedule, and runs the set, coordinating cast and crew. She's the director's right hand." He pointed to a pretty blonde with a walkie-talkie, a crowd around her. "Nina's our First AD."

I must have looked confused, because he patted my shoulder and said, "Lola's not a bad egg. She merely occupies a . . . unique state of reality." He handed me a card. "If you need anything." His name was Clark.

My vision of waltzing onto the lot and heroically pulling the Nikon lens free from the legendary stone in which it was embedded, fulfilling the prophecy to become the Chosen Image Taker, was ludicrous. Los Angeles wasn't Unknown. I wouldn't be talking my way into a job here.

It was 9:30 p.m. when Laura found me drooping into my tea. Waiters had begun to give me the eye. I was desperate to put my head down somewhere designed for sleep.

Laura looked frazzled. "What a day!" She plopped down. "You're lucky, you've been kicking back."

I blinked at her. "Let's go lie like vegetables on the couch." The idea was heaven on earth.

"Hmmm? Yeah, for a minute. Minka's coming at ten." She looked at her watch. "Oh Gawd! I barely have time to change!" She jumped up.

"Change?" I left a generous tip and trailed after her.

"I can't wear this, silly!" She smiled. "It's Wednesday! Wednesdays are Buffalo Club."

"A club?" My mind struggled. "Wait . . . my car," I remembered. "I have to get Oliver."

"Oliver?" That stopped her.

"My bird," I reminded.

"You brought your bird?"

I frowned. "Of course. What else would I do with him?"

"Oh. I dunno. Leave it or give it away." My mouth dropped open. She registered it. "Okay, okay." She followed me to where I was parked, muttering, "Minka's gonna be pissed if I'm not ready. . . ."

We drove down an alley in Venice Beach and parked by a dilapidated entrance to a more dilapidated unit in a dirty stucco building. The apartment was filthy. A biscuit-sized living room held a battered mustard sofa, an ancient TV, and a scarred coffee table piled high with *Us Weekly*, *Star*, *OK!*, and *In Touch* magazines. Volcanoes of clothing and pizza boxes obscured the dismal putty-colored carpeting. The adjacent kitchen was stocked with appliances from 1952. I peeked through the only doorway to see an even smaller bedroom. I looked back at the sofa and decided I was going to become quite acquainted with the water stain on the ceiling above it.

I returned after retrieving Oliver and my suitcase from the car to find Laura decked out in a tulle-swathed costume rejected by *Swan Lake*. She was considering an array of gaudy beads when an equally exquisite vision pranced in. Her dress looked like a belted garbage bag designed by Spock.

"Oooh, I *love* the turquoise belt," Laura squealed.

"Those pink go-go boots are *darling*." The

Minka creature stuck to script. "It's soooo *Lola!* Perez Hilton is gonna love them!"

"Do you think so?" Laura squealed. Oliver squawked in protest. This brought their attention to me. Silence fell. "You can't wear that." Laura spoke first.

"Oh." I regarded my perfectly normal jeans and T-shirt. Then saw my easy out. "I *know*. I'm *soooo bummed*. Everything I have is all packed and wrinkled. I *can't* go like *this*. You guys go ahead." Big sigh. Sad face. "Really—you guys go. I'll be ready next week!"

"Next week?" Minka giggled. "Tomorrow is Villa!" With that they were gone, and I was left with blessed calm. I opened the fridge and found some withered carrot sticks and half a lemon. The freezer held a dozen Butterfingers, two bottles of vodka, and the aura of an eating disorder. I took a Butterfinger. Laura hadn't given me a key, so a food foray was out. I gave Oliver a wilted carrot.

"At least we can get some sleep," I said.

I shook out my sleeping bag. I didn't want direct contact with the couch. I tried not to think about mold spores. My eyes strayed to my suitcase. I rooted in it and gently withdrew the story. *My* story. I curled against the cushions, already soothed as I started to read about a girl who loved to climb trees.

WITHIN two weeks, life in LA had settled into a pattern. Naturally, the studio job offers that Laura promised would fall like golden rain never materialized. After a few conversations that felt like trying to capture mist in a box, I gave up pressing her.

Unworried, I'd hit Main Street, starting with the Italian restaurant closest to Laura's place. You could always get a job waiting tables. Except, apparently, in LA. In a town teeming with aspiring actors, service jobs were gold. Surprisingly, Laura was unconcerned. "Don't sweat it," she said. "It took me a while, too." Living with her wasn't terrible, though the outfits were hard on the eyes. For a while, she and Minka dragged me around the party circuit until I could beg off and go home. Soon Laura stopped protesting when I elected to stay in, and I spent most of my nights reading or watching movies.

In the mornings I would rise, release Oliver, and start my day of rejection at local restaurants and cafés. When I spiraled into

the inevitable panic, I would stave off hyper-
ventilation by going for longer and longer
runs. The marathon was going to be a snap.

The only variation in the California scen-
ery was whether I ran north toward Malibu
or south toward Manhattan Beach. Either
way, I clocked the end of my run by the same
landmarks—the giant predator metal statue,
the pizza sign, the hookah café. I would slow
to a walk in front of my favorite tattoo parlor,
Do You Tattoo, and study the tattoos through
the window, feeling further from permanence
than ever, a dandelion fluff with no home, no
job, no tattoo. If I ran and never stopped, it
wouldn't matter to anyone but Oliver.

"You can't get a tattoo through the glass."
A voice made me jump one day. The speaker
was a tattoo-covered Mr. Clean in a sleeve-
less Hannah Montana concert shirt. He
looked at his watch. "I'm guessing about sixteen to eighteen miles today?" My mouth
dropped open. He laughed and tapped the
window. "It's glass. You can see in; we can
see out. C'mon in. I'll make tea."

I followed him. The shop was empty but
for a gothically pale skinny man in black
jeans and a black T-shirt with a skull on it.

He squealed when he looked up. "The little chicken came in!"

"Be nice, Jacob," Mr. Clean said. To me, he said, "This is Jacob. I'm Marion."

"Maeve," I said. "Are you hiring?"

"Nope. But there's no charge for hanging out." And, just like that, my routine expanded to include Marion and Jacob. I still had no job, but now I had something to do in the afternoons, drinking tea and pestering them to let me try my hand at tattooing.

"I'LL never meet Mr. Right," I moaned.

"I read something once that said love isn't about finding the right person, but about finding the right wrong person." Marion was concentrating on the design he was drawing. "The idea is, we're all different flavors of wrong . . ."

"Can I be Rainbow Sherbet Wrong?" I giggled.

"I want to be Triple Pistachio Wrong," Jacob called from his perch near the cash register.

Marion pinned us each with the look the real Mr. Clean gave shower scum. I shut up in a hurry. The shower scum always lost.

"By the time we're mature enough to have a relationship," Marion said, "it's because we're all a little wrong. We've got our quirks and issues and know what they are. That's essential for a real connection. If you don't know yourself, you don't know what works with you. When you've figured out *how* you're wrong, you can find a mate who complements that."

"I thought you were supposed to end up with the person who thinks you're perfect."

"Sounds exhausting and impossible to me. Can't change what you are, and you can't go back to who you were before life stamped some problems on you. It's like a tattoo— once you got it, you got it. Even if you remove it, there's a different kind of mark."

"Know thy scars?" I was intrigued. "So we're looking for someone who fits nicely against our unsolvable problems?"

" 'Zactly. If I don't know my true shape . . ."

"Try barrel-shaped, with an accent of pear," Jacob called.

". . . then I can't find the wrong shape that fits with me. Though if I look for a string-bean-shaped num-num-head in a tiresome eighties Goth T-shirt, I might be close."

It made sense to me. It was easier to contemplate working with my flaws than trying to magically become perfect. "I'm looking for Mr. Wrong."

"Not just any Mr. Wrong. The one you look at with love and think, 'This is the problem I want to have for the rest of my life, that I want to be my first and last problem of every day.' " Marion shot an affectionate look toward Jacob.

"I'm touched," Jacob said. "And I mean that in a very salt-touching-my-open-wound kind of way."

Chapter Twelve

Hilton Lows to Loews High

I WAS irritable as I jogged back to Laura-Lola's (as I now thought of her) place. My run had been very unsatisfactory. My heart had jerked alarmingly no fewer than three times as the corner of my eye saw one man with a back identical to Noah's, another with Noah's stride, and a third driving Noah's truck into a parking lot.

"This is ridiculous." I cursed. "Why am I obsessing about someone six hundred miles away who drives me mad?" It'd been over a month. I tried to recapture the outrage I'd felt pulling out of Unknown, but it eluded me. I couldn't even remember the reason I'd been angry, which, of course, made me angry. I'd worked myself into an excellent state by the time I walked in the door.

Laura-Lola, it seemed, had, too. Hers appeared to be one of exuberance. She was hopping excitedly around the living room. "You're not going to believe it!" she squealed excitedly. "I just found out that Perez Hilton is going to be at the Lisa Kline spring-line launch party tonight at her store on Robinson, and *I'm going to be there, too!* Minka got us on the list through her uncle!"

"Oh." I struggled for a response.

"Maeve, this is it. I know Perez and I are meant to be." She sighed, her eyes in a far-off place. "Once we meet, Perez will instantly recognize the depth of our connection."

I boggled over Laura-Lola's disconnect with reality. Perez Hilton was so openly gay that Elton John was jealous. "You're talking about Perez Hilton, the *Queen* of Media," I explored.

"Yes. He is so *insightful* about celebrities and how they really feel. He insults only the ones who are shallow and mean or on drugs."

"Mmm-hmm. Doesn't he out a lot of gay actors as well?"

"He's committed to honesty in the industry."

I recognized that I wasn't getting anywhere. "Let's get you ready, Betty. You've got a big night out."

"Oh, yeah, about that," Laura-Lola said, without any real concern. "You need to find someplace else to crash tonight. I don't know Perez's situation, so we could end up coming back here."

I boggled again. "Are you serious?"

She frowned. "Of course I'm serious. It's *my* house, isn't it?"

"I've got nowhere to go." Desperation tinged my tone.

"Can't you go visit Madelynn or whoever?" Her tone was disinterested as she sifted through a pile of clothes.

"It's Marion, and I can't just show up asking to stay!"

"Why not?" She threw over her shoulder the genuinely surprised look of the sublimely selfish.

"Laura, Perez Hilton is gay," I yelled.

Laura-Lola froze. Slowly she turned, face like a raptor.

"My . . . name . . . is . . . *Lola*," she pinched out. "Perez is a catch admittedly out of your league, but there is no need to cast aspirations on his character. I think you should leave now. You can come back to-morrow night."

"Road trip, don't forget the bird," said Oliver, the tension in the room making him anxious.

Laura-Lola rolled her eyes. "Don't worry about your bird. I kind of like him. He's al-ways telling me I look thinner."

My agitation subsided. Oliver's safety be-ing settled, my temporary homelessness didn't seem like that big a deal. I'd slept in Elsie before.

It was after six when I hit the boardwalk and wandered down to Do You Tattoo to see Marion. Maybe today I might be able to convince him to give me a tattoo lesson. But I skipped up to a dark store and a dismissive "Closed. We Went Camping" sign.

I turned away, stalking off to . . . where? I didn't know. I turned east toward Main Street and passed O'Brien's Pub. The patio was rollicking with happy, lively people; they annoyed me. The World Café, Joe's Diner, even the Coffee Bean were hopping. The Library Alehouse seemed less packed, so I braved my way in. I spotted one lonely stool at the bar. I elbowed through and grabbed it.

"Waiting for someone?" gleamed the bartender-actor, or "bactor."

"Johnny Depp will be here any minute." I pasted on a fake smile. "Can I have the Racer Five IPA?" I ordered my favorite beer.

He winked good-naturedly and turned to get my drink.

"Aren't people in LA so happy you can't stand it?" said the guy next to me.

I checked him out. He was about my height, skinny, and had a face you liked. Open brown eyes and a grin that said, "I get it and I was about to make the same joke."

"To tell the truth, it sort of makes me feel inadequate that I'm not happy all the time. What are *they* drinking?" I demanded.

"Well, it sure as hell doesn't have calories

or taste like this." He raised his pint of beer. On cue, Smiley-Bactor-Man returned with mine. I clinked my new friend.

"I'm Judd Wooten."

"I'm Maeve Connelly. My delusional roommate kicked me out for the night because *she* thinks *she's* going to seduce Perez Hilton at the Lisa Kline spring launch party."

Judd let out a guffaw. "You new to LA?"

"A month," I admitted. "I'm from North Carolina."

"Why did you come here?"

"I had cancer." The words came out. "I had leukemia when I was in college. It surprised everyone when I beat it. I thought it'd be easier to start over somewhere far away."

Judd assessed me. "Your hair is long."

I ducked my head in shame. "Yeah, I'm not at all heroic. I took a long time."

"Kudos to you, kid," he said seriously. "I lost my dad to cancer. How long have you been in remission?"

"Two years, seven months," I whispered.

Judd's face split into a wide smile. "You're cured! The two-year benchmark means a lot."

I was having this conversation in a bar after evading survivors' groups for so long. Judd signaled for his check, and I felt anticipatory loss for my newfound friend.

"So what do you do, Maeve Connelly?"

I slouched. "At the moment, I run on the beach, take pictures, and try to figure out what the hell I'm going to do."

"What kind of pictures?" Judd looked interested.

"Oh, you know, just people doing what they do. I used to get paid for it."

Judd signed his credit card receipt. "You like taking pictures?"

"I love it."

"You want to shoot, you call me." He slid me a card. "I run a company that photographs special events." He smiled. "I'd love to have you on board, purely because I like the way you think and I'm partial to long braids." He tugged one, but it didn't feel predatory. This was the first person in LA other than Marion who seemed to be himself. "Organize a serious portfolio. I'll pitch you to my partners and we'll see what we can do."

I looked at his card. It was professional: WOOT PRINTS PHOTOGRAPHY.

"Wow, Judd. Thanks!" Was it possible that for once, timing had worked in my favor, planting me next to this guy?

Judd stood, slinging a camera bag from the floor over his shoulder. "I've got to go. I've got to cover a fashion event party at Lisa Kline tonight." He winked as my mouth dropped open. "I'll try to get some good ones of the 'seduction' for you."

I WAS headed down Main Street toward the Santa Monica Promenade when my cell phone rang.

"Maeve?"

I sucked in my breath, frozen. After phantom sightings of Noah all day, the real one was saying my name. Repeatedly.

"Maeve? Are you there? Hello? Maeve, can you hear me?"

I smiled at his impatience. "What's up, duck?"

"Oh, there you are." His voice was relieved.

"I'm here, Big Ears. How the hell are you?" I forced casual cheer.

"At the moment, hungry and in need of a drink."

Huh. Well. Okay. "Too far away to help, I'm afraid."

"Actually, I'm in Santa Monica. At the Loews Hotel."

My heart stopped. Then started like a bird trying to fly out of my chest. He'd come for me! Noah was here to take me home!

"I'm in town for an independent book-sellers' conference."

His words shot the bird like an arrow. But my happiness was only slightly diminished. He was *here*. Near me.

"So I was hoping you'd meet me?"

"You betcha." I tried not to sound overly enthusiastic. "There's this great little dive right there called Chez Jay. For Irish pubs we have Finn's and O'Brien's. Or there's—"

Noah's voice had an unseen smile when he interrupted my verbal flow. "Why don't you come to the hotel? If it's not too far for you." Always courteous.

"Sure, sure. I'm close. Ten minutes?"

"I'll be at the bar."

It was less than ten minutes before I was smiling at the doorman as I stepped into the Loews lobby. It exuded understated luxury and the scent of expensive floral arrangements. I located the bar and headed toward it.

I spotted his back instantly, and felt the same jolt as earlier. Only this time it *was* his back. Inhale. Exhale. As if feeling my presence, he turned, and something warm flooded my body. I crossed the distance as he slid off his stool and stepped to me, meeting in a hug that increased from tight to bone-crushing. Finally he released me and smiled down from six foot four.

"You look great." His green eyes were warm. I grinned back.

"You should've warned me to wear sunglasses, pasty," I joked.

"I've been trapped inside a store." He shook his head, face rueful. "I just can't keep good help." Now my smile spread, and we beamed goofily at each other like awkward teenagers. Noah recovered first.

"My lady." Ever the gentleman, he assisted me onto a barstool. "I was about to order something to eat. Will you join me?"

My stomach's loud rumble would have overpowered a sonic boom. Noah started, then laughed. Without a word, he gave my braid a tug and turned to the bartender.

"We'll have one filet, medium, please, and one of the halibut, miso broth on the side, peas steamed with no butter. And a bottle of your Cambria Pinot Noir."

"But . . ."

"And we'll start with the crab cake appetizer." He looked at me. "You like crab cakes, right?" He didn't wait for an answer. He shut the menu with a satisfied snap.

I felt a little panicky at the thought of the cost. "Noah . . ."

"Maeve, allow your old boss to buy you dinner. This is on the corporate tab."

I gestured to the lavish surroundings and raised an eyebrow. "This is pretty swish for an independent bookshop. Dipping a hand into the till, are we? Wait until the boss finds out. You're canned."

He laughed, but his right eyebrow did the thing where it creased down on one side. It was his tell. There was something he wasn't saying. He noticed me noticing, and looked shifty.

"Tell me about this independent booksellers' conference."

His gaze flicked away. "Nothing very exciting. Room full of people looking worried."

Definitely. There was definitely something he was withholding. I pondered it. Then horror flooded my body.

"You got married," I accused, feeling sick. I felt miserable.

His eyes flew back to mine, astounded. "What? Maeve, no . . . that's just ridiculous. Preposterous, even. Beth and I—"

"There's something you're not telling me," I interrupted. I didn't want to hear about Beth. "You have the worst poker face, Noah."

He was smiling again. He tapped my hand on the bar and began to absentmindedly play with my fingers. "It's not that big a deal." He gave a laugh, embarrassed. "I've been flown out by a studio. They're interested in *The Boy Who Could Fly.* They've optioned the rights to make a film. They're trying to impress me Hollywood style, hence the highbrow food and hotel."

"Noah, that's incredible!" I launched across the space between our barstools, throwing my arms around him. He reflexively wrapped his around me and returned the hug. It felt so good to be captured against his chest that I couldn't move. Someday I'd have to face the reality that he belonged to another. But not tonight. We held each other until it wasn't about congratulations anymore. I didn't pull away until the sound of his cell phone jarred the mood.

"Hello?" Then his expression became strange. "Beth." He mouthed "Excuse me" in my direction and hurried away from the bar, phone close to his mouth. After five minutes, he returned, seeming agitated.

"How's Beth?" I faked interest.

"Demanding." He frowned. "Maeve—"

"Okay, then, crab cakes?" The bartender interrupted him, placing a dish in front of us. Beth might be dominant in Noah's life, but I didn't want to hear about it. I seized my fork and took a bite. Noah opened his mouth, then closed it. After a pause, he picked up his fork as well. Diversion successful. "So tell me more about it."

"My agent called a few weeks ago with an offer. But it doesn't mean they'll actually make the movie," he warned. "It just means they've bought the right to be the only ones who can decide to make the movie for the next two years."

I swatted him. "I *have* learned a thing or

two about Hollywood since I got here."

"You've really taken to LA. I was impressed with your social savvy, suggesting all the places we could go. You definitely don't miss Unknown." Noah's voice was funny.

Oh, but I do, I wanted to say. Instead I said, "How's that Ronnie Two Shoes been behaving?"

After a while our main courses arrived. We salted and peppered and somewhere in there a second bottle of wine appeared. Noah asked me about life in LA. I asked about the Monkey Flower Festival plans. I felt a pang at the thought of missing the festival.

"And are you happy?" Noah asked.

"Yeah, sure." I didn't meet his eyes.

Noah looked at his watch. It was midnight. He looked at me regretfully. "I should probably get to bed. I have an early flight tomorrow."

"But you haven't been to the beach yet! Let's go."

"Now?" he asked in disbelief.

"Yes. It'll be perfect. Santa Monica by moonlight." I was already rising from my stool when he stopped me with a hand on my arm.

"Maeve, what's going on?" His face was concerned.

"Nothing's going on. It just seems like we should hang out. Who knows when we'll see each other again?" I had a brainstorm. "Hey, I know! Let's stay up all night and watch the sunrise!"

"Unfortunately, I'll practically see the sunrise if I want to make my flight. So I'm going to have to put you in a taxi, I'm afraid."

"Taxi? Oh no. I'm not taking a taxi." I accepted defeat, but refused to have him know the mess I was in.

"Don't be ridiculous. I'll pay for it. I'm not letting you wander into the night after two bottles of wine."

"It's not that. It's . . . I mean, I prefer to walk."

"That's it." He crossed his arms. "What's going on?"

I opened my mouth. Then I closed it. Exhaustion washed over me. I was tired of taking care of myself. I wanted someone else to share the load. "I have nowhere to go," I confessed.

"What do you mean?" He looked confused. I explained, bracing myself for his upbraid at getting myself into this predicament. Instead, he broke into a laugh. "You silly goose, you can stay with me. Why didn't you say something hours ago?"

I shook my head, bemused.

"C'mon." He stood, and I followed him, like a puppy.

The room he let us into was spacious and attractive, dominated by a king bed. I felt awkward. Noah caught my hesitation and tugged my hand. "C'mon, settle in. We'll watch TV until you're sleepy."

We flopped onto the bed, burrowing in against the pillows.

"Where's the remote?" I feigned casual, trying not to be aware of his body stretched out next to mine. We both looked around.

"Uh-oh." Noah pointed. The remote was across the room, on top of the TV.

"Well, go get it," I said.

"You go get it," he said.

"I'm the guest," I argued.

"I rescued you," he disputed. "You should show me gratitude."

I turned on my side, propped up on my elbow. "Oh yeah? Well I rescued you from being that lonely guy at the bar drinking and eating alone. You should show *me* gratitude."

"I paid for that dinner."

"No, you didn't. The studio did," I countered.

"Well I gave you a job when you were broke and desperate."

"Oh, please. You were a mess. I saved that place for you."

His look was incredulous. "Cheeky monkey. I graciously hired your unemployable self, *and* I chauffeured you around Arizona."

"I made you sandwiches when you would have starved to death, *and* organized your life, *and* made sure you paid your taxes."

He shook his head, smiling. "It figures that I finally get you into my bed and we're arguing."

I frowned at him. Surely he didn't mean . . .

Noah laughed and pressed his index finger on the crease between my eyebrows. "Watch out," he teased. "Your divot is showing."

"I see London, I see Kent, I see someone's forehead dent." I paraphrased childhood lyrics. I thrilled at his touch.

"You seem unperturbed." He was surprised.

I flopped on my back. "It's funny," I said. "I worried so much about that divot." I let the truth come out. "Some days they were pumping chemicals in my body designed to kill half my cells, and I directed all my energy to maintaining a placid facial expression. I'm not sure why I thought I could control that one wrinkle when I couldn't control my cells, my hair, my dry skin, my chapped lips. But I was going to block that furrow, no matter what. And you know why?" I looked up at him again. "Because I knew I was going to die," I said out loud. And paused to catch my breath. Noah's gaze stayed steady. "I knew I was going to die, and I didn't want to be lying in my coffin with a divot on my forehead. I wanted to be a good-looking corpse."

"And now?" Were Noah's eyes shimmering? I'd definitely had a lot of wine.

"And now I'm going to live a hell of a long time," I gloated. "I won. I'm going to do so many things in my life and have so many wrinkles that by the time I'm done, I'll be a wizened old crab apple. I have a life. And this"—I pointed at my forehead—"this is the first stamp on my passport."

I smiled up at him. He leaned down and kissed me. It was so sudden I didn't realize it was happening until it was. The moment his lips touched mine, we locked in an embrace, pent-up longing coursing between us. Time suspended as the kiss went on and on. It was beyond anything I had dreamed of in all my imagined Noah fantasies. I gave myself completely to the kiss.

He pulled back at last and gently brushed my bangs off my forehead. "Thank God for you," he murmured. "I can't imagine a world without Maeve." He kissed me again and smiled, bumping his nose against mine.

Emotions were raging through me. They must have reflected on my face, because Noah frowned and jerked back. His expression became frozen. "I'm sorry. You weren't expecting to get jumped. I promised you a safe place to stay—here you were opening up to me and I leaped on you. God, what's wrong with me? I'm so sorry, Maeve." He released me and rolled on his back, looking wretched.

I stared at the man I loved. I wanted him so badly. I grabbed a fistful of his shirt and pulled him back against me. "Stop talking," I commanded against his mouth, unbuttoning his shirt.

I AWOKE to a boxing match between disorientation and cottonmouth. Disorientation had an early advantage as I absorbed a bed too comfortable to be Laura-Lola's futon. Shock flooded my system, along with the memory that last night I'd slept with another woman's boyfriend.

I began to cry. Noah hadn't behaved above reproof, but I was worse, keeping him at the bar long after he intended to go to bed, attacking him when he'd only given me a kiss. He was the wrong "wrong person" for me. I couldn't fix the ways I wasn't perfect, but I could avoid what made me imperfect in ways I couldn't live with.

Enough was enough. I'd been waiting for Los Angeles to fix itself for me, and that hadn't happened. It was time to get off my ass. Things were going to be different, starting today.

I dragged on last night's clothes and was heading for the door when I saw the $20 bill on the dresser with a note that said "For a cab—N." I froze in shock. Tears started again and I was pulling out my phone to call my sister when a wave of nausea hit. I raced to the bathroom, stumbling as I reached to brace myself on the toilet. The porcelain knocked my phone into the toilet, and I had only a moment to watch it sink to the bottom before I threw up on top of it.

It'd been a cheap phone to start with and would never survive this. For once I didn't curse my bad luck. This punishment was deserved. I turned to go, pausing only to take the $20 and crumple the note. I was going to need a new cell phone, after all, so Noah could call and explain why he left me money after cheating on his girlfriend.

When I got back to Venice, Laura was sitting on the sofa, listlessly flipping channels. I tried to gauge her mood. I'd bet my whole twenty dollars on Not Good. "Hey," I said. "How was last night?"

She looked about to break into tears. "I'm a complete idiot."

"Oh, hey! Lau— *Lola,* no."

She gave a snotty burble of a laugh. "You can call me Laura." Her lip started to tremble. "But really, I think I'm not very smart."

"Hey." I scooted over and put my arm around her. "You are plenty smart. You have a heart of gold, sister, and don't you forget it. Look at how you've taken care of me."

"Taken care of you?" she scoffed. "You're the last person in the world that needs taking care of. You're not afraid of anything. You came all the way out here by yourself. In about a minute you'll have it all figured out and be way more successful than I'll ever be." From where her head rested on my shoulder, she couldn't see my fly-catching mouth. "Besides, I was awful to you last night."

"No . . ."

"Yes, I was. Can you believe I thought I was going to hook up with Perez Hilton?" Her tone rose to a wail. I was about to say that I would never have guessed Marion was gay, when she cried, "He had a *million* girls with him. He didn't even *look* at me. I'm so stupid." I shut my mouth. "So where'd you stay last night? I'm really sorry I kicked you out."

I opened my mouth to make a dismissive joke and turn the conversation back to her. Then I paused. And changed my mind.

"You won't believe it," I said, and began to tell her the story.

A WEEK LATER, JUDD sifted through the photos spread on the desk before him. I'd spent most of the week creating a portfolio for him.

"I'm impressed." He looked at me. "We all were. A little too impressed. I'm not sure you'll find the work we do . . . uh . . . artistically stimulating."

"There's an art to paying rent," I said.

"You're hired."

I exhaled in relief. "Now I can replace the cell phone I dropped in the toilet."

"I wondered about your, er, complicated messaging system." Judd raised an eyebrow.

I snorted. It'd been a nightmare since I'd lost my phone. Until I could afford a replacement, I was dependent on Laura to field messages and let me use her phone to return calls. It was my penance. Not that it mattered. He hadn't called. It hurt.

"Anyway, your missions for Woot Prints," Judd went on, "are mostly charity events where no one remembers the charity, exclusive private parties that exist merely to be crashed by those higher on the Hollywood food chain—who never do—and promotional launches that attempt to convince

meaningless twits that their indistinguish-
able product is indispensable."

"So what do I actually do?"

"Every gig is swarming with the B-and-
lower list. You're there to catch their good
side. Consider it a challenge. If you can catch
one of these creatures showing genuine self
without artifice, that'll be a masterpiece."

We decided that I would shadow Judd for
a few events, learn the dance steps, then start
solo with some small gigs.

"Fantastic. See you Wednesday!"

"Just out of curiosity . . ." Judd stopped
me as I gathered my things. He tapped a
print. "Who's this?"

Stab of pain. The picture caught Noah,
chin resting on his hands as he stared at his
computer. "No one," I said.

"Right." Judd didn't buy it. "See you
Wednesday."

It was the truth. Noah didn't exist for me
anymore. Despite me making very sure that
Tuesday had Laura's number, with strict instructions to give it to "everyone," he hadn't
called, making it very clear what he thought
of me—or, rather, that he didn't. I had too
much pride to call him. When people had

bailed on me when I got cancer, I was smart enough to blame the cancer, not myself. Noah hadn't called because he didn't feel like it. End of story.

When I walked into Do You Tattoo, Marion didn't even look up from the *Semper Fi* he was inking on a Marine.

"Go ahead," he grunted.

I headed for the phone.

"Aloha," came the lyrical greeting.

"Tuesday! I got a job! I'm an event photographer."

"I'm happy for you. Well, sort of happy. I kind of hoped you'd come back. Noah refuses to hire anyone—"

"Tuesday." I cut her off. She was under strict instructions. If Noah didn't care to talk to me himself, I didn't want to hear about him.

"Ugh, sorry. I swear, the two of you. That must have been one humdinger of a fight that neither of you will talk about."

"Tuesday."

"Okay, Miss Avoidance, what else is new?"

I told her about Laura and Marion and Jacob, but soon I ran dry, because there was this giant thing I couldn't tell her—what had happened with Noah.

"Things sound good," she said. "I'm astonished you got my message. It took me forever to convince your friend Laura that I was *named* Tuesday, instead of wanting you to call me *on* Tuesday."

"I'm glad you did. It's good to talk to you." I was reluctant to end the call but was without the means of extending it.

"Aloha, love," she said, before cutting my connection to Unknown.

Chapter Thirteen

Life

I WAS hot, sweaty, and irritated.

"I'm not sure you got my best side on that one." The collagen-enhanced lips moved as the pink and white gels swept the bleached hair off the Botoxed forehead. I dutifully snapped a picture identical to the first. When the "reality" star turned away, I paused and waited. Within five seconds I was rewarded, and snapped a picture of her gorgeous manicure grasping the expensive silk fabric she wore and unglamorously digging it out of her butt. *Click*.

I slipped through the party. I couldn't complain. It was a good job and paid just fine. It didn't give me the artistic satisfaction my work in Unknown had, but satisfaction had never paid the rent.

After the party I walked down Pacific to a small Venice street, paper clutched in hand. I found the sign for Ozone, double-checked the address, and hurried to number 21. The buzzer sounded, and I took an old-time elevator with a folding iron cage door up to the fourth floor.

When the woman came to the door, I was startled by how pretty she was. Elegant was the word that came to mind.

"Maeve?"

"Dimple?"

"Nice to meet you." We shook hands. "Please come in." Her smile was warm, gesture graceful.

"Thanks for seeing me," I said.

"It's no problem. I think this might work out."

I stepped into the apartment and was instantly in love. This was definitely going to work out. I staged a thoughtful hand to my chin to keep from blurting, "I'll take it!" The front room was all light and windows. The woodwork was bare cedar, walls vanilla. The kitchen wall had inlaid tiles. The corner bedroom was all windows on two walls. The bathroom was tiled in white octagonal tiles with a decorative black pattern.

Dimple gave a nervous laugh. "Don't think this is weird, but if you want to see the room's best feature, lie on the bed."

I didn't skip a beat. I stretched out. "What's the feature?"

"Look toward the ocean."

Without lifting my head from the pillow, I could see an incredible ocean panorama, sailboats dotting the horizon. I bolted upright. "Holy guacamole, was that a dolphin?!"

"Yeah." She grinned. "You can see them most mornings. As soon as you open your eyes."

"So you want to sublet it furnished?" I started the negotiation.

"Mmm-hmm. And you're okay with month to month so long as I give you reasonable notice that I'd like to come back?"

"Yep."

"What can you afford?"

"What do you need?"

As it turned out, we had exactly the same price in mind.

"A true meeting of the minds." I grinned.

"I FOUND a place to live," I reported to Tuesday without preamble when she answered her phone later that day. Relying on Laura's phone had made my calls efficient.

"That's great," she said, but her tone was subdued.

"Is everything okay?"

"No. Yes. I mean . . . I'm just tired." She sighed. "I'm heading home from the hospital." My heart stopped. "It's Child."

"What?"

"It's okay. He's okay. God, I'm crap at this." I could see her biting her lip. "I was about to call you. We were waiting for definite news. He's going to be fine. He was having chest pains."

I was immobile, hand pressed to my eyes, world pulsating.

"He went to see Samuel. The EKG revealed a significant blockage, so they hustled him to the hospital. They had him on the table within thirty minutes and put in a stent." Her voice caught a little. "It was a ninety-eight percent blockage."

My breath came easier. "Okay. That's okay. My dad has a stent. In a way this is better. Now we're on alert, and we monitor."

"I know. The doctors said he's fine. It was a little scary, that's all."

"God. You're telling *me*." My relieved laugh was a bark. "That was almost as bad as when I thought Noah and Beth had gotten married!" It slipped out before I could stop it.

"Ha!" Tuesday's snicker was equally relieved. "Married? As if. Those two can barely pass a civil word since they broke up. And it was debatable how much they talked *before* it ended."

There it was again. That moment when time shimmers a beat, like passing through a membrane to another world.

"What did you say?"

"I said I doubt they talked when they were still together. In the beginning, sure, but . . ."

"They broke up?"

"Of course! Before you left. Are you telling me you didn't know?" she demanded. "He was going to tell you when you went to the store to say good-bye. I don't know what the hell happened, since neither one of you will talk about it, but afterward he moped around like a kicked dog."

I swallowed. "But then he—"

"Noah ran into Samuel, and they got to talking. He did the math and realized you had to have broken up with Samuel before you left. Quite coincidentally, all of a sudden he's got meetings and a conference in Los Angeles and is off."

"But Beth called him. When he was here."

"Probably to tell him she was keeping his Jeff Buckley records or something equally witchy." I was speechless. "Are you there?"

I made a strangled sound.

"I don't know what happened out there, but after he got back, he went from being a kicked dog to being a neurotic teenager asking if there'd been any calls every two seconds—even though he had his phone in his hand constantly—to being an aaaaangry bear."

"So." I licked my lips. "So when he was here, in LA, he wasn't . . . he and Beth weren't . . ."

"Weren't even speaking. Correct. And every time he calls you, he gets some girl hyperventilating about the fact that you're out at some fabulous party so exclusive she can't get in. He's convinced you're living the glamorous socialite's life and want nothing to do with a small-town hick like him—his words, not mine."

"What? That's ridiculous," I protested. Noah had called?

"You know you're my little hibiscus, but I don't get it. You return everyone's calls but Noah's. And he was horribly worried about you being too broke for a cab when he saw you. He was ready to wire you every penny he had to make sure you had enough to eat. He almost went mad when he heard you'd lost your phone. It really hurt him to find out you were partying every night."

"I was working! I was photographing events."

"Good luck getting that through his thick head. After fifty-seven unreturned calls, I can't blame him. Why didn't you just call back?"

"I never got any messages!" I was going to strangle Laura-Lola. "I had no idea! I thought he was blowing *me* off."

"You're the only person on the planet who can't see that Noah only has *maka* for you."

"I hope *maka* means 'eyes,' " I muttered.

"So now that you know, what are you going to do?" Tuesday demanded. My lack of answer was notable.

"Don't tell him anything about this while I try to figure it out."

After we hung up, I crossed to Laura's room in two steps. "Did someone named Noah call me?" The words tumbled out so fast they made no sense.

"What?" She looked up from *In Touch* magazine.

"Did. I. Get. Any. Calls. From. A. Man. Named. Noah."

"Oooohhh. You mean No One? There was this guy who called, like, a *million* times, but every time I asked who was calling, he said, 'No one,' or 'No-one-thanks,' like it was one word." She giggled. "He was really polite, but never left his name. I didn't think it was worth mentioning." She shrugged, smile bright. "Mr. No One!"

I sagged against the door frame. "Oh. Thanks."

I rolled back into the living room. So Noah had called. Noah wasn't a cheater. My relief was intense. But, I frowned, was it about Noah? I was over being "taken care of." I was finally doing a pretty good job on my own. Tuesday's question echoed in my mind. *What are you going to do?* "I don't know," I murmured.

I TRIPPED over a box in the dark living room and cursed as my shin collided with the coffee table. An official resident of Venice Beach, I'd been living out of suitcases for a month, and I seriously needed to unpack, but September was the busy season at work, and I'd had no time. All the television premieres held launch parties packed with people craving to be photographed. This was the eighth night in a row I'd gotten home after 2:00 a.m. Too tired to turn on the light, I wanted only to fall into bed.

When I awoke, I experienced the daily spurt of pleasure I'd known since getting my own place. I was exhausted from the amount of work I had to take on to make the rent, but, despite the cost, it was worth it. Every morning I remembered I was living in my own apartment, with my own job, in California, completely self-sufficient. I'd done what I had set out to do.

"Howdy, pardner," Oliver greeted me when I entered the living room.

"Howdy yourself," I said. It felt good to speak aloud. Last week, four days had gone by where I hadn't spoken a word beyond "Hi" and "Thank you" to clerks providing me with goods in exchange for money. I resolved to drop by Marion's tattoo parlor for an overdue visit. Being so busy, I barely saw the few friends I had.

I didn't have a job until evening, so I spent the morning sorting out the apartment. The bruise on my shin demanded it. I hung clothes and put books on the shelves. I wasn't ready to put nails in the walls, even though Dimple had assured me it was fine. Though I'd left more than two months ago, I was still too homesick for Unknown to put up my pictures. The one thing I displayed in pride of place was the card I'd received from my parents when I'd sent them my new address. It read *We couldn't be more proud of you.*

By three, I was down to the last box. I sat on the floor and pulled it toward me. It was labeled "Miscellaneous." At the very bottom, under a jumble of pens and pencils, was *The Girl Who Could*. I carefully extracted the beautiful book. I opened it to the dedication and slowly turned the pages. By the time I came to the end, I'd made a decision.

"Oliver," I told the bird, "we're going home."

"I'M GLAD," Vi said.

"I had to come here, though, to be able to make the choice."

"I get you. When are you going to leave?"

"As soon as I can. I want to find someone trustworthy to take over the apartment sublet. I don't want to screw Dimple. I think Clark, the guy who works with Laura, might take it. I also want to do all the jobs Judd assigned to me. He took a chance on me, so I owe it to him, especially during the busy season. And I want to build a comfortable financial cushion so I don't get myself stranded like I did on the way out."

"Let me send you some money," Vi offered.

"You're still calling me from Marion's phone."

"No." I shook my head. "I can do this on my own. I have a plan."

A week and a few (borrowed) phone calls later, I put my plan into action. First was a trip to buy photo paper and inexpensive mattes and frames. Next, an all-night after-hours printing binge at the Woot Prints darkroom, permission of Judd. Finally, setting up my booth on the boardwalk one busy Saturday.

I displayed for sale both framed and unframed photos of Venice and Unknown. Avid buyers snapped up pictures with enthusiasm. By sunset, I'd sold all my stock.

Three weeks later, Clark and Dimple had agreed on the sublet, I'd had several successful weekends on the boardwalk and a substantial nest egg, and I'd finished my last job for Judd. Elsie had recently had a bath, and my things were in boxes. I was ready to go, almost.

MARION looked up when I walked into the tattoo parlor. I'd said good-bye to Judd and Laura. My last stop was Marion and Jacob.

"How'd it go?" he asked.

"I sold 'em all again." I was flush with profit. "Check it out." I waved my shiny new iPhone at him.

"Nice. But I hate to lose you," he said.

"You're not losing me," I said. "You just have to drive farther."

He handed me a bag. "I got you these." Inside were several pairs of touristy Los Angeles kneesocks. "So you remember us."

"I love you, too," I said. "I got you this." I handed him a miniature Oscar statue that said *Best Friend Award.*

Jacob wandered out. "Hey'ya, chicken."

My smile broadened. "Not this time." I slapped $60 on the counter and tapped the page I'd found in the book. "This one. Right here." I tapped my neck behind my ear.

"Rock on!" Jacob exclaimed. We high-fived.

Marion pulled the book to him and looked at the design. "That's a good one," was all he said, but his voice was gruff.

I knotted my hair and tilted my head so he could ink me with the Chinese symbol for Life. My decision was permanent.

Afterward, Oliver and I walked over the soft white sand down to the water. I sat cross-legged and watched the mesmerizing roll of the waves. I felt the sun on my face, smelled the salt. Oliver tugged strands from my braids. I breathed. I didn't take a picture. I didn't frame the scene. I *was* the scene. Breath, light, warm sand. I wasn't on the outside. I was the center of everything. Breathing. Feeling.

When it was time, I reached into my pack. There was one last thing I needed to do. I couldn't go back in time and give Cameron this last kachina, but I could say good-bye.

I WAS perched on the side of Cameron's bed. For a change, it was just the two of us.

"No more," she begged. We'd been playing "Would You Rather . . . ?" for almost an hour.

"You just don't want to choose between a hairy mole and a third nipple," I chided.

"Hairy mole! It'd be the only hair I've got." Her laugh turned to a cough that turned to gasping for air. She was as pallid as onionskin, except for purple shadows bruising beneath her eyes.

She leaned her head back as she regained control of her breathing. "I think I'm ready for this to be over," she croaked, without opening her eyes.

A flash of agreement, then revolt. Cameron had been the gift God handed me when I needed it the most. I wasn't ready to give her back. "Does it hurt?" I asked.

"Don't ask me that." She silenced me, eyes open now.

"Are you afraid?" I asked.

"No." Her head was comically large for her twig neck, and her shake was more wobble. "You know how it is."

I nodded, but I didn't. I'd never gotten to that place where fear let go. When death had danced close, I'd been afraid. But even when they'd asked if we wanted a priest, they hadn't stopped the fight; chemicals continued to flow. And worked a miracle. Cameron was off the tubes. No more battling. This was a different kind of waiting.

"Tell them," she made me pledge. "Tell them I wasn't afraid. Coming from you, they might believe it."

Again I nodded, wondering what I could possibly say to her family, a twenty-two-year-old trying to comfort broken sixty-year-olds.

Cameron went on. "For years I was the manic, melodramatic cancer-won't-get-the-best-of-me person. But you know what? Cancer sometimes will get the best of you, and that's why it sucks. I'm not saying permanently, just sometimes. Remember that."

"Are you giving me a parting lecture?"

She managed a laugh. "I don't know what I would say for my last lecture." We held eyes, wondering what wisdom we could give each other in our diverging journeys. When she spoke at last, she simply said, *"Live."*

"As long as I can." I made the only promise I could keep.

She made a feeble gesture to her long-abandoned desk. "Get that envelope. It's for you."

"What is it?" I drew out a thick sheet of watercolor paper. Cameron was incredibly talented. She had been an art student.

It was a watercolor comic map of the United States, scattered with caricature icons—a cowboy galloping across Texas, an Amish horse and buggy cantering through Pennsylvania, Mount Rushmore dominating South Dakota, surfers cresting California's coast. In the middle, hanging out of a bright red convertible, waved a blond girl with a wide smile, driving, and Cameron's grinning freckled face on the passenger's side.

"It's all the places we said we'd go when we got better."

I swallowed hard. "I might not get better," I said.

"You might," she said.

"I can't do it alone." I wasn't talking about the road trip.

"Not to sound like Dr. Phil, but you're only as alone as you want to be."

"I think I might want to be." My throat was tight. "For a while."

"That's a choice." Her voice was fading as she tired, but she managed a smile. "But when you're ready"—she indicated the colorful map—"take me with you."

I'd cried a normal amount once—skinned knee, dead dog, broken heart. But when I got sick and had a well of legitimate causes, the tears had dried up. I hadn't wanted to wash away in them. In that moment, the valve burst, and every single tear I'd ever held back erupted. I put my head on her knees and sobbed. The watercolor still bears the blotch that stained the corn palace in Iowa before

Cameron extracted the map to safety. She made shushing noises, hand on my head.

"I'm going to miss you," I burbled through the snot.

She feebly tapped the map. "I'll be right here."

I pulled myself together and mopped my face. "If you live, I'll get you a corn dog and funnel cake at the Minnesota State Fair."

She laughed. "How did you know what I wanted for my last meal?"

"Crazy in the brains!" I scolded. "You need to shop on the right-hand side of the menu. Get the lobster thermidor and baked Alaska."

"How about snow crab legs and artichokes . . ."

We bantered until her parents arrived. I would not be alone with Cameron again before her death three days later. It was years before I was able to say "I love you" to anyone, because I hadn't said it to her.

I EXTRACTED the jar from my bag. I'd been carrying it with me a long time. "I hope you enjoyed the trip," I said to Cameron. "I'm sorry it took so long."

I unsealed my portion of Cameron's ashes and gently shook her into the breeze. Soon I would write her parents and tell them what I had done. I could stop avoiding them.

When the jar was empty, I filled it with Venice Beach sand. In the resulting hollow, I nestled a kachina for Cameron. While her ashes continued her exploration of the world, the sixth kachina would stay on the California beach she'd dreamed of seeing. The statue intertwined a bird, nest, fish, and wave. I wondered if my mom had been thinking of my friend when she created it. It reminded me of Cameron's own drawings. To me, the seamless joining of elements and animals meant belonging. I didn't belong to Los Angeles, but I belonged to myself at last, body and spirit. I was grateful to this place for giving that to me. I didn't need to stay until October. This particular marathon was over, though surely there would be others. I was ready for my new home.

The seventh kachina, the mother figure with the owl, would return with me. It was mine to keep, to remind me of where I began, and of the six others that marked my journey to where I was now. With a last gaze at the ocean, I walked to where Elsie was waiting to take me to the desert.

"Where're you headed?" The parking attendant looked at my packed car. "You're loaded."

What he didn't know was how free I finally was. "Destination Unknown." I smiled.

WHEN I pulled into Unknown, it was a far different scene from my shadowy arrival many months ago. Though it was after dark, the town square was bustling with preparations for the Monkey Flower Festival. I could see Bruce and Ronnie bickering over how to erect the tent. Liz Goldberg and Jenny Up were hanging paper lanterns on the bandstand, while Helen Rausch skulked nearby, ready to pounce on flaws in their work. Fairy lights were strung from every possible branch and structure. I could see Tuesday's work in clusters of misshapen paper flowers. I didn't see Noah's tall frame among the crowd, but that didn't worry me. I headed home to Ruby's. I had all the time in the world.

Epilogue

"RED wine?"

"Yes, thanks. Did you get the popcorn?"

Pause.

"You remembered to get the popcorn, right?"

Cough.

"Are you kidding me? You forgot the popcorn! What's movie night without popcorn?"

"I had a deadline! I was focused on getting chapters out."

"Spare me. You spent the entire day distracting me while I was trying to research the impact of Indonesian imports on domestic cement production for *Cement Times: Solid Facts.*"

"I didn't notice you complaining." Haughty.

"*Whatever*, clever. Let's watch the movie."

"Where's the remote?"

Silence.

"It's on the TV."

"Well, go get it."

"You go get it."

"I'm the guest."

"Right. You have more stuff here than I do. There's no room for *my* socks anymore!"

"If you can call those socks."

"There is nothing wrong with black socks."

Snort. "Fine. If you won't get the remote, we'll just sit here."

"Fine." Quiet. "I can think of something to do . . ."

Giggle. "That tickles."

Pause. "Want me to stop?"

"Not on your life. C'mere . . ."

Long silence.

"Maeve?"

"Yes, Noah?"

"What's this I hear about you opening a tattoo parlor in the corner of the bookstore?"

CHARLES MARTIN

What gave Charles Martin the idea to write *The Mountain Between Us*? "A friend and I were climbing the Woody Ridge Trail in the eastern U.S. It gains 3,400 vertical feet in 2.2 miles. The conditions were horrible. My friend dehydrated a few hundred feet from the top. Started having decision-making trouble and losing fine motor skills. The temp dropped to about zero, snow was blowing sideways, and I figured we needed to get our Florida selves in a tent fast. We did. I got him changed—out of wet and into dry—and we listened to the wind try and rip us

© Deborah Feingold

off the mountaintop. Hovering over my Jetboil in that tent, I began thinking, If a few variables changed, then this could get messy. My imagination took over from there."

KERRY REICHS

Driving across the United States while researching *Leaving Unknown*, Kerry Reichs discovered that "if you plan ahead poorly and find there is no room at the inn, you can, in fact, sleep comfortably in a Mini Cooper. . . . I've spent the equivalent of a weekend in every state but North Dakota. I've been to the corn palace, Cadillac Ranch, and the world's largest wooden bucket. I've visited Why, Odd, Normal, Surprise, Truth or Consequences, and Last Chance."

Reichs practiced law for six years before taking a sabbatical to write. "I always intended to write a book. In my mind, it was to be when I was older and I had something to say. . . . As I approached thirty-five, I realized that I did have something to say."

Keith D. Arnold

Helping to enrich the lives of thousands of visually impaired individuals every day
www.rdpfs.org

Reader's Digest Partners for Sight is a non-profit foundation established in 1955 by DeWitt Wallace, co-founder of Reader's Digest. Originally created with the purpose of publishing high-quality reading material for the visually impaired, the Foundation has helped to enrich the lives of thousands of visually impaired individuals.

Now, through its program of carefully directed charitable grants to qualifying organizations, the Foundation is also a vital source of support on local, regional, and national levels for the blind and visually impaired community. **Partners for Sight** supports the grant program as it continues to provide new technology, new opportunity, and new hope for the visually impaired.

If you would like to contact the Foundation, write to: **Reader's Digest Partners for Sight Foundation, Inc.,** 44 South Broadway, White Plains, NY 10601.